BURNING SKY

WESTON OCHSE

SOLARIS

First published 2018 by Solaris
an imprint of Rebellion Publishing Ltd,
Riverside House, Osney Mead,
Oxford, OX2 0ES, UK

www.solarisbooks.com

ISBN: 978 1 78108 530 1

10 9 8 7 6 5 4 3 2 1

A CIP catalogue record for this book is available
from the British Library.

Designed & typeset by Rebellion Publishing

Printed in Denmark by Nørhaven

BURNING SKY

Other titles by this author

The Task Force Ombra Series
Grunt Life
Grunt Traitor
Grunt Hero

Seal Team 666 Series
Seal Team 666
Age of Blood
Reign of Evil
Border Dog

The Afterblight Chronicles
Blood Ocean

Tomes of the Dead
Empire of Salt

Multiplex Fandango
Halfway House
FUBAR

For everyone who has ever served in Afghanistan,
knows the taste of dust in their mouths,
hates driving down the pot-holed roads,
stares warily at passersby,
and looks lovingly at T-Walls.
This book is for you.

The universe is no narrow thing and the order within it is not constrained by any latitude in its conception to repeat what exists in one part in any other part. Even in this world, more things exist without our knowledge than with it and the order in creation which you see is that which you have put there, like a string in a maze, so that you shall not lose your way. For existence has its own order and that no man's mind can compass, that mind itself being but a fact among others.

— Cormac McCarthy, *Blood Meridian,*
or *The Evening Redness in the West*

PROLOGUE

BLOOD MERIDIAN WAS Boy Scout's favorite book despite the author's love of gruesome details like baby heads hanging from trees and scalps fluttering in the air like birds. The reason for his appreciation had more to do with the spirit of the narrative, a theme that Boy Scout universally understood... a theme of unrelenting madness, much like he'd experienced in Afghanistan over the last few years. The constant fighting, the ever-present threat of violence, and the seeming inexorable backwardism of the populace could have been transposed from the book or vice versa with no loss of intellectual impact, especially the madness he'd felt that single night four months ago when he just couldn't take it any longer.

Boy Scout's left eye twitched as he blinked the memory away. He couldn't relive that moment now. There was too much at stake. Memories such as that were best saved for a solitary night in a shadowed corner with a bottle of something strong. It would do him and his mission no good reliving what he'd done... what he'd been forced to do by an absentee God.

He gave his crew a visual check, ensuring that they were still on mission, then resumed his vigil. Staring across the jagged and lifeless horizon, red dust-filled sky bleeding into earth of the same color, Boy Scout reflected on how similar it seemed to the *terra damnata* in *Blood Meridian*. Although Afghanistan was geographically different from the fictional landscape described by Cormac McCarthy in his book, it still held the same genus of *condemned earth*. As in the book, so it was in real life, the landscape of the damned included the souls of those who lived upon it. The main character had been a runaway kid, forced to witness terrible things. At times like this, Boy Scout thought about that fictional kid, wondering what he'd be thinking standing in Boy Scout's shoes, the leader of a six-person security detail instead of companion to scalp hunters, eager to paint their history in blood. Boy Scout wondered how the boy would feel, knowing that there were real places where good men were sometimes forced to do evil things, just because it was the right thing to do... places like Afghanistan, where no one could escape without earning a little *damnata* of their very own.

He tore himself away from the memory of both his deed and the terrible book, raised his binos to his eyes, and observed the mountain to the convoy's nine. He didn't like their choice for a hunker-down site... no, that was too soft a word. He *hated* the choice. Although the road ran flat before them, keeping anyone from successfully hiding, the mountains to either side held too many dark clutches of brush-filled hollows. A sniper could be lying in any of them, some *mooj* who'd been shooting invaders ever since the first Russian tank crossed the Amu River forty-plus years ago.

Boy Scout had seen the results firsthand of what a fifty-caliber bullet could do to the human body, even if it was shot from a rifle that was first made in an 1800s English factory, dropped by some unlucky British soldier during the First Battle of Kabul. The weapon might be old and the dusky skin around the eyes sighting down the Martini-Enfield's barrel might be wrinkled, but at three hundred meters, a round could still shatter a leg, remove a hand, or smash through an unprotected head as well as a round from any modern weapon.

"B.S., you seeing what I'm seeing?" Narco asked over their multi-band inter-team radios (MBITR).

Boy Scout spoke into the mic as he kept scanning his sector. "Not seeing anything you see, Narco, because I'm on my own sector."

Narco delayed responding, which meant he was probably rolling his eyes. Boy Scout made a note to talk to him later in private. Dakota Jimmison, aka Dak, call sign Narco, was always a bit fast and loose, but while on mission, Boy Scout needed the man to remain focused.

"Vehicle approaching from twelve o'clock," Narco said, all business now.

Was this the rendezvous or was it something else? Aloud, he said, "You and Preacher's Daughter take it out if it gets closer than fifty feet."

A smoky female voice joined the coms. "Guess who gets to break out the RPG?" After a pause she added,

"This girl."

Boy Scout could almost see the smile on her face through the coms. Glad she was happy, but he hoped they didn't need to use the weapon. If they did, it meant they were in the shit and that all his worries were right. In this case, he'd rather not be right at all.

"Vehicle still moving. Clock it at two kilometers and closing," Narco said.

Boy Scout needed to move forward to manage the situation but he was unwilling to disregard possible attacks from their flanks. They'd taken a three-vehicle convoy out of Mazar-e Sharif five hours ago just to hunker down on a set of GPS coordinates. That this location had been pre-selected for them hadn't thrilled Boy Scout. The location had been Alpha's idea. They could have reached the location by helicopter in an hour, but Alpha again had insisted they travel by land. Boy Scout had tried to argue that Alpha's safety would be compromised if they prosecuted the mission as ordered, but Boy Scout was told in no uncertain terms that he and his team had one mission, which was to carry Alpha to and from an important rendezvous while maintaining secrecy and security… and since Alpha was a JSOC general officer, there was no getting around it.

"McQueen, keep Alpha secure inside vehicle. Criminal, you take my sector."

"You want me to move back there so you can move up front, boss?" came another female voice, this one hard-edged, bordering on nasty. She was the newest member of the team. Her name was Sarasota Chavez. Her parents called her Sara, but to the team she was Bully.

After a second of thought, "Roger. Let's do that."

"WILCO," she said, the word like a slice from a blade.

Boy Scout felt a pat on the shoulder as she left the side of the middle vehicle and took his position. She'd once been a convoy driver. She'd also been an MMA fighter. He felt confident with her at his back.

He nodded to Criminal, who was also watching the rear. The twenty-seven-year-old former MARSOC marine wore the same body armor vest as the rest of them, but his was decorated with a various assortment of My Little Pony patches. His name was Oscar James. His friends called him Oz, but because of his ability to procure absolutely anything, Boy Scout had fondly given him the call sign Criminal. His HK 416 automatic rifle hung from a sling around his neck, ready to be raised. But for now, he had his hands on his binos.

Even knowing he didn't need to say it, Boy Scout said, "You and Bully watch our flanks. Engage anything that moves."

"Got it, B.S.," Criminal said, referring to Boy Scout's call sign and his real name, Bryan Starling.

Boy Scout strode forward. He glanced once through the armor-plated glass at Alpha sitting in the middle SUV. Chaz McQueen, former Special Forces Warrant Officer and now contractor, sat beside the GO, as stoic as he was muscular.

Boy Scout continued to the first vehicle.

Preacher's Daughter, or Laurie May, aka Lore, former Army intelligence lieutenant now government civilian, was grinning from ear-to-ear as she held her RPG-32 cocked jauntily on her hip, grenade pointing skyward.

Narco, former Army military policeman now shit-hot adrenaline-junkie contractor, stood next to her, spying down the scope of a long rifle. Part Cherokee and part German, he had the soft and hard features of both nationalities. He and Criminal were fast friends. While Criminal wore My Little Pony patches, Narco wore Brony patches to fuck with him. He thought it was hilarious, but it only pissed Criminal off.

"What we got, Narco?"

"Up armored SUV by how low it rides. Land Cruiser. Same as ours. Think they're friendlies?"

It didn't make sense for them to be. If Alpha wanted to establish a meeting with friendlies, he could have done it any number of ways. Meeting out in the middle of bum fuck Afghanistan was such a waste of manpower and time. Unless...

Boy Scout spun and strode to the middle SUV. He jerked open the door and glared at the JSOC general. "Seriously? We're your taxi ride?"

The general, whose face bore the desert tan and scars from a dozen Middle Eastern and African countries, didn't change his expression when he said, "You're an Operational Support Team. Your job is to support operations and transport VIPs. I'm a JSOC brigadier general. Mission accomplished."

Boy Scout scowled on the inside. There were so many things he wanted to say. So many things he wanted to do at this moment. But he needed to keep it professional. He needed to do what his old boss Pastora had once said: *Be gracious even in the face of an imbecile.*

"How many and from what unit, General?" he asked.

"They'll be JSOC. Don't know how many."

"The reason I need to know, sir, is because in about ten seconds, I'm going to command Preacher's Daughter to send an RPG round down the throat of that oncoming SUV. As long as they don't identify themselves, I have to treat them as enemy combatants."

"Vehicle now one kilometer and closing," Narco said.

"That's now five seconds, General."

Alpha pulled out an Iridium Sat Phone and punched three quick numbers. He held up a hand for Boy Scout to wait.

"Three, two, one." Boy Scout turned to Preacher's Daughter. "Prepare to fire."

"Delighted to," she said, shouldering the weapon and stepping away from the vehicles to make sure no one behind her was in the back blast area.

"If they are your pick-up team, have them slow to a stop and flash their lights three times. You have three seconds."

Alpha shouted into the phone, resulting in the oncoming SUV skidding to a stop. When the dust cleared, it was pitched sideways and less than a hundred meters away. The headlights flashed three times in what seemed like a grudging fashion.

To McQueen, who sat in the driver's seat of the SUV in which Alpha was currently sitting, Boy Scout said, "Why don't you help the general out of the vehicle, McQueen."

A fire hydrant of a man, McQueen was old school Special Forces and had recently retired so that he could better embrace his alternative lifestyle. He grinned wide beneath his boonie cap as he exited the front seat and held open the rear door. "Sir, if you will?"

The general blinked in surprise. "You want me to walk?"

McQueen squinted down the road for a moment, slowly glanced right, then left, then nodded. "It's not far. We'll cover you. Not to worry."

The JSOC general gave Boy Scout a sour look, but otherwise said nothing. He stood, pocketed his Iridium, and grabbed his rucksack, which was bulging with God knew what.

Boy Scout and McQueen followed him to the head of their convoy then stopped and watched him walk the hundred meters to the waiting SUV.

"Were we really only a taxi service?" Narco asked.

"Seems so," Boy Scout replied.

"Ten-hour round trip," Criminal said from the rear. "That sucks balls."

"What Oz said," Preacher's Daughter grumbled.

"What she said," McQueen added, scowling. "Ever get tired of the feeling of being used?"

Boy Scout shook his head. "Enough of that. What's done is done. I'm sure he had good reason to bring us out here."

"Like taking out ten kilos of black tar heroin behind Uncle Sam's back," Narco murmured. And he should know. He'd spent three years with the DEA after a stellar career in the infantry working Mexican border interdiction ops. It was the DEA who'd given him the call sign because he could sense drugs like he was psychic. And then, of course, there was that time he'd been caught dealing himself, the reason the DEA had let him go, and why it had been so hard for Boy Scout to get the guy a clearance.

Even knowing Narco's ability, Boy Scout couldn't help but ask, "What makes you say that?"

"Why else are we out here in the middle of nowhere with no security other than our happy asses and close enough to the border one could drive over? If we went by helo, he'd have to have filed a flight plan. Now there's nothing to prove we were even here."

Boy Scout nodded. Narco's logic was impeccable. The question was, why would a general need black tar heroin... if that's what he had?

Bully cried out from the rear. "Object at seven o'clock and moving fast."

Everyone spun to that direction.

Boy Scout brought up his binos but only saw a flash of hot white light.

"Identify," he called.

"Missile!" shouted Oz.

Boy Scout lowered his binos and saw the flash of light heading towards the general's SUV. Damn. Boy Scout began to shout an order, but it died in his throat as the image stopped in midair, as no missile could ever do.

"WTF," Criminal and Narco said as one.

Boy Scout commanded, "Lore, fire!"

Preacher's Daughter still had the RPG on her shoulder.

She prepared to fire, but then a savage barrage of gunfire erupted from the other SUV, targeting the object.

Glints of light flared from the mysterious object as each round found its mark. Boy Scout could see that it was roughly shaped like an immense medieval knight's shield but so bright that it was difficult to watch without blinking furiously. The object had a distorted aura, like a mirage, the sky behind it skewed and melted.

"What is it? A UAV? Taliban have UAVs like that?" Bully asked.

"Taliban don't even have paper airplanes," Narco said. "Must be Russian."

Boy Scout doubted that it was even Russian. Something about it was off. Way off.

The general's SUV began to back away, then turn. The driver floored it, dust spinning into a storm, as someone continued to fire out a window.

Two more objects appeared in the air beside the first one, as if they'd been there all the time and had just now become visible. Before the general's SUV could get twenty meters, the objects attacked it, lances of fire shooting out from their centers, slamming into the vehicle. The SUV swerved, then flipped and rolled. After a few seconds, it exploded, sending pieces of metal and men high in the air.

Bully took a step back. "Oh shit!"

"I'd say the general should have filed a flight plan," Narco said.

Boy Scout had to think quickly. Mounting up didn't seem the right thing to do. But if they didn't, then they were too out in the open.

The three objects turned toward them and began to move, leaving in their wake white-hot mirage-like distortions.

"Lore, carefully. Wait until they're close, then fire. Dak, I want you to reload her as fast as you can." He paused, then added. "When she fires, everyone give everything you got."

He heard metal on metal as everyone readied. He didn't even bother raising a weapon. He seriously doubted it would help.

Still, they had to try.

They had to do *something*.

Dying like sardines in a can like the general had was no option.

He detected a faint humming emanating from the objects that grew louder the closer they came.

When the trio of burning shields stopped in front of them at an altitude of about thirty meters, Preacher's Daughter slowly raised her RPG, gave a whispered prayer to St. Michael, then fired.

The middle object exploded in a shower of impossible sparks, and began to spin in the air, faster and faster, pieces of it falling to the earth while others shot into non-existence.

All around Boy Scout, his TST opened up with everything they had—four HK 416s pouring dozens of 5.56-mm rounds per second into the two remaining targets.

Narco pulled out a new rocket propelled grenade and inserted it into the launcher.

Boy Scout stood, locked in wonder, as what was left of

the middle object began to fall... right on top of them. For a brief second, everything seemed familiar, then the world became brighter and brighter and brighter until the humming sound turned into a scream. Boy Scout slammed his hands to his ears and closed his eyes to the new *terra damnata* as a white-hot meridian bore through his eyelids and consumed him whole.

Chapter One

Six Months Later, Los Feliz, Suburb of LA.

BRYAN STARLING AWOKE in a pile of his own vomit, the taste of bile-coated Fritos, beer, and pepperoni pizza coating his cheeks, nose, and lips. His eyes beheld a sideways universe where the floor was one wall, and the kitchen was another. Stacks of pizza boxes and plates rested against the counter, miraculously not falling, even though they were at an angle to the ground. A brown creature stroked its mandible beside his eye. Then he watched as it reached out and blurred, now too close for his eyes to adjust.

He groaned, causing the creature to run.

He blinked once, then fell back into a stuporous sleep where a thin white goat held by a young girl in a dress lapped water from an underground cistern. He watched the creature for a dream eternity, until it turned to him and bleated.

His eyes snapped open and he felt leathery whiskers tickling his face.

The creature fell off and backed away, seeming to appraise him.

His eyes widened. A cockroach—it had been chewing on his eyelashes.

He scooted away, brushing frantically at his face.

His sideways world tilted right side up as the wall became a floor, sending his stomach lurching at the shift. He dry-heaved, a thin string of stinging bile finding its way out of his mouth. He spat it onto the floor, then turned and sat roughly on one haunch, trying to think what the last thing was he could remember.

Flashes of—

A line of half-snorted coke.

The glowing orange end of a joint, then him toking like a furious Hunter S. Thompson.

A neon sign with the image of a girl sitting in a martini glass, legs askew.

A knife smearing peanut butter onto a pepperoni pizza, then shaking a bag of crushed Fritos onto it.

The bulging eyes of a dying Afghan man, tongue protruding.

Starling slammed his eyes shut and vigorously rubbed his face, as if the motion could wipe away the images, but the visage of the man stayed with him until the life was choked out of him and his head sagged to the side.

That hadn't happened last night.

That had been a long time ago... the problem was that it hadn't been long *enough* ago.

Starling shoved himself unsteadily to his feet. His mouth tasted like a dry lake where frat boys had thrown the mother of all parties. He stumbled to the bathroom and caught the nightmare of his face in the mirror. Bags under his eyes, sallow skin, crusted puke at the corners of his mouth: he was anything but a boy scout. He'd fallen far and fast, only he didn't know why. It seemed like just a few days ago when he'd been the leader of an Operational Support Team, finishing a successful tour, his team members going their own ways, deployment cash and danger pay filling their pockets, fueling their dreams.

And now look at what he'd become.

He'd been a tall six-foot-four, two hundred-pound US Army Ranger who'd left the service after eleven years to work contracts in and out of Afghanistan. After a couple black-ops contracts that were more sitting than doing, he'd found himself leading an operational support team and recognized that the multiple daily missions gave him the necessary adrenaline he needed to fuel his excitement-junkie soul. With wide broad features and red hair, he'd been the quintessential Midwestern boy next door. He'd gone to church every Sunday, been an Eagle Scout, and had a bachelor's in American literature from Iowa State University. He'd been that guy everyone wanted to be.

Until now.

Now he was roach food.

Sure, he was still six-foot-four, but now he weighed two hundred forty pounds, most of it packed onto his gut, making him slump, bent forward like a man twenty years his senior. His once perfect hair was now stringy with sweat and dull from being unwashed. His eyes were hollow, devoid of any of the passion that had once powered his every breath.

Staring at himself, he hated what he was seeing and slammed his fist into the mirror, shattering it. Blood blossomed from his hand and dripped into the dirty sink. He turned on the faucet, ignoring the shards in the basin, and ran water over his cut knuckles. The water went from red to pink and he shook his head in defeat, droplets spraying everywhere.

How much longer could he live like this, if you could even call it living?

He felt a vibrating in his left pocket.

He shoved his hand in, felt around, and came out with a phone. Without thinking, he answered it. "What is it?"

"That's all I get. No hello? No good morning?"

Starling flipped through his mental Rolodex. Who the hell was this?

"What's wrong, Bryan with a Y? Cat got your tongue?"

Larsson. Fucking Larsson. "What do you want, Larrson?"

"I have an address for you."

"What's the deal?"

"You'll know what to do when you get there."

"What's the price?"

"Five large."

"Make it ten."

"Five."

"How about eight?"

"Five."

"Six?"

"It's five, Bryan with a Y. Now get your ass over there

and take care of business."

Starling wrote the address in blood on the wall beside the broken mirror, then took a picture of it with his phone.

He cleaned up as best he could, finding the least dirty pair of jeans and an old shirt that said Army of One amidst a wave of wrinkled gray. Rather than wash his hair, he took an electric razor to it and shaved it to a stubble that matched what he wore on his face. He didn't have any Band-Aids, but he did find some duct tape. He took a kitchen towel, tore it into strips and used it to bind his bleeding knuckles, then used the duct tape to keep the towel in place.

When he was ready to go, Starling searched around and spied a half-open bottle of water. He took it, sniffed it to make sure that's what it was, then slung it down. He grabbed the 9mm from where he kept it under the sofa cushion and slid it into a holster in the small of his back. He shook his T-shirt to ensure it covered the area, then he was out the door.

He waited at the bus stop with two homeless men, an elderly woman going grocery shopping, and a kid with a skateboard. He watched as the kid appraised each of them. Starling tried to stand a little straighter and a little taller. Even though his clothes were of the same caliber and cleanliness as the homeless men, he didn't want to be categorized with them. The kid must have noticed because he sneered and shook his head.

Starling turned away and stared at the graffiti painted on the metal side of the bus stop.

TRES DIABLOS
FREE BLOWJOBS CALL 1-800-YOU-SUCK
SUZIE LOVES ~~STEVE~~
COCK
MISSING GIRL – HAVE YOU SEEN HER

His gaze focused on the last line. An emptiness filled him until he wanted to sob. His body was a vessel full of nothing and that nothing weighed him down until he felt like falling to his knees. He turned sluggishly, his vision narrowed to a claustrophobic monocular, as if he were living from the end of a telescope. Then, as if as an afterthought, he noticed vaguely that the world had stopped, everything freeze-framed and silent. He reveled in the oddness of it, honing in on the minute details of everything to help him forget the vacuum inside. Then something moved at the corner of his vision. Deep blue skin glinted in firelight. Talons curved at the end of long fingers. A hunger began to eat at him. He tasted blood in his mouth.

A metal-on-metal squealing jerked everything back. The sound of the big city hit him. The sudden movement dizzied him. He grabbed onto the side of the bus stop with his duct-taped hand to steady himself.

"Fucking crackhead," said the skateboarder, a look of disappointment on his face, as if he were his mother or drill sergeant or both. Then the kid shook his head and skipped through the door and to the rear of the bus where he found a back seat to slump in.

Starling let the others on the bus ahead of him as he regained his senses, then found a seat next to a man eating a giant pretzel, white salt turning his lap and the front of his shirt into ski slopes in miniature. Pretzel man gave Starling a wary eye and shifted so that he could eat his killer carb load in semi-privacy.

Starling lived in a third-floor apartment in the Los Feliz neighborhood of Los Angeles. He had a view of the hills from his window, but other than that, it was just what it was—a studio he could afford in a community that was as lost as he was. Two transfers and seven blocks later, Starling found himself walking down 8th Street in Koreatown. He passed a flower shop next to a market, then a noodle shop. At Harvard, he turned south and headed down to the next block. Three houses in on the left, he found the bloody address on his phone. A sprawling multi-family unit took up the corner, surrounded by a fence. The second structure in was a tiny Craftsman with a ten-foot fence—the sort of barrier he'd expect in an industrial section and not around a home. Strange. The third house was also a Craftsman and didn't have a fence. No cars were parked in the driveway. Nothing lived in the dirt front yard.

A Korean man walking his dog gave him a long look, the sort of look you'd do when you figured you might need to give a description to the police. The dog looked like a muscular miniature poodle whose pure-bred mother had probably been had by a stray Pitbull. The upturned nose matched that of its owner.

There were two kinds of people who lived in this neighborhood, and Starling was neither of them. Koreatown was in the middle of the city and was treasured for its location. This was an older neighborhood filled with Koreans who hadn't been priced out by gentrification. The occasional Lexus or Land Rover in a fenced driveway told of upwardly mobile professionals who could afford to drop dime on run-down older Craftsmen homes and turn them into showcases. Starling saw evidence of this here and there along both sides of the street.

Starling rubbed his newly shaven head and grinned at the older gentleman.

The Korean's expression never changed—probably *click, click, click*—taking mental pictures for a future line up.

Starling waited for the man to turn the corner. When he did, Starling hurried up the home's broken sidewalk. He stepped onto the porch and tried to see through the curtain on the door's window, but it was too opaque. He tried the knob. It was locked.

Glancing behind him, he moved to the right side of the porch, vaulted over the railing, and landed on the driveway. He almost fell but was able to catch his balance at the last second. He followed the driveway around the side of the house. A few stubborn clutches of grass wouldn't give into the imminent domain creep of dirt. On the right was a detached garage, doors closed. A colorful mélange of shirts and pants hung on a clothesline. He could see by the way they moved in the breeze that they were all but dry. That made his job simpler.

There were stairs to the back door, but also a handicapped ramp. He found a place beside the back steps and squatted down to wait. He kept his mind dull and his body alert, much like he'd done on countless operations, waiting for the enemy to show, willing the action to happen.

Ten minutes later, the doorknob turned and the inner door opened. The screen door protested, then slammed back in place. A twenty-something Korean woman in yoga pants, tennis shoes and a bathrobe hurried down the ramp to the clothes. She stuffed them into the plastic basket she'd brought out with her. When she was finished, she turned and went back to her house. It wasn't until she was almost to the back door that she saw him squatting against the side of the house.

He barely had to lift the pistol in his hand to make her understand his purpose.

Together they strode inside, tears in her eyes, his own heart turning to stone for what he was about to do.

Chapter Two

Later, Koreatown

Starling followed her through a sparse kitchen with an old Formica table and matching red vinyl and chrome chairs that hearkened back to the sixties. A twenty-year-old refrigerator hummed loudly, almost covering the sound of his boots on the wood floor. The interior smelled of pine oil with a hint of something rancid.

She left the basket of clothes on the table, then continued into the living room with him close behind. She bypassed the couch and threw herself into a low-slung library chair—one of a pair that faced the couch. She pulled an E-cig from the pocket of her bathrobe and took a deep drag. Then she blew out a prodigious amount of vapor, which temporarily hid her face. When the cloud dispersed, he noticed that her lower lip had curled into what could only be a sideways grin. Gone was her defeat, now replaced with a look of irritation.

Starling glanced around the room. Four corners. A sofa

.other chair. A glass coffee table rested on a flower-
.erned throw rug. The wood-paneled walls made the
oom look dark. A fireplace took up half of one wall.
Stairs and a hallway took up the opposite. A large picture
window with the curtain pulled was by the front door.
The only brightness in the entire room was the white
popcorn ceiling.

"What's your name?" Starling asked, his pistol at his
side rather than pointing at the girl.

"Don't you know?" she asked. Her words still held a
vestige of her Korean heritage.

He regarded her for a moment. Her hair was cut into
a bob, which accentuated her high cheekbones and long
neck. He shook his head. "Sometimes I'm surprised at the
sheer amount of shit I don't know. I'll ask again. What's
your name?"

"Joon. Joon Park."

"Do you know why I'm here, Joon?"

She stared at him for a long moment, inhaling, then
exhaling. Finally, instead of answering she asked, "Why
do you keep doing this to me?"

This took him aback. "What do you mean? I've never
seen you before."

"That's what you always say."

"I've never been here. You must be mistaken."

She took another drag from her e-cig and stared at him.

"Are you saying you know me?" he asked.

She sighed. "You always act so innocent until you're not."

He began to pace. "This makes no sense." He rubbed
the tip of the pistol against his temple, then tapped it hard

against the side of his head. He glanced at her and shook his head. "Why would you say any of this?"

Her half smile fell as she pushed herself back in the chair, lifting her feet into it and hugging her legs. "Please don't hurt me again."

His eyes narrowed as he tried to understand the sudden shift. Just a second ago, she hadn't been afraid of him even though he carried a gun. Nothing had changed. All that had passed between them was the same thing that would have passed between two strangers in a store, with the exception of his pistol and the fact that Larrson had sent him. Then he realized what he'd been doing with the pistol.

"What makes you say that?" He waggled the pistol in the air for a moment, then slid it back where it belonged. "Why do you think I'm going to hurt you?"

"You really don't know, do you?" she asked. She relaxed a little and took another drag off her E-cig and on the exhale said, "I think you're messing with me. You come here acting like you don't know anything, but we know different, don't we?"

His frustration crescendoed. He felt like punching Larrson in the face. What was it he was supposed to do? As it was, he felt damn stupid standing in the middle of a Koreatown house not knowing why the fuck he was supposed to be there. His usual job of evicting crack addicts who'd taken occupancy of abandoned homes or of getting money from street thugs they owed their loan shark was something he could handle.

But this?

Whatever this was, he didn't want to be part of it.

He started to back away.

"Larrson sent you, didn't he?"

This stopped him. "How do you know?"

"He always sends you."

"Me?" He swallowed. "Did you say he *always* sends me?"

Instead of answering, she asked, "Ever wonder if you're a character in the wrong story?"

"What is it you've done?" he asked.

"They never tell me."

They? Who is they? "But you must know."

"I don't know anything. I just want you to stop coming."

How many people had Larrson sent? What was it she'd done? Why was he here? Normally, it was an obvious answer: a coffee table full of coke and cash, a pimp with a bruised and black-eyed woman gripping his sleeve, or even a drunk with a dented fender, blood and hair still clinging to the metal. But this was something completely different.

"You have to tell me what you've done so I can fix this somehow."

She let one of her feet stray from the protection of the chair and onto the floor. She took another immense drag of her E-Cig and blew it out. "I haven't done anything. I'm just me."

"*I'm just me,*" he repeated. "You have to have done something, Joon."

"You're certain about that?"

He sighed. "There's very little I'm certain of nowadays."

He glanced around the room, searching for evidence of her life—pictures, trophies, knickknacks brought back from Disneyland or Hawaii or Mexico... anything. But there was nothing, not even any photos. The mantle was empty. The walls were empty. Even the table between the chairs only held a lamp. It was like he'd walked onto a Hollywood set instead of into a house. He spun, turning, searching, eyes narrowing. There had to be something. She had a basket of clothes. The kitchen was lived in. There had to be some evidence that she existed.

"What's wrong with him, Mommy?"

Starling turned to the new voice and almost fell backwards.

It was a boy, perhaps ten years old, with wide eyes. He was Korean like his mother, but had a pure California kid accent. His black hair was tousled. He had on shorts and a shirt that read *I Heart Venice Beach* with an actual heart in place of the word. But the physical blow that shoved Starling to his knees was the rest of what he saw. The boy sat in a low-slung wheelchair, the kind you steer with your mouth. His legs ended at nubs where his knees had been. His arms ended at nubs where his elbows should have been.

"What happened to him?" he managed to stammer.

"Freddie was born that way. Congenital amputation."

The room seemed to dissolve almost as if it were a mirage, miles away. The image of another young boy in a wheelchair replaced this one. This time it was a young Afghan boy of eight with arms and legs that didn't work thanks to an IED. He'd been used for something he never should have been used for. Bile rose in Starling's throat. He struggled to stand. The image of the boy was suddenly replaced by that of the goat in his dream, its mouth inexpertly sewn shut, its devil eyes judging him, the girl standing imperiously behind.

He backed away until his rear end touched the fireplace.

He desperately needed to regain control of his mind and the situation. The drugs and booze had left him a washed-out old soldier on the edge of sanity. Barring a sudden and immediate stay at an all-expenses-paid detox joint of his choosing, he was going to totally lose his shit. The girl. The goat. The shy boy from Afghanistan. And now this Korean woman—Joon—who claimed to know him. And her son. The bile continued to rise. He stumbled from the living room to the kitchen and unleashed his stomach into the sink, covering the breakfast dishes, including one that had a smiling Big Bird on the bottom with the words *JOB WELL DONE*, with vomit.

He heard from the other room, "Mommy, is the man going to hurt you again?"

"I don't think so, Freddie. This time it seems different."

"But he's sick, just like the last time."

"It's going to be okay, I think, Freddie. Now go back to your room."

With both of Starling's hands gripping the sink and his head hung low, he listened as the boy maneuvered the wheelchair, then moved down the hall. Starling jumped a little when a door slammed.

A moment later, Joon entered the kitchen. She barely glanced at the vomit, reached up into a cabinet for a glass, then filled it with water from a gallon jug in the refrigerator. She handed it to him.

"Here. Sit down." She pulled out a chair from the table.

He accepted the glass, then sat. He took a sip, then drank half. After he swallowed, he rolled the cool glass across his forehead. He regarded Joon, who stood across from him, her back against the counter.

"Who's the father?"

"You wouldn't know him," she said.

Starling considered his position in the mess. "Let me guess. He comes from money and he wants little Freddie to come live with him."

Her face pinched, menacing. "He can have him when I'm dead."

"I think that was one of the options. It's why they sent me."

She shook her head. "You ever killed a woman?"

"Once," he said, reliving the moment. "I had to. She ran at me and wouldn't stop. Turns out she had on a suicide vest. We checked her out afterwards. She had three kids and a husband. It was the husband who made her do it. It was either her or him and he was too much a coward to do what the Taliban told him to."

"What'd you do to the husband?"

"Something that made him wish he'd strapped the bomb on himself."

She regarded him for a moment, then as he finished his glass, she took the jug from the refrigerator and refilled it.

"You some big time soldier?" she asked.

Big time. Had he ever been big time? "Nah, I was just the guy you turned to when you needed something fixed... when you needed help."

"Like a boy scout."

He laughed.

"What? I say it wrong?"

"No, you said it right. It's just that Boy Scout used to be my call sign—what they called me in Afghanistan."

"You're not a boy scout anymore?"

"It's been a long time since I've been anything close to a boy scout."

"You going to do what Larrson wants?" she asked.

He noticed that her hand was close to the kitchen knives. "If it means taking the boy, then no."

Her hand retreated an inch. "You shouldn't cross Larrson."

"How do you know him?"

"He got me this place."

"You have anywhere else to go?"

She shook her head. "My father and mother say I disgraced them. My brother was killed in Iraq. All my other family is in Korea and they're even worse than my father."

"What was your plan?"

"The boy's father was going to give me enough money to live on and to take care of him."

"And now?"

"Now he wants my son so he can put him in a state home. His wife found out about the monthly payments and he wants to shut them off."

"Larrson tell you this? How did he know?"

"The boy's father used him as a go-between. Count on that asshole to know criminals."

"If I don't come back with the boy, there's going to be hell to pay."

"Can you pay the hell back?" she asked, twisting the words to mean something else.

Starling downed the rest of the water and placed the glass on the table, then nodded. "Yeah. I think I can. Let me make a call."

Chapter Two

Chapter Three

STARLING WAS WELL aware that he was about to cross a line he couldn't uncross, but he saw it as an opportunity rather than a negative. He'd been silently begging the universe to throw him a lifeline for months. He couldn't tell how he'd stumbled onto this downward path, but he'd desperately wanted to get off it. Helping Joon and her son would be the first major step back to being who he'd been. And he'd need the help of the only member of his former team he was still in contact with: Chaz McQueen.

As Starling dialed the number, he remembered that he owed McQueen three hundred bucks, which was what the big man wanted to talk about right after they said their pleasantries. Of course, he also wasn't surprised when Starling wanted to talk about something else. When presented with the intriguing problem, McQueen was more than willing to do something that lent relevancy to his existence—not that bouncing the door at West Hollywood's most exclusive gay bar wasn't relevant—but he couldn't make it until after his shift was over at one a.m. Starling pressed him, but McQueen was firm. He'd made a commitment to the club and wouldn't leave them in the lurch. Starling was a little bemused as he hung up. It seemed as if at least one of them still knew what the word *duty* meant.

The next call was a little trickier.

He walked deeper into the backyard, found a spot to stand next to the clothesline, then hit redial on a number.

"Is it done?" Larrson asked.

"Is what done?"

"Don't play games with me."

"Who's playing games? I asked you what the mission was and you said I'd know when I got there. Well, I'm here and I don't know what the fucking mission is."

"I'm not going to spell it out on the phone. No telling who's listening."

"Just tell me one thing."

"What's that?"

"What do I do with the girl?"

A moment of silence was followed by a salacious laugh. "Whatever you want, big boy."

Starling gritted his teeth and turned to look back at the house. Joon stood behind the screen door, staring out at him, clutching her E-cig against her breast. He wondered if she knew how her future was absolutely in his hands.

"No, seriously," he said.

"I am being serious. About the boy…" Larrson paused and shouted to someone off-phone. "About the boy. Package him up and deliver him to me by six."

"It's ten now. What do you want me to do the rest of

the day?"

"Babysit. Fuck, I got to tell you everything?"

"Why wait?"

"Because I'm in fucking San Bernardino taking care of another *schmoe* who can't tie his shoes without asking why. You don't want to be that guy, Starling. You don't ever want to be that guy." Then he began yelling at someone again. After a few seconds, he hung up.

"Don't be that guy," Starling said to himself. "Too late. I *am* that guy."

He pocketed the phone and strolled up the walk to the back porch.

Joon didn't move as she watched him come back to the door.

"What did he tell you to do with me?" she asked.

"Whatever I wanted."

Her jaw dropped and her eyes widened. He could see her playing out possible futures in her mind. "Did he say that?" she asked, each word measured.

"In so many words." He lifted his hand to the screen door handle. "Can I come in?"

She regarded him for a moment, then backed away.

When he stepped inside, she nodded to the sink. "Feel free to clean up your mess." Then she turned on her heel, grabbed the laundry, and headed into the living room and down the hall, presumably to her room.

Starling glanced at the vomit in the sink and shook his head. Being *that guy* wasn't so hot after all, but it seemed as if it was necessary if he was ever going to get back to the boy scout he'd once been. Going against Larrson felt right. This was different than the other times he'd been the man's stalking dog. Starling was in sort of a rehabilitation phase, one where he had to clean up his own vomit. On the bright side, at least it was in the sink.

After washing away his addition to the sink, he cleaned Joon and Freddie Park's breakfast dishes.

Certainly when he failed to bring the kid around at the appointed time, Starling would become *that guy*. It would probably take an hour or two for Larrson to send his crew, which meant they'd probably be safe until about 8 p.m. The problem was that McQueen wasn't arriving until after midnight. Starling was going to have to come up with a plan.

After he was done at the sink, he helped himself to two pieces of bread and some peanut butter. He ate ravenously, making small animal sounds as he chewed open-mouthed. He chugged some water then made another sandwich. He was halfway through eating when he heard a humming noise, which was soon followed by the appearance of Freddie in his wheelchair. Starling stopped in mid-chew, as if he was a thief who'd been caught in the act. Then he slowly resumed chewing.

"You stealing my peanut butter?"

"I've got to get some food in my stomach," he said.

"That's our food," the kid said.

"True, but since I'm helping you, I figured I could have some."

"You should have asked."

Starling considered arguing, but the kid was right. He should have asked.

"Want me to fix you one?" Starling asked instead.

"I had breakfast." The kid watched him for a moment, then asked, "Are you a criminal?"

Starling felt a blow to his soul. Was he? He supposed the law would see some of the things he'd done as a crime. It was funny. He used to see things in black and white. There was a right and a wrong and no space between them. He had guys on his team like Dak and Oz, who both lived in the gray zone between the two. But for Starling—at least how it used to be—there had been no gray zone... until now.

"I don't think I am," he said.

"Then what are you?"

Starling thought for a moment, then slowly said, "I'm just a guy who's going to try and get you and your mother out of a jam."

The kid blinked several times at the answer, then put the steering pole into his mouth, spun the wheelchair around and headed out of the kitchen.

"Where's your mother?" Starling called after.

"Putting together a suitcase."

"She better not take much stuff. We need to be able to move fast."

The kid halted the progress of the wheelchair. "I can't move too fast."

"Then I'll figure something out."

"You won't leave me, will you?" the kid asked in a small voice.

"No, kid. I won't leave you."

The wheelchair started up again and Starling watched as Freddie turned down the hall and headed towards his bedroom.

The day went faster than he'd expected. Starling had figured early on that they couldn't merely stay in the house. He was only one man and there were too many ways to get in. No, he needed to find a place for them to hide until McQueen came for them. He considered taking him back to his apartment, but two things discouraged that idea. The first was that he lived in a third floor walk-up, which would make it hard for Freddie to get up there, much less flee if the need arose. And the second was that Starling didn't know if Larrson had set up surveillance. It could be either technical or personal, but if there was someone or something looking for them, especially the obvious biometrics of a wheelchair, they'd be in worse shape than they already were.

So he'd decided to look for something closer to home. After a long conversation with Joon, he discovered that the house next door with the high fence belonged to a neighbor who was on a twelve-day cruise. She'd given Joon the keys to the gate and the home and asked her to water her plants and put the mail inside. Joon said the woman was a little paranoid when it came to security. An older Korean woman, she didn't appreciate at all the influx of non-Koreans and blamed every bad thing on their intrusion.

After several visual circuits of the home, Starling escorted both Joon and Freddie out the back, helping him guide the wheelchair down the ramp, across the yard, and into the back alley. They hurried to the gate at the house next door. While Joon unlocked the padlock,

Starling looked up and down the street, waiting for a car to swing around either corner and plough towards them.

Soon they were inside with the tall gate locked behind them. This home was another 1930s Craftsman, but the two couldn't be more different. Where one had cracked and peeling paint and more dirt in the yard than grass, this one was pristine. Even the grass in the back yard looked manicured. Starling noted that the wheelchair left distinguishing lines in the grass, so he went behind and used his feet to rub them away.

After Joon opened the door, he lifted the wheelchair onto the porch and they went inside. She hurriedly punched a code into the security alarm, telling Starling the numbers as she did so. The model home look continued inside. With a Spartan yet elegant touch, everything had a place. A hint of lavender remained in the air, reminding Starling that this home belonged to an old woman. They made their way into the living room. Joon positioned the chair near the fireplace. She sat on the loveseat next to it, then pulled an iPad from her bag and installed it into an electronic cradle attached to the front of the wheelchair. Using the steering rod, Freddie began to play a game.

Starling left them and checked the house. Once he was satisfied it was empty and all the doors and windows were locked, he settled into a chair by the front window and prepared himself mentally for the siege. It was like putting on an old familiar uniform. How often had he done the same thing during his protection details as a TST commander? He'd lost count. Hundreds. Maybe thousands. He couldn't help smiling as he recognized that he was once again becoming who he used to be.

By five, however, he began craving a drink. Anything. A beer. Wine. Scotch. Vodka. He'd even settle for a bottle of strawberry Boone's Farm. He got up and went to the kitchen and poured himself a glass of water. His hands were trembling enough that he was afraid he'd drop the glass. He drank two glasses of water, then washed and dried the glass and put it back on the shelf.

Glancing around the kitchen, he searched visually for where a bottle might be if the older Korean woman was so inclined. It wouldn't be where people would normally see it. She'd make sure that it was available but hidden as well. After all, it was her business if she wanted to have a nip or two, but no one else's.

He tried the small cabinet over the refrigerator but saw that it only held a crockpot.

Of course—it was too high.

If you were an older Korean woman, where would you put your booze?

Then Starling leaned down, searched under the sink, and saw a bottle of Maker's Mark behind the ant and roach killer. He pulled the bottle free and held it as if it were a precious child.

"Is that what this is about?" came Joon's voice from the doorway. "You going to get drunk and then protect us?"

Starling fought the urge to say something back. He licked his lips and stared hard at the bottle.

"Do you want a straw, big man?" she asked.

He unscrewed the cap and inhaled the rich acrid smell of barrel-aged bourbon. Then, with shaking hands, he put the cap back on, put the bottle back under the sink, and closed the door. When he straightened up, he looked Joon in the eye.

"I told you I'd protect you and I will."

Then he stalked out of the kitchen, his throat the ass end of the Sahara, his will all but broken as he put distance between himself and the liquor he so desperately wanted to baptize himself in.

Every second of the next hour was a battle of will. He almost gave in a thousand times, but fought against it.

"How long have you been drinking?" Joon asked.

"Better ask how long I haven't."

"Why do you do it?"

He thought about it. Images of that night and the boy in the wheelchair flashed by so fast he barely saw them, but it didn't matter. Those transitional moments of justice had been forever etched into the back of his skull. Try as he might, he'd never forget.

"I honestly don't know," he said, and then his phone rang.

He checked the time. 18:11.

"Where are they?" Larrson growled.

"I don't know what you're talking about," Starling said.

After a moment of silence, "I knew you'd act this way. Fucking wannabe boy scout."

"Then why'd you give me this one?"

"I thought you'd be too far gone to care."

And there it was. That's how the universe saw him... too far gone to care. Steel slid into his spine. He stood a little straighter. Head high. Eyes steady. "I guess you were wrong."

"Yeah, I guess I was. You know I'm coming for you, right?"

"I was counting on it."

"Well, then. Ready or not, here I come."

Starling held the phone against his ear, listening to the dial tone. After a moment, he slowly lowered the phone, then put it away.

"What'd he say?" Joon asked.

Freddie stared at him as well, waiting for the answer.

"He said he's coming."

She let out a lungful of air and nodded, her complexion now pale.

"Then we better be ready." She got up, went into the kitchen, rifled around for a moment, then returned with a low-ball glass filled halfway with a dark liquid. "Here," she said, holding out the glass.

Starling stared at it. He glanced into her eyes and saw that she had her own steel ready. He took the glass, hesitated a second, then slung back the warm bourbon. He closed his eyes as it burned all the way down. He needed this. He could handle this. Just a little to keep that steel in his spine.

When he opened his eyes, she was no longer there. He sipped the last few drops from the glass, then placed it on the table.

Chapter Four

STARLING FOUND JOON standing at the front window looking out.

"How much time do we have?" she asked.

"Depends if they anticipated my response. They could have a team ready to go or they might have to get across town. Either way we have to be ready."

His phone buzzed. He pulled it out and saw a text from McQueen.

WILL BE THERE BY NINE. HANG ON. GOT A REPLACEMENT.

That was good news. Now they only had to hold out for a few more hours. He texted McQueen back, telling him where they were. When he finished, something suddenly occurred to him.

"Where's your phone?" he asked.

She nodded to her purse. "In there. Why?"

"Who gave it to you?"

"Larrson. Said my husband wanted me to have one in case he needed to talk to Freddie."

"Has he ever called?"

"Not once."

"Let me see the phone."

She hesitated, then went to her purse, rifled through it, and then came out with a smartphone. She handed it to him.

He noted that it was unlocked and began to sort through the apps until he found what he was looking for. TRACKMYPHONE. He pointed at it. "This way he knows wherever you are."

Her eyes widened. "Shit."

"What about the kid's iPad?"

"I bought that."

"Larrson or his dad never touched it?"

"Never."

"Good. Then I'll just deal with this."

"What's your plan?"

"Not sure. But you and Freddie stay put. Whatever you do, don't show yourselves. I'm going to put something together that's better than waiting for the storm to come."

She stared at him and nodded, her eyes now filled with worry. He shoved her phone into his back pocket, then opened a map app on his phone and took a close look at his position. They could be coming from any direction, but there were some more obvious routes that they'd probably take. What he needed was a location that would benefit him in the event that he had to fight a group. Then he saw it. Two blocks down was a church that had a narrow corridor between the main building and an out building, running to a central courtyard.

Starling left by the back door, locking it behind him.

Then he strode to the back gate and turned right. To anyone who might be watching, it looked like he wasn't paying attention to his surroundings, but he actually was. He'd taken a course on surveillance detection from a contracting agency back when he was with Ranger Regiment and had put it in practice all through his time on a TST. The idea was to determine his surveillance status without those watching knowing what he was doing. The alley was empty except for the occasional trashcan or piece of broken furniture. He strolled one block, then another. Once he thought he saw a car filled with Korean men turn onto Harvard, but he kept going. They'd find out soon enough that the house was empty, call Larsson, and he would tell them about the tracking app. By then, Starling wanted to be in place and ready. Then again, this was Koreatown, so there were probably lots of cars filled with Korean men.

The church was a two-story brick Episcopal structure. The narrow corridor between it and what looked like a fellowship hall was blocked, but it was nothing to move aside the board that covered the space, then go through and do the same at the other end. He had to turn sideways to get through. The corridor ended in a courtyard filled with an assortment of playground equipment. A high fence topped with razor wire promised that no one was going to get in that way. Visibility through the fence was blocked by fabric woven between the metal pieces, much like the sniper fencing he was used to seeing in the Middle East to deter enemy observation. He checked the back door of the church and saw that it was locked. Pulling out his wallet, he grabbed two picks, worked the mechanism for a moment, then got it unlocked.

The door opened into a kitchen. He pulled open the drawers until he found a set of knives. He kept one and placed the others around the back yard, jamming them into the earth, grips upward. Then he returned to the kitchen and began opening cabinets. Nothing else seemed usable.

Next, he tried the fellowship hall. It was locked as well, but it took him only half as long to open the old locks on this door. Inside he found a long hall with tables and chairs. He rifled through several wall lockers and found a bag of aluminum baseball bats. These he took with him, laying some in places he was sure he would remember.

When he was done preparing, he took Joon's phone and placed it on one of the seats of the swing set. Then he sat to the right of the corridor, baseball bat in hand, and waited. Ten minutes in, using his own phone, he texted McQueen the address just in case McQueen needed to recover a body.

Time moved slowly. He listened to the night sounds of Los Angeles—car horns, plane landings, helicopters, shouts in a dozen different languages both friendly and hostile. Twice he heard a car pass the entrance, but it didn't slow. He kept checking the time and as it crept inexorably towards twenty hundred hours, he wondered if he had been wrong after all. What if the app was just automatically installed? What if Larrson hadn't placed it there? What if a gang of thugs had found the pair and were gang-raping Joon? Those and a dozen other doubts crept through his mind on little cat feet, but he ignored them, just as he'd ignored such doubts while on the TST or on one of the hundreds of sentry duties he'd performed during his career. He had to trust his instincts. He had to trust the mission.

Then he heard it.

Rough whispers in the dark.

Starling tensed, readied himself.

He vectored in on the whispers, which were coming from the back alley. Two voices seemed to be at odds with each other, then someone rattled the fence in frustration. The razor wire. Starling recognized the language— Korean. They'd tried the back, now they'd try the front. Two minutes later, the whispering returned. He heard them curse, then their feet dragged on the dry grass as they tried to creep stealthily down the corridor. He didn't know how many there were, but he presumed more than five. He ran through several different scenarios with enough moves to make a dance instructor dizzy, then firmed up his grip on the bat.

The first head popped free of the corridor, turned and looked towards the back door of the church, then back towards the swing. He was about to look in Starling's direction, when the man behind him prodded him forward.

Starling took this as a sign, and as the first guy cleared the opening, Starling brought the Louisville Slugger Model 516 aluminum bat around in a wicked swing, intersecting the second man's knees in a sickening crack.

The man's screams made the first man turn and Starling launched himself up, bringing the bat with him, catching the first man square under his chin and shattering his jaw. He fell unconscious to the ground as teeth rained like confetti.

The other man was still screaming, grabbing at his legs as more men behind him tried to get through.

Starling swung the bat down into the second man's crotch, feeling the impact of his balls on the metal. His screams turned to breathless shrieks.

Starling hurled the bat at the third man's head, catching him in the nose. He fell unconscious atop the second man, muffling the sounds of agony.

Starling cursed as he noted that the law of unintended consequences was now in effect. Where the second man had been blocking the way, the third fell on him, creating a bridge. Soon the remaining four were running over the body and spreading themselves out in the back yard, surrounding him. They were dressed like male models: silk shirts tucked into sleek pants and high-end shoes.

Starling was already breathing heavily, the result of six months of no physical training and several hundred empty pizza boxes. He could pull out his pistol at any moment and potentially end the fight, but with LAPD's ShotSpotter spread throughout the city, the last thing he needed was attention from them.

It seemed as if the four arrayed against him felt the same because none of them were armed except the guy who'd been smart enough to pick up the bat.

Starling stepped carefully as they surrounded him. The scene reminded him of Bruce Lee in *Fists of Fury*—the movie where old Bruce got his ass beat the first two thirds of the movie because of a vow he'd made to his sister, then finally kicked the shit out of the entire planet the last third. If only he had Bruce Lee's skill. But Starling wasn't without moves of his own. He'd gone through Level Three Army Combatives Training and had used his skills against hajis while clearing buildings and on operations, as well as brawled with marines and SEALs. Now, faced with four young Korean thugs who probably knew Tae Kwon Do, he felt he could do okay, even if he was the fat version of a US Army Ranger.

Then he felt his back scream with pain as something sharp sliced into it. His reminiscence had allowed him to let his guard down for the time it took for one of his assailants to step forward and stab him.

He cursed at his over-confidence, took a step forward, then fell backwards in a controlled fall, using his momentum to get to his target, where he swept the man's feet out from under him. Starling recovered, reached over and pulled a kitchen knife from the dirt and shoved it into the man's throat, pinning him to the ground.

The man's hands came up to it as his eyes bulged and his airway stopped working, but he hadn't the strength or coordination to remove the blade.

Starling then rolled to his left and got to his feet just as one of his assailants slammed a foot down where he'd been.

The same man spun around and barely missed Starling's chin with a reverse hook kick. But the man recovered too slowly. He failed to control his momentum and let his foot fall farther forward than it should.

Starling pulled another knife from the ground and slammed it into the top of the man's knee. The guy opened his mouth to scream and Starling kicked him in the face.

Now the odds were better.

Two on one.

"You boys want to double team me, or take me on one at a time?" he asked.

"Fuck you, gringo," the one on the left said.

"That's Mexican. Can't you say white boy in your own language?"

The other said *"baeg-in namja,"* which Starling had heard enough times from Korean soldiers he was training to know that it was exactly the right words.

"That's better." He grinned, stepping around so he could be closer to one of his planted weapons. Gringo Korean must have anticipated that, because he, too, pulled one of Starling's weapons out of the ground. "Look what you found," Starling said.

"Dak cho!" Gringo Korean said, glancing fearfully around at his fallen friends.

"You want me to shut up? I can't, especially when fighting. You see, I'm a talker." He felt the wound on his back and came away with a red wet hand. It didn't seem life threatening, but it would need stitches.

The other Korean ran at him and launched a vicious set of punches and kicks.

All Starling could do was to back away until he was at the fence. He took two kicks to the ribs and one to the gut before he was able to grab one of his attacker's legs. Then the guy began to punch him in the face, and *damn* but those hurt. He let go of the leg and managed to get a fistful of the man's shirt in each hand. They grappled for a moment, then Starling stepped aside and threw him to the ground. Just as he was about to kick him, Gringo Korean ran at him with the knife.

Starling dove out of the way but landed roughly on the ground. By the time he picked himself up, both the Koreans were on their feet and advancing. Starling turned and ran, limping into the fellowship hall. They followed close behind.

He grabbed one of his bats, but the first man who'd kicked him found and grabbed another.

Starling stumbled backwards, aware that he was losing blood from the knife slash in his back. His blood was dripping on clean white tile floor as he pushed the tables out of the way.

The two Korean bangers advanced on either side of the room, neither in a hurry. But by the narrowness of their eyes and the tension of their lips, Starling had no doubt their intention was to kill him, if for nothing else than to avenge what he'd done to their mates.

Starling considered pulling his pistol and just getting this over with, yet even as he backed up, pushing aside more tables and chairs, a knife wound in his back, he felt better than he had in weeks. He was winded though, breathing more heavily than he should. He also felt the strain in his shoulders and knees. All this hard living and no exercise had left its mark. Still, he only had these two to deal with before he could get back to Joon and her son.

His phone vibrated in his pocket.

He ignored it as he leaped out of the way of a bat swung in his direction.

"What if I was to say to you, *shi bai kepu seck yi*?" he

said to the one with the knife.

The man snarled and leaped forward.

Clearly, he didn't like the idea that Starling would have unconventional sex with his mother.

Starling kicked a chair in the Korean's direction, making him trip and become entangled with the chair legs. Starling stepped aside as he fell. As the man on the ground tried to get up, Starling kicked him in the chest and knocked him over. The downed man's face was awash with pain and anger.

And then it began to... *change*.

The features liquefied and rearranged. Gone was the long face, the grim smile, and the epicanthic folds. In its place were the sharp, exaggerated features of something that should have been in a horror movie. Starling wasn't sure what it was, but certainly not human. Demon? He glanced at the other Korean and saw that his face had changed as well. What were these things? Their skin was almost white with deep gray mottling. Glowing golden eyes regarded him as both of the beings growled.

Fear shredded Starling's confidence with Wolverine claws. He spared a look behind him, searching for the front door, ready to flee. He spied it not fifteen feet away and was ready to get the hell out, but when he looked back, the two were back to normal. Not demons, just two Korean men, eager for his destruction.

What the hell had just happened?

Had his eyes played a trick on him?

Was it the adrenalin, or a leftover from the drugs he'd ingested the night before?

His phone vibrated again. It had to be Larrson.

Starling answered with his left hand while swinging the bat with his right to clear a space in front of him. He eyed the two Koreans warily, worried they might change again.

"Yeah," he said into the phone.

"We've been looking for you."

Both Koreans lunged at him.

"A little busy now," he said, grunting as he leaped back. He slid across the top of a table, then once on the other side, kicked it at his attackers.

"That's what I want to talk to you about. It's all over. We have the kid."

What the hell?

"What do you mean?"

"Just what I said. We got him."

No more screwing around. Starling threw the bat at one of the men, then pulled his pistol and shot both in the gut before turning and kicking open the front door. He shoved the pistol back into the holster in the small of his back, then ran limping down the street and into the alley. Realizing he still had the phone in his hand, he managed to say, "If you hurt them, I'll kill you."

"You're in no position to dictate terms. This isn't even your concern. If I see you again, I'll kill *you.*" Larrson hung up.

Starling cursed and kept running. He turned down the alley behind Joon's house and sprinted. Then halfway down the block, he slowed to a stop. Breathing heavily, hands on his knees, he thought about the call from Larrson. Why would he call? Why then?

He heard sirens from the direction he'd come. Without thinking, he stepped to the side and shoved his pistol deep between the cushions of an old couch. He walked as calmly as he could past the rear of the Park's home. Larrson stood on the back porch, shouting into a phone. Several Korean men stood beside him, nervously looking at their boss. As Larrson looked toward the alley, Starling turned his face away. Soon he was past. He turned a corner and hiked to Olympic with a smile on his face. He'd almost fallen for the ruse. Larrson didn't have the boy. He didn't have anyone. Starling had noted as he passed that the house next door was as silent and empty as a tomb.

Chapter Five

STARLING HAD SPENT the time waiting for McQueen hunched over a bag containing a forty-ounce beer, leaning against the side of a Koreatown plaza off Western Avenue. Part of his reasoning was to blend in with the other human detritus. The other part had to do with hiding the slash on his back. He'd occasionally hold out his hand and ask for some money. Most of the Koreans glared at him—stupid, white, poor addict—but a rare few seemed to feel sorry for him and gave him money. During the time he'd been there, he'd garnered $27.32.

McQueen finally arrived in one of his employer's vans. If he'd meant to blend in, he was an utter failure. The van was painted Day-Glo pink with two giant men's faces silhouetted and kissing. The words CLOSETS ARE FOR CLOTHES and COME JOIN US AT HANK'S were painted on the side in rainbow letters. The van pulled into an empty space in the parking lot and waited.

Starling couldn't help rolling his eyes as he deposited the bag and the empty forty in a trash bin, then opened the door to the back.

McQueen was dressed in a skin-tight pink company shirt with the image of a raised fist over his breast and the words COME YANK AT HANK'S. He wore jeans and combat boots. On his hands were fingerless gloves. He had a full head of brown hair with a hipster beard and mustache. When Starling opened the door, he said, "Close the door and take off your shirt."

"Bet you say that to all the guys," Starling said.

"You wish." McQueen opened a combat medic bag and pulled out alcohol and some swabs. He'd tugged off his fingerless gloves and pulled on rubber ones. "You're not my type."

"What? You like tall, dark and handsome?" Starling said, wincing as McQueen turned him.

"I'll take them as tall, dark and clean. Jesus, Starling, what happened to you?"

"No reason to call me Jesus." He winced again. "Just been down on my luck, I guess."

McQueen had been an 18D in the army—MOS designator for Special Forces Medic. He'd retired as a warrant officer after commanding two ODAs in Iraq. All his men and fellow operators had known about his sexual preferences. A few made jokes, which he'd never minded, but none really cared. Starling understood that Special Forces was a brotherhood much like his rangers, and there were few things that could disturb that. Certainly, who you went to bed with wasn't one of them.

"'Down on your luck,'" McQueen repeated. "That another way to say alcoholic?"

"I'm not an alcoholic. That was a disguise."

"You wear it pretty well, my friend." McQueen applied bandages to Starling's back, then handed him a T-shirt to match his own.

Starling furrowed his brow but couldn't think of any reasonable excuse not to wear it. Grimacing, he shrugged it on. "There. How do I look?"

McQueen cocked his head and twizzled an end of his mustache. "Like someone I used to know."

Starling felt his smile drop a little. He hadn't seen McQueen in person for five months, and seeing him now brought back a lot of good memories and a lot of missions they'd been on in Afghanistan. McQueen was the most solid person Starling knew. They weren't friends. They were closer than that. Starling felt that McQueen could have easily been the TST commander. That he'd never fought or argued for the assignment had always made Starling wonder. That was why Starling had made him second in charge. Now, seeing how normal McQueen looked compared to himself made Starling realize how hard he'd fallen.

"How have you been doing since you got back?" Starling asked. "I got to tell you, you're looking pretty good... in a purely heterosexual way."

"Is this a serious question or are you just giving me a yank?"

"Serious." Starling gestured to himself. "You can see what happened to me, but you look the same as you did."

McQueen shook his head. "Anything but." He ran a hand through his hair and began to put away the medical supplies. "Can't sleep, and then when I do, I see shit."

"What sort of shit?"

"Weird, dreamy shit." McQueen shook his head. "I don't know. I'm no shrink."

"Like a girl and a goat, maybe."

McQueen gave Starling a startled look, then swallowed. "I don't want to talk about it."

"You *have* seen them," Starling pressed, but he couldn't get McQueen to respond. "Brother, I can't even nap without seeing them." Starling whistled the theme music to *The Twilight Zone*. "What about other things? Have strange things been happening to you?"

"I bounce the door of a gay bar. My definition of strange might not be the same as yours."

Starling barely heard the comment as he remembered the faces of the two Koreans that had morphed. It wasn't something he was prepared to share. He was already close to looking stupid and didn't want to be the one who shoved himself over the edge.

Starling shook his head and changed the subject. "Thanks for coming out."

"Anything to help an old friend. Where are they now?"

"Hopefully still holed up. Ready to enact Plan B?"

"Let's get it rolling."

"Got that burner phone I ordered?"

"One better." He handed Starling a pink-cased iPhone.

"Whose is this?"

"A little asshole who keeps selling Special K and X over at the club. I swiped it from him last night after I beat his ass. We can make all the calls we need on this puppy."

Starling stared at McQueen. The guy was normally quiet to the point of being taciturn. Starling wasn't used to seeing him this animated, much less this free with his language. Starling shrugged inwardly, then made the call.

"911, what's your emergency?"

"There are intruders in the house across the street. Looks like a whole Korean gang is doing a number there."

"Are you safe, sir?"

"Oh, sure. I'm just down by the window... oh shit. They have guns."

"Did they see you, sir?"

"I don't think so... shit!"

"Can you give us the address, sir?"

He gave the address, then said breathlessly, "I think they might be coming for me. I gotta go." He hung up and tossed the phone to McQueen.

"What now?" McQueen asked, tossing the phone out the window.

"Let's find a place down the street to watch the fireworks."

By the time they found a spot a block down Harvard Street, all hell was breaking loose at Joon's old house. Four squad cars had pulled in front of it and the cops had their weapons trained on those inside, screaming for them to come out. McQueen and Starling were wondering if they might have created a standoff, but after about fifteen minutes and the arrival of five more squad cars, the men filed out of the home, hands on their heads and were soon eating the street as they were segregated, frisked, and cuffed.

After about an hour all but one squad car left the area.

From watching police procedurals, Starling guessed it was waiting for the crime scene techs to arrive. Not enough to bother anything they'd be doing.

After another fifteen minutes, he said, "Okay, let's go."

They pulled around the block and then up to the front gate of the house next door, where hopefully Joon and Freddie were still safe. The officer watched them warily, but when Starling got out of the van and waved, the cop couldn't help smirk at the day glow pink shirt and the *Come Yank at Hank's* logo.

McQueen honked the horn and flashed his lights.

Starling went to the gate and rattled it.

This got the cop's attention. He headed over, thumbs hooked in his belt.

"Hey, Joon! It's me. Ready to go?" Starling glanced nonchalantly at the officer, then shouted, "Joon, open up!"

The cop kept coming.

Where was she? Larrson hadn't figured it out, had he? Starling remembered seeing a stack of mail in the kitchen of Joon's house. Had that been hers or the neighbor's? Would Larrson have been smart enough to realize she might be next door?

"What's going on?"

Starling spun and met the policeman, Office McKinney by his nameplate.

"I asked a question."

"Just waiting on my sister," Starling said regretting the words the moment they left his mouth.

"Your sister?" the cop said, his eyes unreadable.

"Yes sir, officer."

"Show me some ID," the cop said.

"Right now?"

The cop took a step back, the equivalent of a threat.

Starling's eyes widened. This was the last thing he needed. He glanced at McQueen, who sat steadfastly behind the wheel... like he should. At this point any movement could result in something bad. Starling knew that if he was in the TST and was presented with a man who wouldn't cooperate, depending on the circumstances, he was cleared hot to kill.

He swallowed. "No problem, officer." He reached for his wallet, moving slowly, nothing in his stance aggressive.

Just then the front door to the house opened. Joon pushed Freddie out onto the porch, left him there, then ran down the stairs and to the gate.

"I was wondering what happened to you," she said to Starling.

"Just getting a van, sis," he said, not taking his eye off the police officer.

Starling watched as the cop assessed Joon, then turned back to Starling, an eyebrow raised in question.

"Adopted," Starling said. He shrugged.

"Can you help us with my son, officer?" Joon said, unlocking the front gate, keys and chain rattling against the metal.

The cop turned toward the front porch.

"It's my nephew," Starling said. "We're taking him to Disneyland tomorrow. He's always wanted to go." Lies piling on top of lies.

Joon swept open the gate.

Starling stopped reaching for his wallet. "We'll bring the van into the driveway to load him in. We might need help, though, getting him down the steps."

He waved and McQueen slowly drove the van up, stopping so the headlights illuminated Freddie, who was in his wheelchair on the wide front porch of the Craftsman. A set of four stairs rose from the ground to the porch.

Starling walked forward, putting his back to the cop, trying to pretend that loading a hand- and footless kid into the back of a pink van advertising a gay bar in the middle of Koreatown was the most natural thing in the world.

"Hold on a minute," the cop said, stepping towards them.

Now Joon, McQueen, and Starling turned, all with their hands on the wheelchair.

The cop watched them for a moment, then nodded. "Let me give you a hand with that." He approached the boy in the wheelchair. "What's up, kid," he said, ruffling the boy's hair. "You doing okay?"

"Awesome, officer. Gonna see Mickey tomorrow."

Starling knew then that the Oscar was going to Freddie.

The cop grabbed one side of the wheelchair while McQueen grabbed the other.

Joon hurried to the back doors of the van and opened both of them.

Starling climbed inside and squatted, waiting to receive the chair. Out of the corner of his eye he saw the remnants of his bloody shirt and hastily shoved it under the passenger seat.

Another few minutes and the chair was inside and

strapped down, and they were driving away from the residence.

No one said a word for five blocks.

Finally, Joon said from the back, "I didn't know if you were coming back."

"I promised," Starling said. "I don't break promises."

McQueen shot him a look but didn't say a word, then introduced himself using the rearview mirror.

After the introduction, she asked, "What now?"

"Now we find somewhere to stash you. I know the perfect place." Starling turned to McQueen. "And you've spoken to Lore about this?"

The bigger man shook his head. "Been trying to get ahold of her, but no luck. When's the last time you talked to her?"

Starling thought about it and couldn't remember. That was so odd. He'd always remained in contact with his TST members. He still knew the phone numbers of old members of his regiment he hadn't seen in a dozen years. But for the life of him, he couldn't recall Lore's number, her address, or even what she was doing these days. He said as much.

"It seems to me that you haven't been in touch with anyone. No offense, Starling, but the only reason we've been in contact was because you owe me money."

The embarrassment of the situation struck Starling and he felt the heat of Joon's and her son's gazes on the back of his neck. "I'm trying to fix that. What's up with Lore these days?" he asked, trying to shift the attention away from him. The embarrassment was bad enough, but the disappointment was something he couldn't bear.

"She's fallen farther than you, I'm afraid." Then McQueen added, "No insult intended."

Starling sighed.

"She has a trailer east of Corona," McQueen said. "Supposed to be raising vegetables and living her crazy yoga-vegan lifestyle."

Supposed to be. "So she's not then. What happened?"

"Drugs, man. She's been back and forth from detox, but the last two times I spoke with her she was clean as a whistle and even considering another tour back in the box."

"What's the box?" Freddie asked, making Starling realize that he might be too young for some of the things they were saying.

"The box is downrange," he said, then realized he needed to explain it. "Downrange means a deployment, usually to a warzone, so when we say take a tour in the box, we mean some place like Afghanistan and Iraq."

"Have you been there?" Freddie asked.

"Been to both places," Starling replied. He wanted to add *and they were both shitholes,* but he kept that to himself.

"You mean you were in the army?" Freddie asked a little too incredulously.

Starling bit back another sigh and caught the grin on McQueen's face. "Yeah. I was in the army. In fact, I was a US Army Ranger. Do you know what rangers are, son?"

"I played them in *Call of Duty*. They're special-ops forces."

"*Call of Duty*? You mean the game?" Starling remembered it being pretty damned gory, stopping just short of slasher movie SFX. The profanity was also over-the-top, however realistic it might be. Most civilians had no idea how much cursing really went on in the military. Then he remembered the kid had no arms, so how was he... oh. The steering mechanism must pull double duty as a game controller.

"It's pretty bad," Joon admitted from the back. "But we talk about it and he realizes that real life isn't as graphic."

Starling flashed back to the aftermaths of a dozen real battles and bit his tongue.

"I liked the scenarios they have, especially the one where I become a spy in Russia. I think that's cool." Freddie paused, then added, "And they help kill zombies."

Starling furrowed his brow, wondering.

McQueen stepped into the conversation. "Starling here was in charge of a team of us."

"I thought you were in charge," Freddie said.

"Me? I'm just the driver and the muscle."

"The muscle?" Freddie asked.

"I keep anything bad from happening to my friends, and now that you're my friend that means you too."

As they headed south and east, Starling kept trying to contact Lore. Once they hit I-15, the going got faster. They stopped to get some food at an In-N-Out Burger, then continued on their way. They finally reached Lore's house by 23:15 hours. It was a double-wide amid hard scrabble about a mile off a side-road. The nearest house was several acres over. Like the driveway, the road was unlit, but the interior of the house was flashing like a rave was going on inside.

McQueen pulled to a stop near the home and turned off the ignition, the slamming sound of techno replacing the engine noise. They sat and listened to the *THUNKA THUNKA THUNKA* beat emanating from the home. The music was so loud that the trailer seemed to pulsate. Odd sequences of colored lights flashed furiously to the music. It was like the trailer was a living thing, screaming for its life.

"Well, that explains why she never answers her phone," McQueen said.

Then a face slammed against the nearest window of the trailer, leaving a long, bloody smear.

Chapter Six

Corona Regional Medical Center

STARLING SAT IN the hospital waiting room, his eyes wide, still not believing what he'd seen, the words *zaxhem mahal keh dar ahn noor shoma vared ast* still ringing in his ears. It sounded Middle Eastern, but it could very well have been Martian. All he was certain of was that he'd never forget them, each syllable screamed from the bloody mouth of Lore as she was thrown back and forth across the trailer by a giant, invisible hand. As crazy as it sounded, it had to have been a hand, because that's exactly what it had looked like when they entered. Lore, once a fierce army lieutenant, being rag-dolled back and forth, absolutely not in control of her limbs. The only thing he'd ever seen like that was years ago when he'd fallen asleep with the television on, only to wake up to *The Exorcist* on television, the gory face of the girl leering into the TV camera with green bile dripping from her lips.

Starling shook his head to free himself of the image and sipped the tepid coffee he'd scrounged from the nurse's station. McQueen was in the room with Lore. He'd told the hospital staff he was her brother, which sort of made sense since it was him who'd brought her to the hospital. The ride to the emergency room had been terrifying; Lore had fought against Starling as he'd restrained her—spitting, snarling, and gouging, her trying to break free while he held her on the floor of the van.

Poor Freddie had cried the entire way, with Joon trying desperately to calm him.

Starling's wrists had withstood the worst of Lore's struggles, scratches from mid-arm all the way down to his hands, bloody red trophies of where he'd held her down. It should have hurt, but all he could think of was that first moment when they'd broken down the door to her doublewide. The inside was completely devoid of furniture except for a wall unit holding a stereo and speakers affixed to the far wall. A multicolored light was wired to a corner of the room with a fan in front of it to continually shutter the light. The carpet had been ripped away, revealing wooden flooring that had been drawn on with strange sigils and letters. These markings matched those on the walls, which covered almost every inch of the once white surface along with images of various triangles with rays shooting from them in every direction. Everything that had been done had essentially transformed the room into one immense, mystical mosh pit.

But what he saw of Lore was much worse. Her hair had been cut on the sides in what he could only describe as a punk haircut. The back of her head still had long hair, but it had been tied into intricate braids interspersed with sticks and pieces of garbage. Her face had been marked like the walls, with hundreds of tiny letters and sigils written helter-skelter across her features. And that's where all normality stopped. Beneath her chin was another matter altogether. Her breasts and groin were wrapped with black duct tape. It looked like an entire roll had been used. Beneath the tape and covering every other inch of skin except for her hands and feet, she was wrapped with tinfoil. The shiny metal crinkled as she moved. Atop everything else, she'd wrapped herself in cellophane. This had made it hard for Starling to hold her down, his hands constantly slipping.

McQueen appeared at the door to her room, exhaustion in his eyes. He ran his right hand through his hair, then subconsciously smoothed his beard. He came over and plopped into the seat next to Starling with a groan.

"How is she?" Starling asked. He glanced over to where Joon sat, curled up in a molded chair beside her son in his wheelchair.

"BP and heart rate are now normal. She's breathing unassisted. They gave her something to sleep, so she'll be that way for a few more hours. We'll know more when she wakes up."

"If she's coherent," added Starling.

"Right. If she's coherent."

"What was she on?"

McQueen shook his head. "That's the funny thing. She wasn't on anything."

"Bullshit."

"Tox screen came back clean."

"Then what was all that about?"

McQueen shrugged. "Your guess is as good as mine." He pushed himself to his feet. "Where'd you get that coffee?"

Starling told him and McQueen shuffled off towards the nurse's station.

Starling remembered Lore in the last mission. They'd been attacked by an unidentified UAV, and she'd taken it down with an RPG. Another pair of UAVs had arrived, but they departed as soon as the first one was destroyed. Whomever the operators were, they'd probably been unwilling to lose another of the high-tech gadgets. He could still picture her in her Kevlar helmet, Oakley sunglasses, and body armor, leaning back and laughing at the UAV as it broke into a hundred flaming pieces. So confident. So accomplished. So unlike the Lore he'd seen in her home. And to believe McQueen, she hadn't been on anything.

Starling spent the next half hour trying to figure out how it happened. Then he noticed that Joon was staring at him.

She asked how Lore was and he told her what McQueen had related.

Then he remembered something she'd said earlier, something that had been bothering him. "What is it I do?" he asked.

Joon gave him a questioning look.

"Your son said I hurt you sometimes." He shook his head at the illogic of it, but pressed on nonetheless. "Let's just say there's a Groundhog Day effect or something crazy. Let's say I have come before. What is it that I do?"

"I remember you hitting me once." She held up her right hand and pointed to the back of it. "With this, right here," she said, pointing at her cheek.

His eyes widened. "Me? I hit you?"

She nodded but watched him carefully.

"Impossible," he scoffed, shaking his head. Then seeing her wide, adamant eyes, he asked, "Is that all? Is that all I did? Not that hitting you wasn't bad enough, but…" By the look in her eyes he could tell there was more. "What else?"

"You kicked me."

"I couldn't have." He'd never kicked a woman in his entire life. He couldn't even imagine the scenario where he'd consider such a thing unless it was in combat.

"As you say then." She turned away, curling into herself on the chair.

He stared at her back. The entire conversation was insane, but he felt compelled to push through it.

"Where?" he asked breathlessly.

"In the stomach." She didn't turn around.

He grinned at the absurdity of it, then his expression was washed away with concern and confusion. "You're having me on. I'd never…" But as she turned, he saw the hurt and truth of it in her eyes—the fear—the memories. "How many times?"

She considered the question, then asked, "How many times did you kick me or how many times did you come back to kick me?"

He put his hands on the sides of his head and wished he had hair so he could pull it out. "Okay, what's the worst I did to you?"

She looked at him for a long time without saying something, then said, "I think you killed me... once."

"You think I... you're not sure... how?" he whispered, barely audible. "How is that possible?"

She turned and stared at a poster on the wall warning against choking hazards. Her voice was low and monotone as she said, "I remember you grabbing my hair. I remember the pain as you bashed my head against the fireplace repeatedly, screaming about a boy and a girl and a goat. You even began to bleat like the animal. You sounded like an animal. You were an animal... and then... darkness." She licked her lips. "I remember that darkness. It was so quiet. So gentle. You know how when you're in a dark room, there's all sorts of worry because of sharp corners and objects you don't want to knock onto the floor? This wasn't that kind of darkness. This was a darkness where I felt safe. Where the idea of pain didn't exist. Where it was just me and the universe and nothing."

Now it was his turn to stare at her. The women he'd killed... the woman he'd kicked... the woman he'd— "How did you know about the girl and the goat?" he asked suddenly.

"You were screaming about them."

"Me? Screaming?" He shook his head. "When did this happen? The kicking." He inhaled. "The killing."

She regarded him before she spoke. "Not now. Before. It's not as clear as it should be."

"Let me ask you this," he said. "How is it that you and the boy can remember me, but I can't remember you?"

She shrugged. "Maybe you're in our story instead of us

being in yours."

She ended it there. Freddie was awake and needed to use the bathroom.

Starling watched as she stood, then pushed him down the hall into a family bathroom that was wheelchair accessible.

He was still staring when McQueen returned with a large coffee and a burrito.

"Looks like you're going to be sick," he said, sitting down and taking an immense bite of the burrito. He chewed, then swallowed, his gaze on Starling the entire time. "Want a bite?"

"What? Uh, no thanks." Starling leaned back in his chair and exhaled loudly. After a moment, he asked, "Ever feel like you're a character in a story and not real?"

McQueen stopped chewing momentarily, then chewed fast and swallowed so he could answer. "I don't know what that means."

Starling shook his head. "That makes two of us, brother."

"Who'd you hear that from?"

"Joon. She and her son say they've seen me before."

"Maybe you were in the same store or restaurant. LA is big, but it's really just a small town."

"No, they say I did things to them."

"When you say things, you mean...?"

"Hurting them. Maybe even killing them."

With half the burrito gone, McQueen shook his head. "I think they're having you on."

Starling nodded. "That's what I thought too, but to what end? What is it they have to gain?"

McQueen seemed to consider this as he chewed. He finished the burrito, wadded up the wrapper, and found a trash can to place it in. Then he wiped his hands with a napkin and dumped it too. When he returned to his seat, he sipped his coffee. As his hand got next to his face, he sniffed his fingers and made a face. "I hate it when my hands smell like food."

He went to the nurse's station where there was a sanitizer dispenser and spent several minutes wiping it into his hands, then smelling them. Once he was satisfied, he returned to his seat.

Starling watched him all the while, remembering how fastidious McQueen had always been with his gear and person. It would be too easy to label it as a mark of his gayness. As Starling had learned, it was more of a control mechanism. McQueen liked order and hated surprises so he kept everything around him neat and prepared. He'd squared off with Narco on several occasions, the smaller, leaner member of the TST, their Charlie Brown equivalent of Pig-Pen.

After a few sips of coffee and one more sniff of his fingers, McQueen said, "Who are they anyway? You don't know them. You've never seen them before."

"Yet they seem to think they've seen me."

"Don't you know how impossible that is? Listen, I know you've been using. You have the DTs right now." Starling began to protest, and McQueen held up a hand. "Stop it. I can see it in the color of your eyes, the way your pupils are dilated, and the way your hands are shaking. This is an air-conditioned hospital and you're sweating. I bet you're not even hungry right now."

Starling shook his head.

"You should be." He checked his watch. "It's two in the morning. Last time you ate was at least seven hours ago. You should be ravenous. I sure was. The point is that you're not thinking straight."

Starling knew McQueen was right, but damned if he was going to admit it. These were his DTs and he'd deal with them in his own way. "I asked her *how is it that you and the boy can remember me, but I can't remember you* and she said, *maybe you're in our story instead of us being in yours.* Haven't you felt out of sorts? Haven't you felt like you aren't yourself?"

"I keep a tight rein on who I am," McQueen said with finality.

"Well, bully for you. I don't feel like myself at all. I feel like a character that someone else is writing. My call sign was Boy Scout, for God's sake. I didn't choose it, you all gave it to me." He thumped himself in the chest. "Do I look like a fucking boy scout to you?"

A nurse walking by carrying a clipboard gave him a stern look.

"The point," Starling continued, his voice lower, "is that as crazy as she sounds, I feel so out of place that it might just explain who I am and what's going on."

McQueen leaned in close, speaking directly into Starling's ear. "Or it could be them taking advantage of a good man trying to self-medicate for severe PTSD. I know what you've seen. I know what you've done. Remember, I was there when you killed that colonel. You've killed a ton of hajis over the years, but that killing was different. It was murder, plain and simple, and who knows what the weight of it is doing to your soul, much less your psyche."

Murder, plain and simple. There was nothing plain nor simple about that murder. Starling hated the word. It was the grammatical equivalent of a hand grenade. He'd rather call what he'd done *revenge by proxy*, but he kept his mouth shut. Now wasn't the time for that memory to surface; then he really would need something to cloud his mind. He subconsciously licked his lips as the ghost of scotch teased him.

"So you think they're having me on," he said slowly.

"We brought them along, didn't we? If they hadn't said all of those things to you, would they still be with us? Seems as if they're getting everything they want."

"Larrson was a real threat."

"I'm sure he was and you've saved them from him. Let me ask you this, what do you plan on doing with them now?"

Starling had absolutely no idea.

The door down the hall opened and Joon backed her son out.

"I'll tell you what." McQueen said, preparing to stand. "You need to figure this out quickly. I think helping them out in the short term was a good idea, but they need an end game. Especially now. Lore is my focus from here on out. We need to help her. We need to figure out what's going on. Because you're right. If she wasn't on any drugs, then what the hell was she doing?" Then he got up and headed down the hall.

As he passed Joon and her son, he nodded.

Chapter Seven

STARLING WATCHED AS Joon and Freddie resumed their places in the waiting room. What *was* he going to do with them? He couldn't just leave them. They were his responsibility. Sure, he hadn't signed a hand receipt for them, nor was he under any order to remain responsible, but if he ever wanted to regain even a semblance of the man he'd once been, he needed to see this through. All that said, he was well aware that without money, resources, or any place for them to go, it was an iffy, if not impossible, proposition.

After an hour—now four in the morning—Joon got up and stretched. She checked on her son, whose head was slumped forward in his chair, then looked around. When she spied the coffee maker at the nurse's station, she ambled over and poured herself a cup. After adding milk and sugar and stirring, she blew across the surface of the hot liquid as she pushed a fist into the small of her back.

Starling joined her. He was aware that he needed a shower, or at least to clean up. He could smell a slight sour odor, probably sweat from his exertions with the

Korean gangbangers.

"Seats aren't that comfortable," he murmured.

She nodded, barely glancing at him.

He rubbed his face with his right hand and felt the grizzle. What he wouldn't do for a shower... and maybe a gorilla-sized martini. He gritted his teeth as a phantom taste of vodka tickled his lips. Then he laughed hoarsely. "Bet I look like something someone dragged in, huh?"

She glanced at him again. "If you say so."

He felt like an idiot. Clearly, she wasn't up for small talk, but that was fine. He'd been thinking of how to help her. He decided to play her game and see if she had the solution already.

"I've been wondering how we can help you," he said, "but I'm also wondering if you might be able to help yourself."

She turned to him, interest and doubt in her eyes. "I have a little less than fifty bucks and nowhere to go."

"Good to know. Let me ask you this. Have you and I ever had this conversation? I mean, in the hospital, about where you should go to be safe?"

She cocked her head as she chewed the inside of her cheek. She seemed about to answer when her face began to pixelate until it was nothing but unrecognizable static like one would see on a television with no operating channel. Where her dark eyes had been, they now glowed a deep pulsating gold.

Starling backed away as she began to speak.

Her static-laced words sounded like they were coming from underwater.

Starling shook his head to clear the impossible image. Was he dreaming? Was this part of his DTs? What the hell was going on? He glanced at the nurses behind the counter and all of them had the same features... or lack thereof... all with black and white static faces and golden eyes. He was suddenly aware of the blood pumping through his veins, the thud of his heartbeat booming over every other sound. He began to shake. He reached for the counter but missed it, his hand batting at the air. He opened his mouth to speak, but found no air to push words free.

Suddenly Joon's face was right next to his, the static buzz burning through the sound of his own heartbeat. His eyes went wide as she got closer and closer, desperate for her static not to cover his own face. Or was it already? He felt blood leave his head and he was suddenly ice cold.

Then...

Groggily, he opened eyelids that weighed a hundred pounds apiece. It took several tries, but he eventually managed to regain his vision. The first thing he noticed was that he was sitting down. He turned his head sluggishly to regard his right arm. An IV had been affixed to it, and the tube ran to a bag hanging from a tall, silver pole. He was sitting in a chair in the corner of an admitting room, his shoes unlaced and his pants unbuttoned.

"Here comes Cinderella," McQueen said. He moved in so close that Starling's vision blurred. He felt a touch on his head. "Doesn't look like it's going to bleed, but you definitely got an egg there."

"What—what happened?" Starling managed to ask, his mouth dry as a Martian lakebed.

"According to your friend Joon, one minute you were standing there, the next you were taking a nosedive onto the floor."

"Didn't... didn't she catch me?"

"Brother, the way you smell and look, even a homeless man on a bender would be hesitant to touch you."

Starling remembered how her face had turned to static and shuddered. That had possibly been the most terrified he'd ever been.

"Water," he said. "Can I have some water?"

McQueen poured him water from a plastic pitcher.

Starling eagerly grabbed the cup and gulped it. "More," he said, and McQueen gave him more. Four glasses later, he felt better.

"What was my problem?"

"Nurse said dehydration. I agree. They were going to do a tox panel, but I talked them out of it." Then seeing Starling's confusion, he added, "Not knowing what you took, I didn't want there to be a formal record. After all, we're eventually going to go back in the box, right?"

Back in the box. Back in Afghanistan or Iraq. That was the last thing on his mind.

"How's Lore? Is she awake?"

"She's awake and asking for you."

"What's she saying?"

"She won't tell me shit. She wants you and no one else."

"Is she still talking that language?"

"That *language* was Persian," McQueen said. Then anticipating Starling's question added, "I Googled it."

"You Googled it?" Starling licked dry lips. "Of course

you did."

McQueen held up his phone. "It's from Rumi. According to Wikipedia, he was a thirteenth century poet and Sufi mystic."

"What's Lore doing quoting a thirteenth century poet?"

McQueen shrugged. "Better yet, why is she speaking Persian? You saw her bio. She never mentioned speaking Persian. That would have gotten her a better contract. No reason to hide it."

"Did you get her words?"

"I recorded them, then sent the recording through Google. Says, *The wound is the place where the light enters you.*"

"That supposed to mean something?" Starling asked.

McQueen shrugged again. "Same as any poem, I guess. Who knows? You ready to talk to Lore? Think you can stand?"

Starling put weight on his feet and managed to pull himself upright. He was a little dizzy, but otherwise felt strong enough to move. He started to pull out the IV, but McQueen stopped him.

"Let's leave that in until the bag is gone. You need the fluids."

Starling assented but felt like a patient as he shuffled out the door of the room they were in, hand gripping the pole that held the saline bag rolling beside him. Once in the hall, he glanced down to where the elevators were. He could end all the bullshit right now. All he had to do was rip free the needle in his arm and make a break for it. McQueen wouldn't chase after him and, with any luck,

Starling would find a package store where he could pick up a pint of anything... even drain cleaner. He was so thirsty for some booze. He had that twenty-seven dollars plus change he'd begged for in Koreatown. He could really do it. He paused and closed his eyes.

"You okay, man?" McQueen asked.

Starling could feel the man's hand on his arm, the flesh and blood connection of a friend and fellow soldier. They'd shared time together, doing things that no two men should ever have to do. Starling had stood by McQueen when others wouldn't because of his personal tastes. McQueen had stood by Starling even in the darkest of times, especially those moments of obsidian clarity when Starling had understood the totality of his actions against the Afghan colonel. That there'd been a moment, however fleeting, he'd thought of leaving his friend and Lore, sent a sick shiver through his chest that would have released as a sob had his jaws not been clenched. He held it there and tasted the grimy bile that was his addiction, then swallowed.

"Yeah," he managed to say. "I'll be fine." Which wasn't the same as being *okay,* but it showed an optimism he was just beginning to feel. Alone he was nothing; he'd proven that to himself and the seedy underbelly of Los Angeles. Together, as a team, he was everything. A single moment of lucidity laid out what had to be done before him... for Lore... for McQueen and the rest, wherever they were. It was time to get the team back together.

They moved down the antiseptic hall to the open door to the room were Lore was lying, awake, her face a mix of anger and confusion.

The nurses had succeeded in wiping off most of the symbols on her face, but there were still enough there that she'd draw looks if she were to go out in public. Starling wondered what they stood for. McQueen had been smart enough to record her voice. Starling hoped he'd also photographed the symbols so that they could go to the oracle of Google later and see what they meant.

He stood in the doorway staring at her, trying to divine what had happened to the once proud and professional woman.

Fifteen seconds passed until her head turned toward the doorway. When she saw him, her eyes narrowed. "Who the hell are you? The fat version of Boy Scout?"

He couldn't help laugh and entered the room.

McQueen came behind him.

"In the flesh, Lore. And what about you? I loved your new outfit. You looked ravishing in your tinfoil."

"And your makeup," McQueen said. "I haven't seen that sort of creativity since the last Satyr Motorcycle Club rave in Tahoe."

Both Lore and Starling turned to McQueen.

"What? The Satyrs. They're an actual MC. A gay MC."

"I don't think it's the same thing," Starling said.

"Definitely not the same thing," Lore added. "Can I guess what happens at these raves?"

McQueen blinked, then grinned. "Okay, fine. Not the same thing." Changing the subject, he asked, "How you feeling, Laurie?"

"Like I was rolled hard and put away wet."

Starling loved that about her. She was tough as nails, cursed like a Navy chief, but could easily be found wearing a dress and makeup at a niece's cotillion.

"Care to tell us what happened?" Starling asked.

He could see her working through a possible answer, her eyes widening, then going to slits. Finally a tear fell from her left eye. "We need to go back."

As she said it, Starling knew it was true. Still, he wanted to hear her words, so he asked, "Where? Afghanistan?"

She nodded. "For weeks now, I've been fighting it. It started as a dream of us back in Afghanistan waiting for something, then it changed and I saw a girl and she had a—"

"Goat. She had a goat," Starling said. "Was its mouth sewn shut?"

"Yes, a goat," she said, pushing herself up to a sitting position. "But in my dream its mouth was just a mouth. So you dreamed it too?"

Starling nodded.

She turned to McQueen. "And you?"

McQueen glanced at Starling, then nodded.

"I knew it!" Starling said. "I knew you dreamed about that goat."

"Was he playing tough guy?" Lore asked.

"When isn't he?" Starling responded.

"There was that time in Herat when he found that waif of an Italian major. What was his name?"

"Antonio something. Wasn't it Antonio?" Starling asked.

"I think that's right," Lore said. "Maltefano was the

last name. Antonio Maltefano. He was a hot guy, if you liked them in miniature."

"He couldn't have been more than five feet tall," Starling said. "He literally disappeared in McQueen's shadow."

McQueen cleared his throat and said, "You know I'm in the room, right?"

"Just making sure you know your place," Lore said.

"What's that supposed to mean?"

"That you're not a roadie. You're with the band. Part of the team. You like to play this aloof gay ninja warrior, and it probably works in some circles, but not here. We've seen you without your makeup and in curlers."

"I'm not a ninja."

"And I'm not as crazy as I look."

McQueen smiled. "I see Lore is back to her old self. Good girl. I think I'll go check on Joon and her son, though," he said.

After he left, Lore asked, "Joon and her son?"

"Long story. Weird story." He noted that the saline bag was empty and pulled out the needle. He let it fall, hanging from the bag, then pushed the contraption against the wall. He approached the bed as he held a piece of tissue against the place where the needle had been. "So what happened? Why are you quoting thirteenth century poetry in Persian?" He touched her cheek. "Why the marks?"

Her brown eyes burrowed into his. "Oh, Boy Scout. How I've missed you. I was hoping you'd come to my rescue."

"You've never seemed like the rescuing type."

"That was then, this is now." She lowered her gaze. "Things have been… difficult for me."

"It's been weird for me too. I have these dreams and then Joon—this Korean woman I was sent to—well, anyway she thinks we've met before."

"When you saw me, I was at wit's end," she said. "I had these words stuck in my brain. Persian you said? Who the fuck knows Persian?"

"Uh, Iranians?"

"Whatever. I had these words and I didn't know what they meant, but they were everywhere. I'd go to Starbucks and I'd ask for a Triple Chocolate Latte—don't judge—and instead of my order, I'd speak those words. What the fuck, Boy Scout? How does that happen? I'd be at the checkout line at Von's and try and say a simple thank you and, *blam*, those damned words. I lost my job with UPS because every interaction was apparently a practice in thirteenth century Persian poetry and my boss thought I was crazy. It got to the point that I stopped talking entirely. I'd write things down like I was a mute. I had a whole stack of stickies back in my trailer. Things like *thank you* for a Starbucks order or *can you pass me a carton of Newport 100s*. Shit like that.

"Oh," she added, sitting fully upright. "I even had one that said *Fuck You Very Much,* which I reserved for this one ass hat clerk at the last working video store in Riverside, who took it upon himself to decide which videos someone could watch like he was the king of video or something. Bottom line was I had these words stuck in me so, I cleared my trailer and got ready, then had my own fucking mystical rave."

Starling's eyes narrowed. "That was all you? You set that up? And the tinfoil?"

She grinned. "Seemed like a good idea at the time." Then she laughed, full and throaty. "How many times have we said that? Huh, Boy Scout?"

"Stop calling me that," he said.

"What? Boy Scout?"

"Yeah."

"But that's who you are."

He shook his head. "Was."

She paused a moment, then asked, "So there's a weight limit to being a Boy Scout? That why you don't want to go by your call sign?"

"We don't call you Preacher's Daughter except in the box."

Her eyes narrowed. "No, you don't. Say, you're not feeling all right are you, Boy Sc—I mean, Starling."

"I've been better. I've had my own crazy shit to deal with."

"Crazy like tinfoil, Saran Wrap, and the entire encyclopedia of religious icons drawn on your skin?"

"Crazy like eight balls of coke, X, Special K, and the old fall back, Windowpane, along with a shitload of pizza and vitamin V."

"Oh," she said, drawing out the word like everyone's mother. "You were self-medicating. Yeah, I tried that, but it didn't work for me. I'd pass out and get stuck in dreams about the girl and the goat. Fucking weird, right?"

"Totally fucking weird," Starling said, suddenly

impossibly happy to have Lore back in his life.

"What's the plan?" she asked.

"Why you asking me?"

"You're team lead. If you want to get back to being Boy Scout you need to start making decisions. So what's next, El Jefe?"

Starling sighed and looked inward. "We seem to be having the same dream. We both have this idea that something's been left undone. I can't explain this feeling I have… this need that's been gnawing at me. I have no rational explanation for saying this, but I feel… I feel that if we go back, we'll figure out what all of this means."

After a moment to take it in, Lore said, "I've been feeling the same." Then she laughed self-consciously. "Didn't you see my fashion statement?" Then she got serious. "But we can't just go back to Afghanistan. It's not like we can take a cruise or anything. We need a contract. Think you can get us one?"

"I think so. Maybe. Depends. If we're going to get the team back together, we need to make a stop in Phoenix first."

"Oh yeah? What's there?"

"Narco."

"And you think he can help?"

"We need his connections."

Suddenly a commotion erupted from the hall. A loud voice, punctuated by an "I don't think so" by McQueen, followed by a scuffle, then the sound of a body hitting the floor.

Chapter Eight

STARLING SAID TO Lore, "Get your things. I think we're about to move, and fast."

By the time Lore swung her feet off the side of the bed and was ripping her IV out, Starling was at the door, watching as two stunned nurses and a doctor stared down at a rent-a-cop unconscious on the floor. McQueen stood over him, violence coloring his cheeks.

The downed security guard was Asian. Probably Korean. Starling lunged forward and knelt beside the unconscious man. He fumbled through the pockets of the guy's padded jacket until he came out with a cell phone. He swiped it on and checked the last numbers called. He recognized it immediately, then stood.

"McQueen, report."

"Mall cop here said he recognized me from an APB that was just posted."

Starling shook his head. "That's bullshit. Larrson was the last number called."

And there were probably more on the way. Starling

glanced worriedly at the elevator, which showed that the car was on the first floor. "You know what this means, right?"

"GTFO," McQueen said.

"GTFO," Starling repeated.

Starling stood and began addressing doctors, nurses, techs, other patients, and his friends. "Here's the situation. A criminal gang is after us. They are bad, we are good. This man alerted them to our presence, which makes him bad. Very soon the criminals are going to come here. They are not after any of you. They are after us."

A doctor stepped forward, gesturing towards Starling. "What sort of horseshit is this? You're in a hospital, not a—"

The doctor fell to his knees as McQueen grabbed his fingers and ground them together.

"Let the nice man talk," McQueen said in a gentle voice. "He has a plan. Don't you, Boy Scout?"

Starling jerked at the use of his old call sign, then shook his head. "See if the doctor has a cell phone."

McQueen let go of the doctor's hand and held out his own. The doctor whimpered as he pulled out a phone and handed it to McQueen.

"What's your number?"

As soon as the doctor said it, Starling typed it into the security guard's phone, then made a call. The doctor's phone buzzed in McQueen's hand.

"Now we have coms. Go and get us transport. And not what we drove in here with," he added, thumbing the logo on his shirt. He glanced down the hall. "Make sure we can fit the boy too."

McQueen broke into a run. He ignored the elevator and headed further down the hall.

As soon as the big man left, the doctor stood and said, "I'm going to sue him for this."

"Do what you need to do," Starling said.

"I'm going to call the police is what I'm going to do," the doctor said.

Starling nodded. "Do that. In fact, do it now and do it quick. Remember what I said? The bad guys are coming." When he saw the doctor hesitate, Starling yelled, "I said call them. There are worse people than us out there and they'll be here soon." Starling called over his shoulder, "Lore, you ready to go?"

"All set, boss," she said.

"Then let's get going. On me," he said, and began moving toward Joon and her son at a brisk walk. When he was close, he said, "Follow me, Joon."

Lore was following but using the wall to steady herself.

Starling considered helping her, but she saw him and shook her head.

Starling knew that it would be the police who would probably get there first. Possibly several were in the hospital already. Hospital security would also be notified. Larrson couldn't have co-opted all of them. Whatever was going on, Starling had little doubt they were being tracked by the hospital security cameras.

They rushed down the hall. When Starling saw the room he wanted, they all ducked inside the staff lounge. Once the door was closed, he whirled on Joon.

"Why'd you call him?" he asked Joon.

"I didn't," she said, backing away.

"You had to have."

She shook her head as tears burst at the corners of frightened eyes. "But I didn't."

He turned to the kid and snatched free the iPad from its holder. He closed the game being played, then checked and noted that the WiFi was on.

"You been talking to anyone?"

The kid swallowed.

"Who? Who have you been talking to?"

"I—I wasn't ta—talking. It was my dad. He messaged me."

"Did you tell him where we were?"

The kid shook his head. "He asked, but I told him I wasn't allowed to say. He got mad."

"Who bought this?" Lore asked, stepping forward.

"I did," Joon answered.

"With whose money?"

"His father gave me a credit card to use. And no, I haven't used it in days."

Lore thought hard. "Did you also use it to open the iTunes account?"

Joon nodded.

"Then he has access." Lore turned to Starling. "It's not enough to get rid of the Find My Phone Apps or their like. You can search for a connected Apple device through iTunes." To the kid, she asked, "Did he ask for your iTunes password?"

"Yes, but I didn't—" Tears burst from Freddie's eyes.

"There you have it." She turned off the WiFi and

handed to Joon. "He can keep it but the WiFi has to be turned off."

Joon took the pad and put it back into the clips on the chair.

"What is it about him?" Starling asked softly. "Why does he want the kid so much? What aren't you telling me?"

Joon glanced nervously at him but wouldn't meet his eyes.

"If you don't tell me, I'm leaving the both of you here."

Lore peeked out the door. She was still wearing her hospital gown and her butt slipped free of the ties. "Starling, we need to go."

"You really need to tell me," Starling said.

But Joon stood her ground, staring at the floor. The only sign of her nervousness were her fingers working furtively at her sides.

"Then that's it. I'm going."

He turned and strode to the door.

"Coast clear?" he asked.

"Hardly. Security is down the hall."

"How many?"

"Two."

"Can you take them?"

She snorted, then removed her hospital gown and strode into the hall stark raving naked, her gown draped around one arm.

Starling let the door close, but put his ear to it to listen.

"Can someone help me with the ties?" she asked in the sweetest voice. "They're just so hard to get to."

"Miss, put your clothes on," said a deep voice.

Another voice, the doctor's, said, "She's one of them."

Joon approached Starling with her hands out. "Please. You can't leave us."

Starling eyed her but said nothing.

"One of who?" Lore asked. "Who am I one of?"

"Ma'am, put your clothes on," said the deep voice, now closer.

"He'll kill me and lock up the boy," Joon said.

But Starling remained silent.

"Ma'am, you really should—"

Several thuds were followed by a sickly smack against the floor, then the sound of boots running his way.

Then more thuds, followed by a pathetic whimper.

Joon grabbed Starling by the shirt. "It's his organs. His father made him for his organs. He arranged for his sperm to be donated to me so that I could raise him and watch over him."

Lore pushed open the door. She was now wearing a security jacket and a smile. "We need to get going."

Starling couldn't take his eyes off of Joon's imploring face. *Made him for his organs. I watch over him.* Was she a mother or an organ caretaker? How could she be either of those things? Disgust, hatred, and confusion washed through him in a sick rainbow.

Lore grabbed his shoulder. "Now!"

Starling's eyes narrowed, then he shook he head. He put his hands around Joon's wrists and made her let go of his shirt. "You take care, now," he said in a dead voice. Then he slipped into the hallway. He closed the door behind him.

Chapter Nine

CONFUSION REIGNED BACK by the nurse's station as men and women argued about what to do. The doctor who'd caused the trouble earlier seemed to be at the center of everyone's attention. When he saw Starling, he shouted and pointed.

Still wearing only the security guard's leather jacket, Lore led the way as they raced down the hall. At the end, when they turned the corner, they saw a police officer heading their way. They backtracked and found a flight of stairs down a side hall. Instead of going down, they went up. Footsteps rang from below, heading up as well. They only had two stories to go to get to the roof. Starling pushed open the door, let Lore through, then closed it. He spun, searching for a way off the roof, but all he could see was the door they'd entered from, the electrical boxes for two elevators, and a helicopter to which Lore was already running. Everything else was dark LA night.

"Can you fly it?" he asked, not remembering any flight experience in her records.

"No, but we don't have to."

She rifled in the back of the chopper and came out with a hundred foot rope with D-rings attached to each end. She began to tie off one end to the helicopter skid nearest the edge.

"Hey, you!"

Starling spun. A police officer had his gun drawn and was pinning him with the beam of a flashlight in his other hand.

"Stop where you are." Into his microphone the cop said, "Two of them on the roof. The others' whereabouts still unknown."

"Ready, Lore?" Starling asked.

"Ready."

"Ladies first."

When the cop saw what she was preparing to do, he straightened. "Hey! Stop right there."

"Later, Slater," Starling said with a wave, then backed away and ran towards the helicopter. He felt an itch in the center of his back where the cop was aiming but was fairly confident that the man wouldn't shoot. After all, it wasn't as if they were murderers or anything. All they'd done was crack a few skulls.

He grabbed up the rope from the ground as he ran. When he got to the edge of the building he leaped, wrapping the rope around his side and pulling a loop through his legs as he started to plummet. But the rope caught him and he was soon hurtling to the side of the building. He brought his feet up to stop the impact but slammed into the building on his back, breath shooting from him. Although he couldn't breathe and every bone in his body now hurt, he managed to turn around and set his feet. Then, in five great leaps, he rappelled down the side of the building and onto the roof of a one story structure, where he fell heavily to the ground.

Lore was already halfway across it.

Starling limped after her.

His phone buzzed in his pocket, or rather the guard's phone. He answered it while running.

"Meet me on the east side," McQueen said.

Starling scanned the horizon. They were going the wrong way. He glanced back and saw the cop beginning to descend the rope.

"Can't do it." He spied a sign down the road, big and red and bright. "Meet us at Tommy's Burgers."

"You finally hungry?"

Starling grinned. "Actually, yeah." Then he tossed the phone to the ground.

It was nothing to slip off the single story and onto the grass. A bum sleeping in the bushes complained about the noise. They ran around the corner of the building, then came up short.

Five Korean men in tracksuits and dress shoes stood by one of the doors looking like they were ready to make a Bruce Lee movie. Three were smoking while the others were eagerly staring at the exit door. While Starling thought that he and Lore could probably take them, he couldn't spare the time. And it looked as if they didn't have to. A police car skidded to a stop at the curb and two cops got out.

The five thugs immediately straightened and threw on their *I'm not really a gangbanger* smiles.

The cops barely gave them the time of day as they pushed past them.

Starling took the opportunity to sprint across the grass to the sidewalk, then ducked behind a panel truck stuffed with ladders and painting supplies.

Lore was right behind him, but it seemed that they'd drawn the interest of at least one of the bangers.

Starling nodded to Lore, who peeled away, sprinting low into the parking lot, using the truck as a visual barrier between her and the men at the front door.

A Korean rounded the corner of the truck.

Starling looked over at him, adjusting one of the ropes holding down a ladder.

"What's up?" he said.

Lore had already gone to ground so there was nothing for the Korean to see.

He glanced at Starling, then sneered. "What you looking at?"

Starling lowered his gaze and went back to pretending to adjust the rope. "Sorry," he said loud enough to be heard.

The Korean watched him for a moment, then snorted.

Starling counted to five after the guy left, then sprinted as best he could after Lore, remembering when he'd done this without all the extra pounds. God, did he feel fat.

Soon they were in the back of a panel van that said *Chu's Glass Cleaning* on the side and going through the Tommy Burgers' drive in.

"Not exactly a generic van, is it?" Starling said.

McQueen nodded. "Watched a young man take his wife into the emergency room in labor. Left the keys in the ignition and the engine running. He's not going to miss it anytime soon."

"What happened to Joon and the kid?" McQueen asked.

"I was going to ask you. What was it she was saying?" Lore asked.

"Had to leave them behind. There was no way we were getting them out of there."

"We going to get them back?" McQueen asked.

The perverted idea of a man birthing a son just so he could have spare parts had been boiling in Starling since he'd first heard the poisoned words. He wanted to be mad at the mother, but he couldn't. She'd done nothing other than be the mother she could be under the circumstances. But the father and Larrson were other matters entirely. Starling wanted to punish them. He wanted to hurt them.

"I said, we're going back to get them, right?" McQueen said again.

Starling let out a breath. "I'd like to, but I can't figure out a way to do it." Then he relayed what Joon had told her about the son being an organ storage facility for the father and explained Larrson and his connection to the vile enterprise.

McQueen cursed.

Lore got a sick look on her face. Then after a moment, she said, "Give me the phone. I have an idea."

While McQueen pulled forward and got their take-out order, she tried several times to call up a number from memory but with no success. Then she dialed 911; when it was answered, she asked to be transferred to the non-emergency line. There she asked to be put through to Lt. Danny Mayorga. While she was on hold she told them, "He works in the LA gang unit. It's a stretch, but maybe… just maybe."

After a few moments, she spoke, "Danny, it's me, Lore. Yeah. I know it's early, but—and I'm sorry I stood you up, but—" She shrugged and rolled her eyes. "You're right. I should have called, but—right. You're definitely right. I just thought I'd call and give you a scoop. Okay, you're not a newspaper. A lead, then. Right. A lead. That's what you law enforcement types call them, right?"

She spent the next ten minutes explaining everything Starling had told her, including the fact that Joon and her son were probably currently being held by the police at Corona Regional Medical Center. There was a small window of opportunity for him to get to Joon, because if she was released, she'd be disappeared and the kid would be in the wind. When Lore got to the point about the kid being an organ factory, she had to hold the phone away from her head because of Mayorga's angry cursing. When it died down, they talked for another five minutes, then she disconnected.

McQueen glanced at her in the rearview mirror.

Starling stared openly. "So what's going on?"

Instead of answering, she rifled through the food bags and found her hamburger, which was already cold. She unwrapped it and took a huge bite, her eyes rolling into her head as she groaned with the unmitigated pleasure of biting into a burger. She chewed heartily, then ripped another equally impressive bite free, much like a hyena might from the hind of a downed wildebeest. When she was finished with that bite, she wiped her mouth clean with the sleeve of the security guard's jacket she was still wearing, found a Coke, then took a long sip.

Finally, she came up for air.

"Sorry, boys. You ate your food while I did all the work."

"So what gives?" Starling asked.

"They've been trying to get to this Larrson character for years. Danny thinks this is the perfect opportunity. He already called and arranged for Joon to be held while I was talking to him. If everything works out, he's going to get them into protective custody."

Starling felt an overwhelming sense of peace when he heard those words. Joon's constant comments about how he'd previously hurt her and done things to her had engendered in him a feeling of ownership for her future. He'd left her in the hospital knowing it was the only thing he could do to get away. Now that her safety was assured, he felt a great weight lift from his soul, if only knowing that he wouldn't do to her again what she'd said he'd done before.

"Happy now?" Lore asked, shoving a handful of fries into her mouth.

"It's a little better," he said, reaching over and grabbing a napkin. He dabbed at the right corner of her cheek where a dollop of ketchup had found a home. "I'll really be happy when we figure out what's going on."

"You mean the girl and the goat," she said.

He nodded. "And why you kept quoting a thirteenth century mystic."

She took a slow contemplative bite from one of her fries. "Yeah. That."

Chapter Ten

I-10 heading East

THE SUN ROSE over the continental United States as they approached Indio, California, and with it, morning commuter traffic heading into Palm Springs and Los Angeles. Their progress slowed to a crawl as they moved east along Interstate 10. They decided it would be a perfect time for a new vehicle. Trading the panel van for a black Chevy Tahoe wasn't difficult in the airport long-term parking lot. At the exit, McQueen apologized for not having a ticket and slipped the nice man behind the glass a fifty to assuage his concern.

Up and over Chiriaco Summit and past the home of World War II hero General George S. Patton, they made Blythe two hours later. It wasn't hard to find a Walmart. They each needed a change of clothes and hygiene products, as well as enough gear to get them back to the box. McQueen and Starling took turns going inside, each of them grabbing what they needed along with duffle bags to carry their stuff. McQueen also got enough clothes for Lore so that she could go inside and do the same.

Starling was happy to get out of his pink *Come Yank at Hank's* shirt and exchanged it for a few generic polo shirts. He also grabbed a burner phone that he put to immediate use, calling everyone he knew at both Luke AFB in Phoenix and Davis-Monthan AFB in Tucson. Either place would have a bird heading to the Middle East and if they'd find answers anywhere, it would be there.

Lore sat in the back seat with a mirror and some wipes and started working at wiping away the worst of her sigils.

After a while, Starling put the phone in his lap and sighed.

"Any luck?" she asked.

"Not at all. Either everyone I know is gone, or no one will give me the time of day because we're out and not on contract."

"They don't like tourists mucking around their war zone," she said.

"But we're not tourists," he replied, frustration evident in his voice.

"If we aren't working for the government in some capacity, then we are exactly tourists," McQueen said from the front seat.

"I've got a line on that, I think." Starling rubbed his freshly shaved face. "You know who could help with that?"

"Elon Musk?" Lore asked.

"Bill Gates?" McQueen offered.

"No, you dummies. Narco. Dakota Jimmison. He can help. He knows everyone."

Lore gave Starling a look. "He should, especially if he

went back to dealing."

"Yeah, but he's our guy. I didn't see you complaining when you wanted to get antibiotics for the woman's shelter in Kandahar. I didn't see any of us complaining when he was able to get the three dogs at NKC that were going to be euthanized onto a C130 bound for Germany."

"Still, you have to admit he's sketchy," she insisted.

"He's our own Radar O'Reilly," Starling asserted, resurrecting the affable, grape Nehi-drinking character from the old TV show *M.A.S.H.*

She scoffed. "He's nowhere near Radar O'Reilly."

Before Starling could comment, McQueen shook his head from the front seat and interrupted. "Save your breath, kids. He's not helping anyone. He's working off his latest DUI with the infamous Sheriff Joe Arpaio."

"That the guy who said eff you to the governor?" Starling said, remembering the brewha from a late-night TV news program he'd watched while tripping on meth.

"One and the same. Narco's girl called me asking for help, but there was nothing I could do." McQueen shrugged but kept his hands on the wheel. "It's his fifth or sixth, she said."

"How does he even get a clearance?" Lore asked.

"He knows where all the bodies are buried," McQueen said. "And what is it with you two? I noticed the last couple of missions that you and he barely speak."

Starling looked at Lore. Was that true? Why hadn't he noticed that? He was usually up on team dynamics.

"It's nothing," she said, staring out the window at the passing desert landscape.

"Oh, it's something." McQueen grinned. "Did he hit on you?"

She shook her head.

"Did you hit on him and he declined?"

She gave the back of McQueen's head a sour look, then stared out the window.

"Is that it?" Starling asked, trying to suppress the laughter that was begging to be released. "Did he turn you down?"

She sighed heavily. "Listen, you two. Let's keep this professional."

"Professional? Weren't you the one who wanted to turn a professional relationship into a personal one?" Starling shook his head. "Seriously. I think it's funny as shit that he turned you down, but I can't have members of the team getting into any sort of relationship that interferes with our mission."

She sighed again.

"What?" he said.

"That's what Dak said to me. He said even if he wanted to, you'd get pissed."

"He was right."

"But that's not why she's mad, boss," McQueen said.

Starling thought about it for a second, then he had it. His eyes widened. "*Even if he wanted to* is what he said. So instead of a cold turn down, he couched it in better terms. That's not so bad."

"But he smiles at me," she said.

"What does that have to do with anything? I smile at you, too. See? I just did it. So what?"

"It's not the same kind of smile," she murmured.

"What kind of smile is it?" Both McQueen and Starling asked simultaneously.

"You or him?" she asked.

"Him."

"It's the *Oh look, there's that girl who wanted to date me but I had to let her down easy because she's not pretty enough and not smart enough and not whatever the fuck it is enough for me to date her.*" She looked each of them pointedly in the eye, then returned to itemize and inventory the cacti as they flew by.

No one said a word for a full minute.

Finally, Starling said, "I don't think that's the kind of smile he gave you."

She flicked her hand. "Whatever."

"No, seriously. That's not it."

She turned to Starling. "Then what is?"

"You're not his type."

"Not his type?" She repeated, each word louder than the other. She held out her right hand and ticked off her attributes with her left. "One, I'm fit. Two, I've grown my own boobs and they're more than adequate. Right, McQueen?"

"I'm the wrong one to ask, dear."

"Oh, right. Three, I'm intelligent. I have a master's degree in religious studies, for God's sake. Four, I'm a better shot than he is, proven at least a dozen times on the range. And five, I think I happen to be pretty damn good looking. I've even been called hot, and not just deployment hot. So if he has a type, what part of me isn't his type? Does he like short, flat-chested, obese dumb girls who can't shoot?" Quickly adding, "Not that there's anything wrong with those sorts of gals."

Starling caught himself smiling and tried to stop but couldn't. "All of those things about you are true," he told her. "You're also polite, sharing, caring, considerate, and will go out of your way to help a fellow human."

"Who's not a fucking terrorist," she added.

"Yes. Who will go out of her way to help a fellow human who's not a fucking terrorist. But none of that is what Narco likes. He likes hot trashy women who aren't smart enough to realize that they shouldn't be dating him and won't ask many questions. He doesn't want a commitment. You would be a commitment. It very possibly could be that he isn't ready for you."

All through his speech, Lore's eyes had gotten narrower and narrower. "How can you be sure?"

"McQueen?"

"Yes, boss."

"You get Narco's girlfriend's name?" Starling asked, keeping his eyes on Lore.

She stared right back.

"Yes, boss."

"Well, can you share it with us?"

"Her name is Charlene. But don't call her that. She likes to go by Char, like what you'd do to a steak if it's overcooked."

"And what does Charlene do?" Starling asked, pronouncing the hard *CH* in the name.

"She told me that she's an astrologer by trade but has to supplement her income by being a hairdresser."

"An astrologer?"

"Yes, boss. Mercury in retrograde and that shit."

Starling crossed his arms and sat back, never once having looked away from Lore.

"So?" he said, raising his eyebrows.

After a moment, she laughed. "You guys practice that Vaudeville act or what?"

"No, sis. This is all true," McQueen said.

"Just an educated guess," Starling said.

She cocked her head and thought about it.

"Have I ever lied to you?" McQueen asked.

"No," she admitted.

"Think I'd start now?"

"Probably not," she mumbled.

"Probably not," he repeated.

"I mean, no," she said. "So it's true then."

"Absolutely. And just to prove it, you can meet her."

"We're going to meet Charlene?" she asked also pronouncing it with the hard CH.

"Absolutely. If we're going to break Narco out of his Sheriff Arpaio chain gang, we're going to need to talk to her and get some background." Then he added, "Know what I think?"

"What?"

"I think once you meet Charlene that you two are going to be the best of friends." To McQueen he asked, "What's that saying that Bully makes?"

"'Closer than two rabbits screwing in a wool sock,'" McQueen said flatly.

Starling adopted an exaggerated Southern accent and

said, "Lore, I think once you meet Charlene that you two are going to be closer than two rabbits screwing in a wool sock."

She stared at him, then snorted. "I can't wait." Then she snorted again.

Chapter Eleven

Guadalupe, Arizona

CHARLENE, AS IT turned out, lived in a two-bedroom whitewashed adobe in the Phoenix suburb of Guadalupe. Just south of the college suburb of Tempe and north of the bedroom community of Ahwatukee, Guadalupe came straight out of Hollywood central casting if you wanted to see a dusty poor Mexican town. Somehow, because of the great wall of I-10 to its west and the highland canal to its east, amidst all the glitz and palm trees Phoenix had to offer tourists visiting the more than five hundred hotels and forty resorts the metropolis had to offer, Guadalupe lived as the gritty throwback antithesis. There were no sidewalks. The streets were as dusty as the yards. Even a tumbleweed rolled languidly across their path, chasing after a coyote that eyed them suspiciously.

An El Camino on blocks sat in the driveway of Charlene's home. A rusty yellow Tonka dump truck and a Big Wheel were the only color in the dirt yard. A metal leash tied to the water spigot on the wall spoke of an uncertain tragedy with a disturbingly empty collar dangling at the end.

McQueen parked the Tahoe on the street in front and they all climbed out.

Three taps at the door and it opened, revealing Charlene in all of her glory. Her candy-apple red hair piled on top of her head like a 1960s sorority girl perfectly matched the hue of her lipstick. She was beautiful in the way women can be only when they spend five hours a day preparing themselves. She wore a silk house coat over shorts and a tank top that read *I'm a Pisces, Let's Save Time and Assume I'm Never Wrong*. She held a TV remote in one hand and an iPhone in the other.

"I'll talk to you later, Maizy. They're here. No, they don't look dangerous. Just some fat guy, a big gay hipster, and woman with tattoos on her neck."

At the comment, Lore raised a hand to one of the sigils that had stubbornly resisted her attempts at removal.

Starling couldn't help frowning at his description.

McQueen remained McQueen and did nothing.

"They're Dakota's friends," she continued. "No, not that kind of friend. Real friends. I think they were deployed together." She grinned and waved them inside as she rolled her eyes and shook her head, holding up the phone. She mouthed the word *Sorry*. "Yes, Afghanistan. Or at least I think it was Afghanistan."

Starling nodded.

"The fat guy said yes. Afghanistan."

She waved them in and they complied.

Once inside, she closed the door with her foot.

"I'm sure it's nowhere we want to go. All the dust and dirt and roadside bombs. I think they make the women wear sheets or something."

"Burkas," Lore said.

"Gesundheit," said Charlene. "Listen, Maizy, I really do have to be going. I have company and you know how I like to be polite." She paused, then opened her mouth in surprise. "He did not. Are you serious? Did you call the police? And you say he took your feathers too?" She shook her head and stormed down the hall, slamming the door behind her.

After a moment, McQueen said without batting an eye, "Either she's batshit crazy or she's talking to her parakeet on a cell phone."

Starling was still wincing at being called fat.

The living room was well appointed in that rent-a-furniture sort of way. Everything was new and matched, but it was cheap. The most expensive thing was the seventy-inch high definition television on the wall across from the couch. The picture was so clear they could see the sweat on Jerry Springer's upper lip as he watched two immense black woman re-enacting a past sumo wrestling championship.

The opposite wall had pictures of a young boy in varying stages of growth, the oldest being around ten.

The couch was framed by two matching easy chairs facing inward toward a low-slung coffee table.

The kitchen table was covered with boxes of hair products, as if Charlene had just shop-lifted the entire inventory of a hair salon.

Starling detected the faint smell of cinnamon.

He turned to Lore and McQueen, who were still standing where they'd been when Charlene had left them. Starling shrugged, then caught movement from the television. He turned to it and watched as a fist-fight faded to a commercial. It began in a desert somewhere with a single white spot in the middle of nowhere. The camera panned in from a forty-five degree God's view. Closer and closer. A pit opened in his stomach and he felt a wave of sickness surge into the space. It was the girl. The girl with the long hair, shoeless, wearing a simple Sunday dress. The girl from his dreams. She stood, holding a thin rope that was attached to a white goat. She and the goat were looking the other way. He followed their gaze and saw that the sky was now on fire, burning with a brightness that made him bring his hand up to shield his eyes.

What was the commercial? What were they advertising?

"I see it too," said a voice beside him.

"What is it you see?"

"It's a girl. She has stringy hair and wears a robin's egg blue dress. She's holding a rope attached to a white goat."

"Who is she?"

"Don't you already know?"

"Hey, boss? What's going on?" McQueen asked, breaking the spell.

Starling blinked. The commercial evaporated and was replaced by a man selling RVs wearing a gorilla suit.

"Didn't you guys see that?" he said as he turned, noting that Charlene was right beside him.

"Did you see the goat?" Lore asked.

Starling looked from one to the other. "Are you telling me you didn't see anything? Lore? McQueen?"

They both shook their heads.

"Then who said…" It dawned on him that it had been Charlene who'd seen it. "How?" he asked.

She offered a thin smile. "It's what I do. Dakota saw the same thing. It was driving him crazy."

"Did you really see it?" Lore challenged. "Or are you just relaying what Dak told you?"

Charlene turned to Lore and appraised her, like she'd probably appraised every woman she saw as a challenge. "I saw."

Lore met the other woman's gaze, then shook her head. "It's not something you can prove, so I guess it doesn't matter."

"It's not something you can disprove either." Charlene pointed the remote at the television and it snapped off. She dropped the remote on the coffee table and found one of the easy chairs. "Come on. Sit down."

Starling took the other chair facing Charlene.

Lore and McQueen sat on the sofa.

"What you are seeing is a psychopomp," Charlene said.

"What's a psychopump?" Starling asked.

Charlene opened her mouth to answer, but Lore beat her to it.

"Pomp. Psychopomp. It comes from the Greek *psychopompos,* which means the guider of souls. Notably Charon, who guides the souls of the dead across the River Styx, is a psychopomp. A modern cultural assimilation of the psychopomp would be the grim reaper." She gave

Charlene a hard look and added, "Masters in religious studies. UCLA." Then she looked back at Starling and smiled like a darling.

"The death's head with the scythe? That grim reaper?" Starling asked.

Lore nodded.

"Does that mean we're dead?" Starling looked from Lore to Charlene.

"Not necessarily," Charlene said. "In fact, I doubt you are actually dead. What I do know is that you have a shared psychopomp. I saw it because you saw it. Dakota's seen it. You know, Jungian psychology addressed the idea of a psychopomp and treats it as a mediator between the conscious and the unconscious." Then she gave Lore a hard look. "Nine hours at Maricopa Community College."

Lore exhaled heavily and pursed her lips.

"I still don't understand," Starling said.

"What I can't figure out is the girl," Charlene said. She turned to examine Lore. "Could it be you?"

"I'm certainly not the goat," Lore said.

"What do you mean?" Starling asked. "Isn't she the psychopomp?"

"Oh, no. The goat is the psychopomp. The girl is holding it at bay."

Lore thumped her chest. "That's me, holding back the goat."

"But the goat's not trying to get away," he said.

Charlene shook her head. "Doesn't matter. The leash or rope or whatever," she flicked her hand, "is what controls it. The leash is not a leash just as the goat is not a goat. It's metaphor."

"What would happen if the goat got free?" Starling asked.

"I've only seen a psychopomp once before," Charlene said. "It was a golden retriever that had died and then showed up in an old man's bedroom."

"What happened?"

"The man came to see me and I knew right away he was going to die."

"Did you tell him?" McQueen asked, speaking up for the first time.

"I did. The golden rule of psychics is to always tell the truth. And he died that night. The purpose of the presence of the animal's spirit can't be entirely known, but I suppose it was to guide the spirit of its master into the afterlife."

Starling rethought his initial impression of Charlene. On the outside she was the model of trailer trash iconography, but on the inside she was an intellectual psychic with an acute understanding of the afterlife... or at least that's how she appeared. Dak was definitely out of his league if he thought she was his type. In fact, he probably did because Charlene knew how to act the part around him.

"How do we know you're a psychic?" Lore challenged.

Charlene smiled and cocked her head. "How does it feel to wear tinfoil? I'd imagine that it chafes," she paused, "especially in the more tender places."

Lore's mouth fell open. She looked from McQueen to Starling and back.

"I didn't say anything," Starling said.

"Neither did I," McQueen said carefully.

Charlene continued. "I hear loud music and see you dancing. You were trying to get rid of something... something that was stuck in your head. I can hear the words, but I don't understand them."

"It's Persian," Lore said slowly.

"Ah, that's why," Charlene said. "Whatever it is, it's as important as the presence of the girl. Pay attention to them. Listen to the words. Watch the girl. When the girl disappears, then you know that something terrible is going to happen."

"What about the sky on fire?" Lore asked, apparently no longer trying to outdo Charlene. "What about the burning sky?"

"Okay, give me a moment and let me see. What I need you to do is to imagine the burning sky. All of you. The more you can concentrate, the better I'm able to focus." Charlene closed her eyes. She inhaled and exhaled heavily through her nose. "Burning sky. I'm looking for burning sky. Imagine it. Bring it to me. Yes. There. I can see it. The sky's on fire. Oh my, but isn't that bright. It's almost blinding." She brought her hand to her eyes even though they were closed. "I can see why you keep seeing it. There's something there. This is different. This is very different. I can't see through it but there's something on the other side... something—"

Her head jerked back and both hands grabbed the arms of her chair, nails biting in so hard that two of them snapped off. The veins in her arms popped as her elbows locked. The corners of her mouth peeled back as the skin on her face tightened. A high-pitched whine started in her throat and leaked from her mouth like air hissing from a tire.

Starling, Lore, and McQueen shot to their feet.

Starling swept the coffee table out of the way and reached out to touch her but the moment his fingers wrapped around her forearm he felt a searing heat transfer from her into him. He gritted his teeth and bit back a scream. The pain was so intense that he was certain his skin was melting. His vision went white… no, not white, he was *seeing* white. He screamed at the same time Charlene did, and for one split second he thought he saw darkness on the other side of the burning sky… darkness in the shape of a figure.

Then it was as if a light switch flipped and everything went black.

Starling's hand released and he fell backward, stumbling. He felt hands support him and found his balance. His vision returned. He quickly checked his hand, sure that it would be ruined, but it was free of any wound and as normal as it had been earlier in the day. Relief washed over him.

Charlene tried to stand but fell back in her chair.

"Wa-water," she said. "Fridge. Water."

Lore stepped quickly into the kitchen and slung open the refrigerator, retrieved two bottles of water, and returned to the living room. She unscrewed one and placed it in the shaking hands of Charlene. Then she unscrewed the other and did the same for Starling.

Both Charlene and Starling sucked down half of their bottles before they came up for air.

"What was that?" Starling asked, glancing momentarily at his hand before running it over his head. "Felt like I was on fire."

"You were. We were," Char said. She drank the rest of the bottle and let the empty fall in her lap. "As to what that is? I've never encountered anything like it before."

"Are you okay?" Lore asked Starling. "What did you see?"

"Something on the other side of the light. I think it was a figure."

Charlene nodded. "It felt like a presence. It was more than just a figure, it was…" She hesitated, then said breathlessly, "I don't know what it was."

But Lore wouldn't let her off the hook so easily. "Come on. You know something you're not telling."

Charlene shook her head. "I'm just not sure. I can't really say."

"I'm dropping the bullshit flag in the end zone on that one. You know. I can tell you know. I'm a professional interrogator, among other things, and your tells are giving you away."

Charlene's eyes narrowed. "I have tells?"

Lore shoved her hands on her hips. "You have tells."

"What are they?" Charlene asked.

Lore seemed about to answer, then grinned and shook her head slowly. She brought a hand up and waggled a finger. "Oh no you don't. You're not changing the subject. What exactly was it that you saw on the other side of the burning?"

Starling interjected. "Lore. That's enough."

Lore stared at him with a wounded gaze. "But Starling, she knows something."

Starling was about to reply, then noticed Charlene shaking her head slowly. "I understand your frustration. I really do. But I think it's important that I don't speculate. I don't want to confuse you on your own journey of discovery."

"I thought you said that psychics had to be honest," Lore protested.

Charlene considered the comment, then smiled. "Anyone want some water? It's cold."

"Oh, this is so much bullshit," Lore said, turning and throwing herself into a seat on the couch.

Starling knew that they'd eventually find the answer. If Charlene didn't want to tell them, it was probably for a good reason. He had a good feeling about her and knew that if something bad was going to happen that she'd let them know. Whatever it was, the answer wasn't here. The answer was somewhere in Afghanistan. The problem was getting there, which was their current problem. But first they had to find a way to free Narco.

Chapter Twelve

Surprise, Arizona

DAKOTA JIMMISON, AKA Dak, aka Narco, was a former MARSOC Gunnery Sergeant with more awards than any three marines, including a Silver Star for rescuing a reporter and her crew who'd gotten too close to the action during the Battle of Fallujah. He was an expert in almost any weapon, could pick off a haji from over a thousand meters with a Barrett .50, and was one of the first people you'd ask to join you in a fight. But Dak had demons just like everyone who'd ever seen a buddy killed or a kid lying lonely and dead along the side of a Third World road. During combat, he was a tactically focused military machine, but whenever there was a lull, he'd invariably find himself seeking solace from the bottom of a bottle. Which was why Narco was currently wearing an orange jumpsuit with the letters ADOJ on the front and back, picking up trash along Highway 60, which ran between the cities of Surprise and Sun Lakes West. These two places had two things in common. One, the average age was seventy-three years old; two, there were more golf carts than there were cars.

Eighteen hours ago, Starling and the others didn't know what they were going to do to spring Narco. Since the TST was a bunch of good guys, they couldn't go around shooting deputy sheriffs, nor could they substantially break the law—their previous two Grand Theft Autos not included. But the combined brainpower of a former Special Forces team sergeant, a former US Army Ranger, a former human intelligence specialist gun porn addict, and a psychic hairdresser with a heart of gold had devised a plot that if briefed to a room full of colonels would have had the lot of them digging foxholes in the middle of Death Valley. Still, they had to work with what they had, and with a computer, a big Yellow Pages, the local newspaper, and the compelling need to get to Afghanistan as fast as they could, they put together something that could work while causing the least amount of harm.

The camels had been the most difficult part of the plan.

The Garcia Brothers Circus had been performing three shows daily in several fields near the Happy Trails Adult RV and Resort on the western edge of Surprise. Not only did they have carnival rides and a midway, but they had a big top whose highlight was an act with a dozen camels ridden by midgets juggling burning batons. Starling hadn't understood the draw, but it was evidently a popular act. Or at least it had been. The circus had all but shut down months ago. For whatever reason, the circus hadn't moved on to the next venue. The rides were silent and still as a cemetery stones, more tumbleweeds tore down the midway than customers, and the big top was permanently closed. Which was why the advertisement in the paper that twelve camels were for sale had been the germination of their very psychotic plan.

Now Starling sat in the front of a moving van in the parking lot of a big box store, tremendous thumps and brays from the back so loud he was worried someone would call the police on him. In this part of the country, moving vans were frequently used to transport immigrants who hadn't gone through the proper legal channels, so people looked at the vans differently. In Arizona, a moving van wasn't merely a moving van. That his moving van held six recently-purchased camels would definitely be a surprise to whichever officer decided he wanted to check and see what Starling was transporting.

Starling prayed that he didn't garner any more attention than was necessary.

He checked his watch. They had less than five minutes before OPERATION NARCO CAMEL went into effect.

Dak had called the night before and cryptically let Charlene know where he'd be picking up trash. He was on a twelve-man crew dressed in dashing orange jumpsuits and guarded by three deputy sheriffs. They weren't cuffed or chained. The only thing that kept them from walking off were the steely eyes of the deputies and the knowledge that if they ran, life would be much worse for them when they were caught. As for Dak, he wouldn't be caught. And if Starling was right, they'd be able to find a general officer somewhere in Afghanistan who would sign off on a memo stating that Dak's presence in the combat zone had been of the utmost importance, top secret mission, blah blah blah. Starling was confident that Dak would figure out what to say. And if he didn't... well, at least he'd have an all-expenses paid vacation in a well-lighted facility where the only alcohol you could drink was raisin hooch brewed by desperate men in the comfort of their two-man cells.

As absurd as it was, OPERATION NARCO CAMEL had in its roots another operation Starling had planned and led three years ago. And like NARCO CAMEL, it began with deception. Only instead of camels bought from a dying circus, they'd had the Dallas Cowboy cheerleaders, who were rotating through Afghanistan on a USO tour. Traditionally, Afghan army officers weren't allowed to be part of USO ceremonies because it was a time for US service men and women to let their hair down and get a little wild. In this case, through the mediation of an air force two star who owed the TST a favor, the entire staff of Afghan National Army battalion commander Lieutenant Colonel Sharif was invited to attend as VIPs. Lieutenant Colonel Sharif didn't attend such things, which was both the reason Starling had been so enraged, and the reason it became easier to get at him.

Afghanistan had a secret they didn't want anyone in the West to know. Yet much of the West knew and did nothing about it. The practice of *bacha bazi,* also known as *bacchá,* literally means 'playing with boys.' The ancient Pashtu custom of selling pre-pubescent boys to wealthy and high-powered Afghan men was widespread across Afghanistan, as was their *use.*

Starling had been stunned when he'd first heard about it. When he'd asked their terp what he knew of it, he'd merely shrugged and said, "It is custom. Everyone does it. Girls are dirty but the boys are clean." Then he'd given Starling a leer that had caused McQueen to manhandle him before he had a chance to wring the terp's neck.

But the terp was right.

It was said that every Afghan man of power had a *chai boy,* or a *dancing boy* as they were sometimes called. When Starling had escorted a VIP to a meeting and seen a boy as young as eight years old serving tea to an older high-ranking official, his guts churned, knowing that the boy could be forced to do anything at any given time. Starling had wanted to kill every one of them, or at the very least beat them within an inch of their lives, which was very unlike Starling. He'd always been a reasonable man and conscientious leader. He'd always adhered to MDMP, the seven step military decision making process drilled into soldiers from their first leadership course. MDMP was the rule. Every mission, every sortie outside of Camp Eggers, which was their home base, was the result of MDMP, concentrating on mission analysis and developing courses of action. Except when he saw *shy boys,* what he'd come to call them—then all reasoning left him. It got to the point where he was unable to accompany his VIPs into meetings and had to send a member of his team in his stead.

And none was worse than Lieutenant Colonel Amanullah Sharif. He'd been a high-ranking police officer from Uruzgan Province before he'd been appointed to the

Afghan National Army. In his home province, they referred to *shy boys* as *bacha bereesh*—boys without beards. Sharif had brought his own *bacha bereesh* when he'd become assigned to Kabul and the very sight of the poor child set a plot into motion from which Starling would never return.

So it was with somber righteousness that Starling, dressed completely in black, including a black balaclava to hide his face, slipped over the wall of Sharif's personal compound in the Farza District of Kabul, and into Sharif's home. As a US Army Ranger, Starling was part of one of the world's elite fighting forces. He'd been trained in multiple ways to kill and disable, and had tried virtually every one. One thing they'd never been trained in was the use of the French garrote. Once inside, Starling could hear the laughter from the guard force as they gathered around cell phones and watched the broadcast feed provided by Sharif's senior men of the USO show and the cheerleaders. It was nothing for Starling to make it to Sharif's room, open the door, confront the evil, and remove it from the planet. Then Starling took the small, broken figure of the boy who'd been sexually abused for years and gave it to a woman he knew in the Afghan Hands Program. He didn't have to say anything. Once she saw the young boy, she knew what needed to be done.

No one except McQueen knew what he'd done.

The killing had been truly righteous... but it was still murder and was a line that once crossed could never be un-crossed. No matter how much it had needed to be done, no matter how correct he'd been in saving the child, Starling was in a country whose customs allowed for such a thing. He was also a member of a military whose very own commanders had a strict order not lift a finger to help the *shy boys*, because evidently killing Taliban was more important than the destruction of a child's soul.

Starling breathed for a full moment, hungover from the memory that had come unbidden, shaken free from the mental niche in which he'd had it jammed. Then he saw the daylight and the parking lot and the colors from the big box home makeover store. A camel brayed from the back. A Mustang drove by. America. He sighed, embracing the current reality of OPERATION NARCO CAMEL.

He started up his Penske moving van just as the U-Haul rental truck in front of him pulled away. He gave it ten seconds, then pulled onto the road. They headed northwest on Highway 60. The highway had two northbound lanes and two southbound lanes separated by a median. A mile ahead twelve inmates wearing orange jumpsuits were picking up trash on the right side of the highway. They were being watched by three deputies. One sat in his car at the intersection of Highway 60 and Pantera Road so he could view all the inmates in front of him. Another sat in his SUV at the intersection of Highway 60 and Mountain Avenue so he could keep the inmates in his rearview mirror. The distance between the two vehicles was about a hundred and fifty meters. A deputy on foot holding a shotgun stood on the side of the road, in the middle of the two vehicles, chatting to one of the inmates and watching the others. The temperature outside was one hundred and three without a lick of humidity.

The camels were demonstrating their unhappiness behind him. One kicked the side of the truck so hard that it wobbled on four wheels. Very soon they'd get the fresh air they desired.

When McQueen's U-Haul reached the corner of Mountain Avenue, he tried to take a right turn from the left lane, cutting off the car in that lane, which laid on its horn. By now McQueen would have the instant attention of the deputy in the SUV. McQueen stopped the truck, which now blocked both lanes of traffic. The plan was for McQueen to knife his front tire and pretend it popped itself.

Traffic slowed, then accordioned to a stop, putting Starling's Penske van about even with the deputy on foot.

Horns honked.

Several people shouted out their windows.

Nothing was moving.

McQueen came around the front of his truck with both hands on his head in the universal *Why is this happening to me?* sign. The deputy in the SUV got out and asked McQueen something, who in turn shrugged, and pointed to the other side of his truck where the front tire was quickly deflating.

Starling glanced to the right. Every inmate, along with the deputy, was looking forward.

Starling killed the engine and threw the keys behind the seat. He got out and moved to the back of the truck. An old school beige and rusting Lincoln had pulled within three feet of the back of the truck. A chunky kid in a Cardinal's cap sat behind the wheel. Starling met the kid's gaze for a second, then turned to the truck and yanked out the metal ramp. Because there wasn't enough room between the front of the car and the back of the truck, he let it slam down on the hood, smashing flat the hood emblem.

The kid's eyes widened and he shouted obscenities Starling didn't need a lip reader to understand from the cool confines of what had probably been his grandfather's car.

Starling ignored him, climbed onto the ramp, then jerked open the door. The interior smelled of crackers, oily hair, and camel shit, which was how camels generally smelled, except their confinement in the close quarters of the van had intensified the odor until it was almost overwhelming. Certainly, had Starling had time, he could bottle it and sell it to a Third World dictator as a biological weapon.

Each camel had a white sheet thrown over its back and tied in place by a rope girdle. On each side of the sheet was an enlarged photo of Sheriff Joe Arpaio wearing a cowboy hat and pointing out at something. Above the picture were the words JOE WANTS YOU TO. Below the picture of Sheriff Joe on this particular camel were the words GET DEPORTED. The other camels had similar sheets. Everything was identical except for the text surrounding each picture.

Each camel also had an old school boom box affixed to the back of its neck using bungee cords.

By now, the kid was out of the car, calling Starling every name in the book. But he fell silent as Starling pressed play on the CD player and ushered the first camel down the ramp and onto the kid's car. *Flight of the Valkyries* began to play at a nuisance level of noise from the camel's speaker as it stepped into stopped traffic.

Starling didn't take time to watch whether it was going to have the desired effect.

Instead, he turned on the CD players for and ushered out camels wearing sheets advertising GET DOWN ON ALL FOURS, FREE HIS WILLY, SMOKE A BOWL, SUCK HIS COCK, and KILL ALL MEXICANS. They'd laughed uproariously as they'd made the sheets in Charlene's apartment last night. But now came the serious moment. Starling took a second to watch as KILL ALL MEXICANS trundled happily down the ramp and onto the kid's front hood.

People were already out of their cars.

Some laughing.

Some taking cell phone pictures or videos—probably both—because this was definitely a social media moment.

Some, however, were clearly pissed.

A large Mexican man with a chin the size of a shovel blade started forward towards KILL ALL MEXICANS. When he saw a red haired white woman laughing at it, he confronted her and soon there was an all-out argument.

Whatever they were saying, Starling couldn't tell. Six versions of *Flight of the Valkyries* blocked out all noise. So he simply climbed down from the back of the truck, turned right and walked across the median into the southbound lanes of the highway, where traffic had stopped to watch the incredible camel-inspired shenanigans taking place.

Starling didn't know if the deputies were watching him.

For all he knew, they were running after him. He felt the tickle of possible attention on the back of his head but ignored it. He kept up a moderate loping walk as he crested the curb on the other side of the road, walked around a gaggle of rubberneckers at the bus stop and over to the grocery store where his Uber ride waited for him.

He climbed in.

"You Dak Jimmison?" the man behind the wheel asked.

"That's me." Starling showed the driver the cell phone screen with Dak's information but his own picture.

"What's going on over there?" the driver asked.

"Something political," Starling said, closing the door. "Someone was crazy enough to make fun of Sheriff Joe."

The driver, who was clearly of Middle East descent, snorted. "And camels, too."

"Yes. And camels, too."

Chapter Thirteen

Casa Grande, Arizona

THREE HOURS LATER, they were having dinner at Mimi's Café in Casa Grande, roughly halfway between Phoenix and Tucson.

"No one. I mean, *no one*, expected to see what you guys did today. I bet they still don't know that they've been had." Narco was one huge grin. He threw back his beer, got the attention of the waitress, and nodded for another.

Starling watched Narco celebrate his escape. He'd let the kid have a few more drinks, then shut it down. No reason to pee in his Wheaties after such a successful prison break. Especially since the improbable had happened. He had to believe that if there were such a thing as multiple timelines there were versions of the events where they were all caught and locked up in one of Sheriff Joe Arpaio's famous prison tents. So the fact that they'd succeeded should definitely be celebrated.

While the deputies had been trying to contain the chaos

created by the camels—people fighting, arguing, blocking the way as they pressed forward to take pictures—it had been no trouble for Narco to slip back fifty feet where Lore waited in the Tahoe. He grabbed onto the driver's side mirror and hugged it as she took off. The deputy who was on foot saw the action too late and took off running, but he was no match for the SUV.

Lore took three turns then pulled the vehicle to the curb.

She got out, punched Narco in the shoulder, gave him a shining grin, and beckoned him to follow.

They ran between two homes then hit a parallel street, where they got into a Honda Civic waiting at the curb. The Civic had a Pizza Hut roof topper, the kind a deliveryman would use. With both Lore and Narco laying as flat as they could in the backseat, Charlene eased the car forward and quickly exited the area. A patrol car and a sheriff car passed her coming into the housing subdivision, but no one looked at them twice. She was a pizza delivery person. She was invisible.

Lore sat next to Starling in the restaurant booth. Narco and McQueen were wedged into the other side. The American-French fusion restaurant was virtually empty mid-afternoon on a Tuesday. Other than a few older ladies chatting over coffees and croissants, the four had the place to themselves.

"I can't thank you guys enough for springing me," Narco said for the tenth or twentieth time.

"It's not like you were in solitary confinement," Starling said.

"Wasn't exactly Alcatraz," McQueen added.

"Still… camels? How'd you come up with that?"

Lore pointed to Starling. "Was all the boss's plan."

Starling shrugged. "You're the one who paid for it."

Narco's smile fell. His eyes narrowed. He took a quick drink then put the beer down on the table. "What's that supposed to mean?"

"Charlene had your credit cards," Starling said. "We weren't exactly rolling in it. So you paid for everything."

Narco looked from one to the other. "When you say everything, you mean what?"

"Everything. You bought the camels. You bought the boom boxes at Best Buy. You bought the CDs for the music. The sheets. The posters. The bill from Staples, where we printed enlarged pictures of Sheriff Joe Arpaio. You rented the two trucks. You paid for my Uber ride. Everything."

Narco was silent for a moment, then asked, "How much does it cost to buy a camel?"

"Normally it's around three thousand dollars, but I talked them down to nine hundred."

Narco mouthed the words, then closed his eyes. "So what you're telling me is that not only am I a wanted man for escaping jail, but I'm also seriously in debt."

All three of the others nodded. "Pretty much."

Starling shrugged. "It's not like we had a choice."

The waitress came and cleared their appetizer plates, then quickly returned to deliver their dinners. Four French cheeseburgers on brioche buns with Freedom Fries. The anachronism wasn't lost on Starling. He poured a pool of ketchup for his fries to swim in, then passed the bottle to Lore, who did the same.

No one said anything until they were halfway through the meal. Gone was the need to talk. The stress and the frustration of the last seventy-two hours bled away as the medium rare meat popped in Starling's mouth. He'd never felt more ravenous. He'd also never felt more alive. His senses had been deadened for so long by drugs and booze. This was the first time in months his system had been so clean.

McQueen finished first. His cell buzzed and he checked it. Excusing himself, he got up and went outside. After about a minute, he returned. To Starling he said, "That was Charlene on the burner we bought her."

Starling raised his eyebrows.

"They picked her up as expected. But they didn't find anything. She let them check her real phone for location services and it alibied her not leaving the house. Because she'd stashed the burner phone in her mailbox, they never found that either. There's no proof she was involved so they had to let her go."

"She's going to be okay?" Narco asked.

Lore gave him a quick glance, then looked away, concentrating on her Freedom Fries as if they were the inner workings of a bomb.

McQueen nodded. "She's going to be fine. But she did say something odd I couldn't figure out."

"What's that?" Narco asked.

"She said, *I'll see you all soon if this doesn't work.*"

"If what doesn't work?" Lore asked without looking up.

"I asked her the same thing," McQueen said. "But all she said was, *You'll understand soon enough.*"

Everyone paused for a moment, then Narco barked a laugh. "That's Char for you. Always the cryptic one. Realest psychic I've ever been with, though. And did you see her legs? They go right up to her chin." He grinned and popped a fry into his mouth.

Starling slid his gaze over to Lore without moving his head. She was focused on her fries, but she wasn't eating anymore. Her mouth was a grim line. How is it that he'd never known about her feelings? He'd have to pay better attention from now on.

"What's next?" Narco asked. He'd finished his beer and was about to ask for another when he saw Starling slowly shaking his head.

"What? Is this an op?"

"Yes, it is." Starling pushed his plate forward, then put both elbows on the table. He spoke softly. "We need you to get us a ride on the first thing burning out of here."

"Where's here?

"Can't go to Luke. That's back in Phoenix. So it's Davis-Monthan in Tucson. If not there, then Biggs in El Paso."

"Where we going?"

"Back," said McQueen.

"Back where... Afghanistan?" Narco's eyes widened. Then he shook his head. "I'm so done with that place. No way am I going back."

"I'm afraid we have to," Starling said. "And you're coming with."

Narco sat back and crossed his arms. "I'm not going back, boss. I'm out and done. Contract is up."

McQueen gave the approaching waitress a death glare

and the woman decided that this moment wasn't a good time to clear plates. She headed back toward the kitchen.

"There's a reason we put our asses on the line for you, Narco," Starling began.

But Narco wouldn't let him continue. "You put your asses on the line for yourself. I was fine with doing my time. I had six more weeks, then I was free of that asshole sheriff. You wanted me to do something for you. That's the selfish reason you had, so don't pin any of this on me."

Starling sat back, silent. Narco spoke truth and he couldn't argue with it. Well, he could, but then he'd look like an asshole.

"How's your sleep?" Lore asked, still not looking up.

"It's fine. How's yours?" Narco snapped back.

"Not so good," Lore responded, looking from her plate into Dak's eyes. "Not so good at all. I have these reoccurring dreams. So do McQueen and Starling. And you know what's weird about it? We're all having the same dream. But then you wouldn't know about that, would you, because your sleep is so fine. It's like you're a sweet baby laying his head to rest on a pillow shared with angels. So soft. So perfect. So nice."

Narco's defensive grin fell. He didn't move his head, but his gaze cut to Starling, who was staring right back at him.

Lore continued. "McQueen pretends he doesn't have dreams, but he's always been the most hard-assed of our lot. I suppose he can just take it. Starling here has been following your recipe for success, drinking and popping everything and anything that comes within his reach. Look at the boss. Isn't he the model of a TST leader? Or didn't you notice, because you were busy thinking about getting some nice, perfect sleep.

"And then there's me. Not only have I been having the same dreams as these two, but I also had phrases in my head that kept repeating over and over until I went insane. Know how these guys found me? I was slam-dancing inside my trailer, wearing duct tape and tinfoil jammies. Perfectly normal. And then there's you, Dakota Jimmison. Your sleep is so perfect you got picked up for yet another DUI. I'm sure the drinking wasn't to obliterate your brain cells so you wouldn't dream. I'm so fucking sure of it."

The waitress appeared in the uncomfortable silence that ensued. She cleared the table, then hurriedly laid the check in the middle. A smiley face was written on the back along with the words *Thank You!!!* followed by the name *Clarissa*. Then she hurriedly left.

"Monster," McQueen said.

Lore turned to him. "What did you call me?"

McQueen shook his head and brought a hand up to twist the end of his mustache. "Monster energy drinks. I have about six a day to keep me up. Sometimes I'm able to stay awake forty-eight hours. Once I was up to sixty hours before I crashed. When I do sleep, my body needs it so much it doesn't have time to dream." He twisted the other side of his mustache. "I'm no different than Starling. I just chose a different vice."

Everyone was silent.

"What about Bully? She having the dreams?" Narco asked.

"We don't know where she is," Starling said. Then

he grabbed the bill. He took out several twenties he'd received from the ATM after getting a cash withdrawal from Narco's credit card before they bought the camels. He knew that once OPERATION NARCO CAMEL was over the credit card couldn't be used. As it stood, they had a little over four hundred dollars. When that was gone, he didn't know what they were going to do.

"So I probably have the dreams too," Narco said, a sullen missive into the silence.

"Same dream every night?" Lore asked.

"Yes."

"We already knew," she said. "Charlene told us."

Narco stared at her, then let out a sigh. "Then why all this bullshit?"

"I said all that bullshit so you'd understand how desperate we are. I get that you don't want to go back to Afghanistan. None of us do. It's the shit-hole of all shitholes. It's the hair on the mole on the rectum of a nasty god. But the fact is we're compelled to go back. We all have a feeling something's been left undone. Something important. Something dire. And then there's the dream. The girl and the goat. They have some serious significance, only we aren't exactly sure what that is. Your girlfriend gave us an idea, but that's not the whole of it."

"Don't forget the burning sky," Narco added.

"Right. And let's not forget the burning sky."

"Yeah. I have the same fucked up dreams," Narco said. He glanced around the table. "So you think going to Afghanistan will make the dreams go away?"

"I do," Starling said.

"And you, Big Ugly," Narco asked McQueen, using his pet name for his partner and friend.

"I do, Little Jerk," McQueen said.

Narco shook his head. "Fuck fuck *fuck*."

"Does this mean you'll do it?" Starling asked.

Narco cradled his head in his hands and rocked back and forth. His mouth moved, but no words came out. They didn't have to. He was merely repeating to himself silently what he'd just said aloud.

"So?" Starling asked again.

Narco glanced up, then straightened. He sighed. "If it means getting that girl out of my head, then hell yes."

"You should be more worried about the goat," Lore said.

Narco stared at Lore for a moment, not understanding. "Whatever. You got a burner phone?" he asked Starling.

Starling pulled it out and set it on the table.

Narco grabbed it, then pushed sullenly out of the booth and headed towards the front door. Before he left the building, he was already on it, talking animatedly to someone about a plane trip and a return to the place none of them wanted to go.

Chapter Fourteen

Tucson, Arizona

As IT TURNED out, Narco had a line on the last of their TST—Criminal aka Oz aka Oscar Jesse James, who was currently acting as a HUMANTECH Contract Coordinator at Al Udeid Air Base in Doha, Qatar. HUMANTECH was the contract company that handled the Department of Defense Tactical Support Team contracts and had hiring authority. At first, Criminal didn't want to be bothered with their problem, but two things changed his mind.

One, he thought Narco's improbable story of arrest and escape was the most hilarious thing he'd ever heard. Oz didn't have the call sign Criminal for just any reason. The affectation was far from random, because Oz *was* a criminal. That he hadn't been caught was an indictment on various judicial systems rather than his personal ideals. Criminal had his own opinions about property rights and professed a more egalitarian theory of ownership. Thus he was constantly redistributing other persons' perceived wealth and making it available to others.

Starling hadn't known this when he'd reviewed Criminal's file. Had he known, he would have found a way to get Oz reassigned to another team. But once assigned, he discovered Criminal to be intensely loyal. Although he was quick to acquire things with questionable provenance, his activities were mostly harmless. From the seventy-inch flat screen he'd installed in the team room to the Russian-made RPGs they'd used on the last mission to the forty pounds of live lobster he'd lifted from a truck bound for the CIA base, his acquisitions often benefited the team.

Still, Starling had had to mollify the senior CIA official who missed his lobster.

Then, of course, there had been the situation with a local Kabul district politician who'd approached Starling because Criminal had allegedly stolen his American-made Corvette and smashed it into a T-wall. Criminal, of course, had denied it. Starling would have pressed the issue, but the politician dropped his protest. Two days later, an IG investigation was initiated because of the misplacement of twenty kilos of black tar heroin that had gone missing from the DEA warehouse on Bagram Air Force Base.

Starling could think of half a dozen other instances where Criminal's proclivities had caused him pain. So it came as no surprise that Criminal would appreciate Narco's experience.

The other thing that changed Criminal's mind was mention of the girl and the goat. Even halfway around the world, he hadn't been spared the same haunting dream they'd all experienced. He'd been thinking that he was alone, but knowing now that this was a shared thing caused him to want to find the underlying cause of this puzzling imagery.

But they had two problems.

There was no way that Narco could travel. His name had already been placed on the No Fly List, which the military had to honor by regulation. They needed an identity for him. The second problem was that there was no current need for TST contract fills. All the contracts were full. But instead of seeing this as a road block, Criminal treated them as speed bumps.

The four spent the night in a motel room near the main gate of Davis-Monthan Air Force Base. A C5 Galaxy was leaving tomorrow afternoon with space available. Starling had tried to get at least three of them on the manifest, but without movement orders, the load master wouldn't allow them to board the plane. Plus, they needed military Common Access Cards or CACs. No CAC, no travel.

They received a Skype call from Criminal at 06:31 the following morning.

Starling answered it. He'd already been up since four worrying. Well, that, and wanting something to get his system moving... something he shouldn't have. Had he been in the hotel room alone, he would have gone out and scored something, picked up a fifth of vodka. But with the others in the room, he was loath to go out. McQueen would know right away, then the others shortly after. He was trying to treat this whole chasing-a-nightmare thing as a military mission, and as such, needed to act appropriately. So when he answered the Skype call, he was dressed, cleaned up and ready for action.

"Oh, hey boss. What's up with you?" Criminal said, grinning from half the world away.

He looked like the same kid from on their last mission. Half-cocked smile amidst a black goatee. Sharp Hispanic cheek bones from his mother. High forehead and blue eyes from his father. It always seemed like he was about to break into laughter.

"Waiting on you, Criminal. Were you able to track down Bully?"

"She's not in any system. No contracts. No mailing address. It's like she fell off the planet."

"Seriously? Nothing?"

"If I can't find her, boss, nobody can."

Starling shook his head. Without her, the team wouldn't be whole. "Were you able to come through with the rest of it?"

"What have you been doing over there? Not only is Narco on the No Fly List, but you and McQueen are, too."

"Shit happens. Still, we need to get back. We need to get to Afghanistan. How are you going to make that happen?"

Criminal stared back at him for a long moment. "It's not the easiest thing in the world."

"I got it. Now, how are you going to make it happen?"

"Damn, boss. You're acting like we're back together and you're in charge."

"That's the plan. Better get used to it. Now how are you—"

"Going to make this happen. I got you. I even feel you. So listen. I need the three of you to hit up a friend of mine at his address. He's going to give you new IDs. Once you get those, you can get on base, go to the Contracting Facility, and get CAC cards issued in your new names. You'll have orders by then and be able to travel. I've booked four seats on the C5. You'll land in Dover, then board another C5 five hours later, which will land in Aviano, Italy. From there you'll board contract air to Doha, where I'll meet you."

"That sounds pretty simple and straight forward," Starling said.

"Boss, if you knew how many strings I had to pull and favors I had to pay back, you'd be..."

"What'd I be?" Starling asked.

"I don't know, boss. It was just a lot of work."

"Don't you think we're worth it?" Lore asked, coming up behind Starling, a toothbrush hanging out of the corner of her mouth.

Criminal waved. "Hey, PD. Good to see you."

"Good to be seen. You got us hooked up?"

He grinned. "You were easy, girl. No one has an APB, BOLO, or arrest warrant on you."

"So sad. I suppose it's something to which I can aspire."

Starling had a pen and paper in hand. "Give me the contact info so we can get going."

Thus began a self-imposed bureaucratic to and fro as they traveled, first to an apartment in the South Tucson barrio to the home of Victor Escalante. His apartment complex was surrounded by a ten-foot-high chain link fence with cyclone wire across the top. If it weren't for the bangers hanging out at the entrance checking all who entered, it would have seemed more like a place where people were imprisoned than where people were protected.

Victor was all business. The apartment complex was set up with apartments for unwed males on the first floor. The second floor held families. The third floor held Escalante's offices and one grand apartment comprised of four apartments merged together. He and his staff worked with such efficiency that it was almost like they were on a military base being taken care of by ID card services. An hour after they'd arrived, the group left, three new ID suites in hand, each including a military CAC, a driver's license, and a social security card.

Three hours later they'd signed contracts with HUMANTECH and received movement orders.

They had some cash left, which they spent at the Base Exchange buying personal items, clothes and something to carry them in.

Starling was worried they might get bumped on the C5 because there were a lot of blue-suiter air force personnel who also had orders. Uniformed personnel always came first. Then civilians and contractors with military orders. Then came those using the aircraft for free personal movement. He spied several families eager to get a free flight for their vacation. One older, probably retired, Pacific Islander and his family of six looked like they'd been traveling for days, one of the problems with flying Space A. Retirees and their families were the last in the pecking order and were only allowed to fly once all the others had boarded. And a family of six, nonetheless. He hoped that they'd make it and also hoped that if they didn't, it wasn't his four that contributed to it.

Starling stood with Lore, Narco, and McQueen. They wore classic contractor apparel: Merrell shoes, cargo pants, tucked in polo shirts, and thin jackets. Each of them held a small pack in their left hand. Starling had a water bottle, as did Narco. McQueen held a GQ magazine he'd dive into once he got on—*if* he got on. And Lore grabbed a Brian Keene novel from the store's racks, something called *The Complex*.

It was getting toward the end of boarding when a tech sergeant approached them and gave them documents to get on the plane. They all looked at each other with collective relief and boarded. A C5 Galaxy was exactly like a civilian aircraft on the inside—if the civilian aircraft had all the seats facing backwards, no windows, and no flight attendants, only grumpy loadmasters and airmen. Because the plane was almost full, they had to find seats where they could. Narco and Lore found seats where they sat alone. Starling and McQueen found a pair next to each other. C5 passenger seats were larger than civilian seats, so as Starling settled in, he let out a sigh.

Right before they closed boarding, the family of six made it on. Everyone was forced to sit by themselves, but a couple of young uniformed officers found a way for the two younger kids to sit near their mother.

Starling didn't notice much after that. The stress of the last seventy-two hours, especially the constant feeling that they'd be found out during the last twenty-four, had weighed on him. He was soon asleep, where he dreamed of a dark, wet place. He couldn't see very well, but he knew he was somewhere underground. Multiple sounds of breathing told him he wasn't alone. But try as he might, he couldn't get his eyes to open more than slits. The only other sound beyond the breathing and the occasional drip of water was an electrical buzzing, like an old light bulb but louder, and somehow it existed as something sentient. He tried to turn to the sound, but he couldn't move, frozen in a dream fist that held him tight and rigid.

Then came another sound that his mind immediately processed and recognized. The bleat of a goat. His whole body shook with the noise, muscles vibrating, skin on fire, bones resonating. Then it came again. His body rattled, almost exploding with the energy of the bleat. And with this came a shift of view.

Now Starling saw something new, something that glowed and somehow rested in midair. He tried to process the shape, but without the whole, it was an impossible feat, like trying to imagine the universe by seeing only a single star. Yet his mind somehow resolved the shape and labeled it as a thigh... a human thigh. But that was impossible. How could a thigh glow and float of its own accord?

The bleat came again, shaking his universe until he felt like his very bones would fly out of his skin. Then he was attacked. He fought madly, suddenly able to move, clawing, scratching, but something held him with more power than he possessed.

"Easy, man. Wake up. Be cool." The words came in sharp staccato whispers.

Starling kept trying to fight, but he was unable to move his arms.

"Open your damned eyes."

The goat bleated once more, shattering galaxies.

His eyes snapped open.

McQueen held him by the wrists, the bigger man's forearm and triceps muscles bulging.

Several people near them were staring.

McQueen hissed at them, "Haven't you ever deployed before?"

They all turned away.

Starling's mouth was so dry he had difficulty speaking. "Sorry." He pulled at his hands and McQueen let go. "It was a dream."

"Some dream."

Even as he tried to summon what it had been, reinvent what he'd seen, it was gone.

"You were bleating like a damned goat," McQueen said.

He did remember the goat. "That was me? I thought it was…" He rubbed the side of his face. "Damn. I'll be glad when this is all done." He looked around the darkened cabin. "Where are we?"

"Somewhere over the middle of America." McQueen placed a small box on his lap along with a water bottle. "Here. You missed dinner."

"Oh, joy. What is it?"

"Bologna sandwich, carrots, and yogurt."

Hunger was the last thing on Starling's mind.

"Thanks," he said.

He let the food and water rest on his lap and closed his eyes. He tried to will his dream to return to the glowing thing… yes, the glowing thing in the dark place. He needed to know what it was. A certain desperation had grown within him that begged to know. But try as he might, the dream eluded him. Instead of a dark place, he found himself in a place so bright it was almost blinding—the Middle Eastern sun so reflective it hurt to stare without good sunglasses. And there he was again, in Iraq in 2009 when he'd seen his first body, or part of one… a foot inside of a shoe that had been sheared off mid-calf by the power of a roadside bomb. It rested on the ground next to what turned out to be the boy's father, who'd been at work when the child had been killed. Neighbors had run to him with the news and he'd come home to find the only piece of his son that he recognized. Through the terp, Starling had learned that the shoes had been the boy's dream for two years. He'd gone by the same shop, staring in the window, aching for the shoes. He'd begged his father to buy them for him. The kid promised that they would make him run faster than any shoes out there. He'd be the fastest on the football pitch and be able to outrun a jihadi's bullet. As it turned out, the shoes *had* made him fast.

But fast as he was, the eleven-year-old could not outrun the hatred embodied by a hollow metal gas tank filled with projectiles and explosives.

The shoe was bright orange and white and looked like it had just been sitting on a shelf in a store, not lying on the side of a dusty Iraqi road with the foot and soul of a child snug within it. Starling even remembered the brand, the word Paralitefoot emblazed across the heel. Starling had had his own dreams of summer running, but he came from a world where there were fireflies instead of firefights... a place where there were grassy parks instead of empty fields filled with land mines... a place where the worst that could happen was being a latch-key kid instead of having one or both parents dead, killed by the ambivalence of a well-placed bomb.

When Starling eventually woke, tears had dried at the corners of his eyes.

In the darkened cabin, he chewed slowly on his bologna sandwich. Then he rushed to the bathroom, where the contents of his stomach came up. He vomited with his eyes closed, hoping this time he'd lose the memory of the bloody stump of the boy's foot, lonely and dead on the killing fields of the Middle East.

Chapter Fifteen

Al Udied Air Force Base, Doha, Qatar

Two MORE PLANES and ten thousand miles later, they found themselves in the blast furnace known as Doha. Criminal was waiting for them on the tarmac. He was leaning against a white double cab Toyota Hilux, an infectious grin on his face, a Raiders cap on his head. With the C130's ramp lowered, the passengers filed around the two cargo pallets and into the white-hot heat of Qatar.

After an exchange of pleasantries, they got in the truck and Criminal drove them away. Thirty minutes later, they pulled into a fenced area with the words HUMANTECH displayed everywhere. Several other SUVs were present, but no one was outside. Nor would they be in the 109 degree heat.

Finally inside the air conditioned trailer Criminal used as an office, he handed them ID cards with their actual names and corresponding contracts and movement orders—everything they'd need to get into Afghanistan and stay awhile. He took their fake IDs, placed them in an envelope, and jammed it in the back of a filing cabinet.

Besides Criminal's desk, there were two more desks. The walls were covered with HUMANTECH recruiting posters, to include one shot of the TST—geared up propagandist gun porn designed to attract recently retired operators back into the fold.

"Where are yours?" Boy Scout asked after they destroyed the first set of docs.

"My what?" Criminal sat in the office, feet up on his desk.

"Your orders. You're coming with us, you know," Boy Scout said flatly.

Criminal shook his head. "Don't think so. I have a job here."

"This is more than just a job, Oz," Lore began.

But Criminal cut her off by rolling his eyes and saying, "You're chasing a dream... a dream you can't catch."

"Who said we can't catch it... figure this out?" Boy Scout challenged.

Criminal laughed. "Look at you. The four of you. All serious and shit about figuring out what a girl and a goat are doing in your dreams. It probably means nothing and you know that."

"We don't know that," Narco said. "Listen, man. I didn't want to come either, but what Boy Scout is saying is right. We need to track this down. We need to figure this out." Seeing Oz's eyes roll, he added, "And don't go telling me you don't feel like you left something behind... something undone."

Criminal put his feet on the floor and leaned forward,

one elbow on the desk, his other hand pointing at the group. "Sure I feel it. So what? I also feel like I should have dated Sissy Jenkins in high school. I feel like I shouldn't have entered that building in Fallujah and I wouldn't have been shot. I also feel like I've bent over double to help you guys and I'd appreciate a little fucking thank you."

"Okay," Boy Scout said. "Thank you. Feel better?"

Criminal waved his hand and sat back heavily. "Fuck off. You want to go so badly, there's a bird leaving this afternoon and you have seats on it."

"But Oz, you're part of the team," Lore said. "You can't just stay here."

"Watch me."

"We could use you, Criminal," McQueen said.

"There's plenty out there like me. Maybe not as good or as handsome, but plenty. I'm sure if you need a fifth you can find someone dumb enough to go back."

"You're scared," Lore said, the words coming out as she thought them.

Criminal's head snapped around. "You don't know what you're talking about."

"I know scared when I see it," she said.

"Whatever you say, Preacher's Daughter." He shook his head. "Whatever you say."

"So that's it." Boy Scout glared at him. "You're really not coming."

"Nope. I'm staying right here in Doha where I can collect hazard pay without any of the hazard."

"And that's your final say?" Boy Scout asked.

"That's my final say."

Boy Scout and Criminal locked eyes for a full thirty seconds.

McQueen broke the contact by grabbing Boy Scout by the shoulder. "Come on. Let's go and get kitted out. They're not going to let us on a bird without body armor and some weapons."

Boy Scout felt like he had to say something else, but he just couldn't think of anything more. He'd had the feeling that everyone was on board, that everyone wanted to find out what was going on inside their heads, but apparently that feeling wasn't shared by Criminal. Boy Scout didn't make a face. He didn't shake his head. He merely looked at McQueen and said, "You're right. Lore, Narco. You want to join us?"

Lore said, "Right behind you."

Narco said, "Gimme a moment. I'll be there."

Boy Scout turned and left the trailer. He walked across the parking lot to another trailer, this one with bars on the windows. He opened the door and saw an older woman sitting behind a desk that was three feet inside the door and situated so that to get into the rest of the trailer, one had to pass the desk. She had steely gray hair and wore a strand of pearls around her neck. She had on the same contractor clothes they did, except her polo shirt had the words HUMANTECH over her left breast.

"Afternoon, Nancy," he said.

"Good afternoon, Mr. Starling."

"Can't say I'm surprised to see you here."

"You know I haven't rotated back home in six years."

Boy Scout shook his head. Nancy Coon was nearly seventy years old and was everyone's stand-in mother. She'd spent her first two years paying off debt she'd discovered her deceased husband had racked up. One it was paid off, she realized she hadn't really missed anything back in America that she couldn't get here on the air force base. She'd then decided to buy a house and pay it down so that by the time she did rotate back, it would be hers, free and clear.

"How much longer until you pay off the house?"

"I paid that off a few months ago."

"Then why are you still here, Nancy?"

"I need a new car. Been thinking about an Acura, or maybe a Lexus."

"You're never going to leave here, are you?"

Instead of answering, she pointed to a form on the desk. "I need you to sign here. We have body armor, a Sig Sauer P229, and an HK 416 ready for you. Not sure how much ammo you want, but make sure you log it before you leave."

"Yes ma'am." He signed the form, then stepped to the back of the trailer and started to put on his gear.

McQueen and Lore came next.

Finally, Narco entered the trailer.

Boy Scout looked over to where Narco stood, ready to sign his own form. When they made eye contact, Narco shook his head.

Boy Scout returned to adjusting his body armor. Because of his added weight, he had to work the straps to get it to fit. He'd hoped that Narco would be able to convince Criminal to join them. The two were alike in so many ways, but it looked like that had failed.

Narco said a few words to Nancy, then joined them in the back.

Nancy disappeared for ten minutes. When she returned, Criminal was on her heels. When she got to the desk, she sat down, pulled out a piece of paper, and he quickly bent down to sign it.

Then he joined the four members of the TST and began putting on his own gear.

"I thought you weren't coming," Lore said.

"I don't want to talk about it." Criminal snapped on his body armor, then said, without looking at anyone, "I'll be with you for one week. If we don't figure this out in one week, you'll have to do it without me."

"I understand," Boy Scout said.

On the way out, he stopped at Nancy's desk.

"Can I help you?" she asked.

"Looks like Oz is joining us."

She beamed at Boy Scout. "Isn't that nice. The team's now back together."

Boy Scout nodded. He wanted to talk more, but there was something predatory about that smile. Something behind the happiness that promised to snap and bite. He was convinced she'd said something to Criminal, but she'd never tell him what it was and Boy Scout couldn't ask.

"Well, you take care, Nancy."

"I will, Mr. Starling. You take care, too." She beamed another smile. "And make sure you get Oz back to me safe and sound."

Boy Scout tipped an invisible hat. "WILCO, ma'am."

Chapter Sixteen

Kabul, Afghanistan

BOY SCOUT BELIEVED that if a country were to have a national car, Afghanistan would have the Toyota Corolla. They were so omnipresent one could stand in the center of Massoud Circle and see nothing but Corollas for several minutes before a pickup truck carrying eggs from the hinterlands or a motor scooter carrying boxes drove by. What was funny was that many of those cars had originated in America and Canada. He could tell this because he'd seen bumper stickers that read *Obama '08* or *My Great Dane is Smarter Than Your Honor Student* or *My Kid Is in the Honor Roll at Tyner Junior High*. What usually brought a smile to his face was when he saw a Corolla with a *Jesus Saves* bumper sticker. The irony of the driver not knowing what it meant but still having it on his car wasn't lost on Boy Scout. If it wasn't for the Toyota Land Cruisers and Chevrolet Suburbans used by NATO and NGOs, one could've designated Afghanistan as the Land of the Corolla, arguing with a certain amount of credibility that a silhouette of the vehicle should appear on the national flag instead of a mosque.

Here the Corollas were interspersed with the occasional green pickup belonging to the Afghan National Army, whose members openly carried their machine guns, often brandishing them to help get through traffic, even though no one really paid them much attention. When Boy Scout had first come to Afghanistan, the ANA soldiers worried him, possible perpetrators of what NATO called Green on Blue Attacks—an ANA soldier killing an American soldier—that had happened with alarming regularity just a few years ago. But he soon learned that these were less a danger than the faux police cars and trucks. Often owned by a local warlord, these usually high-end vehicles had sirens and lights to assist them getting through roads designed to serve several hundred thousand in a city with closer to four million people. These men often wore face masks and body armor and were known to pop off at NATO SUVs with a round or two just to impress their warlords.

But neither Jesus Saves Corollas, green ANA pickups loaded with soldiers, or Afghan gangbangers in their warlords' rides impacted the usual TST mission. That's because they had one hard fast rule when moving through the city. Never stop... which was a rule they were often forced to break with stupefying regularity. Gridlock was the norm, especially at the city's natural chokepoints.

Boy Scout had been in country less than a week when he'd encountered his first incident. They'd been in a three-vehicle convoy, pretty much like they always were. Boy Scout and Preacher's Daughter were in the middle vehicle with the package—a pair of civilians from the Defense Intelligence Agency. While each of the civilians had their own weapons, they'd been ordered to keep them holstered. The last thing Boy Scout needed was for two barely trained civies to get in the way of his team in the event of a firefight. Both of the civies had acquiesced, understanding that if something happened, their best chance at living rested with the six men and women of the TST who'd been trained specifically to keep them alive.

The lead vehicle was driven by McQueen with Criminal as gunner.

The trail vehicle was driven by Narco.

Boy Scout had received the BOLO list just that morning with pictures of three sedans, two motorcycles, and a bicycle. Each had been placed on the *Be On the Look Out* list because they'd been seen lingering near various US positions in the Kabul base cluster. He was well aware of the dangers presented by vehicle borne improvised explosive devices or VBIEDs. Not only could one of the sedans have an engine packed with plastic explosives, but one of the motorcycles or bicycles could slip through congested traffic and slap an IED with adhesive or magnets to the side of one of their vehicles. Although their SUVs were armored, he wouldn't want to test the vehicle's structural integrity against the explosive power of an IED.

Each of the men and women of his team had more than a hundred hours of combat driving training, not to mention real world experience in either Iraq, Afghanistan, Syria, or both. But all the training in the world couldn't defeat a terrorist intent on attacking a vehicle convoy, especially one locked in the dead-stop traffic of Massoud Circle.

Named after Ahmad Shah Massoud, known also as the Lion of Panjshir for his contributions in driving the Soviets out of Afghanistan, the center of the circle was dominated by a tall monument with an immense blue ball atop it, around which vehicles vied for access to the six roads that ran from it. There were no vehicular lanes. There were no lines. Entry into the circle was on a first come, first served basis. Because almost all the cars were Corollas it became an ant farm, with identically sized vehicles vying for a position that would allow them to depart the circle on one of the connecting roads.

On this occasion they were deadlocked, his three-vehicle convoy pinned in by a herd of angry Corollas. Because of its geophysical relationship to the Green Zone and its locus for the road to Kabul International Airport, the circle was a place one was forced to transit, which was why every member of the TST had their head on a swivel, hyper-aware for anything that could possibly be a threat. They'd locked their bumpers so that no one could get between them and separate the convoy, and were eagerly inching forward as traffic tetrissed around the monument.

The problem started when the DIA employee sitting behind the front passenger seat began to lose it. About fifty and seriously overweight, the body armor so tight that it was probably cutting off blood flow, "Gotta go, gotta go, gotta go," rattled under his breath.

The other employee, a man half his age and weight, said, "Take it easy, man."

But the big guy wasn't listening. "Gotta go, gotta go, gotta go," he chanted, increasingly loud.

Lore turned in her seat. "Everything is fine," she said in a voice that was the model of calm. "We do this every day and it's not a thing."

The big guy stared at Lore with bulging eyes, then bit back the chant. He glared fearfully out through the bulletproof glass on his door.

Suddenly the MBITR crackled to life.

"Five men working through the vehicles from our four o'clock," said Narco.

Lore spun and Boy Scout turned. She had her 9mm drawn but kept beneath the level of the window.

"We see them," Boy Scout said. "Do you clock any weapons?"

"Negative. But two are wearing man jammies, so they could be carrying."

The men were walking through the traffic, staring into windows as if they were looking for something.

"McQueen, can you get us a way out of here?"

"Only if I push," he said, meaning gun the engine and push the smaller cars out of his way, doing whatever damage was going to happen, his cement-filled metal bumper the modern equivalent of a battering ram.

"Hold off on the push," Boy Scout said. To Lore, he added, "Watch them."

"Pretty easy thing to do. They're coming right at us," she said.

"Gotta go, gotta go, gotta go." The man was now loud enough that everyone could hear it.

"You need to calm your friend," Lore said without turning around, her attention fully on the five men coming towards them.

"Sam," said the younger man. "Come on, Sam. Keep it cool."

"Can't. Gotta go, gotta go, gotta go."

The first of the five men was almost upon them. Two of the men had stopped at a car with its windows down and were reaching in. A man was fighting them as the men tried to pull things from his backseat.

Boy Scout had already clocked two ANA soldiers standing in the center of the circle, their AKs on their hips, watching the five men. Either the men had a working relationship with the soldiers, or the soldiers just didn't care. Either way, it was evident that the men placed in the circle to keep the peace weren't going to lift a finger. One of them lit a cigarette. The other looked away.

"Sam. Calm the fuck down," the younger man urged.

Lore glanced into the back seat and the guy gave her a look like, *I'm trying but he's freaking out and I can't stop him.*

"Gotta go, gotta go, gotta go, gotta go." Now he was almost yelling.

Just then one of the five men approached Lore's window. He was a dark-skinned Afghan with a sparse, short beard. He grinned because he evidently thought that by showing his rotting teeth, Lore would let him in. He tapped his knuckles on the window and bent down to peer in.

"Go away," she said, locking gazes with him.

But the man kept knocking.

She lifted the pistol so it was clearly visible, the barrel still pointing at the ground.

The man kept knocking.

She turned the working end of the pistol and aimed it at the man's face.

But he merely grinned wider. He knew the score. He was as safe behind the bulletproof glass as she was inside the vehicle.

"Gotta go, gotta go, gotta go."

Boy Scout wondered why the man had even deployed. If he couldn't take the stress of driving in Kabul, how was he going to react to being shot at?

Then things happened faster than he could stop them.

The man began pawing at the door handle. It was Boy Scout's responsibility to lock everyone in the car. The backseats were supposed to have been child locked. But he was driving a brand-new vehicle and hadn't yet set them up. So when the man pawed at the door handle a fifth time, the handle engaged and the door sprung open.

The Afghani man at Lore's window immediately filled the space, reaching in and grabbing at the fat man, who was now shrieking.

Lore spun in her seat and pressed the tip of her pistol against the side of the intruder's head at the same time that Boy Scout drew his pistol free from his chest rig and brought his right hand over and behind so the barrel of his pistol was on the intruder's forehead.

"Push! Push! Push!" he commanded through coms.

He felt the jerk as Narco shoved them from behind.

The intruder's eyes had gone wide and his face trembled. He raised his hands, then disappeared from view as the vehicles pressed through the crowd of stopped cars.

Lore reached back and slammed the door shut from the inside.

She glanced at Boy Scout. He knew what she wanted to say, but that wasn't how they acted. If she wanted to bitch, she could do it later. For now, it was all professional. And she knew it.

Instead, she turned to the DIA men in the back seat. "Let's not touch the door knobs again, okay?"

"Yes, ma'am," said the younger man.

Their three-car train plowed through a dozen cars, pushing each of them out of the way until they ended up pointing every which way. Once clear, Boy Scout gunned the vehicle. A space opened between their SUVs and they raced down the road.

The older man had passed out.

"Is he alive?" Boy Scout asked, seeing this in the mirror.

The younger man nodded. "Yeah. And he pissed himself, too." He blanched. "Sorry about that."

Lore gave Boy Scout another look.

They'd have to clean that up later, too.

But they were safe. As he drove, the stress of the moment bled away with each kilometer between them and the circle, until finally he was calm again. He glanced back at the passed out DIA employee. He doubted they were going to make their meeting. The funny thing was, to get them back to their base, they'd have to go right back through Massoud Circle.

That incident seemed like it had happened decades ago, but it was really a little over seventeen months. This would make Boy Scout's third rotation with virtually the same team. Although it wasn't unheard of, it was a rarity to be able to work with the same people. Personnel turnover in a war zone could be dizzying. One moment you have a great working relationship with someone, the next they've redeployed and you have to learn the idiosyncrasies of another. That they were all contractors working for the same company was in their favor. HUMANTECH knew they worked well together and tried to keep them together because in the end, it was all about making the customer happy and in this case the customer was the United States government.

They'd hit Kabul three days ago. One day to set up their team room, get cars issued and cleared, and establish a routine, then two days of missions. Three full days and they were nowhere closer to figuring out the significance of the girl and the goat. Three full days and they still had a maddening feeling that they were missing something. Then there was the unexpected attention they'd been receiving. It was a small thing. In fact, it might not have even been a thing. At first, he'd thought he was making it all up in his head. But then Lore mentioned it too. Either his paranoia was catching, or they were receiving more attention than they deserved.

The eyes.

Everyone's eyes.

They didn't look away.

They didn't look down.

Afghanistan was much like some of the more dangerous places in America, whether it be South Central Los Angeles or South Chicago. You didn't meet someone else's gaze. To do so was to challenge them... a challenge most often ending with a gunfight. The same went for Afghanistan. It was the *mode de guerre*. Women didn't look at anyone except other women or children. Men looked at other men they knew but kept their attention away from those they didn't. The only persons who truly had the freedom to stare openly were children, and then only because of the universal imprimatur of childhood curiosity.

Something had definitely changed in Kabul since their last rotation.

The TST found that it was impossible to pass unnoticed because it seemed that everyone was watching them. Not out of the corners of their eyes, but full out staring, as if they were the center of everyone's attention. Wherever Boy Scout would drive, everyone was already looking in his direction as if they'd been expecting them. Even in Massoud Circle, the eyes of every driver and passenger followed them, watching their every move. The faces were impassive, but the eyes moved with them.

There'd been an ill-chosen moment in high school when Boy Scout had agreed to be in a Neil Simon play, the one that Jane Fonda and Robert Redford had made famous on the silver screen. Like most things he'd done in high school, he'd agreed to do it because of a girl. The idea of memorizing lines to be regurgitated in front of a crowd of five hundred fellow students hadn't bothered him when he'd signed up to appear in *Barefoot in the Park*. It had never occurred to him that so much attention would bother him. But then lights, camera, action, and a few moments later he was stepping through a prop window as the Upper West Side letch, Victor Velasco, to the cheers and jeers of his fellow students in Phipps Auditorium. Instead of remembering his lines, he'd focused on the thousand eyes staring directly at him, pinning him to the stage, and he knew that such attention was absolutely the last thing he'd ever want. He hadn't been afraid. Instead, he'd been immediately sick, his lines barely passing the fist-sized lump of vomit that had wedged in his throat.

He was brought back to that moment now because of the attention they'd been receiving in Kabul... a situation so eerie that he found himself not as vigilant as he should have been. The combined gazes of everyone he passed on the street weighed on him enough so that he found it difficult to watch what he was supposed to watch.

Everything came to a head on the morning of the fourth day. They had a mission to carry three members of the embassy econ council to the Afghan Ministry of Finance. From the very start, Boy Scout had felt something was off. The norm was for the TST to arrive and everyone be happy to see them. After all, they were the ones putting themselves in harm's way. His appearance had always engendered smiles, handshakes, and even high fives on occasion. They were the hired beasts to keep the other beasts at bay.

But by the conspiratorial way the embassy folks stared at him then mumbled to each other, the TST's appearance seemed anything but popular. By the looks in the eyes of the two men and one woman, it was plain that they weren't even wanted. It was as if their existence was accepted with reservations. Sideways looks and heavy-lidded stares put a pall over the entire movement.

The TST employed their usual three-vehicle convoy. The embassy was packed in the center of the Green Zone and abutting Resolute Support (RS) HQ. Because of the sensitivity and its location, there were almost a dozen checkpoints to go through before they rolled into Massoud Circle. At each checkpoint, Boy Scout would glance in the rearview mirror and immediately lock gazes with his passengers. After a moment, they'd drop their gazes and lower their heads together, their conversation much like those of crows in the midst of a murder. Whatever they were saying, it was conveyed with the slow shaking of heads, conspiratorial glances his way, and whispered words, taking him once more back to high school where the cruel cool kids would talk amongst themselves about the others—and Boy Scout had always been an *other*.

Navigating Massoud Circle turned out a simpler task than most other times and they soon found themselves pulling into the Ministry of Finance compound. The guards at the compound gate checked their vehicular IDs, then the NATO identification plate on the dashboard. By rule, the TST never left a vehicle. Many of the other official travelers were made to disembark vehicles, allow for explosive sweeps, and forced to unload weapons at the various checkpoints in and around Kabul... but not the TST.

Never the TST.

Except this time.

An ANA soldier stood in front of the first vehicle with his AK47 at the ready. Several other ANA soldiers had formed a rough arc inside the compound, all facing him. An ANA major with a clipboard gestured for those in McQueen's vehicle to disembark.

McQueen radioed from the first vehicle, where Narco sat beside him in the passenger's seat.

"Boss, you seeing what I'm seeing?"

"Roger," Boy Scout acknowledged. "Remain fast." He honked the horn to get the ANA major's attention.

The man glanced in his direction, then proceeded to ignore him. He walked up and rapped his knuckles on McQueen's window.

"For God's sake, what's taking so long?" asked one of their passengers.

Boy Scout glanced in the rearview mirror, but no one was looking at him. Instead, all three of them had their heads together once again. Finally, one glanced at him and sneered. It was the woman, her red-lipsticked lips pulling back until it seemed the corners touched her ears. He felt a cavity open in his stomach, reminded suddenly of a version of Caliban he'd seen in a horror movie version of Shakespeare's *The Tempest*. This Caliban had pokey teeth that enabled him to suck the blood from dying children in a hospital. As long as he stared, the creepy grin remained, his eyes locked with the woman.

Then McQueen called. "Boss, he wants me to roll down the window."

Boy Scout flicked his gaze to the SUV in front of him,

then to the backseat, but the woman was no longer looking at him and her mouth was a thin flat line as the men whispered to her.

"This isn't right," Lore said from the passenger seat. "Criminal, watch our six. Whatever happens, we need a way to get out."

They were closing the gate behind them.

Criminal eased his SUV backwards to keep them from closing the gate completely, his SUV now a four thousand pound door stop.

Several ANA soldiers yelled for him to move, but he merely hung his arms over the steering wheel and grinned at them.

Classic Criminal.

Someone from the back seat hissed, "Will you just fucking open the door?"

But when Boy Scout looked, they were still huddled together. It wasn't apparent who had spoken. It didn't seem as if anyone had spoken.

"Excuse me?" he asked.

But they ignored him.

Part of their rules of engagement was to not let the client get under their skin. They were to remain professional at all times. "I said, excuse me. Did one of you just say something?"

The woman suddenly sat up, staring openly at him.

His full attention was on her lips as he waited for her to resume that blood-thirsty horror movie Caliban thing she'd been doing with her lips.

"Boss, this has gone to DEFCON one," McQueen said,

referring to the most serious nuclear readiness stance America could have—the brink of war.

Boy Scout glanced once again at the activity forward and saw that the ANA soldier in front of McQueen had locked and loaded his AK, had shouldered it, and was sighting down the barrel, preparing to fire. The other ANA soldiers in the arc had likewise pulled their weapons and brought them to bear. If they opened fire, the SUVs windows would hold enough for them to be able to back out if they were lucky, but this was all wrong. Why the confrontation? His and the other TSTs had been here hundreds of times, escorting various government entities intent on helping the ever-failing Afghan economy from total collapse. Why was the ANA suddenly antagonistic to them?

"We shouldn't be here," the woman said in a monotone.

"Excuse me?" Lore said, flipping through her movement orders. "We were to pick you up at the embassy and deliver you to the Ministry of Finance by eleven hundred hours. Current time hack is eleven oh four. We'd have been on time had it not been for the shenanigans—"

"Shut your cunt," one of the men hissed.

Now all three were sitting up straight, staring at Boy Scout.

"Excuse me?" he said again, eyes narrowing, about ready to throw the ROE out the window. While he'd expect such behavior from a drunken colonel, he'd never seen or heard embassy personnel speak this way.

"He told the cunt to shut up," the woman said, the Caliban grin flicking in and out of existence.

"Let us go," said the remaining man.

"Yes, let us go," the woman said. Caliban grin, then back to normal.

Suddenly the man who'd first spoke began to bang on the window next to him and started to scream unintelligibly.

The inhuman sound sent simultaneous shivers of confusion and fear down Boy Scout's spine.

While the man screamed, the other man and woman chanted, "Let us go, let us go, let us go, let us go."

"Uh, boss, still waiting on orders," came McQueen's voice over the coms.

But Boy Scout was too stunned to reply. His gaze was locked on the woman's, whose mouth kept flicking back and forth from normal to Caliban then back again as she chanted *let us go* at the top of her lungs. He became aware that Lore was staring at him and saying something, but he couldn't hear it over the cacophony of screams and chants.

Then sudden silence as the back doors clicked unlocked.

"You want out?" Lore growled from the front seat. "Then get the fuck out, you fucking cunt."

The three lowered their eyes, grabbed their briefcases, and exited the vehicle. The second they were outside, they returned to normal, suddenly chatty with the ANA as they started walking towards the front steps of the ministry.

The ANA soldiers who'd been aiming at the lead vehicle lowered their weapons and moved back into position.

The ANA major greeted the woman with a handshake.

She shook his hand, then followed him up the stairs into the massive, Soviet-built cement building.

Boy Scout had been waiting for the woman to turn around, to give him one last Caliban grin, even acknowledge them, but it was like once the embassy personnel were out of the vehicle, the TST had ceased to exist.

He caught Lore staring at him from her seat.

"Boss, I am so sorry I said that. I don't know what came over me, it's just that—"

He held up a hand and she stopped talking.

"Call the J3 and get another detail here. We're heading back to the house," he said.

He contacted the rest of the team and they backed out of the compound. They were soon heading to their team room. Boy Scout knew he was shaken but wouldn't admit it. What had gone down had been the strangest protection mission he'd ever been on. Even now, as they re-entered the Green Zone, the woman's crazy monster smile remained as the ghost of an image in his mind. With her smile superimposed over much of what he saw, he still noticed that everyone was waiting for them, everyone was watching, eyes on them as they moved from place to place to place, as if life was a television show and they were the stars.

What was it that Joon had asked him? *Ever wonder if you're a character in the wrong story?* What would happen if Tarzan suddenly showed up in an Alice in Wonderland tale? What would happen if Godzilla showed up in *The Hunger Games*? What would be the result of Harry Potter showing up in *Fifty Shades of Gray*? As characters in a story, they knew their place. They knew their part. No matter how many times the story was told, they knew and expected an outcome defined by the story's creator. So when Harry Potter or Tarzan or Godzilla appeared out of synch, wouldn't the characters in the original story notice and wonder why they were there? Is that what was happening? Was Boy Scout an armored-up Harry Potter? Was the TST Godzilla? Were they living in the land of *Fifty Shades of Gray* and didn't know it?

While it was all metaphor, just thinking along these lines made his brain hurt. He definitely had trouble thinking straight. When they pulled into their own compound, the memory of the woman's smile was all but gone, but what lingered was the idea that they were definitely in the wrong story, even though it looked exactly like the one they should be in.

Chapter Seventeen

HE LAY IN bed remembering the vitriolic heat of their argument. It had been just short of a knock-down, drag-out fight. In fact, it'd been so bad that Boy Scout knew he'd lost them as a leader, which was why, despite the exhaustion and alcohol, he couldn't sleep.

It could have begun earlier, after they'd returned from the Ministry of Finance, but each of them had gone to their own compensating devices.

McQueen had gone to work out in the RS gym.

Lore had gone on an eight-mile run.

Narco had disappeared but had ultimately found a 4th Infantry Division soldier selling Mollies.

Criminal had gone to the embassy pool for a swim.

And Boy Scout had gone to talk to the chaplain... something he hadn't done since his mother had died while he'd been deployed to Iraq and his company commander had made him go. On that occasion, the young chaplain from Vermont had levied the necessary platitudes, signed a paper which allowed a young Starling to return home and bury his mother, then gone on to talk about how everything was part of God's plan.

God's plan.

If there were two words in the English language Boy Scout hated more, it was someone sliming the memory of something wonderful with the ridiculous platitude that his mother's death had been part of God's plan.

If the chaplain had been right, then God's plan sure was complicated.

His mother had been sitting in a Starbucks drinking a macchiato mocha. She liked extra foam and she liked cinnamon. He imagined that at the moment of impact she'd been checking Facebook on her phone, a freckled dollop of foam on the tip of her nose, probably getting ready to post a comment on one of her friend's dog pictures. He liked to tease her that the only reason she was even on Facebook was the pet porn. She'd poo-poo his attitude and remind him that if it wasn't for Facebook, she wouldn't even know where he was and what he was doing. Although her comment stung, she was right, and he took the velvet-gloved slap to the face with his head down and his heart large. Facebook really was their only way to connect, and after her death he'd spend the rest of his life regretting the missed phone calls and the simple perfection of a short letter addressed by hand and sent the way all letters from war had gone since the beginning of time.

They said she hadn't felt a thing, but he'd always wondered if that were true. Did God's plan always allow for painless deaths? It didn't seem so. He'd seen enough dismembered children to know that was at least a very bad ecumenical joke.

The Starbucks she'd been sitting in was in a stand-alone building next to Northgate Mall. They'd found the Go-Pro camera later and pieced together the scenario. His name had been Damien Wayne and he'd been at the helm of a lime green Kawasaki KLX 140. The police video forensics unit said he'd begun filming at the bottom of a parking garage. They traced his line of travel up the five stories of the garage, then across the top level. He'd accelerated there, hit his prepositioned ramp and soared the thirty feet between the garage and the roof of the mall. He'd landed on the roof, wobbled a bit, but held his seat despite the rooftop gravel that had come loose from the pitch.

As to what had happened next, no one knew whether it was planned or if it had been a spur of the moment decision. After traversing the mall's roof back and forth a few times, he inexplicably accelerated, jumped off the roof and onto the roof of an empty parked vehicle transport that had recently unloaded cars for nearby Kelly's Nissan. Damien hit the roof and roared down the truck's vehicle discharge ramp like he'd been possessed by the ghost of Evel Knievel. And like the super stunt biker himself, he made the jump... but he couldn't stick the landing. When he'd hit the pavement at what the vehicular forensics unit gauged to be fifty miles an hour, he'd gone into a skid. Instead of crashing, he'd laid the motorcycle down. Wearing armored cycling gear, he would have survived had not a speeding BMW M5 picked that moment to skid around the corner and run him over. Although it wasn't much of a speed bump, Wayne's helmet tore the muffler housing free, and with it his head, where it rolled underneath a parked Jeep Cherokee to be found later by an elderly man and his dog. The motorcycle continued in a divine trajectory, hitting a curb that sent it airborne and crashing through a window and then straight through Julie Suzanne Starling's face.

Later, when Starling had found out the Go Cam had been attached to the handlebars and there was rumor that there'd been footage of the accident, he'd gone to the police and begged to see it. At first they'd absolutely denied the existence of the footage, but with the help of a former Army Ranger who was now a police sergeant, Starling had been given a USB with the complete footage of the wreck from start to finish, including the beginning where the excited voice of Damien Wayne addressed the camera, donned his helmet, then took off to kill Boy Scout's mother.

With only a few staticky seconds missing, sitting in his Trans Am in the parking lot in front of the very same Starbucks his mother had died in, he'd watched Damien's transitory journey from adventurer to murderer, or what the News 11 team had called *an unfortunate and freaky death*. Boy Scout had barely breathed as he'd journeyed with Damien from the parking structure jump to the top of the mall. He'd been impressed with the landing on the roof of the truck, then had watched with dread as the view of the camera shifted with the bike. Grinding across the pavement, the view was off to the right. He caught the Starbucks' sign and a glimpse of a couple leaving the coffee shop.

Then miraculously, or callously—he still didn't know which—the bike shifted as it hit the curb and he was given a straight on view of his mother. She had been on Facebook doing her daily session of pet porn before work when something had caused her to look up, probably the breaking glass. He saw in her eyes not fear, but confusion. After all, lime green motorcycles weren't supposed to come flying through the window of her favorite coffee shop. Her eyes were wide. He could see the band of freckles across the top of her nose that she'd had since the summer of her thirteenth year when her mother and father had taken her for a holiday in the Adirondacks. Pausing the video for the hundredth time, he could almost count them. But what got him was the expression on her face. Sure, her eyes showed a galaxy of confusion, but her mouth held a small smile, one she'd eagerly give to anyone. She seemed curious. She was smiling as if greeting the motorcycle that was coming to end her life was the most common thing. *It's easier to be polite than it is to be mean, little man. Smile first and ask questions later. You'll see how well it works.* Sage advice for the third grader who wasn't getting along with his new classmates, but little protection against a hundred pounds of metal and plastic flying at you.

Boy Scout had stared through the new window to where a teenager was sitting on a square patterned couch. His mother had been sitting there. For a brief moment he juxtaposed her image from the video to that of the boy's through the window. Then the boy looked up, as if he felt the attention. For a second the boy smiled, as if the ghost of Starling's mother inhabited him, then he frowned and looked away, irritated in the way only teens can be when someone disturbs their universe, even if it was merely by looking at them.

Attention again on the video feed, Boy Scout watched as the image from the Go Cam shifted to a barista whose face was a mask of horror. Evidently the impact with the glass altered the bike's trajectory, because it was through another's eyes that he saw the bike's rear tire intersect his mother's face.

Instantly said the coroner.

Unfortunate and freaky said the award-winning TV news team.

God's plan said the chaplain.

Boy Scout hadn't thought about his mother's death in months, but his current visit to the chaplain had given it new life. The chaplain himself hadn't been much help. In fact, he'd barely said a word as Starling recounted the events of the morning and the way the woman's smile seemed inhuman and monstrous.

Finally, the chaplain had said, "What do you want me to do about it?" then had added, "Maybe they're right. Maybe you should let us go!" Then he'd excused himself and had hurried out of the room.

With the death of his mother still fresh in his mind, Boy Scout returned to the house and found a bottle of Jack Daniels. Grabbing a coke, he made the first of a dozen half and halfs, drowning the memory of his mother, the events of the morning, the father with only his son's foot, and a hundred other terrible memories soldiers in faraway places are unable to organize into neat little memory boxes.

No longer did he feel like the Boy Scout he'd once again become. His skin felt like a Halloween costume or Spiderman pajamas that every other ten-year-old boy liked to wear. The idea that the guy who'd been popping pills, snorting coke, and leaning on deadbeats to get them to pay at least the vig for what they owned Larrson could somehow be transformed into a lean, mean, TST-leading machine was fucking ludicrous, and somewhere between his second and third drink he'd decided that he was going to return to merely being Starling the Fuck Up.

But now, as he lay in bed, twisting and turning with the memory of slapping McQueen across the face, he'd wished he'd found another outlet for his confused misery.

The look on the man's face, the devastation he'd caused in his friend and follower's belief, trust and faith in Boy Scout was antithetical to the last moment of his mother's life. Where she'd looked up with an honest smile, ready to welcome even the harbinger of her own death, McQueen's glare of anger had dissolved into something akin to disgust, a mask that matched the single word he'd launched back in retaliation: *pathetic*.

Then the room-clearing confrontation between Criminal and Narco. There were two kinds of fights among friends. There was the half-hearted slap-punch that led to an apologetic exchange of hugs that occurred often enough after a harried mission where they were blowing off steam and needed to purge the adrenaline that had built up. Then there were the titanic brawls, where neither would give up an inch of metaphorical or real territory, their punches and kicks harder and worse because it was a friend perceived to have become an enemy, the presumed treachery the fire for even greater anger.

It was the second that had fueled their clash, each one trying to own the low ground. The problem between the pair was that they weren't the best fighters when they were drunk and high. Haymakers came from the constellation of Orion and kicks came from somewhere south of Australia. The more they missed, the angrier they became, and it wasn't until Lore tried to intervene and was kicked in the crotch by Narco that the fight switched into overdrive.

The moment the accidental kick connected, Narco froze, clearly freaked by the inaccuracy of his assault.

Criminal took advantage and clocked him on the side of the head with a right cross.

Feeling that the fight should have been stopped because of Lore's pain, Narco took the blow the same way England took the bombing of World War II: he launched his own Normandy Beach invasion, which was actually a fast and furious flurry of punches and kicks, accurate only because Criminal wouldn't or couldn't get out of the way. Their friendship flipped to hatred only as friends were able, hating each other because each knew the other better than anyone.

The lovely evening had ended with everyone cursing everyone else and promising that in the morning, they were voiding their contracts and heading back to America, regardless of what law enforcement agency was looking for them... *And fuck that goddamned girl and her goat!* Lore cried, the last and final words of an extraordinary and terrible evening.

That would have been that except someone began banging on the door of the team room at 3:53 in the morning. Everyone had their own bedroom and Lore was the one to open the door just as Starling exited his own room, wearing nothing but a pair of boxers. Lore had on a pair of black shorts with a T-shirt bearing the Army of One logo.

Their night guard apologized for waking them, then informed them that someone wanted to see them. He admitted that he'd tried to turn the person away, but the person wouldn't go. When asked who it was, the guard said it was a strange child.

The idea that a child was trying to contact them at almost four in the morning intrigued Lore, so before Starling, who really no longer had a right to say anything, could open his mouth, she told the guard to let the child in.

Criminal and Narco came out next, each one eyeing the other, their faces and bare chests quilts of multicolored welts and wounds.

McQueen came last, completely dressed, a pistol at his side, ready for whatever the rest weren't.

Right after that, the guard led a girl into the room. She had long brown hair and wore a Robin's egg blue dressed. They knew her at once.

Lore backed away as the girl entered the room like she

owned it, walking with far more authority than a child ever should.

The girl stared openly at each of them for a moment, then said, "*As-Salaam Alaikum.*" Her speech was a world-weary tenor.

"*Alaikum as-Salaam,*" replied Lore in a trembling voice. "My name is Ms. May. And you?"

The girl sighed and smiled sadly. "I am you and I am here to fetch you."

Starling felt a pit open in his stomach and he knew right then that something terrible was about to happen.

"Fetch us?" Lore turned to Starling, but he had no answer.

"Who are you? What are you?" Narco asked.

"It's time to come home," the girl said.

"Come on, kid. What the hell do you want with us?" Criminal asked, tears appearing in his eyes.

The girl turned to him. "You need to separate. You need to be a part."

"Where's the goat?" McQueen asked.

The girl turned to him. "That's a much better question."

Then Narco disappeared.

Everyone, including the ever-stoic McQueen, backed up a step to let the *what the fuck moment* fill the space. Because when Narco disappeared, he was just... *gone*.

Starling was the first one to speak. "Narco? Narco?" He turned to Lore. "Where'd he go?"

She seemed about to speak, then she disappeared as well. Just gone. One second she was there. The next nothing.

Criminal screamed something intelligible that was cut

off as he, too, disappeared.

Starling turned to McQueen, whose eyes were so narrowed the cleft between his eyes was a dark black. Starling began to walk to his old friend, but before he was halfway there, McQueen said, "Oh," as if in surprise—

Then he was gone.

Now Starling stood in the middle of the house. Just him and the girl.

Starling didn't know what to say, so he asked, "Who are you really?"

Instead of answering, the girl stepped up to him and grabbed him by his shoulders. She pulled Starling down with impossible strength. She whispered into Starling's ear, and the more Starling heard, the wider his eyes became. Then suddenly he straightened.

"Is this true?" he said with a rush of hope.

The girl nodded and backed away.

Starling opened his mouth, but everything went black. He managed to say, "Oh hell," but he didn't know if it was in his head or in real life. A second later he felt something he hadn't felt in years—intense exhaustion and incredible pain—and it wasn't until he opened his eyes that he truly understood what had happened to him... again.

Chapter Eighteen

Kholm, Afghanistan

THEY SAY THAT despair has a smell that once experienced is forever recognized. The acridness of fresh vomit, the pungent sweat forced to the skin by pulses of fear, and the cloying aroma of steaming feces all combined into a miasmatic fragrance worn by those who had abandoned hope long ago. Boy Scout had smelled it once in Darfur when they'd liberated a South Sudanese prisoner camp. The surviving warriors were a third of themselves—gristle, bone, and diseased flesh. Their eyes were sunken into sockets that looked carved out. Cheekbones jutted like knives, ready to tear flesh if an improbable smile might visit their misery. Every bone and tendon was displayed as if torn from an anatomy text, visible beneath the taut, scarred and tortured skin. But what he remembered most of all was their stench... a stench he now wore himself, in a nowhere place he seemed unable to escape.

His chin rested on tepid water, the rest of him submerged

beneath the viscous surface. He brought his hands to his face, noticing the water-logged whiteness of them. His dizzied gaze followed the length of his skin, down his arm and over to his shoulder. Reaching down, he felt his crotch, which was naked and shriveled. He coughed, the exhalation disturbing the water, creating tiny ripples that surged outward with at first tremendous force, then dissipated inches from the disturbance before finally vanishing.

At first, he thought he was standing, but he wasn't. He felt a rough, round stone beneath him, upon which he was seated. He flexed his toes and felt silt swoosh around them, then settle.

As he became aware of himself, he also became increasingly aware of his surroundings. He wanted to stand up and examine this place, but it was like he'd been in some sort of mystical fugue and was only now waking up… he thought of using the term *coming to his senses,* but in no way did any of this make sense.

He became aware of other sounds. An echoing, dripping sound, produced at regular intervals:

Drip.

Drop.

Drip.

Drop.

The staccato sounds were metronomic in their regularity and served to lull him for a moment… an hour… a day… an epoch… but then he heard a cough. Not his, but similar to his own.

Weak.

Alone.

The cough came again. Beside and behind him. He tried to turn, but he felt like his body was the size of a giant with only muscle enough to move a little boy. Still, he tried. What seemed like a decade later he saw the face of a tortured man, features sagging, full beard matted and grimy. The man's eyes were open, but just barely. He stared at the water a few inches from his face. Eventually, Starling became aware of movement. It was the only movement on the man's face. It was his eyebrow. It twitched in a way an eyebrow shouldn't twitch, as if it had come alive. The man coughed again and the cockroach that had been chewing on the man's eyelashes lost its purchase and fell into the water.

Starling watched as it swam back to the man, climbed up his arm, then found his face once more. It teased around in the man's nose for a time, antennae momentarily exploring the inside of the man's nostrils, then found his eyelashes and stayed there, as if they were a sweeter part of the human to eat.

Starling wanted to swat away the nasty insect, but he lacked the strength. No man should have to accept being eaten alive by such a vile creature. He remembered his own life when a cockroach had eaten away at his eyelashes. It seemed so near, yet so far. When was it?

Then the man's features snapped into place.

McQueen.

But it was a McQueen who had aged but hadn't shaved in months. It was a sickly McQueen. Not one who could protect them as he always had. Not the one Starling had just slapped in a drunken stupor. This was a McQueen from Darfur... so much nearer to death than life.

Starling tried to speak. Despite the water, his mouth was too dry to function. He lowered his chin until his lips were under the revolting liquid and let it fill his mouth. The taste was enough to make him gag. Instead of speaking, he found himself unable to breath. His mouth filled with such vileness that his body rejected it. He gasped and gagged. Blackness sparked at the edge of his vision as his body craved the oxygen it wouldn't, couldn't, let in. He tried to stop hacking but was unable to even control the smallest of his muscles.

Then, at the last moment when he was sinking, the water cresting above his eyes and over his head, ready to drown and embrace eternity, he felt strong muscles lift him free. He was dragged backward, heels sliding along the silty bottom then onto wet stone, then free of the water altogether and onto dryness. He was tossed down and turned over onto his back. A weight pressed down on him. His face was turned to the side and something heavy compressed his chest over and over until the contents of his lungs emptied onto the stone beneath him.

The weight was removed. He tried to open his eyes, but he was far too exhausted.

Then a bell sounded, clear and tremulous.

The sound snapped something that had been holding him.

Strings, cables, webbing, and all sorts of metaphorical bindings were instantly severed.

He opened his eyes wide, now feeling like he was at full power. He beheld a curved ceiling high above. The room's walls had been drawn upon by myriad hands, the subjects all different in their varied levels of preciseness.

Then a figure appeared above him... a figure he hadn't seen in an age. He knew this figure... he'd missed this figure. He reached out to it, his back arching from the ground, still on one elbow. He was desperate to touch it. He needed to know it was real.

Then he felt it reach down a hand and touch him.

The warmth was overwhelming.

He felt it enter him and fill him until he was no longer cold.

Then the bell sounded again.

A whine came from his mouth as the figure receded.

Then he fell back.

Into darkness.

Chapter Nineteen

HE WOKE TO the face of an angel... if an angel had had her eyebrows stitched and a tattoo of a dragon crawling up the right side of her neck until its tongue was flicking in her ear. This angel's nose was pierced and she had a finger-long scar beneath her left eye.

"That's it, boss." She wiped his face with a cold rag. Whenever it touched his skin, he relished the sensation. "Just a little longer. Just a bit more. You remembering yet?"

The angel had both Hispanic and Asian features yet spoke with a Southern accent. The lower part of her face, especially the strong jaw, was definitely Hispanic. But the folds around her kindly eyes revealed additional ancestry. Seeing her in the macro he noted that she was wearing an OD green T-shirt with a set of dog tags hanging around her neck. He noticed her breasts only because they were surrounded by muscle. Her shoulders and pectoral muscles were outlandish in their frame. The triceps on her arms would make most men jealous. But all of this didn't really matter, as long as the angel kept bathing him with the cool water.

"That's right," she said, watching his eyes and applying some fresh water to his face. "Take a good look at me, boss. You know me. Hell, you hired me. Do you remember?"

Sarasota. The word came unbidden to his mind. What was it about that Florida town that linked this angel to him?

"I was assigned to that god-awful truck battalion doing convoys back and forth from Basra to Nasiriyah. Back in Desert Storm they called it the Highway of Death after we bombed the hell out of all the fleeing Iraqis who were stealing everything in Kuwait that wasn't nailed down. Remember Master Sergeant Sykes? Remember how he always put me in the lead vehicle because as a female I was the easiest to lose?"

"Sarasota?" Starling rasped.

"That's right. I'm Sarasota. Sara for short. And remember when we were transporting your rangers forward and you saw me fighting the others?"

One girl—strike that—one woman, against two male soldiers. Fighting while a fat slob of a wannabe master sergeant looked on. The cargo trucks had been pulled into a U-shape and everyone on the convoy took bets on who would win. Right away, Starling could tell that it was rigged. The odds were in favor of the master sergeant, who was secretly directing the female soldier to take her time drubbing the two fit male soldiers. By the time it was all over, the female soldier had a black eye and a bloody nose, but her two opponents were unconscious. The shame of it was that she could have done it without getting hurt, but the audience needed a show.

"I remember," he said.

"Then later," she said, smiling, "you confronted my master sergeant in front of the entire platoon. You twisted his arm until he cried... not just out loud, but real tears. Then you had me transferred to your unit even though there was no such thing back then as a female ranger."

Then he remembered. He licked his lips. "You would have made a good ranger."

She motioned with her hand. "And miss all this? I don't think so."

His eyes snapped into focus. He grabbed her wrist and locked eyes with her. He breathed through his nose as memories flooded back.

"How long this time?" he asked.

Her face grew serious. "Two months."

"That long? What happened?"

"Same as every time. You only get so far and the entire thing breaks down."

"And the others?"

"McQueen is having the hardest time of it. Lore, Narco, and Criminal are doing fine. You're the first one to wake."

He felt the fugue leaving him in waves. He knew that he'd be nearly eighty percent soon. He shifted to a sitting position. He was naked but made no move to cover himself. He turned to look at the other four, pulled out of the water just as he'd been. Narco and Criminal were moving their hands. Lore's leg twitched like a dreaming dog's.

"It always seems so real." He glanced over to where he knew the Sufi was sitting, watching, waiting. A bell stood nearby... probably the bell that had awoken him. Who was the old man? Then he remembered. They called him Sufi Sam. He had another name, but Starling had forgotten it. He was the damned master mystic the dervishes put in charge of their travels. Boy Scout slowly drew his attention back to his angel, images extending and dragging with him until his gaze focused on the woman's face. "It definitely seemed real, but then again it probably was. The whole enterprise was so complicated."

"So you remember me now?" his angel asked.

He wet his lips so he could speak. "Former specialist Sarasota Chavez," he began, his voice returning to him. "Now just Sara Chavez. Hot shit driver, an even better fighter, and professional mother to a bunch of lousy bed wetters."

She laughed. "Thanks, boss. I needed that. I've had no one to talk to since you... you know, except for Sufi Sam over there and his conversations are about as scintillating as kicks to the groin."

Starling winced.

"Too much?" she asked, playing an old game.

"Better stick to simpler metaphors."

"A stick up the ass."

"Lighter."

"A straw up the ass?"

"Maybe lose the ass."

"Just a straw?"

"How about as much fun as sucking dirt through a straw?"

She made a face. "Now that's gross."

He laughed and she smiled. He could tell how happy she was that he'd made it back. He couldn't say he was as happy, but he was still alive, so there was that. She reached down and easily pulled him to his feet.

"Clothes in the usual place?"

She nodded.

"Go take care of the others. Let me get dressed and I'll be back to help."

She nodded again, then moved onto where Criminal lay. He was coming to and beginning to moan.

Starling watched her work for a moment, then headed to the back. They were in an underground cistern complex dating back to the early 800s; before that it had been a system of wells that had been built long before Alexander the Great had been through the region. Starling passed the Sufi and as he did so, placed a hand on the man's shoulder. He glanced down and they locked eyes a moment. He felt the weight of the old man's knowledge and was awed by it.

Maybe next time, if they were able to try again.

Anything to keep his team alive... anything to save the world.

Then he went back to a room that had been set up like a barracks. Only one of the beds looked like it had been used. Poor Sara Chaves, aka Bully. Originally, it had been McQueen to draw the short straw, but then she'd jumped in and volunteered. She felt that she had the most to add doing what she was doing now than transitioning back and forth across realities. Three beds lined each wall. He went to his at the end and grabbed soap and a towel.

There were eight cisterns in the complex and they liked to use the second one as a bath. Using a large bowl and a bar of soap, he cleaned as best he could, noting that he'd lost weight. In the latest reality, he'd been well over two hundred pounds. But he was really about one sixty—twenty pounds less than what he was used to. The problem was that what he'd lost was mostly muscle. The Sufi's fugue state somehow slowed all of their bodily functions. Time wasn't a one-for-one exchange in those cases. He was weak, but not as weak as he should have been. A lot of that also had to do with the gruel they were fed. They'd once asked what was in it, but Sufi Sam had merely smiled, unwilling to give away the secret to the magical elixir. The Sufi made it and Sara fed them once a day, giving everyone enough to survive the depravities of the cistern without experiencing any of the harsh side effects of their immobility and fugue.

Starling was feeling better by the second. He stood waist deep in cold water and scooped heaps of it over his body. His head had been all but shaved bare by Sara, per his directions. Once clean, he toweled dry, then changed into his uniform—5.11 pants, TST shirt, boots, and a baseball cap. He left his weapons and kit under his bunk, then headed back to help the others.

Criminal was up and about. When he saw Starling, he nodded recognition, then shook his head to indicate his disappointment.

Starling did the same.

Then, before he went to help the others, he did the thing he'd been putting off. He raised his gaze to the back of the cistern and acknowledged the thing that had put them in this place. The thing that had locked them in this godforsaken cistern until they could find a way to release it or kill it without dying.

Starling had been told it was a *daeva*.

Lore, who had degrees in world religions, had explained it to him. The Zoastrians, which she called the mother religion of both Islam and Christianity, referred to the Old Gods as *daeva*, beings that had been around so long they preceded religion. One of the more recent interpretations was that the *daeva* was the source of the *devi*, or *devil*. Lore had explained that original narratives dating back to fifth century BCE called the *daeva* the *people of the lie* and there was much scholarly consternation as to what that meant. Scholars aside, the TST had somehow managed to kill two *daeva* and wound one.

The last fugue had made it seem like they'd been merely UAVs. That couldn't have been more wrong. The appearance of the *daeva* in their aircraft had been the inciting incident for their current state. The memory of the event plowed through everything.

They'd blown up two shield-shaped vehicles and the *daeva* within. They blew up the third vehicle, or *vimana* as Lore called them, and its driver had been thrown free. Unconscious and unmoving, they'd managed to tie the immense supernatural being to the front of one of the SUVs, like they'd just hunted it down on safari. Its glow had diminished but wasn't completely gone. Driving into Kholm had created a stampede—locals fleeing into their low-slung, white-washed buildings and hurrying down alleys, abandoning their carts and stalls. It wasn't until the TST was almost on the other side of the town that two men appeared in the street before them dressed in billowing pants tucked into knee-high leather boots, tunics over blouses, and oval hats similar to rounded fezzes. Their attire looked like it came from a fifth century re-enactor's catalogue, or perhaps even *Raiders of the Lost Ark*, but it was very real, right down to the scimitars at their waists.

Instead of plowing into them, the convoy halted.

The TST was soon surrounded by more than twenty of these men, who Boy Scout would later learn were dervishes.

Back to the present, Starling beheld the surviving creature. With a chain around each wrist and ankle, it was suspended above the cistern. Though human in shape, it wasn't human at all. It glowed with a dark blue aura. Its over-large almond-shaped eyes were closed. The Sufi and the dervishes had put it in a fugue, and it traveled in its own unreality. Once it had been a ball of fire in the sky, and now it was a ten-foot tall super being whose screams had sent nightmares crashing through them the one time it had awoken.

He was thankful it wasn't awake now.

He was thankful it was in a fugue.

But he would have been more thankful had they never been on this damned mission at all.

Chapter Twenty

McQUEEN WAS IN a coma. Try as he might, Sufi Sam couldn't arouse him, so he'd left to consult with the other dervishes. In the meantime, the TST licked their physical and psychological wounds, still stunned that they hadn't been in reality but instead in a dervish fugue created by the mysterious branch of Mevlevi dervishes and monitored by Sufi Sam. The dervish whirling had as much to do with lateral time management as it did with their worshipping of God. With an aeon of Sufi knowledge to draw upon, the Mevlevi partnered with the traditional mystics to create a complex pattern of dance that allowed them to move easily through other realities.

The TST had been using this as an opportunity to go back to the moment before they'd encountered the *daeva* and try and undo what they did. Not only did their lives depend upon their success, but possibly the fate of the planet.

Now, back in their room with everyone cleaned up, it was Boy Scout who had difficulty coming terms with his return to reality, especially with McQueen still locked in his coma.

"But you never did those things so you can't take responsibility for them," Lore said, shaking her head, which had also been closely shorn by Sara.

"I thought I did them." Boy Scout stared morosely at McQueen. "It seemed like just a few hours ago that I hit him. McQueen, my friend."

"It never happened," Lore said.

An image of Joon came to him followed by an imperfect image of him kicking her from an outside perspective. Had he really done that to her? Had he really kicked her? Had he killed her in one of these travels like she'd said?

"I just can't shake it," he said.

Lore placed a hand on his arm. "It's not the same, boss. Reality is all that matters."

He stared at her hand, then placed his on it for a moment. "But it's not, now is it. If reality was what mattered, what we were doing would have no significance."

"Ever seen that show about a western fantasy?" Criminal asked. He was reclining on his bunk, pillow behind him, legs crossed, cleaning his HK 416 rifle.

All eyes turned toward him.

"I think one of the pay-per-view channels is remaking it, or maybe already has." Criminal laughed. "Now I can't be sure what was fugue and what was real. Still, the flick I'm talking about is the one with Yul Bryner... you know, the bald guy from *The Magnificent Seven*." His eyes narrowed. "What was it called?"

"*Westworld*." Narco looked up from where he was tying his boots. "That's the one where the amusement park is filled with robots and people can do whatever they want to them."

"You mean that bald guy from *The King and I*?" Lore asked.

"What the fuck is *The King and I*?" Criminal asked.

"Never mind," Lore said. "What about it? What about *Westworld*?"

"It's like what these dervishes create. It's not real, but it seems to be." Criminal cocked his head. "People go to this Westworld to do something they wouldn't do in public... in reality. Many of them go there to rape and murder."

Narco raised his eyebrows. "So what?"

Criminal stared at him. "So what? Even if it's a fake world, the rape and murder still counts."

"Bullshit," Narco said.

"Fuck you," Criminal responded. Then he turned to Boy Scout. "It's true. Westworld is not a place where you can go do anything, even those things that you can't legally do anywhere else. Westworld is a place where your morality is weighed and measured. It's an opportunity for you to test your own idea of who you are."

"That's pretty deep," Lore said.

"Pretty deep shit, you mean," Narco added.

"No," Lore continued. "What he says is true, I think. I know what I said before, but Criminal has a point. The difference is that when we are in the realities the dervishes put us in, we don't know they aren't real."

"Which makes it all the worse," Boy Scout murmured.

Sara spoke for the first time. "I haven't traveled with you, but I was there when the dervishes first talked about it. I've spoken to Sufi Sam about it when you're under.

When you're in that state, you aren't only you; you're pieces of each one of you. Each one of your memories and experiences go to create puzzle pieces of the reality. Who you see and who you interact with are inventions of the lot of you. You're used to controlling who you are, but can you be responsible for controlling those pieces of you that aren't a part of you?"

"Talk about deep," Criminal said, giving her a respectful nod. "Now I'm totally fucking confused."

"Like that's a hard thing to do," Narco said. "Still, it's all make-believe. Who cares what you do in a make-believe place? Who cares what you do in Westworld? Raping and murdering is why it was made in the first place."

"Said by no one but a psycho," Criminal murmured.

"Even if you do something or see something in another reality… this fugue y'all were in," Sara continued, "it can still affect you. PTSD is still possible. Ever try and watch that Berg beheading on YouTube? I know people who can't unsee it and have been ruined for life."

Boy Scout remembered the first time, their failure to return to that moment and not capture a *daeva*, and how the old Sufi had been so earnest.

"*You must go back under. You must try again. Even now, it begins to wake. I can only hold it for a time and without the combined might of your minds, it will break free and kill us all.*"

"*I don't want to go back*," Boy Scout had said.

"*It was not I who sought to capture a* daeva. *I am but a vessel to assist you in your life's journey. To save your life. To save the lives of your people, you must go under*

*again. Heed the bell, follow the goat, and allow me to
move you sideways to another place."*

"What is this sideways? I don't get it."

*"It is neither forward nor back. It is neither here nor
there. It is no place and everyplace."*

"You sound like a fortune cookie on acid."

*"I am only who I am. Rumi anticipated your question.
He said, 'I am so close, I may look distant. So completely
mixed with you, I may look separate. So out in the open, I
appear hidden. So silent, because I am constantly talking
with you.'"*

"But I'm not looking for this Rumi character."

*"Rumi is not a character. He is our spiritual leader. The
poem is not about Rumi. It is about yourself. Your true
self. The self who has the answers."*

"Boy Scout?" Something shook him. "Boy Scout, are
you paying attention?"

Boy Scout realized he'd closed his eyes. He opened
them to see Lore right in front of him, her hands on both
shoulders.

"Yeah. What is it?"

"McQueen. He's back and wants to talk to you."

Boy Scout pushed her out of the way, then rushed to
his friend in the other room. He fell to his knees next to
McQueen. "There you are. You had me worried."

McQueen's eyes were droopy. His breathing was
shallow but steady.

"I went away," McQueen managed to say.

Boy Scout cupped his cheek, then checked his forehead.
"We all did."

"No. I went away again."

"Where did you go?"

"To a place of light. A place where nothing existed. It was so bright that I couldn't even see myself. I tried to look at my hands, but even in front of my face they weren't visible." He sobbed once. "I was terrified."

Sufi Sam entered the cistern with one of the younger dervishes. The newcomer's name was Faood and he'd been educated at Oxford. He had a quick smile but serious dark eyes. "What your friend saw was the *Sefid*. It is not a good place."

"What is the *Sefid*?" Boy Scout asked.

"The *Sefid* is The White. It's the nothingness between places. Think of time as a strip of film. The blank strip between pictures is the void." He came and knelt beside McQueen. Then he leaned his head in and sniffed along McQueen's blanket-covered body. "I can smell it on him. And more." To McQueen he asked, "What else did you see?"

"A pinhole of darkness. At first it wasn't there, but then it was."

"Did you go to it?"

McQueen glanced fearfully at Boy Scout before answering. "No. It started coming toward me and I ran from it."

Faood frowned, then glanced at Sufi Sam, who nodded. "Interesting that you ran. What made you afraid?"

McQueen shook his head. "It didn't seem right. I don't know."

"It was fear that saved you," Faood said to McQueen.

"The *Sefid* has a way of seeping into you. It makes you accept it. It makes you want to be there, but there are things that live in the *Sefid*. Terrible things. Sometimes they were once like us. Sometimes they become lost and changed. Then there are those things we put there." He inclined his head toward the main cistern behind him. "We put the *daeva* in that place. It doesn't know it has a body still, but if it finds out, it will be able to escape."

"Was that what was chasing me?" McQueen asked.

Faood shrugged. "Could be. Could also be something else."

"You said sometimes they change? Travelers like us? Is that what you mean?"

"We dervish, we travel, as you know. It is why we dance the way we do. Rumi taught us this long ago, and we do it because of him. Sometimes one of us will become lost. We try and find him, but there are so many places and spaces between places that it's very often they go lost forever. Then, without humanity, without warmth, without love, they become creatures of need... creatures of desperation." He looked around the room. "Have any of you been in the *Sefid*?"

Everyone shook their heads.

"It's common for someone who travels into the *Sefid* and back out to have one of these changed creatures and not even know it. They... how do you say? Replace you... add themselves to you... is there a word for this?"

"Possess," Lore said. "We call this possession."

"Yes," Faood said. "I remember now. Like in *The Exorcist*."

"Jesus," Narco said, getting up and backing away. Finally, he turned and walked to the other end of the room. "What is this bullshit? Time travel... possession... will it never end?"

Boy Scout stood. "Okay, let's give McQueen some room. Narco, come and help me get him to the cleaning room."

"I can do it myself," McQueen said softly.

"Not this time, my friend," Boy Scout said. He took one of the big man's elbows and helped him off the ground.

Once on his feet, Narco came back and took the other.

Boy Scout nodded to Lore. "You work with Faood to figure out when we're going under again. We need to get out of this damned place."

Then he took his old friend into the other room and cleaned him like a brother.

Chapter Twenty-One

MCQUEEN WAS WORSE off than any of them and the differences were staggering. Where he'd been full-muscled with a hipster beard and mustache in the most recent fugue, now he was half that man—sallow cheeks, no beard, no mustache and virtually no hair. Sara had apologized, but her caretaking of the team was difficult enough without having to cultivate a sense of style. She'd done the best she could. His lips were almost whiter than his skin. Any tan that any of them had developed had been leached out by the water and total lack of sunlight. In fact, the water should have had a more severe deleterious effect than it had, but either the nature of the fugue or the gruel they'd ingested somehow protected them.

McQueen's muscle loss was Boy Scout's biggest concern. He looked like a stage four cancer victim, someone nearer death than life. Boy Scout had managed to get some real food—rice and chicken—and was now feeding it to McQueen.

Boy Scout had come out of his own fugue rather quickly,

but McQueen seemed unable to shake it. It was like he was straddling the two realities. Boy Scout wondered if it had to do with his travel to the *Sefid*. The sort of hell that McQueen had described would be enough to drive anyone mad. Whatever it was, Boy Scout wasn't going to allow McQueen to go into another fugue. He wouldn't make it.

McQueen opened his eyes and held Boy Scout's in a steady gaze. After several bites, he put up his hand. "Enough."

Boy Scout put the wooden bowl and spoon down. "Are you full?"

"Yes," he said, then added, "And no." He sighed and wiped the edge of his lips. "That last one did me in, boss. I don't know if I can do another."

Boy Scout agreed. "We'll have Sara join us if you can take care of us while we're gone."

McQueen stared at Boy Scout for a long time... long enough for a single tear to fall.

Boy Scout was shocked. He'd never seen the other man cry. He didn't think he'd had it in him.

Seeing Boy Scout's reaction, McQueen spoke carefully. "There's a lot you don't know about me. I put up a great front, something I've perfected after twenty-four years in the Army. First in basic training, then in infantry training. All the homo jokes. The fag jokes. They never ended. Once I was so offended at some joke this dumb ass cracker made that I failed to laugh like all the others, and he homed in on me right away. He just figured it out. He began calling me a fag. He told me all the things he'd do to me and all the things I did to animals and small children. It was beyond disgusting. So one day toward the end of infantry training he had fireguard from three a.m. to four a.m. Know what I did? I fucking raped him. I beat him up and I stuck my cock so far inside him that he didn't know which hole I'd entered. I was so angry. I was so enraged. I was the gay Hulk and he was my punching bag. No one ever heard us. What I did to him… the anger I bestowed upon him, was epic. Then you know what he did, that fucking cracker? Know what he did? He finished his shift, put on his Class A uniform, and hung himself in the shower. A sorry ass Class A uniform with a Marksman badge and no ribbons. Like that uniform meant anything to him."

Boy Scout burned with a thousand questions but remained silent.

"Turns out that uniform meant everything. He was an ass cracker, but every generation of his cracker family had served in the military since the Battle of Bunker Hill. I took that from him. As bad as he'd been, as hateful as his words had been, they were nothing compared to the act of rage I committed against him. That rape. My fucking shame."

He gazed solidly at Boy Scout. "And you're worried about your soul because of the pedophile officer you killed? You got nothing on me boss. I'm a rapist murderer because I couldn't take a *joke*. I'm hell-bound because I had thin skin. So you know what I did? I grew my skin thicker. I learned how to be aloof. I put on muscle and no one fucked with me, even when I didn't laugh at their silly ass cracker fag jokes. And when the time came to join the teams, I jumped on it. Best thing ever happened to me. Being on a team is different than being in an infantry squad. When you're in squad it's all dick measuring and fighting behind the motor pool. When you're on a team, it's a matter of being part of a band of brothers like none other. And then God had the last laugh."

Boy Scout realized he'd been holding his breath and sucked in a lungful through his teeth. McQueen had never been this forthcoming. To have him unload like this was unprecedented.

"And a last laugh it was. You feeding me just now reminded me of it. And to think I'd pushed that memory way into the back with the dust mops and getting caught playing with Barbies by my father. I was on my team for two years, then we got a new guy. Big, tall, black and beautiful. He called himself the Black Kojak because he always went around with a sucker in his mouth and liked to say, 'Who loves ya baby.' We connected right away. He was the best lover, the most attentive lover, I ever had. It was—he was—

"Then I went on a hundred and twenty-day mission to support a SOCOM special mission unit while he deployed with the team to Iraq. By the time I got back, he was in the hospital. It wasn't an IED. It wasn't a haji with a lucky shot from his AK. No, it was a fucking taco that brought Rudy down. A fucking street taco, then boom, gastrointestinal anthrax. Had the doctors gotten to it sooner, he might not have died, but those fucking doctors had no clue. They medevaced him to Germany, then to Walter Reed Army Hospital, where they were finally able to give the proper diagnosis. By then it was too late. His body was too toxic. I spent a week feeding him Jell-o with a plastic spoon, just like you did me, before he died."

McQueen abruptly looked at Boy Scout, then at the ground, as if he'd just discovered what he'd done... what he'd said.

"Jesus, McQueen, get it under control," he said to himself. "Sorry to unload like that, boss. I just... I just... you helping me like you did reminded me of everything." He knocked on his forehead with his fist hard enough to make Boy Scout wince. "What's up there needs to stay up there and not get out."

"I think it's okay to let some light shine into those dark corners," Boy Scout said. "Stuff can rot and infect other memories if you don't keep that clean up there." He cupped McQueen's cheek.

McQueen let Boy Scout's hand stay there for a moment, then shook it off and laughed softly. "You're the only straight man who has ever held my face like that. Why do you do it?"

"My grandfather used to hold my face like that and it made me feel connected instead of all alone."

McQueen nodded. "Your grandfather was onto something." He looked around, then let out a long, sorrowful sigh with just a hint of a sob at the end.

"Hey," Boy Scout said.

"What?"

"What was that cracker's name?"

"Why do you want to know?"

"I think it's important that you say it out loud."

"Is this a form of therapy?"

"Maybe." Boy Scout leaned forward. "Maybe I just want to know. You know, a detail. Like the *red* house or the *nasty* smell. A detail."

McQueen exhaled. He glanced at Boy Scout several times before he finally spoke. "His name was Billy Picket and he'd been my best friend until he found out I was gay." Then McQueen slammed his face into his hands and bawled.

Details.

Cleaning out the closet.

And to discover that the man McQueen had raped had been his best friend.

Boy Scout thought about that for a moment, then got up and left the room to give McQueen some time alone with his specters.

Sometimes Boy Scout forgot that even though they were a team, they were also individuals.

Each one of them came from somewhere.

Each one of them had a past.

Each one of them had done things they'd regret until the day they died.

But very few of them had done something that had left them ashamed… something that was nearly impossible to come back from.

Chapter Twenty-Two

THEY SAY THAT anger is an emotion best kept in a closed fist, but McQueen's anger had the unintended but welcome healing quality of returning whatever vigor the *Sefid* had leached from him. Boy Scout had given him the space and time to grieve, during which the other members of the TST busied themselves by wiping down their weapons and applying oil where necessary. They'd been provided a wooden tray of cheese and fruit and a jug of locally produced wine. Their stomachs weren't used to anything but gruel, so they ate carefully. Had this been a normal military unit during a normal time, they'd be exchanging war stories, making up lies, and bragging about improbable sexual conquests. But what they were now was far from normal. Each dreaded returning to the fugue, but they knew the inevitability of it, they were merely counting down the moments while they were still in the now.

A thousand years ago the *daeva* had been everywhere. They stormed the skies from modern Iraq to the Hindu Kush. As the Mevlevi dervishes had explained, the *daeva* pleasured themselves in war and could be seen burning savagely above battlefields, their very presence filling the embattled with martial rage. But *daeva* couldn't fly by themselves. They used *vimana,* sometimes referred to as chariots of the gods, which allowed them to soar above the earth as they went in search for evidence of man. They couldn't fly high, but when you're a god and flying, you are high enough.

So the *daeva* searched out man, for wherever man was, violence and war was sure to reign.

When Boy Scout asked if anyone had ever seen these *vimana* and their *daeva,* the Mevlevi dervishes had laughed. Predating the Vedic Era of India, which was about 1500 to 500 BCE, there were reports in the earliest writings of mankind about these flying machines and their ability to rain down fire. Alexander the Great wrote about them in a letter to his advisor and tutor, Aristotle. Roman scribe Flavius Philostratus witnessed *vimanas* in India repelling invaders. There was no end to those who had seen the *daeva* riding in their *vimanas*. To the common man, they might seem little more than a disturbance in the sky, but to ancient men they were as real as the sun that warmed them and the air they breathed.

Then, in the thirteenth century, Jalāl ad-Dīn Muhammad Rūmī founded a secret sect of Mevlevi dervishes for the specific purpose of rounding up the *daeva* and imprisoning them, believing that peace would finally reign on Earth with the absence of those beings who inspired and fed upon man's hatred. As the story was told to them, Rumi and his dervishes found an isolated valley ringed with impossibly high mountain ranges in the northwest corner of what was now Afghanistan, and one by one lured the *daeva* into it.

The term *dervish* was generally used to refer to an initiate following the Sufi path, while the whirling was part of a dance to celebrate the *Sama* ceremony. The *dhikr* was the dance that was part of that ceremony and was meant to inspire and demonstrate their love of God. But with a few steps added, it allowed the dervishes the ability to move sideways through realities, an insight that had come to Rumi and inspired his formation of his own personal sect of Mevlevi dervishes.

They built outposts at each entrance to the prison valley. They didn't have weapons other than their hands and feet. They didn't need weapons. What they had was the dance, and whenever a *daeva* would try and leave, they'd dance, slip-sliding in time and sending the *daeva* into a different reality, until all the realities were filled with lost and lonely *daeva*.

The TST's problem—and the problem of the Mevlevi dervishes who'd explained it to them—was that the TST had physically removed a *daeva* from the valley. Their methods of communication with each other were unknown, but since no one had ever heard them speak, the Mevlevi believed that some form of unspoken communication was, indeed, used... which meant if this *daeva* ever awoke, it could communicate the truth of its existence and the Mevlevis to the other daeva, possibly bringing the entire imprisonment down. The idea of releasing thousands of bloodthirsty *daeva* on a planet that already had a death wish was unimaginable. So it was up to the TST to find a way sideways, to where they went on a mission and didn't kill two *daeva* and wound another.

Boy Scout remembered one of their earliest fugues when they'd almost accomplished the mission, but at the last minute they'd had to fire to keep the *daeva* from killing them just as they had the JSOC general and his crew. On yet another mission they'd allowed themselves to be killed... but still ended up back in the cistern with the imprisoned *daeva*. They'd been trying to get back to that point where they'd delivered the JSOC general to the valley, but without being able to reach into that moment and inform themselves, they seemed doomed to repeat everything. Still, they had a strong, though waning belief that they could figure it out, and this was what kept them going. Of course, there was also the unspoken threat of the Mevlevi dervishes. *You made the problem. You fix the problem. And you can't leave until you do it.* None of them had even whispered such a thing, but Boy Scout was aware that it was a possibility.

Boy Scout had just sat down to eat a piece of cheese when McQueen came out of the wash room.

His face was red but there was no evidence of his grief. Lore greeted him and McQueen nodded in return. He went to his bunk, sat on it for a moment, then retrieved his weapons and started disassembling them, clearly using the monotonous labor as a distraction from the reality at hand.

After a few minutes, Lore came over and squatted next to Boy Scout.

"What's going on?" she whispered.

"What do you mean?"

"With McQueen. What happened?"

"Why do you think something happened?"

"Men. You can't tell if something's wrong unless it's in letters scrolling across a woman's forehead. Trust me. As a woman I can tell something is wrong."

Boy Scout stared at her for a moment, then chuckled. He bit off a chunk of cheese and chased it with some of pungent wine. "If you want to know anything, you have to ask him. I'm everyone's rabbi and I don't kiss and tell."

"Yeah, well, I was hoping you were still the fat, doped-up Boy Scout from the last fugue."

Boy Scout rolled his eyes. "Thank God that wasn't real. I was like a walking turnip." She was about to leave, but Boy Scout reached out and stopped her. "Let me pose a question for you."

"Shoot." She returned to her squatting position, hugging her knees with her arms and resting her cheek on them as she gazed at Boy Scout.

"So we go sideways or whatever in these fugues. Because we're trying to recreate an event and change the outcome, we keep going back and back to the same time period." He paused, searching for the words to describe what he wanted to ask.

But Lore saved him. "You want to know about Joon."

"Yes," he said as both a sigh and a word. "How could she know, and I not?"

"You're worried about time travel."

"Yes. I know we're going sideways to different realities, but it seems as if I'm going back to the same place... like in time travel. If I was going sideways, creating different realities each time, then I wouldn't encounter anything a second time. Remember that Ray Bradbury story about the butterfly and the dinosaur?"

"I think so, but you're the English lit guy. I just do religion."

Boy Scout nodded. "It was called 'The Sound of Thunder.' The premise was that scientists had figured out time travel and monetized it. They knew when a T-Rex was about to get its head staved in by a tree and made the whole enterprise into a trophy hunt where hunters could shoot the T-Rex right before it died. Anyway, the protagonist loses his nerve, steps off the levitating path, and accidentally kills a butterfly. And that changes the whole world."

"The butterfly effect," she said. "Right."

"Yes and no. That whole *Jurassic Park* Jeff-Goldbloom-chaos-theory-butterfly-flapping-its-wings-in-Tokyo shit was attributed to the butterfly effect, but it's not the same. That's chaos theory. Bradbury chose a butterfly to demonstrate that even the most inconsequential change to the past could change the present."

"But we're not changing the past. We're changing the…" Her mouth remained open as she sought the right word.

"Right? What would you call it?" he asked.

Her eyes narrowed as she said, "We're changing the *sideways*."

"I guess that's as good as anything. But we keep going back to the same places… and I mean the *exact* same places. The people remember us. It's like if you were reading a book for the fifth time and a character in the book started speaking directly to you and asking you why you keep reading about them."

Lore nodded, then abandoned her squat. She moved up and sat next to him. She took a swig of wine, then grabbed the cheese out of Boy Scout's hand. "You make a valid point. What if we're not really traveling sideways in time?"

"But that's how they described it."

Lore flapped her hand in irritation. "Sure, whatever. Sideways. Upside down. Inside out. Whatevs." She took another bite of cheese, then punctuated her next words with what was left of it in her hand. "What if we don't go anywhere at all but in our heads? I mean, sure we're there all the time anyway, but based on your surprisingly intellectual gyrations, I think I know what it is we're really doing. You see, I don't think this is time travel, sideways, backwards or whatever. Do you know what I think, Boy Scout? I think we're constructing another reality."

"Constructing another... what?"

"You heard me," she said. "We're putting our minds together like a server farm and working in parallel to create something from all the data we have."

"Then why are they trying to tell us this is time travel?" Boy Scout asked.

Lore waggled a finger. "They don't alter time. They cause us to alter our own realities. As to why they're trying to see it as time travel, it might be something we need to find out."

"Okay. Let's back up a minute. I think I sprained a muscle with my—what did you call them—*intellectual gyrations*. I don't understand the difference. I mean, I'm sure it's there, but can you speak in one or two syllable words for the dumb guy here? What's the difference between altering time and altering reality?"

She scoffed. "Right. You're the one with a master's degree, remember?"

"In literature, not philosophy. For me that whole 'the abyss is staring back at you' is creepy as hell."

"Nietzsche," McQueen said from his bunk. "Frederick Nietzsche. German philosopher from the 1800s. He said 'He who fights with monsters should be careful lest he thereby become a monster. And if thou gaze long into an abyss, the abyss will also gaze into thee.'"

Lore chuckled. "Now look who's Mr. Wikipedia."

"Just trying to be specific," he said.

"I think I understand that," Boy Scout said. "But it's still creepy as hell."

"Philosophers are a creepy bunch by nature," McQueen said.

Lore and Boy Scout stared at him.

Finally it was Lore who broke the silence. "You're just going to throw that out there? You're not going to expound… give us examples? Come on, McQueen. Give."

McQueen sighed. "Okay. Descartes had a thing for cross-eyed ladies. Immanuel Kant was an OCD hypochondriac. Kierkegaard believed that his family was cursed. Jean-Paul Sartre had a deep and abiding fear of crustaceans. They were all crazy. I think they spent too much time in their heads."

"Says the man who never speaks but is always thinking," Lore said.

"I speak when necessary," McQueen murmured. "I try and spend my time thinking instead of constantly yammering." He gave her a pointed look, then resumed staring at the ground.

Lore stood up and squared her shoulders. "Did you call me a yammerer?"

Boy Scout shook his head. He'd surrounded himself with brilliant minds and loyal friends, but they were irritating at times. Irritating to distraction.

"Calm down, Lore," Boy Scout said. "We were talking, so it's okay for you to yammer."

The corners of McQueen's lips rose by the merest millimeter, but Lore didn't seem to notice.

Lore frowned and bit back a retort. Or did she? "I'll try and not yammer while I explain my idea." She flashed her eyes at Boy Scout, but he didn't move. "The dervishes don't alter time. We don't go back in time. I don't even think we go sideways. I think we stay in our own reality during the fugue."

"So we're just trapped in our own minds."

"You're not trapped any more than you are now. Their dance isn't magic. When they whirl, they aren't opening up great doorways in time that we step through. I think it's a simple matter of hypnotism."

"So it's a parlor trick."

She chewed on her lip. "It's more than that. Somehow, through their very specific dance, they put us in a state where our minds can function together. We create our own massive multiple online role playing game where nothing is real and we're just characters of our own creation while our bodies rot inside an Afghan cistern."

Boy Scout blinked in confusion. "But I've been working under the assumption that there's something that we have to change... like there are forking paths and we need to go down the right ones until we reach that moment of change."

"Like choose your own adventure books, only ours results in our demise," McQueen added.

"Can't the dervishes just bring us a book with the answers?" Boy Scout asked.

"They might, but even they don't know the answers."

"Makes you wonder how they lured the *daeva* into the valley in the first place," McQueen said.

"Faood mentioned to me that this area has been in constant conflict for more than two thousand years," Lore said. "Most of that reason was because of the very presence of the *daeva*. There was a cluster here to begin with, which was one of the reasons the dervishes chose that valley. Supposedly the Soviets executed more than five thousand Afghan militants here. All the activity drew the *daeva*. But how they lured the rest, I have no idea."

"You've had this idea for some time," Boy Scout commented.

"Not really. It's just something I've been trying to work out. It was your comments about Joon that allowed me to put all the pieces together. You see, if this were time travel and we were going back in time, then she would never know. And if this were sideways travel and we were constantly moving into a different reality, she would never know then either. The only way Joon could recognize you would be because you're going back to the same place over and over... and that place has to be inside our own heads. Joon is a construct that we keep reconstructing. The only problem is that whichever one of us constructs her remembers what happened before and lets that information inform the recreation of her."

Boy Scout turned to McQueen. "What do you think?"

"The force is strong in this one."

"I was thinking the same thing." Boy Scout turned back to Lore. "So then how are we to get the answers?"

She sighed in exasperation. "That I don't know. In fact, I'm not sure we have the whole story. I'm wondering why the dervishes wanted to sell us a time travel bag of goods. I mean, if we can't travel back in time, then we can't change anything."

"Then why are we here?" Boy Scout asked.

She nodded and frowned. "Exactly."

Boy Scout glanced towards the door to the main cistern where the *daeva* hung. "So we're in our heads like a large server farm. My memories are co-mingled with everyone else's memories and we're somehow using that to create our own reality. I remember being fat. I remember being a drunken asshole. I remember you getting kicked in the balls."

She snorted. "I don't have balls."

"You certainly act like you do," he said, grinning. Then, back to the conversation, he added, "So you think we're constructing another reality. Doesn't it have to exist in a place and time?"

"Does it?" She passed the cheese back to him. "I'd die for baked brie right now but this is pretty good. Goat,

I think, but hard." She wiped her hands, then repeated, "Does it have to exist in a place and time? I don't think so. What is it they say? We use only ten percent of our brain? Whatever the number, think of our brains as computer servers and think of our fugues as the world's best reality MMORPGs ever. Blows World of Warcraft and Elder Scrolls out of the water."

Boy Scout waggled a finger. "Don't mess with Master Chief."

Lore laughed. "That's HALO and not an MMO. Still, I would never mess with Master Chief." She flashed a grin. "It's just that I have this belief the dervishes can't—"

Her words were cut off by a shriek so sharp it made them all jerk to their feet.

Chapter Twenty-Three

THE SCREAM CAME again. A scream not of fear, but of anger… of disbelief. Everyone dropped what they were doing and ran toward the sound. By the time Lore and Boy Scout got to the other room, the others were already there, blocking their view of what was going on. Boy Scout glanced at the *daeva*, but it was still chained and in its fugue state.

"You did this! You killed him!" Faood shrieked.

Boy Scout pushed through the wall of people to see Sufi Sam on the ground, his mouth open impossibly wide… so wide it was as though his jaw had become unhinged. All the color had been leached from his skin, leaving it cadaver gray. His eyes were wide open, unseeing, as if whatever had happened to him was a great surprise.

"What happened?"

"Your man killed him," Faood sobbed as he gripped the old man's shoulders. "He was one of the oldest among us. Did you know that he knew Rumi?"

"Now hold on," Boy Scout said. "None of my people were involved. We were all back in the room." He went to put his hand on Faood's shoulder, but the dervish angrily shoved it away. "There has to be another explanation."

"Explanation?" He lowered the dead mystic to the ground and stood. "What would you have?"

"Perhaps the *daeva*," Lore began, but stopped talking when she saw the murder in the dervish's eyes.

"No, it was you," Faood said, approaching McQueen.

He reached out to grab him, but before he could, McQueen shoved Faood square in the chest with the flat of his right hand.

"Do not touch me."

Faood backed away and drew his sword. He danced a few steps, spun twice, and his sword flared in his hand.

Before he'd met the dervishes, Boy Scout had never seen a scimitar in real life outside of a video game. This one looked immense, sharp, and deadly. The broadness of the wide, curved blade in the hands of the dervish reminded him of doing bayonet drills on a fog-shrouded field in South Carolina. The idea of being cut or stabbed seemed alien to him as a twenty-first century American. He'd much rather be shot or blown up, but here, with the dervish in this ancient site, it fit perfectly.

Narco and Bully brought up their rifles and aimed them at Faood.

Lore and Boy Scout had left their weapons in the other room.

As had McQueen.

"Whoa—whoa!" Boy Scout said, jumping forward.

Faood took a step back. "Do not make me dance. I will dance you out of existence."

"If you can dance faster than my bullets, then go ahead," Narco said.

"I said stop! Everyone calm down," Boy Scout said. To Faood he asked, "What is it you think happened?"

"That one," he said, pointing at McQueen with his scimitar. "Or another one of you. I've seen this kind of death once before. It's because there is a creature in need. A creature of the *Sefid*."

All eyes turned toward McQueen, who'd readily admitted visiting the place.

He shook his head. "Was not me."

"Then who?" shouted Faood. "One of you has a creature in you. You might not even know it."

That idea scared the shit out of Boy Scout but he kept his fear in check. "Okay, just tell us how to find out. Is there a test?"

"I must touch you. I can feel the wrongness of it."

"Is that all?" Boy Scout asked. "You just need to touch us?"

Faood relaxed a little, but still held his sword ready.

"Okay then, touch me first." Boy Scout held his hands in the air and started walking towards Faood.

"Watch it, boss," Bully said, stepping to the side so that she could have a clear shot at Faood if anything happened. "You hurt Boy Scout and I'll annihilate you," she said to Faood.

"I'll be fine, children. I'm just going to let the nice man touch me." Boy Scout stopped within cutting distance of the scimitar. He eyed it warily, then stepped around it and into Faood's guard.

"Go ahead."

Faood raised his left hand and touched Boy Scout's chest. He felt there for a moment, then adjusted his hand several times to be sure. Finally, he nodded. "You are fine."

Although he hadn't for a second believed he had killed the old mystic, Faood's warning that they might not even know if one was inside of them had been a little nuclear warhead of worry. He stepped to the side.

"Okay, guys. It didn't even hurt a little. McQueen, why don't you come next."

The once big guy leveled his gaze at Boy Scout. He seemed about to comment, then instead strode forward in eight confident steps. He stopped where Boy Scout had, never once allowing his gaze to waver.

Boy Scout held the gaze and didn't let it go until Faood declared that McQueen had also passed the test.

Next came Lore. When she stopped, she angrily said, "If this is all a plan to fondle my breasts, then I have to hand it to you. Good job."

Faood ignored her and soon declared her clean.

Criminal passed, as well.

Bully started to come forward, but Narco said, "You don't have to do this. You weren't even in the fugue."

Bully paused, then looked to Boy Scout, who nodded.

She lowered her rifle and went to Faood.

Boy Scout could see the worry on her face.

But the worry was misplaced. She was fine and soon she wore a relieved smile as she stood beside Criminal.

It was finally Narco's turn. He'd walk through just like the others and Faood would realize that his blame was misplaced. Then they'd finally get to figuring out what really had happened to Sufi Sam... how he'd really died.

"Your turn, Narco."

"I'm not doing it, boss."

"Narco, we all did it. Just do it and get it over with."

"I'm not about to let some Third World John Travolta blackmail me into doing something we all know is ridiculous. Like his touch is somehow equivalent to a supernatural MRI."

Lore took a step in his direction. "Come on, Dakota," she said. "I'm with you and totally agree, but remember the rule of basic training?"

"Cooperate to graduate." He nodded. "I'm just not going to give the bastard the satisfaction."

"It's in him. I know it," Faood said. "I can tell even from here."

"You don't know shit, haji," Narco said. His rifle was snug in his shoulder and his finger was no longer disciplined, now worming above the trigger.

"Dakota Ronald Jimmison," barked Boy Scout. "Lower your weapon and stand down."

Everyone tensed.

Boy Scout wasn't playing around. Either Narco was possessed or he wasn't. This Mexican standoff in the middle of an ancient cistern complex wasn't helping anything.

"Sorry, boss. *This* ain't happening."

"It couldn't have been him," Criminal said. "We were together all the time."

"Always and forever?" Bully asked.

Criminal's earnestness failed then, because he couldn't confirm it.

Lore took another step forward. "Dak, give me your gun. Please." She glanced back at Boy Scout and the others and gave them an encouraging smile. Then she turned around and took another step. She reached out. "Come on, Dak. You and me got this thing. Let's not ruin it with this whole crazy business."

Narco stared at her, then spit onto the ground. "Bitch, we ain't got nothing." Then he shot her in the leg.

She fell to the ground stunned, her hands over the wound to staunch the blood.

Things happened quickly after that.

Faood rushed Narco, but as promised, he wasn't faster than a bullet.

Narco fired three times, hitting Faood in the torso and stomach.

Faood fell to the ground. His scimitar clattered as it bounced then skittered into the water.

Narco spun just as Bully was bringing up her rifle.

When she saw him aiming at her, she paused, the weapon only halfway.

"Drop it, Bully or I'll fucking shoot you next."

"I might get one off."

"And I'll kill the rest of them if you do."

"Dak, what the fuck, man?" Criminal cried.

Boy Scout wanted to wring the boy's neck. If he wasn't possessed, then he'd gone suddenly insane. Still, maybe they could figure out a way to save the kid. It worked in movies—maybe the Mevlevi dervishes had a method.

He glanced at Faood, whose eyes were wide. He was breathing fast through his teeth. Gut shot. Boy Scout knew from experience that the pain was legendary.

"I said drop the fucking weapon. I'm not going to ask again," Narco said, jerking his rifle.

Bully tossed the weapon aside, then crossed her arms, her muscles twitching in irritation.

"Now what are you going to do, Slick?" McQueen said.

"Gonna make like a tree and leave," Narco said. "Gonna make like a shepherd and get the flock out of here." He giggled insanely. "Gonna make like the Red Sea and split."

"Soon that thing inside of you will eat you up," Faood said between gasps. "You must let me help you get it out."

Narco stepped over and looked down at him. "I told you my bullets were faster than your dance."

Faood managed a grin. "But I already danced."

Narco frowned, then grinned again. His face took on an insane look. "Yeah, right. Whatever." He backed out of the room and waved merrily. "Okay, now. Gonna make like a terrorist and blow this place."

Then he was gone.

Silence reigned for about seven seconds until Lore called out, "I can't believe that motherfucking possessed piece of shit Narco shot me."

Chapter Twenty-Four

Kholm, Afghanistan

BOY SCOUT ORDERED Criminal to grab the rifle Bully had tossed and hunt down Narco. Then he had Bully retrieve the first aid kit from their room. McQueen was already seeing to Lore. Boy Scout ran over to make sure everything was okay and knew by the sheer amount of cursing coming from Lore that she'd live. Then he turned to Faood. He, on the other hand, was heading south fast.

Boy Scout kneeled beside the dervish. He pulled off his own shirt and used it to compress the wounds. Although it looked as if it would work, the man's heart was strong and pumped blood straight through the fabric. If they couldn't stop the bleeding, Faood would die within minutes.

Criminal came back into the room. "He's gone. He took one of the Land Cruisers."

Bully came running out with the bag.

Boy Scout called over to her. "Got any QuickClot?"

She rifled through. "Only one patch left," she said.

"And I'm using it on Lore."

Faood nodded. "Fix her first. You're going to need her when you go after him." When he saw the look on Boy Scout's face, he said, "You *are* going after him. You need to get him. You need to see for yourself."

Boy Scout had been wondering exactly what they were going to do when they eventually caught him and voiced that doubt.

"It's going to eat right through him. You need to get him back to me or find another one of us. Only we can—" A spike of pain silenced him.

McQueen ran over with a handful of tubes that looked like huge hypodermics with tiny pill-shaped sponges on the inside.

"Got some X-Stat." He gently shoved Boy Scout aside and removed the blood-sodden shirt. He took one of the hypodermics, placed it into the nearest wound, and depressed the plunger.

"Faood, let me tell you what's going on," he said. "Inside this turkey baster are about ninety tiny sponges. They can soak up to a pint of blood and when they do, they're going to block the other blood from escaping." He dropped the empty hypodermic and grabbed a full one, placed it in another bullet hole, and depressed. "These babies can stop the bleeding within twenty seconds." He paused to look at Faood. "Do they hurt?"

The dervish was woozy but alive. He shook his head.

"Good."

Bully came over. "It was a through and through with Lore. Tissue damage, but no arterial damage and no broken bones."

"Can she walk?" he asked.

"Just fucking try and stop me," Lore yelled from across the cistern.

McQueen applied a third X-Stat to the now unconscious Faood. McQueen checked his vitals.

"His heart is steady, but he's going to need medical attention."

"If we find some of his men, we'll send them back."

"Why not bring him with us?" Boy Scout said.

They both looked at the *daeva*.

"It's not like Faood can do anything in his condition," Boy Scout said. "I'd rather take him with us in the event we find a doctor or some real medicine. It's his only chance. Everyone grab your kit and meet me at the vehicles."

They hurriedly donned their combat kits. With the exception of Bully, their clothes were already hanging off them. Once Boy Scout put on his gear belt and his body armor, he realized how truly and utterly his body had changed. Gone were the muscles he'd carried since ranger school. The body armor was so loose he could slide it on without unbuckling it. McQueen was so thin he looked like he was a child wearing adult armor.

They ran out of the cistern.

"I kept them in working order," Bully was saying. "They might be dusty, but they're running."

"Not anymore," Criminal said, pointing at the wheels.

The front two tires of each vehicle had been punctured.

Lore limped to the back of one and began to remove the spare.

Criminal saw what she was doing and did the same in the back of the other.

Together they removed the front tires of one of the vehicles, then replaced them with the spares.

While they worked, Boy Scout fumed as he adjusted the straps on his body armor, then helped McQueen with his. They grabbed the weapons and ammo bags from the back of the ruined vehicle and put them in the back of the serviceable one.

They wouldn't be driving two SUVs, but they at least had one.

Boy Scout drove with Lore in the passenger seat.

Criminal and Bully sat in the back.

McQueen had loaded Faood in the far back. He was giving the man an IV as Boy Scout started the vehicle and quickly ran through the fuel level and other gauges.

The cistern complex was situated amid a group of ruins in a hidden, bowl-shaped valley. Everything looked like brown moonscape with barely any scrub marring the ground. The valley was about ten miles across in all directions surrounded by low hills. A single dirt track ran east. The dirt clouds created by Narco's passage still hung in the air.

Boy Scout had forgotten how wide and blue the sky could be in Afghanistan. He'd also forgotten how hot it could get. The temperature had to be over a hundred with not a hint of a breeze. He thumbed on the air conditioner, aware that he had to keep an eye on the engine heat indicator. If it started going too high, they'd have to turn off the AC and drive around in the oven.

Boy Scout jerked the Land Rover into gear and gunned the engine.

"Do you know where he's going?" Criminal asked.

"There's only one road out of the ruins and into town," Bully said. "It's a shit road with sheep herds on either side. He can't be going fast."

"Unless he doesn't care about the sheep herds," Lore murmured.

Her words turned out to be prophetic because they hadn't gone a mile before they saw a massacre. By the looks of the bodies, Narco hadn't even slowed down. He'd plowed right through the sheep. At first, there were just dead bodies, but soon they could see sheep with wounded legs. One looked as if its spine had been crushed, but was still alive, bleating weakly.

If the complete disregard for the animals were indicative of the inhuman creature that had its talons in Narco, then they were truly up against a being that lacked any shred of human empathy. For as much as Boy Scout wanted to get to Narco and save him, he wouldn't disregard the sanctity of life unless the lives of his team were at risk. So Boy Scout had to slow the Land Cruiser to almost a crawl at times just so they could weave their way through the minefield of dead and dying animals.

A scrub bush held the bodies of six mutilated sheep in various positions. Boy Scout's eyes fixed on the ignoble slaughter and he slowed to a complete stop as he tried to make sense of it. He couldn't breathe. He felt a tightness in his chest. The scene was alarming and he realized that the reason it affected him was because it was so reminiscent of a notable passage from *Blood Meridian* by Cormac McCarthy. *By and by they came upon a bush that was hung with dead babies. These small victims, seven, eight of them, had holes punched in their underjaws and were hung by their throat from the broken stobs of a mesquite to stare eyeless at the naked sky.* Although these Afghan sheep were far from the babies killed by the Comanche war party in the book, there was an equity of the tragic, a validation of innocence. The murder of the lambs and sheep were no less recreant than those of the babies.

It also wasn't lost on Boy Scout that their chases were mirror images of each other. Where he and his TST were pursuing a possessed soldier across the Afghan wilderness, the hunting party from the book had been chasing the Comanches across the American West, both quarry fashioning a bloody swathe of violence as their signature. Boy Scout wondered who had the potential for more violence. Narco? Or Cormac McCarthy's Comanches?

He finally shoved the SUV back in gear and let the scene pass behind him. Only once did he let his gaze flick back, to see the bloody face of one of the sheep staring sightlessly towards the sky.

At one point, they had to stop while Criminal and Bully dragged three out of the way.

They were a little more than halfway across the killing fields when an Afghan carrying a shepherd's staff ran in their direction, waving his arms and screaming.

"Pissed off haji at four o'clock," Bully said. "What should I do?

"Does he have an RPG?" Boy Scout asked leadenly.

"No."

"Does he have a rifle?"

"Doesn't look like it."

"Then let him rage."

Boy Scout felt his own rage building.

The universe should rage.

"Probably lost a girlfriend in all this carnage," Criminal said.

Lore turned from the front seat and shot him a look. "Not funny."

Criminal's smile evaporated and he nodded to her. "I know. Just a coping mechanism." He turned to stare out the window.

Chapter Twenty-Five

The Killing Fields, Afghanistan

BOY SCOUT DROVE the SUV like an enraged NASCAR driver after they finally left the dead sheep behind them. Narco's double-cross was hitting Boy Scout hard, even if it was because of some entity that had possessed him from the *Sefid*. Had the man tried to fight it, or was it something that had achieved such firm and instant control that Narco had no choice but to do its bidding? Boy Scout had signed Narco to a contract on the recommendation of one of his old friends. Although Narco had his issues, he'd proven to be a major asset for the team and had protected them from attack on several occasions. To lose him to some entity seriously pissed Boy Scout off. He realized that the anger stemmed from his own feeling of inadequacy. As the team lead, he owed it to the team to protect each and every one of them. Boy Scout had utterly failed to protect Narco.

Never mind that he'd never had the opportunity. That's

not how leadership worked. It had been Boy Scout's responsibility. Period. And now instead of helping Narco, he was hunting him down. The rage that surged through him would have made the Hulk explode.

"You okay, boss?" Lore asked.

He opened his mouth to speak, but anger was a hard fist in his throat.

"You look like you could chew through the windshield."

"That's how I feel." He cursed as he slammed his right hand down on the steering wheel. "Fucking Narco."

"No shit, boss. He fucking shot me."

"And now we're going to hunt him down... and then what?"

McQueen spoke from the back. "I don't think Faood's going to make it."

Lore turned around in her seat and looked everyone in the eye. "We try and capture Narco alive. Then after I bitch slap his sorry, possessed ass, we figure out a way to get whatever is in him *out*!"

"I suppose you know how to do that?" Criminal asked.

"Not in the least. I'll let Hollywood inform me. God knows we've seen enough movies about exorcisms. Any one of us could probably do it given a Bible, some holy water, and some restraints."

"That's what I don't get," Criminal said. "How can that shit work if the entity isn't Christian? I mean, what if it's Muslim or Hindu or something? What if it doesn't even have a religion?"

"You're right," Lore said, her voice still angry. "On the whole, exorcisms are conducted within a specific religious community, allowing for shared symbology. The idea of possession in the Catholic and Christian churches at large is one of spiritual trespassing. Where many of the other religions of the world invite what we're referring to as possession, they refer to it as channeling. That said, in Islam, an exorcism is referred to as *ruqya* and is used to repair the damage done by black magic. In Judaism, an exorcism is performed by a rabbi who has mastered the *Kaballah*."

"You sound like Wikipedia," Bully said. "I'd forgotten you've been to college."

Lore grinned. "Some people are experts in breaking other people's bones while others are experts in world religions."

"If you're such the expert, why were you bouncing around in your trailer wearing a tin foil bathing suit?" Boy Scout asked.

"Think of it as a small exorcism. I was trying to get that damned phrase out of my head and it worked."

"What phrase was that?" Bully asked.

"In English it was *The wound is the place where the light enters you*, but I was evidently speaking it in Persian... a language I don't know."

"What does it mean?" Bully asked.

"I have no idea."

"You still haven't answered my question," Criminal noted.

"Maybe all the religious mumbo jumbo isn't to hurt the invading entity, but instead to provide energy to the invaded soul," Lore mused. "I know Narco was Catholic, so perhaps it will speak to the part of him that believed."

Criminal laughed hollowly. "I can't believe Narco was very religious."

Boy Scout glanced in the rearview mirror at Criminal. "You know as well as any of us that God lives in the foxhole."

They crested a rise and all eyes searched for danger.

Suddenly Lore shouted, "There he is!"

They'd left the valley of the cisterns and a great plain rolled out before them. Far ahead, trailing a long line of dust, was a dark speck that could only be Narco in the other Land Cruiser.

"Can you get closer?" Lore asked.

"I'm going as fast as I can," Boy Scout said.

"I don't think we're gaining on him," Criminal said.

"Well thank you, Captain Obvious," Boy Scout replied. "Now I guess we know where we stand."

The dark speck suddenly rose into the air, pushed by a red-and-yellow ball of fire.

"Oh, shit!" Criminal cried.

"Was that an IED?" Bully asked.

"Had to be," Lore said.

Boy Scout slammed his palm against the wheel again. "Keep your eyes peeled and shut down the chatter."

The dust trail fell before them like a funeral shroud as they neared. Dark smoke curled madly into the air. The Land Cruiser lay on its left side. The entire right side looked as if a giant monster had chewed away the doors, ripping and gnashing. Of Narco, there was no sign.

They pulled to within fifty meters and stopped.

"Lore and Bully, you take the right. Criminal and I will take the left."

"I'll take the left with Criminal," McQueen said.

"No, I want you watching over Faood."

"Nothing to watch over. He's dead."

Boy Scout met McQueen's gaze in the mirror. They both knew they'd needed the Medlevi dervish alive to save Narco. Not that it mattered, of course, because now Narco was probably dead, too.

Boy Scout was the last to get out of the vehicle.

Lore was limping from her wound, but still ambulatory. While Bully scanned the ground in front of them, Lore monitored the horizon, the butt of her HK 416 sunk deep in her shoulder.

McQueen and Criminal were doing the same on the left side of the road.

Boy Scout held his rifle at the ready as he walked down the middle of the road. One side of the road was on fire, as was part of the vehicle. The conflagration roared in the silence.

The IED could have been manually detonated by a spotter. They were too far out for a cell phone signal, but a simple FM radio receiver and transmitter could accomplish that—which meant they needed to be wary of someone in the surrounding hills. They were searching for movement or a glint of light—anything. It could also be part of a more sophisticated ambush. There could be dozens of enemy fighters hidden in the scrub grass waiting for them to get on the X. The IED could have been placed there years ago and was auto-detonated by the weight of the vehicle. They were so far out it could have been—

He squelched his MBITR. "Hey Bully."

"Yes, boss," she said over the radio.

"This the road you took into town?"

"The very same."

"You ever have any problems?"

"Never, boss."

"Know what I think?"

"Think they were targeting me?"

He was absolutely sure they were. "Look tight. Everyone get down."

All four of his remaining TST members slid into a tactical crouch.

He got down as well, waiting for the ambush to proceed. There was no doubt that the location of Narco's vehicle was the X. Once the enemy fighters, whoever they were, realized that he and his team had no intention of going there, he hoped that they'd get impatient. They probably carried AKs, so at distance they weren't as accurate as their HKs, but they could still kill. Although his torso was protected by body armor, one lucky head shot would ruin his day.

"McQueen, what's the terrain look like on your side?"

"Flat. Grass is only knee high. Could be lying down but I doubt it."

"Lore, what about yours?"

"Same. Although there seems to be a depression about twenty meters out."

Boy Scout considered what to do next. "McQueen, ascertain Narco's condition. Just don't get blown up. Criminal, establish a fighting position and prepare to cover Bully and Lore. You two prepare to bound back to me."

"Roger, boss," came four voices.

"And if you come under fire, let's do an Aussie Peel."

Again came confirmation of his order.

He sat back on his haunches with his weapon draped across his knees. His eyes and ears were alert for even the slightest movement or sound.

"No sign of Narco," McQueen said.

"What do you mean?"

"What I said. No. Sign. Of. Narco."

Was he thrown clear? Where could he have gone? "Are you sure?"

"He's not there, boss."

Boy Scout couldn't figure it out. "Establish position fifteen meters on the other side of the vehicle. I want to see if we can get some crossfire if they show."

"Roger, boss."

"And everyone keep your eye out for Narco," he added.

"Or else he might shoot you, too," Lore murmured into her coms.

As gallows as her humor was, it could also be prophetic. They needed to not only worry about possible enemy combatants, but Narco as well.

"McQueen, inform when in position."

"I'm there. I also see some blood on the ground."

"Think Narco went through there?"

"Could be. It's fresh. I'm gonna watch my six."

An image of a possessed Narco creeping up on McQueen flashed through Boy Scout's mind.

"McQueen, let's not do that. Move back to Criminal. I don't want anyone alone with Narco out there."

He heard McQueen sigh, but nothing else. Still, he knew the man would do as he said.

"Get ready and get down," Boy Scout said.

Then he removed an F1 Australian fragmentation grenade from his pouch. As a security detail, they weren't supposed to have grenades, but Narco had traded fourteen cases of Jack Daniels to an Australian military unit for four crates of grenades a year ago, and they'd had them in stock ever since. The F1 was roughly the same as the American M67. The F1 contained four thousand steel balls with an effective range of thirty meters.

He pulled the pin and released the spoon. With a five-second cookoff, he threw it right toward the depression indicated by Lore.

"Fire in the hole," he said stonily, then crouched back down.

The explosion came as expected. He could hear the pings and rush of the steel balls as they sought flesh, but no one in the TST was even close. But what came next was exactly what he'd been looking for.

He was sighting down the barrel of his HK when the first two came over the lip of the rise. Both fighters were bloody although there was no way to tell if it was their own blood or someone else's. He put two rounds into each of their chests, sending them backwards.

Then nothing.

He pulled out another grenade and threw it after the first one.

Rinse. Repeat. Explosion.

"Bully, check for casualties. Lore, provide cover."

Bully stepped forward in a tactical crouch, her weapon leading the way. When she got to the edge of the grenade area, she took two quick steps forward, then backed up the same. She adjusted her grip on her rifle and stepped forward more carefully.

"Seven, Boss. You fragged seven of them."

"Any alive?"

"Not that I can see."

"See any affiliation?"

"Looks like Taliban to me."

"Lore, you're clear. Go to Bully and assess. Just don't move any bodies." The latter he said because he didn't want to take the chance that one of them was booby trapped. The former he ordered because Lore was more attuned to the different tribal outfits than Bully, who until last year had been little more than a convoy driver.

When she was on site, Lore spent a few moments walking around the depression. "Definitely Taliban," she said. "Looks like you got them all."

"Talk about anticlimactic," Criminal said over coms.

Boy Scout was about to agree when a bullet shattered his right shoulder, sending him to the ground. It was only after he was on his back, writhing in pain, that he heard the shot. Wherever it had come from, it was from a long way off.

Chapter Twenty-Six

HE FELT HIMSELF being pulled by his body armor, the rough dirt grating against his back. He began to slide out of the armor but grabbed a handful of webbing with his left hand. Whatever was happening to his right hand, it felt like it was attached to a vast ocean of pain.

"Aniewonnowhrethtshtcamefrom," he asked the universe.

The universe responded. "Up on the hill. Criminal and Bully are sussing it out."

The pain enveloped him for a swift instant, then retreated like the outgoing wave of a tsunami, taking with it every possible feeling of good and health, leaving him completely depleted. His shoulder was shattered. That he knew. He'd been shot there once before, but he'd only had soft tissue damage. This was something else altogether. This was something magnificent.

He was suddenly rumbling down an unknown road. He sat shoulder to shoulder with other rangers in a mine resistant armor protected vehicle, or MRAP. They were on mission to take out an IED factory. They'd studied the factory layout and each of them knew everyone else's mission in the event one of them might go down.

Then came the explosion. The MRAP rose into the air like a bucking bronco. Much of the damage and effect of the blast was diverted by the v-shaped hull, but the charge was enough to send the ten-ton vehicle skyward. The front end slammed back to earth with the force of a comet. He felt the driver lose control, turn to the left, then the flip. Soon they were rolling, rangers flying against each other like monkeys in a barrel. Bones breaking, faces bruising, muscles tearing, but not a one of them screamed or complained. Not a sound could be heard louder than a grunt, and it was in this carnival silence that Corporal Bryan Starling realized he might actually die. Up until that moment, he'd been swathed in a carefully woven tapestry of propaganda, preaching his invulnerability as a United States Army Ranger. In the end, he was merely an extremely well-trained and motivated killing machine made of flesh, bone, testosterone, and a healthy slice of American apple pie full of blood.

He blinked and was back to the present, where he recognized McQueen working on him. He could hear gunfire but didn't know who was firing.

Night had fallen. McQueen had a flashlight held between his teeth. His narrow eyes were focused on Boy Scout's right shoulder.

"What... what... what..." Boy Scout struggled to form words.

After a few more seconds, Boy Scout felt a wash of

warmth so sensuous that he almost smiled, remembering a short time with a woman named Pak Hyung Mi in a Korean village, then a long time with a Pinoy named Alsace in a club barely outside the gate of Clark Air Force Base.

"Morphine," McQueen said, removing the flashlight from his mouth and holding it in his right hand so he could examine the wound. "You're fixed up for now. I can't get the bone pieces out, but I did stop the bleeding. You'll need surgery so I think this whole exercise in trying to keep the *daeva* from leaving their valley is over for you."

"*Daeva?*"

"Remember the mission? Remember the speech you gave? We're trying to save the world from destruction and all that *hooraw* shit?"

Amidst the brilliant light of the opiate sun flare, Boy Scout remembered himself standing in the cistern delivering a speech when they'd first learned about the consequences of what they'd done. Yeah, now he remembered... but fuck it. Morphine. And as the solar flare died, it all went black.

HE WOKE UP cold and alone in the dark.

His mouth was a vast desert planet that hadn't seen water in an epoch. He moved and felt the leaden weight of his right shoulder. Then he remembered. He'd been shot. McQueen had done something to him and then given him morphine. He could still feel its leisurely journey through his system, a weight as heavy as the memory of the boy he'd saved from Colonel Amanullah Sharif. The boy who was not just any shy boy, but a paraplegic in a wheel chair whose body was constantly used as a sexual tool for an Afghan military officer's vile needs. Although he'd never actually seen it happen, he'd heard the colonel's innuendo.

"I can see in his eyes that he loves me."

"He frowns like my sister but I know she liked it."

Each word was a land mine of predatory violence and hate. The man he'd garroted hadn't even understood the meaning of love. He hadn't known that to love was to submit. He forever sought to control, and in that controlling had become a monster whose upward mobility was destined to be ended by a former US Army Ranger.

When Boy Scout had reported the suspected molestation of the handicapped boy to a military police officer at Camp Phoenix, he'd been told that Afghan officers weren't his jurisdiction and that if Boy Scout decided to take it to the Afghan police he'd be laughed out of the room.

What was the jurisdiction of human suffering?

Wasn't that everyone's responsibility?

The cold radiating from the dirt through his back brought Boy Scout back to the present.

He struggled to sit, but the volcanic pain in his shoulder made it almost impossible. Any move, even the act of breathing, sent shivers of agony along his arm and down his spine. But not willing to merely lie there for eternity, he managed to lever himself into a seated position. His body armor had been removed and lay beside him, bloody and unfastened, but he let it be. He struggled to his feet, falling twice, while the earth reeled in concert with his opiate-soaked brain. Each time he fell, he blacked out for a time, the pain summoning him to a place of hushed darkness. He finally managed to climb to his feet.

"Lore? Criminal?" He turned around drunkenly. "Bully? McQueen?"

He noted that his rifle and gear belt lay in a pool of cooled and hardening blood... his own.

He reached over and felt the bandage that had been placed over his wound. Looking down, he saw the white gauze and felt grounded by it. His torso was naked underneath, and in the star light he could see the gray pallor of his skin. He looked around again. Narco's SUV was where it had landed after the explosion. The fire was out and it wasn't even smoking. The SUV they'd arrived in was where he'd left it in the middle of the road behind them.

Shakily, he bent and grabbed for his rifle. His left hand wrapped around the barrel. He started walking towards the dead Taliban he'd killed with the grenades. He needed to know that he wasn't crazy or in some alternate sideways reality. If the bodies weren't there, he didn't know where he was... *when* he was. But if they were there, then maybe there was an explanation for his entire team abandoning him. As the fog began to clear from his mind, a plausible idea formed. Maybe they'd lit out after Narco. Maybe they were just over the horizon or just beyond shouting distance.

He stumbled and was forced to use the rifle as a cane to keep him from falling.

Ten feet away he saw the first hint of a body.

What if it was his TST? What if someone had come and killed them and stuffed them in with the dead Taliban? He paused, unsure if he wanted to see... but knowing he had to.

"Come on, Starling," he said to himself, realizing that the morphine still had him under its spell. "Get your shit together."

He took several deep breaths, then stepped forward until he could see every one of the dead bodies. That they were at least there gave him relief. That they weren't his TST gave him joy. Seven dead Taliban. Several with missing arms and legs. One with a missing head. Ruined weaponry. All evidence of his two grenades.

So everything *had* happened the way he remembered it.

The only problem was that he was alone.

He made his way back to the road. After three attempts to bend down and grab his gear, he managed to snatch his bloody utility belt and hang it around his neck. Then he spied the MBITR. Why hadn't he thought of that before? He could radio them. He dropped his rifle and fell to the ground beside it. He held the mic with a shaking hand and spoke into it.

"Anyone.... anyone out there." He stared at the transmitter. He listened for a response but nothing came. He repeated the call. Still nothing. The antenna had been folded over, so he released it to its full length, thinking that might increase his chances. The system had a line-of-sight distance of twelve miles. They couldn't have gone that far, right? He repeated the call and thought that he might have heard a voice through the static. He pushed himself to his feet and stumbled, grasping desperately at the radio with his left hand while his right hand hung uselessly at his side.

"Hello? McQueen? Anyone?"

A ghost of a voice spoke to him but he couldn't understand it.

Still, his heart exploded with hope.

His body was suddenly filled with energy. He managed to climb onto the side of the wrecked SUV for altitude.

"Anyone, can you hear me?"

Then came four static-laced words. "Can't... need... want... support..."

"What is it? I didn't understand. Please repeat?"

Nothing but static responded.

"Hello? Can you hear me?"

Static.

Boy Scout spun, looking for anything, even a wink of light. But there was nothing. Here in the back end of Asscrackistan, all he could see was the half moon, the stars, and a wide swathe of blackness.

He started to run to the working SUV, then stopped. He went back and grabbed his weapon from where he'd dropped it on the ground. He struggled to hold both the rifle and the radio in one hand—his off hand—and finally managed to sling the rifle around his shoulder and run drunkenly to the SUV in a left shoulder high, limping gate. He fumbled with the door, but managed to open it. He threw the rifle, the gear belt from around his neck, and the radio into the front passenger seat, then awkwardly used his left hand to grab the steering wheel and pull himself inside. He reached for the ignition but realized the keys were in his pocket... his *right* pocket. The next two minutes were a slapstick gyrational series of contortions to slide his left hand into his right pocket. Eventually, he managed to liberate the keys, which he slid into the ignition and turned on the vehicle.

The lights snapped on and he cheered, punching the ceiling with his left hand.

He put the SUV in gear, pulled around the burned-out hulk of Narco's stolen SUV, then began rumbling down the road. He traveled three miles and stopped. With his foot on the brake, he reached over and grabbed the radio.

"Hello? McQueen? Lore? Anybody?"

At first the response was nothing but static, until he heard the crystal clear words, "Boy Scout."

He thought it might have sounded like McQueen, but then... it also sounded like Narco.

"Yes! That's me! I'm here! Where are you?"

Static was his only response.

"It's me. Where'd you go?" He felt his face turn red and tears come to his eyes. "Where are you? Hello? Hello? Hello?"

Chapter Twenty-Seven

Boy Scout drove for another hour, ranging back and forth along the road, trying to locate his team through the radio but getting only the flat hiss of static in response. It wasn't until the batteries ran out on the MBITR that he put the radio down and stopped trying. Without any sense of where he was or where his team could be, he drove randomly until dawn, seeing no one except Afghanis in old, rusted Toyota Corollas and pickups. They gave him odd looks, as they would any shirtless white man driving a military grade SUV. The morphine had worn off, sending jolts of electric fire through his shoulder at every bump or jostle. He'd stopped and checked the supplies stacked beneath Faood's body. The dead dervish was beginning to smell, but Boy Scout didn't feel it was proper to dump him on the side of the road. He found a bottle of aspirin which he popped like Tic Tacs.

Boy Scout climbed back into the SUV. He couldn't fathom where the team had gone. And on foot nonetheless. He'd been certain they'd gone off in search of Narco, but why hadn't they come back? Why hadn't one of them stayed with him? Not knowing the answers was infuriating. Not knowing whether they were even alive set his hair on fire.

Sitting at a crossroads, he drank the last of his water from his canteen. His shoulder blazed with pain, but he set that aside. What had Faood said? If they couldn't get Narco back to him, then find other dervishes and they might be able to exorcise him. Boy Scout remembered now that Faood had mentioned something about a palace where other dervishes lived. He struggled to recall the details. It had been partially destroyed by an earthquake in the 1970s... what was it— then it snapped into place. Bagh-e-Jahan nam Palace.

If he could talk to the dervishes, they could help him track down the others. Faood was still in back and he could explain to them what had happened. In fact, after the death of Sufi Sam and Faood, they needed to get someone back to the cistern to keep the *daeva* in its fugue, if it wasn't already gone. Or maybe McQueen and the others had captured Narco and taken him back there. It still didn't explain why they'd left him in the middle of the road, but it made a certain sense.

He pulled the tactical map from the glove compartment and found his location through terrain association. Once he was confident in the direction, Boy Scout headed that way. Eventually he found himself moving through the town of Kholm, its busy bazaar already packed with morning traffic. Old men sat hunched together drinking coffee. Women with no head wraps haggled over vegetables. Children chased one another just like children everywhere, idealistic and oblivious to anything but their carefree existence. Kholm was merely a town ensconced in its own pastoral life, surviving on the edge of a war-torn country. Its residents had no idea that a life-and-death struggle was going on with Boy Scout's TST, or that there was a supernatural creature being kept in an ancient cistern mere miles from where they slid blissfully through their daily activities. They had no idea that dervishes could shape time, or that the sky could burn with the power of an ancient god. Which was as it should be, he supposed. Such ideas, such knowledge, were nuclear blasts to the innocent, who once they had discovered it, could never return to what had been—could never return to what could have been—and were stuck in a universe where things were now never as they seemed.

A boy kicking a soccer ball stopped in the middle of the road. He turned his head to gaze at Boy Scout, as if daring him to run him over.

Boy Scout slowed.

The boy continued to stare. With black tousled hair, he wore a long shirt that covered his legs. Sandals adorned his feet. His expression was neither curious nor mean. He stared like an automaton, his eyes leaden.

It was almost like everything was in slow motion.

Boy Scout slowed even more, until he was creeping along at walking speed. What was the boy doing? Why wasn't he moving out of the way?

Then the boy blinked and it was that blink that broke the spell.

Boy Scout had spent so much time gazing at the boy he'd forgotten to check his surroundings. He could have very well driven into an ambush. Noticing the surrounding buildings for the first time, he realized that he was in a natural choke point.

He was just checking his sides when the boy turned, kicked the soccer ball, then ran after it.

Boy Scout stopped the SUV and stared at the spot the boy had been like there was a mine beneath it. Then he shook his head and pressed the accelerator. He was just too exhausted. He was seeing meaning where there was none.

He continued for another two miles, then after checking his map again, turned right down a road lined with date trees. A hundred meters ahead, twin white stucco columns stood as an entrance to drive through. A ten-foot wall made of the same material extended on both the right and left. He slowed the vehicle, unwilling to drive through such an unknown chokepoint.

Suddenly a figure appeared at the front of the SUV.

Lore!

She slapped her hands on the hood loud enough that it sounded like a shot. Her eyes were wide and a smile broke across her face. She mouthed the words, *Boy Scout*.

He slammed on the brakes.

She ran around to the passenger side and slung open the door. She shot into the seat, shoving his things onto the floor. She slammed the door and pointed off to her left. "Drive there," she commanded.

Boy Scout had a thousand questions, but immediately complied. He went where directed and drove behind a copse of date trees. McQueen stood over the body of Criminal. A piece of cloth was draped over the dead man's face. Once the SUV was completely behind the trees, Lore hopped out and ran around the front of the vehicle. Boy Scout was just getting out when she plowed into him, throwing her arms around him in a vicious hug.

He cried out in pain, causing her to let go.

"We thought you were dead!"

"What gave you that idea?" Boy Scout said, both insanely happy, yet getting more and more pissed as he realized they'd intentionally left him behind.

"Uh, no heartbeat," McQueen said, walking up and clasping Boy Scout's unwounded shoulder.

"I got a heartbeat now," Boy Scout said, pretty sure he was correct in what he was saying.

"I swear to you that you didn't," McQueen said. Seeing the expression on Boy Scout's face, McQueen stepped back and clasped his hands in front of him like a hopeless beggar. "I swear to you, Bryan. You were dead."

Boy Scout couldn't help frowning. "I'm here, aren't I?" He glanced down at Criminal's body. "What happened?"

"Narco shot you," Lore said. "And we went after him."

"How did Criminal die?"

"Narco," McQueen said. "He came up behind him and stabbed him in the face."

Boy Scout bent over and pulled aside the cloth. Criminal stared back at him with a single filmy eye. The other was a black, crusted gash savaged by a blade. Narco's blade. Son of a bitch. He replaced the cloth and stood.

"Where's Bully?" he said.

"Recon. She's due to be back in five mikes," McQueen said.

"Why didn't you take the vehicle?" He wanted to add, *why'd you leave me?* but didn't.

Tears had formed in Lore's eyes. "Narco had us on a serious chase. Once he killed—I mean shot you—we went after him. By the time he took us over the mountain, it didn't make sense to go back." She jerked her chin toward the palace. "We tracked him here and were waiting for dark to go inside."

He couldn't help saying it. "You left me."

Although McQueen couldn't meet his gaze, he was the one who spoke. "I checked your pulse three times. You weren't breathing. I swear to you." Then he met Boy Scout's stare. "I would never have left you behind if I thought you were alive." He shook his head. "I am so ashamed."

"Didn't you hear me on the radio?" Boy Scout asked.

"We didn't hear anything."

"So you weren't the ones responding to me?"

"I'm telling you, man, I didn't hear a thing."

Boy Scout stared at McQueen for a long moment. Finally, he said, "Well, apparently, I'm not dead." He leaned against the SUV.

McQueen was about to speak when Bully appeared. She let out a little yip when she saw Boy Scout.

"You're alive!" she cried.

"If enough people say it, it might actually be true," he said, now definitely sick of the situation.

She ran towards him with the intention of hugging him, but he shied away.

"Shoulder," he said, stopping her in mid hug.

Why everyone felt the need to hug him was beyond his

ken. All he wanted to do was to get to a point where they could save Narco, if they still could, and hopefully get some relief for the pain.

"How… we thought you were—"

"Dead," he finished her sentence. "My demise seems to be a popular mythology."

Her smile was ear to ear and her eyes were bright with happiness. "I knew you were alive. I heard you on the radio… or at least I thought I did… that was you, wasn't it?"

He nodded. "I spoke with someone but the connection wasn't… was you?"

"Yes, I think so." She beamed at him. "I just can't believe you're alive."

"That seems to be the consensus." He sighed. All he wanted was a bottle of good single malt and a handful of Vicodin. He was exhausted and the pain in his shoulder was wearing on him. He turned to McQueen and said, "Report."

"Narco is somewhere inside. We watched him go through the front. He shot the guards and blasted his way into the palace. That was three hours ago. Since then, we've been sitting here waiting for darkness."

"Why are we waiting? Aren't the dervishes our friends? Why didn't you go in and help them fight Narco?"

"About that," Lore said.

"What about that?"

"How do we know they're our friends? I mean, they've trapped us as much as they trapped the *daeva*."

He stared at her. "I'm listening."

"I saw Narco embrace one of the dervishes, then enter. We heard gunfire after."

"Now that is an interesting turn of events. Could it be that he tricked his way inside and shot them?" Boy Scout asked, glancing at McQueen.

"I don't think so," Lore said.

"What do you think it means, then?"

"You should listen to her. She makes sense," McQueen said.

Boy Scout usually found that Lore made more sense than any of them. She'd grown up in the shadow of her domineering preacher father and had spent her life trying to be the smartest person in the room. Most of the time she succeeded.

"I've been thinking about that," she said. "On the surface this seems to be a simple matter of Sufi mystics entrapping old Zoastrian angels. Now with Narco we've discovered that there's the whole ghosts in the *Sefid* business. For a dervish to embrace Narco, it would suggest the idea that that dervish was also possessed by a ghost from the *Sefid*, or at least the ghost in Narco was recognized. If that's the case, what really are those ghosts and why?"

"Do you have an idea of what they are?" he asked.

She made a face and shook her head. "No idea at all, and that's what scares me."

Chapter Twenty-Eight

IN THE END, their plan was a simple one. McQueen and Bully would remain outside and cover them with rifles, while Boy Scout and Lore went inside. They drove the SUV straight to the front door of the palace. The impressive piece of architecture was three stories tall and about seventy feet across. Although it was called a palace, it was really more of a mansion. Still, with its white marble walls and tile decorated sunken windows, it was striking.

The main doors opened as soon as the SUV came to a stop. Two dervishes strode down the marble entrance stairs, their hands on the pommels of their scimitars. One stood at the base of the steps, while the other came to Boy Scout's window. He was tall and had a burn on the right side of his face. He wore silver beaded pants tucked into knee-high black leather boots. Atop this he wore a silver and white whirling shirt that dropped to mid-thigh. He'd hitched the right side up and tucked it over the bejeweled pommel of his scimitar, where his hand now rested.

"What is it, friend?" he said with an English accent almost as polished as Faood's.

Boy Scout spoke through the open window. "In back. Faood. He's dead."

The man frowned and glanced at his partner, who went to the back window and looked in. When he saw Faood's body, he called out in Persian and out came two more dervishes. These held AK47s.

Boy Scout raised an eyebrow. "I thought you didn't like modern weapons."

The initial inviting look presented by the dervish had been replaced by a stiffness that afforded no room for pleasantries. "Sometimes they are needed. Now, step out of the vehicle."

Boy Scout glanced at Lore, who sat stone-faced, taking everything in. He turned off the engine, then stepped out of the SUV. He was unarmed except for an obvious 9mm chest rig on his body armor.

"Give me your weapon," said the dervish, his right hand out, palm flat.

"I don't even know your name," Boy Scout said, giving him the same grin he'd once given a colonel who had asked if he didn't mind being extended for a third time in Iraq.

The dervish didn't even bat an eye. "I am Faral. Weapon, please."

Boy Scout pulled his Sig from the chest rig and handed it over, using the barrel.

Without even a thank you, Faral said, "Please tell your woman to remove herself from the vehicle."

Without turning his head, Boy Scout said, "Faral wants

my woman to remove herself from the vehicle."

Lore snorted but complied.

Once she was standing beside Boy Scout, Faral asked, "How did he die?"

"He was shot back in the cistern along with the old mystic. There is now no one to guard the *daeva*," he said.

"The old mystic?" His brow knitted, then his eyes widened. "Erhan. Erhan is dead?"

"You act surprised," Lore said, but received no response.

Instead, Faral's mouth twisted into a frown. He turned and watched as two dervishes removed Faood from the back of the SUV and carried him up the stairs and into the palace. Then he turned back to Boy Scout. "How long ago was that?"

"Fifteen... maybe sixteen hours," Boy Scout said.

"Why did it take you this long to bring him? You should have brought him right away. We could have saved him."

Boy Scout shook his head. "He was dead. I saw him die."

"Not his life. His soul. We should have been there to collect it."

Lore turned to look at Boy Scout, but he remained facing Faral.

"You could collect his soul?" Boy Scout asked, each word seeded with doubt.

"Of course. We have many old souls among us. Why did it take so long for you to bring him to us?"

"We were chasing his killer."

"Did you catch him?"

"No."

Faral shook his head. "That's unfortunate."

"Yes it is. But things just took a turn for the better," Boy Scout said.

Faral stared at him with dead eyes. "How can that be?"

"We know where he is."

Faral seemed determined to play the game to the end. "Who? The killer? Where is he?"

Boy Scout raised his hand and pointed to the palace. "In there."

Faral let his eyes follow Boy Scout's finger. He stared at the front door a moment, then said, "Ahhh."

"Yes. Ahhh," Boy Scout said.

Faral locked gazes with Boy Scout and neither of them said anything for almost a full minute.

As usual, it was Lore who broke the silence. "Why aren't you concerned about the *daeva* you have chained in the cistern?"

Faral spoke without looking at Lore. "We have that under control."

Lore snorted. "Lots of control you have. Oh look, dead dervish."

That made Faral turn to address her. "Your disrespect is noted."

"You hiding a homicidal maniac is noted."

"About that," Boy Scout added. "We want our man back."

Faral glanced at the palace, then at the ground. "He is no longer your man."

"Indeed he is. We're on contract. I'm his boss."

"There is no contract. There is no boss."

Lore spat, "But you admit you have our friend Narco,

homicidal maniac."

"We have a vessel that has been filled. That is what I know."

Boy Scout let a few seconds pass, then said, "This is how it's going to go down, Faral. You are going to let us go inside your precious palace and speak with our man, Dakota Jimmison. He is an American citizen under a Department of Defense contract. Keeping him against his will is tantamount to declaring war on the United States of America. If I'm not allowed to go inside and if anything happens to either me or Ms. May here, I have my people standing by to contact the 160th Special Operations Air Regiment at Bagram Air Force Base. They will be more than happy to bring all of their power to bear and blow this fucking precious palace to smithereens." Faral stared at Boy Scout with dead eyes, but by the way his lip was almost twitching, Boy Scout knew he'd gotten through.

"Just in case you don't know what smithereens means," Lore said, holding out her hands and wiggling her fingers. "It means into little bitty pieces."

Faral said, "You would also blow yourselves and your man up if that happened."

Boy Scout shrugged. "I guess so. Lore, how do you feel about that?"

She lifted one shoulder, jutting her wounded leg out and crossing her arms. "Whatevs."

Faral's eye twitched as if he wanted to look at Lore but couldn't bring himself to break his own ethos. "As I said, he is not your man. He isn't that person anymore."

Boy Scout nodded. "I hear you and I respect what you're saying, but you know I'm going to have to verify that, right?"

"You both can't come in. Please tell your woman to remain in place."

"If you refer to me as *your woman* one more time, I'm going to—"

Boy Scout raised his hand, cutting her off. "Lore, stay here."

"But you can't go in there without backup."

"I got this."

"But—"

He whirled on her. "What? I gave an order. You. Stay. Here."

She looked hurt by his response, but he couldn't help it. He turned to Faral. "Let's go."

Together they marched up the stairs and through the gigantic double wooden doors. The inside was spartan but regal. Crossed scimitars hung on the entry wall. Here and there upon the marble walls were verses written in Persian. The ceilings were at least twenty feet high. They turned left and walked to a set of wide stairs. They passed a pool of blood that was being cleaned up by a young boy. They went up one floor, then moved down a hallway until they came to a room with a plain door. All along the way, whenever they would pass a dervish, he'd bow his head and put his right hand over his breast. Boy Scout absently wondered what Faral's rank was or if he was some sort of dervish nobility. He had to admit, before the events in the valley with the JSOC general and the *daeva,* he'd only been barely aware that there was such a thing as a whirling dervish.

Faral knocked once, then opened the door.

Narco had changed into full dervish apparel, complete with the long whirling shirt. He knelt on a prayer rug and was praying towards the west, which was the closest to the holy Kaaba in Makkah. That was all fine and good, but Narco wasn't Muslim. He was Catholic. Or at least he had been.

Boy Scout remained silent out of respect. As far as he knew, it wasn't time to pray, so whatever Narco was doing, it didn't fit. After about two minutes, Narco stood, rolled up his prayer rug, and put it in the corner of what looked to be a monk's cell.

He glanced at Boy Scout, then said something to Faral in perfect Persian. Hearing the words from Narco was absolutely the most surreal thing Boy Scout thought he might have witnessed in this entire experience.

Faral spoke back to him in Persian, then in English said, "We're going to speak English, Hamad. You must think of speaking in English, then it will happen. This is a new body. You must trust it."

Narco narrowed his eyes as Faral spoke. Then he opened his mouth a few times. Nothing came out at first. Then the single word: "please." He said this several times, getting the taste of it, then finally nodded and addressed Boy Scout with his hand over his heart. "Pleased to make your acquaintance. May I have your name, please?"

Boy Scout blinked at the formality of it. Never had Narco ever used such language. He licked his lips and answered, putting his hand over his own heart. "My name is Bryan Starling. Some people call me Boy Scout. Pleased to make your acquaintance, Hamad."

Narco grinned from ear to ear. "Boy Scout. You are named after a youth who designs to learn different crafts so that he might earn patches to put on a uniform. Interesting."

"I think they gave me the name because I like to help people, I'm unwavering in my loyalty, and I will give the shirt off my back if you ask." Narco nodded, still grinning happily. "Sorry I made you wait. I've been unable to pray for more than five hundred years. It was the first thing I wanted to do after I cleaned myself."

Faral turned to Boy Scout. "Do you see what I mean? Do you understand now?"

"I don't understand this at all. Where's Narco? Where is my friend?"

"I'm sorry, but your friend no longer exists," Faral said. "He's been replaced."

"Been replaced? Replaced by what?"

"By Hamad, of course."

Boy Scout turned from one man to the other, watching them, waiting on the punch line, but all he got was a stern look from Faral and an almost comical grin from Hamad—no, *Narco*. He was about to say something when everything faded to black.

Chapter Twenty-Nine

The Cistern, Afghanistan

Boy Scout woke in a flash. Unlike other fugue states, he wasn't hung over and was fully conscious of his surroundings. He was clothed and dry, lying beside the water instead of in it. He climbed to his feet, cautious about his right shoulder, but he felt nothing. He examined it. No gauze. No pain. Because the shattered shoulder had never happened.

What had they just done? Had they gone forward in time? And now that they were back, where were they? He searched for Faood's body, but he wasn't there. Neither was the old mystic, Sufi Sam, or Erhan, as Faral had named him. But that hadn't happened because it was in the future or the sideways. Damn, he was confused.

He moved to wake Lore, then McQueen. Lore woke Criminal. It was Criminal who noticed Narco. He was naked, sitting on a stone, captured in a much deeper fugue than they had been in.

"Can anyone tell me what the hell is going on?" Criminal asked.

"I needed to show you what was real," Faood said, entering the room with a tray of food and a jug of water. He set them on the ground, then folded himself down. He gestured for them to join him.

"But you're dead," Boy Scout said, lowering himself next to Faood.

"Like they thought you were dead on the road in the fugue? The attack wasn't my doing, You and your people created that, as they did the dead sheep... or maybe that was you."

"How did you..."

"I was there, like you."

"But that didn't really happen. It was a fugue. So how do we know that our brains didn't just make it up?" Lore asked.

"It's because I was there with you. I came as a dead man, my mind controlling the fugue. Remember how we prepared you for each previous fugue? We'd sit down and talk about where you were going and what you were going to do, then as a group you would make it happen. In this case, because of the spirit in Narco, we had no time. It was I who created the landscape of the fugue. It was I who populated it with what was necessary. You merely added the details from your own experiences." Faood gestured at the food and water. "Eat. Drink. You'll need energy for what's to come."

"So we went into the future," Lore said, glancing and nodding at Boy Scout to make sure he was paying attention.

Faood shook his head as he bit a fig in half and chewed. "It would seem so, but like before, you did not go anywhere. You were here all along."

"I knew it," Lore said, slapping a hand against her thigh.

"So you made it up? Why? So you could escape Narco?" Criminal asked.

"Partly," Faood said, swallowing. "I admit that I was in fear for my life. Wouldn't you have been?" He raised his eyebrows. When no one responded, he continued, "But I wanted you to know the truth of it. For too long you have been duped by my people."

Criminal and McQueen surged to their feet.

McQueen asked in a menacing voice, "What do you mean, duped?"

Bully stood as well, eyes narrow, hands rolled into fists.

Boy Scout looked at the faces of his team and could see their anger rising. "You better explain yourself, Faood." To the others he said, "Sit down. Eat. Let's hear him out."

But no one made any move to sit.

Faood put his hands on his crossed legs and gave everyone a friendly but stern look. "This," he said, "all of this, is a lie." He waved his hand. Then he pointed at the *daeva*. "That is not the threat." He put his hand on his chest. "I am the threat, or at least I was. Your whole reason for being here was a ruse."

Boy Scout's eyes narrowed. "What are you talking about?"

To Boy Scout, Faood said, "Tell them what you saw inside the Bagh-e-Jahan nam Palace."

Boy Scout nodded, then glanced toward the water. "I saw

Narco but it wasn't Narco. He was Muslim and praying. Then when he spoke to me, it was in Narco's voice, but it wasn't his words. He spoke in perfect Persian."

Lore shook her head. Her mouth was stretched in a thin line, like she was sick of it all. "But it wasn't Narco. It was in our heads."

"I took you to what could have been to show you what probably is," Faood said.

Criminal spat, "Fucking dervish bull shit mumble-speak."

"Dickensian," Boy Scout said. Then he frowned, because he knew that if Narco were with them, he would have said something like *Gesundheit*, and they all would have laughed, easing the tension of the moment. Oh, how he missed his friend. He vowed right then to do everything he could to return Narco to what he'd been... or as close a version as he could manage.

"Excuse me, boss? What did you say?" Bully asked.

Boy Scout sighed, the loss of one of them just too much. "Dickensian," he said. "The last fugue we took was Dickensian. I'm talking about the old English author, Charles Dickens. *A Tale of Two Cities*. *Great Expectations*. Or more appropriately, *A Christmas Carol*. Faood was our Ghost of Christmas Future."

Everyone stared at him as if he'd gone crazy.

"Doesn't anyone remember *A Christmas Carol*? Ebenezer Scrooge?"

"Oh, Scrooge," Lore said. "What about it?"

Criminal said, "I saw the Simpsons version of that. Holidays of Future Past."

"Will everyone just shut up!" Bully suddenly screamed. She slapped her hands against her head. "Will you all just shut the fuck up!"

Everybody jerked at her outburst.

Bully surged to her feet, grabbed one of the rifles, then locked and loaded on Faood, the barrel inches from his head. "You just going to sit there and take what he did to us? What he fucking made me do?"

"Easy, Bull—er, Sara," Lore said carefully, getting to her feet. She stood, her hands out, placating as she backed up a few steps.

Faood remained still.

Boy Scout stood slowly.

"Don't tell me to take it easy," Bully said. "You have no idea what I've been doing all of these months while you've been playing in your minds... getting drunk... smoking pot... fucking. Sure it wasn't real, but you didn't know that at the time. It was real enough."

"Sarasota, put the gun down," Boy Scout said.

She whipped her face in his direction. Tears streamed from her eyes. "Didn't you hear him? He said all of this was a lie. He said that fucking thing hanging there isn't a threat... never has been." A sob escaped her in a miserable bark. "I watched it sleep, throbbing and humming like a giant fucking lightbulb all this time, waiting for it to wake up and kill me. The damned dervishes told me stories of how evil it was and what it could do. It was a fucking devil to me. When I was washing you, it was there. When I was cleaning your shit every day like a damned nurse in a coma wing, it was there. When I was picking scabs and cutting your hair, it was there. And you know what? It terrified me. I used to go outside and run ten miles just to make myself tired enough that I could sleep, because I dreaded every new day. I knew it was only going to be more of me cleaning your shit and worrying that the devil was going to wake up." She shoved the barrel of the rifle against Faood's head hard once, then again.

His head rocked with the blows, but he made no move to do anything.

"You didn't know what I was doing. You couldn't know how I was feeling. And now to find out that *this* asshole was the real threat? Boy Scout, you tell me. You're our leader. What's real, huh? What's real anymore?" Abruptly she threw her weapon on safe, dropped the magazine and emptied the chamber of the live round. She tossed it to Lore, then ran out the door.

Boy Scout, Criminal, and Lore stared at each other, then turned their attention back to Faood. His head was bleeding where the barrel had struck him, but he made no move to wipe the blood away.

Faood shook his head. "We used you. We used you just as we've used people for almost a thousand years. She's right and I deserve whatever you do to me, but I want the chance to make it right."

"Why'd you do it?" Boy Scout asked, his voice barely a whisper.

Faood took a deep breath. "We put you in a fugue and told you a lie so you'd create overly complex realities so that you could draw near to *Sefid*. The *daeva* here isn't the one you shot down. That one is elsewhere. We've had this one for over a century. It gives us the power to create the fugue, to invent realities. We use its mind as a pathway."

"But *why*?" Criminal asked, his voice cracking. "Why would you do such a thing? Why would you make us spend our lives thinking we had to save the world from that?" he asked, pointing at the *daeva*.

Boy Scout shook his head. They were a victim of their own addiction to responsibility.

"The world doesn't need any more *daeva*," Faood said. "Yes, they are a threat to peace, just not to you. Not here. Not now."

"Then why? McQueen asked.

"To find Rumi. Our master. Our lord. His mind became lost in the great *Sefid* and we believe he still exists out there. Travelers have mentioned finding him. Speaking with him. We travel now to find him. We also send those such as you. Those we can..." He glanced up at the three, then away. "Trick into finding him in the hopes that he could live again inside you... or one of us, if we were so lucky." He placed his hand over his heart. His voice deepened as he said, "Then it all changed."

"What changed?" Lore asked in a hushed whisper.

"We discovered that that there were other beings in the *Sefid,* and that if you brought them back and tamed them, you could live forever. Some of them are from before and we don't know who they are. Some of them are from past travelers becoming lost. Narco has one of those beings inside him even now."

"So it's not really Hamad," Boy Scout said.

"No. That's but one possibility I showed you."

"Is that why he still sleeps?" Lore asked.

"My people have tainted what had been an honorable mission," Faood said. "Now they no longer search for Rumi. They merely search for a way to extend their lives."

"So they can live forever," Lore said.

"The old mystic. The one you called Sufi Sam." He shook his head. "Such a disrespectful name. I so much wanted to stop you from this disrespect, but he wouldn't let me. He was afraid that you might find us out, so he encouraged the disrespect. His name was Erhan and he was a young child when Rumi became lost. He was one of the first to go and try to find him. He was one of the first to tame the creature inside of him. He was the eldest among us. He said to us that the creature, the spirit that inhabited him, was older than humankind and had existed before the creation of everything we know. He and this creature lived as one. At first, he looked for Rumi like the others, but then when he was able to tame what was inside of him, he wanted to find out more about them. His wasn't a quest to live forever. His was a quest of understanding."

"Until Narco killed him," Criminal said. "Enough of this bullshit. I'm going to find Bully." He turned and stormed out.

"Why are you helping us? Don't you don't want to live forever too?" Lore asked.

Faood blinked abruptly. "It's not that I don't want to live forever... it's just that I won't do it based on a lie."

"What about Narco?" Boy Scout asked.

"I need to go back in and see if I can identify the creature inside of him. There is a process of taming and this is the first step."

"I'm going with you," Boy Scout said.

Faood stood and shook his head. "You can't. It's too dangerous. Unless your mind is right, you can't go directly into *Sefid*. This is why we put you in a fugue as a lure for the *Sefid* to take you."

"But is it possible?" Boy Scout asked. "Is it possible for me to go into this *Sefid* and survive?

Faood stared at Boy Scout.

He pressed. "I asked if it was possible."

Faood nodded reluctantly. "It's been done before. You've been traveling in the fugue long enough that the *Sefid* might welcome you." Then he shook his head. "But your mind has to be trained and you lack this training."

"You don't know what kind of training I have had, Faood. You don't understand what it has taken to be me. I'm going to do this, and by God you should not try and stop me."

"What about me?" Lore asked, turning from Faood, to Boy Scout, and back again.

"You and the other two are going to protect us while we're in the *Sefid*," Boy Scout said. "I need you to stand over us. Watch everything. Now go find them and bring them to me. I don't know how long we have."

"And me?" McQueen asked.

Boy Scout nodded to Faood, then guided McQueen into the other room. When he was sure he was out of earshot of the dervish, he said, "I want you to prepare a battle plan. What they did to us... what they did to

Bully... I won't let it stand. After I finish saving Narco, we're going to get our own pounds of flesh back and then some. Think you can handle that, old friend?"

"Doesn't sound too much like something a boy scout would do."

"Well, maybe I'm not a boy scout any longer. Maybe I've become something else."

McQueen looked into Boy Scout's eyes. "Be careful about sudden change, my friend. Be careful about doing things that can't be undone. You know what I'm talking about."

Boy Scout didn't say a word when he turned around and left, because he absolutely did know what McQueen was talking about.

Chapter Thirty

BOY SCOUT WANDERED outside. He needed private time; a few moments to gather his thoughts before he headed into the *Sefid* to rescue Narco. He felt that he'd spent so long being someone else he'd forgotten who he was... who he *really* was.

So he found a spot and sat.

Staring across what was definitely the *terra damnata* of Cormac McCarthy's *Blood Meridian*, he remembered that he'd once wanted to be a teacher. Killing people hadn't been something he'd ever believed he'd do, much less become as accomplished as he was at it. In fact, he'd just finished his master's degree in twentieth century American literature, squeaked through his dissertation on "The Lost Generation's Influence on American Civil Rights" when 9/11 had happened. Like most folks, he'd been absolutely glued to his television, watching, then changing channels whenever a show went to commercial. He'd spent two days on his couch in his apartment, drinking beer, eating take out, sometimes crying because of the terrible loss of life, sometimes just stunned as he sat, slack-jawed and wondering who had possessed the gall to sucker punch America.

As it turned out, it was this relatively unknown terrorist group called Al-Qaeda, led by Osama Bin Laden. But he didn't know that at the time. No one did. Everyone was guessing as the talking heads on television and the PhDs in Washington's think tanks failed to make the connection, all of them as shocked and tearful as Boy Scout had been.

Then he saw a specific image and a forking path was presented to him.

There have been images over time that have caused the world to pause. Images so iconic that they represent a moment in time to perfection. Sometimes these images present themselves immediately. But other times, the images rise like a dead body in a lake, impressing themselves on a nation's psyche.

Boy Scout remembered the first image like that he'd ever seen. The photo was in an immense Time Life book in the basement library of his grandfather's house. Called the "Napalm Girl," the black-and-white photo showed a nine-year-old Vietnamese girl running stark naked down a road, screaming. Napalm roared in shades of gray behind her. Other Vietnamese children ran around her, screaming as well. But they were clothed and it was that clothing that somehow magnified her terror... her situation. Her nakedness made everyone who saw the picture want to stand up, find a blanket, and wrap her, take her away, whispering that we never should have bombed her village and we are so damned terribly sorry.

Then they'd expand their optic and realize that there were American soldiers in the photo. Then they'd blink and wonder. Why weren't they helping the girl? Why weren't they covering her? Then they'd realize that one of the soldiers seemed to be shaking out a cigarette from a pack, uncaring and unconcerned... *inhuman.*

Then Boy Scout remembered the power of the picture of the burning monk in Saigon. In fact, later he'd discovered there was a series of pictures, detailing the events before and after the immolation. But on that first occasion, it was only him, in his grandfather's basement, staring at the picture of a man sitting upright, posture perfect, and completely on fire. The monk had done it intentionally to bring attention to the South Vietnamese regime's discriminatory Buddhist laws. That a person would do something so final to themselves, so viscerally and unimaginably painful, had kept Boy Scout silent for a full day. He hadn't spoken a word after seeing the photo, not until his grandfather had asked him what was wrong.

Boy Scout recalled what his grandfather had said.

"Don't think he did that to himself, Bryan. We did that to him. The South Vietnamese government did that to him. Imagine how desperate a man has to be, imagine how terrible his life must be, for him to do such a thing just so that there would be enough photographers to bring the image to the world, and in small print, the reason for it."

But those images were from a different time... a different war.

The night of 9/11 Boy Scout found his own image.

The image called "The Falling Man."

It was an image taken just after nine in the morning, of a man jumping head first from the North Tower of the World Trade Center. The unknown man wasn't the first to fall or jump from the burning tower. Estimates say that as many as two hundred people leaped to their deaths instead of dying in the flames.

Again with the theme of fire.

Like his own burning sky, a vision he couldn't shake and could barely understand.

Boy Scout would later note that there were many images of the Falling Man, all taken by Associated Press photographer Richard Drew. They showed an unknown man tumbling and out of control, knowing he was going to die, struggling against his gravitational fate. But Drew chose a different image. He chose one he felt was more powerful, and it was forever imprinted on Boy Scout's psyche.

The Falling Man photo was one of a man diving head first, his legs slightly crossed and extended, much akin to Jesus on the cross, his hands behind him as if they were bound. There was no one else in the shot. The background was of the white surface of the World Trade Center. The image was as simple as it was stark—an image that when looked at couldn't be understood. At first the head wants to twist so that it can see the image right side up. Then the eyes go to the hands and wonder why they are at his sides. Then they notice the slightly crossed legs and, having seen a crucifix more than a thousand times, the person immediately makes the comparison.

The Falling Man.

9/11 Jesus.

He died for our sins.

The Falling Man was Boy Scout's forking path.

Either Boy Scout could acknowledge it and continue on his life arc to be a teacher, settling in some Midwestern town, marrying a girl he met at the grocery store, having two kids, a boy and a girl, going to soccer practice, and having weekend barbeques with friends... or he could join the army and become a United States Army Ranger, wearing the Falling Man on his soul as his fellow Rangers wore crosses or emblems of St. Michael on their chests.

He chose the Rangers.

Instead of being a teacher who taught English to white privileged kids, he became a leader of men and women, training them in better ways to kill, effective ways to survive, and how to set up anti-personnel mines in less than thirty seconds. He wasn't going to get married. He'd already decided that he wasn't about to bear the responsibility of bringing children into this fucked-up world. He'd gladly traded it to become the pointy end of the American spear, willingly allowing himself to be poked into the heart of whatever enemy was of concern at the time.

Never once did he forget about the Falling Man.

Or the Napalm Girl.

Or the Burning Monk.

Or the burning *daeva*.

They all stood for something that couldn't be ignored.

They all stood for something larger, grander than themselves.

He wasn't sure what that something was—and he'd

been chasing it ever since—but if he ever found out, he just might be fulfilled enough to stop.

Just maybe.

But until then, he was Boy Scout, former US Army Ranger, now leader of an operation support team deep in the northern Hindu Kush in Afghanistan, prepared to revenge the ass fucking a group of whirling dervishes had bestowed upon them only because the dervishes had figured out a way to fucking live forever. But first, before anything else, he had to save a friend.

He got up and dusted himself off.

Faood stood at the entrance to the cistern complex. As Boy Scout approached, he put his hand over his heart and bowed slightly.

Boy Scout returned the gesture.

"I wanted to apologize to you personally," Faood said. He looked down and shook his head with embarrassment. "Sufi practice is aimed at bringing about the cleansing and awakening of the heart. It was not meant to be a vehicle to find a way to live forever. I never should have allowed the others to... I never should have been part of this thing. It wasn't until recently that I discovered what was going on, and I'm still coming to terms with it." He paused, then said, "I'm from Istanbul, originally. Have you ever been?" Boy Scout shook his head.

"It's a glorious place with such a tapestry of history, it could tell the secrets of Byzantium. Istanbul sits at a crossroads of East and West—Islam and Christendom. The Bosporus strait both separates Europe from Asia and connects the Black Sea to the Sea of Amara and then the

Mediterranean." Faood grinned. "I can see you looking at me, wondering why is he suddenly talking like the Travel Channel."

Boy Scout grinned despite himself. "Something like that."

"Don't judge all Sufis as you judge us. A Sufi is a great worshipper. I came from Istanbul wanting to join the Mevlevi. We, they, strive to perfect the worship of Almighty Allah." He touched his breast and bowed. "We have a rich history, as rich as Istanbul's itself. Do you know that we originated with a pledge? We base our spiritualism on the *bayah*—a pledge of allegiance that was once given to the Prophet Muhammad. This pledge committed Muhammad's followers to the service of Allah. We believe that if we give our own *bayah* to a Sufi shaykh, we have a spiritual link to Muhammad, and then to Allah. They get our allegiance and in return we shall get a great reward."

Faood chuckled before he continued. "I know that the West has made great fun of our seventy-two virgins. I've read your jokes on Facebook. And yes, they are funny. But these virgins are but an aspect of the afterlife. They are one page of a million-page book. Don't you see? Allah has so much more to give. This is why our pledge is so much stronger. The idea was that we would live a life that shines glory onto Allah. Instead, my order has spent its time trying to get their reward before it is even bestowed.

"There are many different kinds of Sufi, just as there are many different nationalities in Istanbul. Tourists complain of headaches because of all the varying languages they hear and all the different people they see. If one isn't used to the place, it can become very confusing. I'm explaining this to you because having realized that what we are doing was wrong, I want you to understand that there are Sufi who believe differently."

"But it was Rumi who discovered you could travel," Boy Scout said.

"Travel to learn. Travel to discover. Not to be who we've become. We Sufi memorize thousands of Rumi sayings. He was truly marvelous with words. Want to know my favorite one? *Forget safety. Live where you fear to live. Destroy your reputation. Be notorious.*"

"Notorious," Boy Scout repeated. "That's a hell of a word. Is that what made you come around?" At Faood's confused expression, he added, "Change sides. Did you want to be notorious?"

"Many things I didn't like, but yes, this saying is central to who I am."

"Well, consider your reputation with Faral destroyed. There is a Faral, right?"

"Yes. He is one of our more militant leaders. He would have us fight jihad, but that's not who we are."

"I once wanted to be a teacher," Boy Scout said. "Then I became a killer. Think there's ever a time I could be a teacher again?"

"*Intellect takes you to the door, but it can't take you into the house,*" Faood recited.

"Was that Rumi again?"

"No. That was from Shams Tabrizi, Rumi's teacher."

Intellect can get you to the door, but it can't get you into the house. "So you say that what I do is necessary then?"

"Everything is necessary. Nothing is necessary. It depends on your design. Listen, these are merely sayings. We have thousands of them. Sayings can mean many things to different people. The meanings of sayings are not owned by those who say them."

"Then why offer me the saying to begin with?"

"Every word is a doorway. Every thought is an egress. Doors are everywhere. There is no shortage of doors. What's important is deciding which one to go through."

"Are you saying you can't go back?"

"Once you are who you are, you can't become someone who you were," Faood said. "Be who you are and become what you want to be."

"You know how that sounds, right?" Boy Scout asked.

Faood blinked and asked, "Like what?"

"You sound like a fortune cookie."

Faood grinned. "You mean I sound like the paper inside a fortune cookie. Ever wonder where that paper comes from?"

"A factory? A machine?"

"Ever wonder why that fortune comes to you?"

"It's random."

"Is it now?" Faood nodded. "Yet the fortune always seems to fit. Interesting." Then he put his hand on Boy Scout's shoulder. "Now go inside and prepare. We will travel shortly." Then he strode out and into the day.

"Where you going?" Boy Scout called after him.

"To pray."

Chapter Thirty-One

The Sefid

LORE HAD BEEN right all along. There wasn't any time travel. There was no such thing as moving sideways through time. It was all pure invention. With the help of these Mevlevi dervishes, each of the TST members had created part of the greater universal landscape of their reality within which to interact. The people, the buildings, the cars… the very air everyone breathed had been invented by the combined weight of the thoughts of the tactical support team. There was no Joon with her crippled son. There were no camels with Joe Arpaio's face on the side. Lore had never worn a tin foil jump suit. Boy Scout was never a fat, drugged-out loser. McQueen was never a bouncer at a gay bar. None of it had happened. That it seemed so real was a testament to the combined might of their brains' abilities to construct something so perfect and seamless.

Because they kept returning to the same time, their

reality took shortcuts and created the same characters with which to interact. This was why some characters were able to remember interactions with the TST's avatars while others didn't. But as strong as the construct was, the active minds of each member, their desires to come to terms with their environment, help others, and solve mysteries, caused ripples throughout the landscape, ripples that could send any of them into the *Sefid* at any moment. Which was why each of them were placed in unlikely positions, doing things they wouldn't ordinarily do, in the hopes that they wouldn't resort to their old selves, that they would become something new.

In Boy Scout's case, he was made to be the very opposite of what he was, playing out a short period of life, then restarting, over and over and over in a controlled loop. His interaction with Joon was normally the end, but there were a few times where he'd not done vile things to her—a very precious few—the memories of what he'd done now fresh in his mind and all in an attempt to tempt the *Sefid* to take him.

Which it had never done.

So it was now a particular irony that he wanted to go there of his own accord.

Faood stood in his *entari,* what Narco had teasingly called the whirling dervish dress. Not really a dress, the *entari* was a garment that covered the body from the top of the chest to the bottom of the ankles. It was wide at the bottom and basically a skirt, so when Faood spun, the fabric flared. He wore a *sikke* atop his head. The conical wool fez was form-fitted to his head and made him look a foot taller. He admitted he didn't have to wear the ensemble to travel through to the *Sefid*, but it helped him focus.

Boy Scout, on the other hand, was stripped to his underwear. He'd need to get in the pool. The water acted as a conduit for the *daeva*'s power. Proximity to the creature was important. But first, Faood needed to dance the variation of the *dhikr* that caused Boy Scout to shift reality. Once Boy Scout was slipstreaming, Faood would join him.

"I could just dance a few steps and put you in a fugue, like I did after Narco attacked, but this is more difficult. I need you to go very deep, so I'm going... how you say? Old school," Faood said.

Bully, Lore, McQueen, and Criminal were in the other room. Seeing his *dhikr* would have a deleterious effect on them, so it was reasoned that they could come out when it was over.

Boy Scout sat on one of the round stones, the water up to his chest. Narco sat slumped beside him, his face barely above the water.

Faood stood on shore.

"Unlike before, where we wanted you to think of yourself in Los Angeles, I want you to instead focus on the image of a burning sky."

"Burning, as in a *daeva*?" Boy Scout asked, glancing at the pulsating creature.

"Think bigger. Think... are you certain you want to do this? It might not work. I might lose you and not be able to find you."

Boy Scout waved his hand impatiently. "I'm going."

Faood licked his lips and nodded. "So imagine a burning sky. Think a hundred *daeva*. Imagine if the entire sky were burning."

"Is that it? Are the *daeva* the key to the *Sefid*?"

"They are the power source that allows us to do what we do. Master Rumi discovered it first, after trapping a *daeva* and experimenting. He also discovered that they are a gateway to the *Sefid*. We must go through their minds to get there."

"Through their minds?"

"Not literally, but it's the best explanation. Our consciousness will touch the consciousness of the *daeva* to allow us to enter the *Sefid*."

Boy Scout had become accustomed to being near the sleeping *daeva*, but only because it had never been awake. The idea of going into its mind was seriously disturbing.

"Just keep concentrating on the burning sky and I will guide you through. Also, never speak with anything. Even if it claims to know you, do not speak with it."

"What'll happen if I speak with it?"

"You don't want to know. Just don't speak."

"What about you? Shouldn't I speak to you?"

"Speak to no one. You won't even know who I am."

"How will I know not to speak? On each of our previous journeys, we weren't even aware that it wasn't real."

"This is different. Your frame of mind dictates what you remember and don't remember. Where before we concentrated on the process being secret, now it's completely out in the open. You're not going to Los Angeles. You're going to the *Sefid* with all of your faculties."

Boy Scout wasn't sure if he understood that last part, but he did have one final question. "You said you've done this before?"

Faood nodded.

"How many times?"

"Once."

"Did it work?"

Faood sighed. "You're the one who pressed to come along. You don't have to come. I can do this without you."

Boy Scout waved his right hand. "No, I understand. I just wanted to know what I was getting into." He paused. "Go ahead. Do the dance."

Faood nodded, then he flexed his arms and stretched his knees for a moment.

"But really," Boy Scout asked. "Did it work?"

Faood began to dance.

As always, Boy Scout's gaze went to the man's feet.

Faood spun slowly at first, then started to pick up speed. His arms were up and his head was cocked to the right, accentuated by the length of the fez. But his feet were the motor for it all. Staying in one place, Faood spun and spun, his feet, propelling him.

Boy Scout became mesmerized by the movement, trying to count the steps.

Then Boy Scout blinked and he was no longer in the cistern.

Wind whipped around him, sending him staggering. He looked down and saw that he was standing on a rough black surface, much like hard tar. He wore tennis shoes and was in gym sweats. His legs and lungs felt as if he'd just tossed off five miles. A gust of wind hit him again, and he went down on one knee. He looked out and saw that he was impossibly high up. He could see all of... where was he? All of New York laid out in front of him.

There up in Midtown rose the Empire State Building, made iconic back in the 1930s with King Kong gripping the needle while swatting at biplanes. Turning to his right, he took in the East River and the Brooklyn Bridge. He kept turning and saw Red Hook, then Governors Island, the Statue of Liberty, facing east and beckoning the world to come into her bosom. And finally, Ellis Island—that first place so many of his country's ancestors had stopped before they made America their home.

Where was he to see all this? Lower Manhattan, certainly. But the only building high enough to have this view would have been... one of the twin towers of the World Trade Center. He jerked his head around and saw the other building, right there. But that would be impossible. Both towers had been destroyed on September 11, 2001, when each had been hit by a plane.

Then came an explosion with a wave of sound so loud it was like heaven was scraped raw and screaming. He was thrown off his feet. He hit the roof hard and rolled as it undulated beneath him. He found himself bouncing from the middle toward the edge, closer and closer. He reached out, desperate to grab something... anything.

And then it stopped.

The screaming sky.

The building shaking itself to pieces.

He was almost back on his feet when the second explosion hit. Although mentally he knew this was the remainder of the fuel blowing from the remains of the first aircraft, it seemed as if another plane had hit right after the first. He flew into the air, straight up. The wind caught him, and like a giant hand smacked him back toward the center of the roof, then slammed him down.

The landing shot the air out of from his lungs. He lay gasping, not only to breathe, but because of his left shoulder. The bursa sac must have ruptured because of the sheer level of exquisite pain he was feeling. A wash of heat and fire suddenly enveloped the top of the roof. Had he not been pushed to the middle, Boy Scout would have become a smoking cinder.

He pushed his way to his feet using his right arm, which then cradled his left, helping to immobilize it to reduce the pain. He could look at his watch, but he didn't need to. He knew what time it was. It was 8:46 a.m. Flight 11, which had left Logan Airport in Boston and was bound for Los Angeles International Airport, had just struck the North Tower of the World Trade Center. Its eighty-one passengers and eleven crew members had perished instantly as the plane entered between the ninety-third and ninety-ninth floors.

As bad as his shoulder felt, his insides twisted at the unimaginable loss of life the world was about to experience. Boy Scout knew he wasn't really there. He was supposed to have gone to the *Sefid*, but he had somehow gotten off track, probably because he'd been recently thinking about the Falling Man. He had an hour and forty-two minutes to stay alive on the North Tower before it collapsed. But he only had seventeen minutes until Flight 175 crashed into the South Tower.

He'd been just finishing working out when the planes hit. He'd driven home oblivious to the events, instead listening to a CD of Pearl Jam's greatest hits and belting out the lyrics to "Jeremy." He'd just gotten out of the shower when his friend Dave Conrad called him and told him to turn on the television. Boy Scout had asked what channel, but Dave had said, *Any of them.* And he'd been right. Even MTV was covering the event.

But now he was here, reliving it.

But to what end?

He stood as close to the edge as he could with the powerful winds and waited.

At 9:02 a.m he saw Flight 175 coming as inexorably as a wave.

At 9:03 he watched in stunned silence as the plane hit the South Tower farther down than the one that hit the North Tower. The explosion was tremendous and parts of the plane flew to the north and east.

A hot wind blew, drying his tears.

He wasn't about to stand here and watch another three thousand murders. He wasn't about to go down with the tower. He screamed, then took off running. He hit the edge at full speed and propelled himself outward. For one brief second, he was weightless. Then gravity yanked him hard. He was falling, tumbling—his view of the ground, then the building, then the plane, then the sky, then the ground. The plaza was beneath him. He could see people looking up at him and pointing. Now at a hundred and twenty-two miles an hour, he couldn't do anything but strike the earth, just as the planes had struck the towers. Right before he hit, he saw a young blond-haired boy, much the same as he had been as a child, standing and holding his mother's hand, a thumb in his mouth, tears in his eyes, watching him. In the boy's eyes, he saw the reflection of the sky—a sky on fire, a burning sky—and the boy and the city and the country and the world would never be the same again.

Then the universe slammed into him.

A brief instance of pain was replaced by nothing.

Sweet nothing. No 9/11. No ruined shoulder. No body. Just. Plain. Nothing. And it was all white.

There was so much white that there was no up. No down. No sideways. Just white. He might as well have been floating in a snowflake. There was nothing to be seen. He held out a hand but there was nothing there. He held out his other. Still nothing. He reached for his face, but there was no reaching and no face. He was an *essence*. And as much as it should matter to him, it didn't. He embraced the white, the nothing that surrounded him. It was a relief from the visage of the boy and the burning sky and the soon-to-collapse buildings, each one a dagger in the innocence of a world where such things only happened in horror books or the very darkest dystopian science fiction novels.

Welcome to the Sefid, he said to himself.

Chapter Thirty-Two

TIME PASSED, OR at least he thought it did. He had zero points of reference. There was no up. There was no down. He couldn't move. He couldn't see anything but white. It was as if he'd ceased to exist, but hadn't really. His thoughts went to one of his sophomore reading assignments: *Johnny Got His Gun*. By the title, he'd thought that the teacher had assigned the class an action book, but it was far from that. Boy Scout learned that Dalton Trumbo, the author, hated war of all types. The book was an anti-war book—a testament to what could happen to an American native son. The main character had been severely wounded in World War I. He'd lost his arms and legs. He also lost his mouth, ears, nose and eyes. All he had was his sense of touch—which was more than Boy Scout currently had. He remembered obsessing about the book, wondering and desperate to know how it felt to be Joe Bonham, the main character. Even now, he could see their parallels, as both Joe and now Boy Scout meandered from reality to remembrance and back, sometimes blurring the lines between.

Back then, Boy Scout had been captivated by the idea of a complete loss of self. He'd even tried to get a graduate assistant in the psych department to let him use a sensory deprivation tank, to no avail. Ultimately he'd moved on, but the idea of Joe had stayed with him. Even as he rode convoys along the Highway of Death he'd thought about what might happen if his truck hit an IED and he ended up like Joe.

And now he was here.

The *Sefid*.

He tried to look around, hoping to see darkness mar the white, but it was impenetrable.

Was he stuck here forever?

Had he done something wrong?

Had his side trip to the Twin Towers thrown him off course?

Then it came to him. Maybe the mode of propulsion in this colorless universe was by thought.

So he thought about moving forward.

Then he thought about moving backward.

Then he stopped thinking altogether. Even if it was working, he had no reference for movement, nothing to mark his passage. In the event he was already in the right place, he didn't want to travel too far away, to risk being lost forever.

His last thought reminded him of Lore, the story she'd told him. It was the formative event that had caused her to be the hard-nosed, intelligent, incredibly competent woman she was today.

She'd been eight years old and her family had gone on

vacation to Franklin, North Carolina. They were staying in a cabin high in the Smokey Mountains. Everything was fine the first night. She and her younger brother got along, but her father had been pining from being away from the pulpit for a full week. Her mother had arranged the outing so that none of them would be near the usual technology—no Internet. No cell phone service. Just the woods, the mountains, and family.

Then the next morning they awoke and little Laurie May wasn't there.

As it turned out, she'd gotten tired of the cabin and had decided to go home. Never mind that it was more than two hundred miles away. Never mind that there was a fresh foot and a half of snow on the ground. She was as determined as her mother and as competent as her father, so she set out on foot. Three hours later they found her, huddled beneath a tree and hypothermic. The tracks in the fresh snow had led them right to her.

Later, she told them that she'd gotten lost and had tried to go back to the cabin, but the darkness and the cold had been too much. After they returned home—vacation cut short—she was determined to learn all she could about the outdoors and how to survive it. Her mother said she should join the Girl Scouts, but Lore would have none of that. As far as she was concerned, even at the age of eight, the Girl Scouts were nothing more than a cookie delivery service. What she wanted was more like the Cub Scouts, and then the Boy Scouts when she got older. While girl's organizations concentrated on family values and community, the boy's clubs worked on small outdoor projects and even went camping. It wasn't long before she discovered that her gender stood as a prohibition for such a thing.

Then she discovered Outward Bound.

Although the program had been designed for struggling teens, she found the outdoor curriculum exactly what she was looking for. She fought with her parents for the chance to go and by the time she turned nine, they finally relented. So for the next eight years, she spent all of her money making certain she could go on at least two Outward Bound events a year—backpacking, canyoneering, canoeing, dog sledding, mountaineering, whitewater rafting, rock climbing, sailing, sea kayaking, skiing, and snowboarding. By the time she was eighteen and ready for college, she received scholarships from dozens of universities because her applications glowed with her outdoor accomplishments and how she'd eventually become an instructor who had positively impacted lives.

The next great adventure club was the military, which she gained by going to ROTC in college and being commissioned in the US Army Reserves at graduation. But instead of staying in the reserves, she'd found a way to immediately go active duty, offering her services as an intelligence officer to special mission units, which assured her that she'd see operational action, if not combat.

All because she'd gotten mad at herself for getting lost in the Smokey Mountain wilderness. To this day she had a tremendous fear of getting lost and always compensated by being the most prepared.

If only Boy Scout had her with him now. He was certain

she'd know what to do.

A sound crept into his consciousness. Creaking. Repetitive creaking. He spun, or at least tried to, then he saw it. A stark black dot on the horizon, growing larger. The creaking became louder. Closer and closer. He felt intense, almost gleeful excitement at seeing something, *anything*. McQueen had run from what had come at him, but all Boy Scout wanted to do was embrace it.

When he finally recognized what it was, his brain misfired. He tried to wrap his thoughts around the image that was appearing before him. How could it get to the *Sefid*? How could this even be here? He'd thought he'd taken care of everything, giving him to the woman at the Afghan Hands program. Hadn't she taken care of the boy? Or had she maybe been forced to give him back? But then to who?

His glee had been replaced with an anchor of dread. He wanted nothing more than to run like McQueen had done, only he didn't know how.

Boy Scout tried to close his eyes, but with no body, that was impossible.

A vast pit of desperation opened inside him as he watched the wheelchair holding the paraplegic shy boy roll up to him. The features of the boy's face were demonic but recognizable. He offered Boy Scout an ugly sneer.

"You left me," he said, his voice like nails on a chalkboard. "You left me and it happened again." New scars had been carved into the boy's face. Several looked like Arabic script. Boy Scout couldn't help but wonder what they said. Then he saw the boy's arms. Round, puckered red and black circles covered every inch of his arms as if an angry octopus had grabbed him. But it was nothing an octopus had done. Boy Scout immediately recognized it and was sickened. Someone had taken an old-fashioned automobile lighter and branded the boy's skin, over and over. Although the boy had never felt it, he could smell the burning skin and hair. Boy Scout wanted to scream.

He was about to speak when he remembered Faood's warning not to.

"The new one," the boy hissed. "The new commander did to me what the other did... what all the others did."

Boy Scout found that unbelievable. The person he'd given the boy to would never have allowed such a thing. Renee was above reproach.

"The things he did to me... shall I itemize them for you?"

Boy Scout wanted to shriek at the universe for it to stop. All he'd wanted to do was save the child from the sexual abuse. What was that old Chinese saying? If you save someone's life, you're responsible for them forever. Could it be true?

"I'm being kept in a closet now. I haven't seen light for months. I'm only fed if I perform." The boy sneered again, then barked out a hollow laugh. "And it's all your fault."

Joon's voice intruded and whispered, "Ever wonder if you're a character in the wrong story?"

Then Boy Scout understood completely. Either he was in an altered parallel universe, or this wasn't his story. First of all, why was the boy speaking English? He'd never been able to before. Secondly, and he couldn't believe that he was now just noticing this, but what was the method of the boy's propulsion? He hadn't the ability to move himself. He'd need a wheelchair like Freddie's—one with a joystick for the mouth. Boy Scout wanted urgently to speak to the phantom and tell it that he knew it wasn't real, but he'd been forbidden to. And it was like the thing knew that, because one moment it was there sneering at him, and the next it was gone.

This time Boy Scout was thankful he was alone. He'd spend a lifetime in *Sefid* if it meant that he could remain free of the specter of the child. Christ on a pogo stick, how had that image appeared? Boy Scout tried to remember what it was about the *Sefid*, but most of what Faood had said was gone. Was it a construct like before? Could he just decide to leave? If so, then he— no. He had to think about Narco. Boy Scout had forced his way into the mission even though Faood could have probably taken care of it without him. Boy Scout would find a way to see it through.

If this was a construct, then whatever damage was done to him inside the *Sefid* wouldn't stay with him. The visit from the specter of the boy had been unnaturally terrifying for several reasons. One, he wasn't accustomed to not having a body. Two, coming so suddenly after his arrival, the specter had caught him before he could prepare himself. And three, he'd secretly been wondering about the kid's fate and was worried that he might have ended up being a shy boy again, so the words of the boy carried much more gravitas than they would have.

So what was the specter? It wasn't something he'd

created and Faood had no idea about the boy, so it couldn't have been him. The only one he'd confided to about the colonel and the shy boy was McQueen, and his old friend would never mention it to anyone. Boy Scout doubted that it was something his own mind had invented. To what end? There was no value other than for someone to see how terrified they could make him.

Was that it? Was something messing with him? Was it the *daeva*? Faood had mentioned that the fugue was powered by the supernatural being. Somehow Boy Scout understood that the *Sefid* was different from a regular fugue. It was certainly more dangerous, but how much so? Faood had said that they'd have to go through the *daeva*'s mind to get to the *Sefid*. Maybe that was the issue. Maybe he was still in the sleeping creature's mind.

Ever wonder if you're a character in the wrong story?

Maybe he was in the *daeva*'s dream... or maybe he was part of its nightmare.

A darkness once more marred the horizon. Boy Scout steadied himself. He knew something was coming, and he hadn't the ability to stop it. It came to him with a low thrum of power. Another wheelchair, but this one powered by Freddie. Even as he steered it toward Boy Scout, the boy had his eyes on him. Freddie still sat in a low-slung wheel chair, the kind you steered with your mouth. His legs ended at nubs where his knees had been. His arms ended where his elbows should have been.

This was different. Freddie wasn't real. He never had been. He'd been constructed by the shared minds of the TST while in a fugue state. So how could he appear here unless someone or something had access to Boy Scout's brain?

The boy stopped his chair in front of Boy Scout. He leaned his head back and appraised Boy Scout. Then the boy frowned slightly and asked in a commanding voice, "Are you notorious?"

Chapter Thirty-Three

Forget safety. Live where you fear to live. Destroy your reputation. Be notorious.

Was he notorious? Had he gone to a place where he might die? Was he afraid? He could answer yes to both of those questions, so yeah. He was notorious. He nodded his head, or at least he thought he did.

"I thought as much. You have the look." Freddie grinned. "Notorious. I'd like to have a conversation with you, about your world."

Since the silent form of communication had worked before, he used it again, only this time shaking his head.

Freddie nodded. "I agree that it's prudent not to talk to the minions of *Sefid*. Many of them are beyond dangerous. But not me." He paused to see if Boy Scout had changed his mind, then continued. "Let me explain to you what it is. This is like a heaven and hell combined. It is a place with no limits and as large as the universe, but it doesn't exist in a dimension which contains our science. You, no doubt, are near a *daeva* and have passed through its mind. This is the normal way of it. Nothing difficult. Did it tax you a memory? Did you replay an important event in your life?"

Boy Scout nodded.

"It always does. Even sleeping, their curiosity cannot be sated. Not to worry. There was no damage done to your memories. It just wanted to know... to experience. I've been studying them from the inside out. Studying *Sefid*. This is the place they go when they die. Did you know that the *daeva* are older than humanity?"

Boy Scout shook his head.

"They are. I've yet to determine how far back they predate us, but I have my hypothesis. They were once everywhere, touching every culture, influencing every tradition. The term devil comes from *daeva*, but I'm sure you knew that already. The Zoastrians called them false gods. In the oldest texts, they were called *those who shouldn't be worshiped*. I find that interesting. The *daeva* are clearly supernatural. They are clearly superhuman. Why wouldn't one want to worship such a thing?

"As humans we rush to worship ideas. We sprint at rumor, praying to it, idolizing it. But to not want to worship something that's clearly worthy makes one wonder if there was a valid reason. Luckily, one doesn't have to look far for that reason. It's simple, really, if you pay attention to the tenets of Zoastrianism. If Ahura created the universe, then how would you explain the *daeva* who were already there? How could something be present before the creation of the universe? Who created *them*? Worship is about connection. Religion is about control. Zoaster decided to not worship them in order to control his followers." Freddie shook his head like he had the weight of the world on it. "The world could do without religion for a while."

Boy Scout had been noticing clues in Freddie's monologue and was beginning to get an idea about who he really was, but he still wasn't willing to talk. It could also be an entity of some sort trying to trick him into believing something else.

"Still, it's an interesting problem that the Zoastrians had with the *daeva* already present, don't you think? Are you a follower of Manes?"

Boy Scout shook his head.

"Zoastrainism is based on cosmogenic duality. Manes described dualistic cosmology as good and evil or light and dark. Dualism. Two things." Suddenly hands appeared on Freddie's congenitally amputated arms. He flexed his fingers and the movement shocked Boy Scout. "Sorry. I was tired of him not being able to move. Where was I? Ah, yes." He opened one hand. "Light." He opened the other hand. "Dark. Not bad, but a little simple. Think of Christianity as a monotheistic cosmological religion. They have a single god as part of their origin story. The Zoastrians have it both ways. They have Ahura Mazda, who created everything. Think of him creating the void. Then he had two sons." Freddie grinned. "Must have been mitosis because there wasn't a Mrs. Mazda. One son was named Spenta Mainyu, who chose truth, light and life. The other was named Angra Mainyu, who preferred deceit, darkness and death. Sound familiar?"

It did, but Boy Scout wasn't going to say anything.

"But Christianity is not only monotheistic. It also has a dual cosmological tenet. God made the universe so he made angels, right? Therefore Satan was of his making, as was Jesus. Dark and light." Once again Freddie's hands opened and closed. Then his eyes brightened. "Or maybe God didn't create angels. Maybe the angels were already here, just like Zoastrianism, the mother religion of Christianity, Judaism, and Islam." Freddie sighed. "Even science has trouble grasping the main problem with cosmology. After all, there is no theoretical model that explains the earliest moments of the universe's existence. Was time created at the moment the universe was created? Or did time exist before the universe? If it did, then other things existed before the universe. Maybe the Big Bang wasn't an explosion, but a bullet shot out of a rifle. The question we should be asking ourselves is who fired the rifle?" Freddie frowned and crossed his arms. "Come now, this is getting boring. I was looking for conversation. I can't converse with my dervishes. All they want is to worship, which defeats my purpose. Also, I could have chosen any form I wanted. Know why I chose this form? Because you made it. This was all you. This form was created as an apology for that poor boy you saved, and this form would be the last one capable of doing you harm."

They stared at each other for several moments while Boy Scout worked through his own arguments. Finally, he did what any ex-Ranger would have when they didn't know what to do next. He said *fuck it* and prepared to wing it.

"I know who you are," Boy Scout said, glad to end his silence.

"I hope so. I left enough clues."

"Or at least I know who you claim to be."

Freddie waved a hand. "Whatever. I don't bite and never have. So back to my question."

Boy Scout thought for a moment. "Who fired the rifle?"

"Exactly. Who was it?"

Boy Scout thought once more. "The *daeva?*"

Freddie's face brightened as a smile lit it up. "Excellent answer. Alas, I don't think it was the *daeva*. I think they are the bullets. Whoever fired them are from the place that was before. They've always been here. They were here before any religion, before man, and have been a footnote that couldn't be explained since the invention of the written word. Sure, many have tried, but the fact remains, someone had to fire the rifle."

"Do you know who it was?"

"I can hear their echoes. I can see their writing on the sand of my dreams. I can even parse the memories of the sleeping *daeva* who remember a different place—a place with more dimensions, where they were many and moved quite differently than they do today."

"Perhaps the explosion that created our universe destroyed theirs," Boy Scout said. Then something Faood had said led him to another leap in thought. "Maybe they were seeded in our universe as muses. Shepherds, perhaps. Something to ensure that a fish would once gain legs so it could become a man who could hold his own rifle."

Freddie clapped his hands. "When the soul lies down in

the grass, the world is too full to talk about. Yes, yes, yes. Keep questioning. Keep seeking possibilities."

"But to what end? Will it save my friend? Will it get us out of here?"

"And he returns to the logic of a soldier. But that's fine. For one bright second you were a seeker of answers, even if you didn't know the right questions. Not knowing the question should never be an obstacle."

"Listen, Rumi. I said this to Faood, but you have a way of sounding like a fortune cookie."

"I see you know me. Call me Jalāl."

"You know they're looking for you, right?"

"I'm aware of that. I occasionally make myself known."

"Are you also aware that they are bringing things out of the *Sefid*? Beings or pieces of beings that are enabling your dervishes to live forever? That this has become their primary mission rather than the search for knowledge?"

"I am aware."

"You don't seem concerned."

"Through their action comes a greater chance at knowledge."

"Did you know that they've been tricking people, enslaving them, like us, to go and find these creatures for them?"

"The many minions of the *Sefid* are aware of my dervishes. They know them and stay away from them. Having fresh searchers is necessary."

Boy Scout could feel his ire rising. "So you know. And you condone this?"

"What are you but a leaf on a tree that will one day

fall? Does the leaf not want to be a tree? For to be a tree it must have a different existence."

"Enough of the fortune cookie nonsense."

Jalal spread his hands. "Your nonsense is someone else's understanding. Look at your world. It's one that I foresaw hundreds of years ago. Wars everywhere. A third of the world is in famine. Gone is your sense of community as people seek those like themselves through electronic means. There was a time when community had a norming effect on society, bringing those with different views together, making them come together, live together. But no longer." Jalāl suddenly seemed to have grown feet. He got out of the wheelchair and, further shocking Boy Scout, put his hands behind his back, pacing back and forth. In the whiteness, it appeared as if he were walking in mid-air. "Again. Sorry to change your construct. It was just so… limiting." Then he stopped pacing and turned to Boy Scout. "You're not insulted, are you?"

Boy Scout found his voice after a moment. "No. I'm not insulted."

"You know you can do this, too? Will yourself into existence."

"What do you see when you see me?" Boy Scout asked.

"Your essence. Like an apparition of you, but barely there. A mirage of what could be if you only were to put in a little effort."

Boy Scout concentrated on bringing his hands into existence, and it was easier than he thought. One second there was nothing, then his arms appeared. Then he willed the rest of his body into existence. Had he known it was this easy, he would have done it long ago. Suddenly, he was flexing his hands and arms. He knew they weren't really there, but they felt real and in that feeling, he became more grounded. He didn't feel as defenseless as he was.

"Thank you," Boy Scout said. Then, eager to return to something that Jalāl had said earlier, Boy Scout said, "I don't believe in the idea that one must break a few eggs to bake a cake. Those eggs are lives. They belong to someone. They are not your eggs to break. They are not your lives to take."

Jalāl stared at Boy Scout, then nodded and resumed his pacing. "Of course you're right. It is good that we have met. I've been disconnected for too long. But let me ask you this, if you knew that your sacrifice could potentially stop all wars and remove all famine, would you do it?"

"Well, yes. Of course."

"What if I knew that your sacrifice could potentially stop all wars and remove famine. Could I then sacrifice you?"

"Well, no. That's different."

"How is this different?"

"Choice. I should have the right to choose my own fate."

"Why is that? Do you have all the information I have at my disposal?"

"No."

"Then how can you make an informed decision? Are you arguing that an uninformed decision has equal weight against an informed decision?"

"No, but don't we have an inalienable right over our own bodies?"

"Even if your right to choose, your inalienable right,

causes the deaths of hundreds... thousands... millions?"

"But how can you be so sure?"

"What I know about the *daeva* is growing. They are the gateway to opening up our universe to something new. Science is working from their end, dark matter, string theory—"

"How do you know all this? I thought you've been in the *Sefid* for more than seven hundred years."

"I have. But there are other travelers such as yourself. I have a way of tying into the sleeping *daeva*. There are also accidental travelers. I learn from them. You noted that I knew how to use this form. Did you ever wonder how I knew? When you were passing through the mind of the *daeva*, I learned what you know. I saw what you've seen. This is my way of learning."

Jalāl paused to see if his words had sunk in, then continued. "As I said, science is working from its end. I'm working from this end. I feel close to being able to discover who fired the rifle. If I can do that, then the universe will open for all of us."

"And it all depends on the *daeva*. You need to keep them alive. Did you really gather them into a valley?"

Jalāl nodded. "Many of them, but not all."

"But you did it to protect them, not to protect humanity."

"This is also true."

Suddenly the *Sefid* was rocked by a shriek so blood-curdling that Boy Scout felt himself blown into a million pieces.

Chapter Thirty-Four

SOMETIMES CRAZY DOESN'T happen incrementally. Sometimes it's full on whacked out all at once. Boy Scout was nowhere and everywhere. He couldn't think. He couldn't see anything except a kaleidoscope of spinning shades of white, dizzying, sickening. His essence had broken into so many parts that he couldn't even form a sentence. Unintelligible jabberings filled his mind. Were these his own thoughts? Or was it from something else?

The spinning was beginning to slow. His mind was coming back together. He could see pieces of himself forming as if he'd been a porcelain doll and his parts were flying back together of their own volition.

A hand.

A forearm

A booted foot.

The mating call of a monkey came from behind him.

He spun, and in his dizziness, fell to the ground. Only there was no ground. He was now upside down in front of the nightmare creature running towards him. In the split second he took to take it in, he saw a giant spider with more than a hundred legs coming toward him. Instead of central eyes, it had a face that was constantly changing into everyone he'd ever known.

Again came that sound, emanating from the lips of his mother's best friend, Rebecca. Then from the mouth of his drill sergeant, Sergeant First Class Reddoor. Then from the mouth of a girl he'd dated three years ago, Connie. The same sound, but different faces.

The monstrous entity was closing in.

More pieces of him were coming together but he wouldn't be whole by the time it arrived.

Boy Scout willed himself to flee, then found himself moving backwards at impossible speed.

Again the universe shrieked like the scream of the King of all Kings and he was once more blown apart.

The dizzying kaleidoscope returned, and after a time of sickness, piece by piece he came together once more.

The mating call of a monkey came once again but this time much softer. Then another and another. There seemed to be dozens of monkeys. Then he saw them. The spider creature had blown to bits as well, but instead of reforming into a whole, it was now hundreds of smaller spiders, all rushing toward him. He'd barely started to reform when three of them crawled up his essence. He batted at them, but he only had a single hand. He struck one and it flew off, shattering into even smaller spider monsters that came back at him. One got onto his back and he tried to reach for it. That was the moment when one skittered onto his face and climbed down his throat.

He gagged, trying to rid himself of it. He could feel its greasy spider legs pulling itself deeper inside of him.

Then another spider entered his mouth, following the first.

He fell to his knees, back arching in dry heaves, trying to spew them from his system. But it was to no avail. They held to his insides, going deeper, clawing at his insides for purchase. Then everything switched. Gone was the pure white of *Sefid*. Boy Scout felt himself slow and his body become someone else's... something else. Something ancient.

Visions—no, memories—began to spin by.

A family chased by a saber-toothed tiger on a flat brown plain. The tiger took down the girl child, ripping into her bowels.

A man on horseback, firing an arrow directly into Boy Scout's point of view, then disintegrating as a ray of white-hot energy was returned.

Alexander the Great's Macedonian phalanx—15,000 Macedonians with sarissas holding off the Persian swords and allowing the phalanx to mow through enemy units.

The Sacred Band of Thebes—he recognized it right away from the point of view of a warrior battling through them.

Sensual sex with an Indian woman of incredible beauty, her lips the color of brown sugar and tasting of mangoes.

An up-close view of a knife fight with another man, his own hands a blur of razor-edged steel, then still as they stopped in his opponent's chest.

And fire in the sky, burning incredibly bright, but feeling joyous at the sight of it.

Then he was ripped free into a moment of pure chaos,

the cacophony deafening.

Machine gun rounds echoed so loud he wanted to cover his ears, but without two hands, how was that possible? He felt roughness against his back. A figure knelt beside him, firing controlled, two round bursts. McQueen! And at that moment he knew he was out of the *Sefid* and back in real time.

"The rounds aren't doing any good!" Bully yelled.

"Then why is it bleeding in two places?" Criminal asked, punctuating his words with firepower.

"Careful not to hit Lore!" McQueen commanded.

Boy Scout struggled to sit up.

Narco was still in the water, but now the *daeva*'s right hand was around his friend's neck.

Faood lay halfway out of the water.

Boy Scout couldn't tell if he was alive or dead.

The *daeva* was awake. Gold light showed from its eyes. Its other hand jerked on the chain that held it, causing pieces of the roof to fall. Already rays of sunlight shot into the cistern, piercing the water, hitting the sand of the bank. No longer did the *daeva* have a dark blue aura. Its skin was now a deep blue, the color of space between the stars. Its mouth remained closed, which Boy Scout appreciated. He could not imagine what fangs or forked tongues could emanate from such a demonic opening and was eager not to discover them.

Then he saw Lore. She had a six-foot metal rod in her arms and was bringing it down, over and over, on the *daeva*'s wrist that held Narco by the neck, but to no avail. The creature was still strangling him.

Boy Scout immediately knew what to do. It was as if his time in the *Sefid* had given him a clarity he hadn't had before. He surged to his feet, falling in the water once before he managed it, then called for a cease-fire.

McQueen stood beside him, but Bully and Criminal continued to fire in controlled bursts. It was obvious that the rounds weren't doing any damage. What was also obvious was that the demon had somehow become wounded.

"Cease fire! You're just wasting ammunition."

Bully and Criminal finally lowered their rifles, but it was clear from their reactions that it was with the utmost reluctance.

"Lore, stop!"

"I... can't... stop... because... it's... choking... Narco!" she said, hitting it after every word.

"Lore, it's not working! Remember what you told me about the light. Remember what you said." He took a deep breath. "You are the girl with the goat. You were meant to save us all along!"

She paused in mid swing and gazed at Boy Scout, her head half cocked.

"What's that?" Criminal asked, pointing to the *daeva*.

Its throat was glowing the same gold color as its eyes. The glow was gaining in intensity, until it seemed as if the creature's neck would burn away. Then it opened its mouth, releasing a bolt of energy that shot across the cistern and hit Criminal squarely in the chest. His entire thorax burned away, dripping flesh and fire, leaving nothing but smoking sinew and bone to hold his arms to his shoulders. For a bright shining moment, his face was alit with wonder, his eyes wide, then he fell hard to the ground in pieces.

"Lore, listen and remember—*The wound is the place where the light enters you*. Do you remember?"

He could tell she remembered but she didn't understand.

"Oh my God," Bully cried. "It's going to do it again."

Another bolt of energy was building in its throat.

"Lore, the light. The reflection!"

"What about it?" she screamed.

"Stab the reflection!"

Then all at once her eyes widened. She adjusted her grip, stared into the water, and thrust her rod into where the light from the broken roof met the reflection of the *daeva*.

The *daeva's* mouth shot open to release a scream and a half-formed bolt of energy surged through the roof, collapsing a section, pieces of solid and molten rock splashing into the water.

Bully dove out of the way, barely missing being crushed by a huge block of stone that hit the sandy bank and tumbled into the water.

For one brief instant, Boy Scout saw the end of the metal rod coming out of the creature's chest, then it was gone... replaced by another one as Lore stabbed the water again.

The *daeva* roared and roared.

But with each strike it got a little weaker, until finally it could cry no more.

The light went out of its eyes.

Its body sagged, including the hand that was still around Narco's throat, pushing him under the water to drown.

Boy Scout and McQueen dove in. They helped Narco

out of the water and pried the dead hand of the demon away from his neck.

Narco coughed, water spilling from his lips.

Boy Scout dragged him onto shore and lightly smacked Narco's cheeks. Would Narco come back as himself or would he still in the grip of the entity?

Finally, Narco reached up and grabbed Boy Scout's wrist. He opened his eyes and said, "Will you please stop hitting me?"

At that moment, Boy Scout knew that his friend was back.

Faood was just getting to his feet. He came over a knelt beside them. His eyes were glazed from just coming out of the fugue. "You killed it," he said, with more than a little awe.

Boy Scout snorted. "You think that's awesome. Guess what? I saw Rumi." Then seeing the confusion on Faood's face, he added, "And he says to fuck off."

Chapter Thirty-Five

The Cistern

"Listen, I don't have time for your lies," Boy Scout said. "One of my men is dead and I'm trying to help the other one you used as fucking bait for some ancient entity."

"You're going to have to make time. The death of the *daeva* caused reverberations in the *Sefid*. The others are going to know. They're going to come investigate."

"I thought all of the *daeva* were locked up in a valley."

"Not all of them."

Boy Scout remembered Rumi saying the same thing. He lurched to his feet. He grabbed Faood's collar and was about to scream at him when he realized he was flying through the air. He hit the ground hard. Sand and grit scraped against his bare skin, but he ignored it as he used the momentum of the throw to roll back to his feet.

Boy Scout managed to balance before falling over. He held his fists out in front of him and moved his fingers for Faood to approach. "Oh, you want to play a little Dervish Fu."

Faood stood unmoving, hands at his sides. "I do not want to fight you."

But Boy Scout wanted nothing more than to fight. His man, the man he was supposed to have protected, was dead. He died because Boy Scout had believed a grand lie, letting his worship of responsibility govern his common sense. To think that if he'd just dismissed the dervish's assertions in the beginning that his man would still be alive and they wouldn't have spent the last seven months sitting in their own filth in a Third World cistern.

He swung a left hook and Faood leaped easily out of the way.

Boy Scout pressed, rushing forward, he feinted a punch, then lashed out a kick that caught Faood on the side of his knee.

The dervish went down, grabbing at the joint.

"Boy Scout!" McQueen shouted.

Boy Scout wanted nothing more than to get into an old-fashioned knuckle-busting fight. He needed some easy Ranger Revenge and his target was right in front of him. His hair-triggered fury only needed a nudge to go nuclear, but when he saw McQueen and Lore in his peripheral vision, their eyes wide, their mouths open, he knew he wasn't in the right. Now wasn't the time to get angry. They needed to prepare. They needed to deal with Narco. They needed to bury a friend. There was just too much to be done to get into a proper fight.

He let his fists fall to his side. Chest heaving with exertion and the emotion of the moment, he said, "I'm just so damned sick and tired of all the lies." He glanced to where Criminal lay. "I don't want to fight either. It's just... Criminal... fuck."

His eyes burned with tears.

McQueen put his arms around him and Boy Scout sobbed into his neck. For a single moment he was a child again and the world was completely out of hand, then he manned up. He pushed away from his friend, then savagely wiped at his eyes. He noted that the others had been crying as well.

Faood still lay on the ground.

"I'm sorry," Boy Scout said, and reaching down, he helped the dervish to his feet. "You've already shown you're willing to help us. You apologized. It was just the knowledge that even your glorious leader didn't mind the others using us for their own gains. He called me a leaf or something that wanted to be a new tree."

"What are you talking about?" Lore asked, wiping away tears.

"Rumi. I met him. Nice fella, if you can get past the fact that he has no problem using us as bait for arcane pre-Zoroastrian entities."

Lore's jaw about dropped to the floor. "You met Rumi?"

"He sought me out. Wanted to chat. McQueen, do an inventory on all our weapons and lay them out here. Bully? Good. I see you're helping Narco. Continue to do so. Lore, talk with Faood. Find out what we'll be facing so we can make up a plan."

"What are you going to do?" she asked.

He turned to stare at her and those who remained. He still felt the urge to fight, but not with his own people.

He knew it was just displaced rage. He swallowed back an initial response, then finally said, "I'm going to bury Criminal." Then he went to his bunk, put his clothes back on, grabbed a blanket from his bed, and rolled Criminal in it.

Narco came to his side. "Here, let me help."

Boy Scout eyed the man. "Are you sure you're okay?"

"Felt like I was rode hard and put away wet. Physically I'm fine." He tapped his head. "Brain's a little spongy, though."

Outside the day was beginning to wane. The sun was low in the sky and already the heat was fleeing, leaving in its wake a bone-chilling cold. Boy Scout retrieved a shovel from the back of one of the Land Cruisers. He found a clearing a hundred feet away, then began to dig. The soil was rocky, but loose.

"How are you really, Narco?"

After a moment, "Angry."

Boy Scout thought about this as he kept digging.

"Ever been in jail, Boy Scout?" Narco asked.

"Got locked up once in Tijuana for trying to steal a mule," he answered. "But they let us out the next morning after we paid a fine."

"You're going to have to tell me that story later," Narco said. "How did it feel to be locked up?"

"Don't really know. We were too drunk to care. Passed out on the floor."

"You're definitely going to have to tell me the story. Promise?"

"Sure."

Boy Scout struck something with the edge of the shovel.

He pushed enough sand away to see that it was a femur. He worked his blade in some more and scraped it against ribs. Someone else had been buried here.

He shoveled the earth back into the hole, moved over a few feet, then dug again.

"I've been locked up a bunch of times, as you know." Narco shoved his hands into his pockets and stared at the ground. "Being locked up has its own freedoms. You don't have to make your own decisions. You don't have any real responsibilities. You know where all your meals are coming from. It's nice, really, if you don't discount that you can't just up and leave. I mean, unless you're talking about a SuperMax, life in our prisons is better than life in about half the world." He shook his head. "That's saying something, I'm sure, but I don't know what."

Boy Scout cursed when he found another body. He refilled this hole, then moved until he found more tightly packed earth.

"Makes you wonder how many are out here," Narco said.

"Figure they've been doing this for hundreds of years," Boy Scout said. "I figure it takes about a year to die, eating their gruel, living in a constant fugue state. You can do the math if you want to."

Neither man spoke for the next few minutes. Boy Scout concentrated on digging. When he got down three feet, the going became easier. He was just waiting to discover yet another body.

"Jail is one thing," resumed Narco, "but the prison I was in was something else. I knew everything that was happening. I strangled that old man. I walked up to him, punched him in the face, climbed onto his chest, strangled the life out of him, then sucked down his soul."

"He was seven hundred years old."

"He... what? Seven hundred? Ah. He had one of those things in him."

"What'd it feel like?"

"I didn't leave the fugue right away. I was in a place of pure light. Like the sky was burning all around and I couldn't see."

"Faood called it *Sefid*. It means white in Persian."

"Yeah, white like it invented white. Then came the spiders."

Boy Scout paused in mid-shovel. "What was that you said?"

"Spiders. I couldn't run from them. One went down my throat. Then I awoke from the fugue."

Narco kept talking, but Boy Scout wasn't listening. He shoveled faster as he remembered his own encounter with the *Sefid* spiders, only he didn't just have one enter him. He'd had many. Was he possessed? Was there something in there waiting for the chance to take over? By God, he didn't want to end up like Narco.

"... it was like I was a bystander to my own life. I saw and felt everything but had no control. I think it would have taken me if Faood hadn't stopped the process so soon by getting me back into a fugue."

"The process?"

"It begins with a whisper."

A whisper. Boy Scout listened to his own mind, but heard nothing except excerpts from a dozen memories and his own voice blaming himself for being in this situation.

The hole was four feet deep by six feet long. Just big enough to secure Criminal. Boy Scout set aside the shovel, then the both of them grabbed the ends of the blanket and gently deposited their friend in his final resting place. They bowed their heads and for a few moments the only sound was the night wind coming through the scrub. After a few reverential moments, Boy Scout grabbed the shovel and began to cover the body.

He felt a hand on his shoulder. "Boss, let me do that."

Boy Scout looked up and saw Narco holding out his hand.

"I want to say a few words anyway."

Boy Scout let the shovel go and headed back to the cistern.

From behind him, he heard, "Criminal, you son of a bitch. The lengths you will go to get out of paying me back a measly hundred bucks. Don't think I'm not going to come after you."

Boy Scout smiled slightly, then let the pair alone.

Inside the cistern, McQueen had laid out a blanket on which to put the weapons and ammunition.

Boy Scout watched him, noting again how thin and frail the man had become. The fugue had hit him the hardest. Why, he didn't know. They'd all been under the same amount of time.

When McQueen was finished, he looked up, a little winded.

On the blanket was all they had left to fight the coming dervishes. Five HK416 long guns. Six Sig Saur P229 pistols. Five grenades. An RPG with one round. Two stacks of ammo, one stack for each kind of weapon. However much it was, it didn't look like it was enough.

Lore came to him with Faood.

Boy Scout nodded. "Report."

"SOP is for them to send three vehicles. Each one with four dervishes. Faood says they have a QRF that is Hezbollah trained, so these guys are going to know what they're doing."

"They have an actual quick reaction force?" Boy Scout shook his head. "What about weapons?"

"AKs. PM pistols. Regular old Soviet stuff."

"So they outnumber us three to one but they have old equipment." He glanced at the broken ceiling of the cistern, then let his gaze linger for a moment on the body of the dead *daeva*. It was decomposing at an alarming rate. The stench of rotting meat rolled off it in waves. "This place was defensible. Now, with the ceiling like it is, I don't trust it. We're going to have to set up an ambush."

"These might help," Bully said, carrying in a wood crate containing nine large bottles. Strips of cloth came out of the tops of each one. "Half lamp oil and half gasoline. I think they used to call this Greek fire."

"Where'd that come from?" Lore asked.

"I used lamp oil and gasoline," Bully said.

Narco's eyes widened. "You made those?"

"I'm not just a pretty face," Bully said.

Boy Scout nodded. "We'll definitely use those. Good work, Bully." He turned to Faood. "If we have any chance at this, you need to tell us your secret."

Faood's face darkened. "It's our closest one."

"What are you talking about, boss?" Lore asked.

"You tell them," he said to Faood.

"We don't have to fight. All we have to do is dance."

"But I thought you needed a *daeva*," Lore said. "We're fresh out."

"The *daeva* helps us establish the fugue. But there was always the dance. It hypnotizes. Once you've had it done before it can work almost instantaneously because your mind is prepared for it… has already been adapted for it."

"So you dance a little jig and then what?" McQueen asked.

"Then nothing. It's like you fall asleep."

"Ahh," Lore said, palming her head. "But there's a way to defeat it."

Faood nodded. "They would kill me if they knew I told you."

"They're going to kill you anyway," Boy Scout said. "Now give."

"It's not good enough to look away. Once you see it, your mind recognizes it for what it is. Especially because you've been fuguing for seven months. But it does help a little."

"Then what do we do?" Bully asked.

"Count backwards by multiples of three."

"Like twelve, nine, six, three?" McQueen asked.

"Yes. It makes sense," Lore said. "Counting isn't enough because you can do that from memory. But by going backwards by multiples, it forces your brain to do something more complex, unfamiliar. But why three?"

"It can be any other number. Two is too simple. Five and ten are too simple as well. We just found out that three is the easiest and most effective."

"Is that what you do?" Bully asked.

"It doesn't affect us." He said something in Persian, then repeated it in English. "A dervish can only move himself."

"Lucky you," Lore said.

"First one I see trying to dance gets shot," Bully said.

Faood frowned, but nodded grudgingly. "A prudent strategy."

"You going to fight with us?" Boy Scout asked.

"What you said earlier was disturbing. I don't know what I'm going to do. I thought I was doing what Rumi would have done. Now I'm not sure."

"I've been thinking about that myself. If it was really Rumi I was speaking to, and I think it was, I have a sense that all the time he's spent in *Sefid* and in other people's heads has served to dehumanize him. To what extent, I don't know. From what little I've read about him, I found him to be a person concerned about the wellbeing of others. You can't spend a day on Facebook without one of his platitudes coursing across your timeline. I just buried one of my men. I found three other bodies and I bet there are thousands. You and yours capture or trick people into doing this fugue because you have... or had... this big bad *daeva*. You keep them in a fugue until they die, then you take them out and bury them."

"Three thousand, nine hundred and forty-two of them," Faood said in a hushed tone.

"Shame on you. Fucking shame on you," Lore said, scowling as she shook her head.

Faood stared at her with liquid eyes. "It *is* our shame."

"Let's pretend Rumi had never left for *Sefid*. What would he say if he came upon you and your dervishes? What would he say about what you've done?" Boy Scout gestured towards the entrance to the complex. "What would he say about the three thousand, nine hundred and forty-two bodies?"

A tear leaked from Faood's left eye, but he remained unmoving.

"Do it for the Rumi who was, instead of the Rumi who is," Boy Scout said.

Everyone was silent for almost a full minute, then Faood roughly wiped his face. "Now look who's talking like a fortune cookie," he said.

Suddenly Narco ran into the cistern, winded, worry lining his face. "I see lights."

"In the sky?" Faood asked.

"Yes, and on the ground as well."

Everyone stared at each other for a moment, then dove for the weapons.

Chapter Thirty-Six

"WHERE WERE THE lights? Were they together?" asked Boy Scout now that he wore his body armor, had the 9mm pistol in a chest rig, and held his rifle. The others were similarly frocked, just as they had been in the fugue, when they thought they were chasing Narco. This time it was real. Or at least Boy Scout thought as much.

"The lights on the ground were coming from the east from the road."

"And in the sky?"

"Two lights coming from the north."

Boy Scout turned to Faood. "What do you think?"

"It could be aircraft. When the *daeva* are flying their *vimana* they're usually stealthy."

"Usually?"

"When they want to get somewhere quick, they have the ability to, say, turn on the 'afterburners.' Is that how you say it?"

"What'll the dervishes be doing now?"

"Waiting for us to die."

"Shit. Faood, you and I are going to hide in the vestibule. The rest of you, disperse inside the cisterns. And remember the rule: *the wound is where the light enters you.*"

The others took off, going deeper into the cistern complex.

Faood and Boy Scout pulled themselves into the vestibule—a small, cramped space a man's width and ten feet deep near the entrance. The opening to the vestibule was hidden from initial sight. One had to be inside the cistern itself in order to see into it.

They were set, when Boy Scout had an idea. He left his rifle and pushed himself free of the space.

"What are you doing?" hissed Faood.

Boy Scout ran to the case of Greek fire, lifted it up, then ran it over to the edge of the cistern. He had an idea and if—

A bright, blinding ball of light filled the entrance—silent and eerie. It didn't take a genius to see that the *vimanas* were landing.

Fucking hell.

Boy Scout hurried with the crate, bottles clinking to the point he thought they might break. When he got to the edge of the water, he set them down. He made to return to the vestibule, but saw a shadow on the interior wall of the cistern as a figure entered. He had no choice but to turn and dive into the putrid depths. He managed to close his mouth, a lucky thing given the generations of body waste in the water, turning the liquid into a plague soup. The body armor pulled him right down to the bottom, allowing his movements to go largely undetected.

Reaching out with his hands, he grabbed the bases of the stones they'd sat upon, propelling himself toward the back of the cistern. He was angling for an immense block of stone that had fallen from the roof. If he could just get behind it, he might be able to hide from the *daeva*. The problem was that as soon as he'd hit the water he lost vector, plus he was taking too much time. He could already feel the strain on his lungs. He kept his eyes closed because of the murkiness of the water, but forced them open before he lost his air. There, in front and to the left, was a large square shadow. He pulled himself to that, then grabbed the edge and yanked himself around to the other side.

There was about three feet of space between the stone and the back wall of the cistern. He fought to ascend slowly when all his body wanted to do was to surge out of the water and gulp air. He managed to breach the water, lips first, sucking in air in a slow, controlled manner. He rose to his feet, keeping his knees bent so he couldn't be seen. The water came up to the lower half of his chest. He pushed his back to the stone, then carefully, silently, drew the 9mm pistol from his chest rig. Water dripped from it, but he wasn't worried about the functionality. It would fire just fine.

He heard movement on the other side of the stone from the direction where the dead *daeva* lay. He started to ease himself around the corner when his left foot went out from under him, slipping on the slick surface of the bottom. His arms shot out to regain his balance and a split second later he was no longer falling. He brought his arms back in, silently cursing himself. He held his pistol to his chest, ready to use it.

The interior of the cistern was eerily silent. Had it been two soldiers recovering the body of a comrade, there'd be muffled curses, small talk, commands. Anything. These creatures didn't speak at all, which lent credence to the idea that they could communicate telepathically.

Boy Scout made sure his footing was solid, then once again leaned to his right so he could peer around the corner.

Two ten-foot-tall narrow beings stared at the emaciated and rotting dead body of one of their kind. Chains still held one of the dead *daeva's* wrists, keeping it from falling completely in the water. The two living *daeva*s' eyes glowed an impossibly bright gold, as if they were giving off hundreds of lumens. A duller glow swirled at their throats and Boy Scout knew what that meant.

A sound came from deep inside the complex—metal on stone.

Both elongated *daeva* heads swiveled toward the sound.

Boy Scout cursed. One of his people—rookie move.

Then his foot went out from under him completely. With a splash, he went under.

A bolt of golden energy struck the water where he'd been, causing it to sizzle and boil.

Boy Scout felt the heat of it on the side of his face, but the bolt had missed him.

He pulled himself behind the stone and rose from the water, again putting his back to the rock. To his left, the stone met the back wall of the cistern. The only way out was for him to go to the right or over the top. If they'd been looking for someone to take their anger out on, he'd given himself to them on a silver platter.

He had an idea that could get him out of here, but it depended on a lot of luck—too much luck for him to try unless he was completely desperate, which was less than a minute away.

Chancing losing his footing again, he jerked his head back around the corner and spied one on the other side of the cistern. The other *daeva* had already entered the water and was creeping towards him.

The one not in the water opened its mouth and released a golden bolt.

Boy Scout peeled back behind the stone and watched as the bolt struck the side of the cistern, shards of rock and mortar exploding in all directions.

Then without thinking, he lowered himself into the water and headed away from his hiding spot, keeping the cistern wall within touch. He pulled himself madly, his pistol still in his right hand. When he felt as if he'd gone far enough, he turned in the direction where he thought the crate of bottles was, got his feet under him, and surged upwards. He shoved the pistol out in front of him and unloaded a magazine into the box. By the time he'd hit it with five shots, the sixth sparked and lit the liquid, which flared, then exploded.

The *daeva* were between where he stood and the bottles on shore. He watched as each of the *daeva* were covered in flaming liquid. But as dangerous as it appeared, where it touched them, there was no effect. Still, they screamed because the water was on fire, and where their refection met the fire, it burned them.

The wound is the place where the light enters you, motherfucker.

Boy Scout climbed onto one of the underwater seats they'd sat on during the fugue and fired into the reflection of the one nearest him. Impacts appeared on the *daeva*'s chest just as if he'd fired directly at the creature.

It reared his head back and a bolt of golden energy shot towards the ceiling.

An immense piece of stone tore free and fell directly onto the *daeva*, driving it to the bottom of the cistern.

Boy Scout dove to his right, calculating the other *daeva's* intentions out of the corner of his eye.

The *daeva* fired, barely missing him, catching the edge of his pants leg on fire. The flame went out as soon as he hit the water. Now underwater, he pulled himself several body lengths away before he rose again. When he did, he saw the remaining *daeva* leap away from the water and run deeper into the cistern, as if it realized its reflection was its worst enemy.

Boy Scout glanced at the giant stone resting atop the other *daeva*, then fought his way free of the pool.

Faood met him when he reached the shore.

"You okay?" he asked.

"Just as I planned," Boy Scout said. Then he rushed into the other room, searching for the creature before it got to his team.

Chapter Thirty-Seven

A SCREAM WAS followed by Lore's voice ringing out, "Come on and get me, you son-of-a-bitch!"

Despite himself, Boy Scout grinned. This was what it was all about. No more of the fugue or the *Sefid* or dealing with the crazy philosophies of the dervishes. They were back to G vs E—good versus evil—full-on combat mode, ready to shoot, blow up, or flat out destroy anything that came their way. And to hear Lore shouting at an advancing superbeing with all the flippancy of road rage at a bad driver was the perfect antidote to the malaise that had found a home inside him since he'd been so combat inactive.

He passed the entrance to their room, then through the cistern they used to clean up, which was the largest of them all. There were eight cisterns in total, each linked together with a single exit—the one he was entering from.

Lore's scream of "Is that the best you can do?" was followed by the sound of an energy bolt scoring stone.

He ran into the fifth cistern and then slowed, seeing

McQueen leaning against a doorway, his rifle ready to fire.

Boy Scout ran up behind McQueen.

"What's going on?" Boy Scout whispered. Then he saw it all.

Like all the cisterns, the fifth cistern was lit by oil lamps fixed to the walls. The fifth cistern was set lower than the others. It was also deeper. Yet as deep as it was, Lore stood in the very center on a raised stone circle, appearing like she was standing on water, the Jesus her father never saw repeating his New Testament romp across the Sea of Galilee. Her face was like a fury, her hands balled into fists at her sides.

The *daeva* stumbled towards her on stiff legs, its ten-foot frame somehow taller as it loomed above her. Its deep blue skin was charred black in the places where the reflected fire had consumed it. Boy Scout's gaze went to the creature's head, where his team had managed to cinch a bag over it. The *daeva* clawed at the cloth and never saw the lip of the water. It staggered, falling to a knee into water illuminated by Narco and Bully who stood to either side shining tactical mag lights onto it.

"Just a little closer, you bastard," Lore called, seething at every word.

Boy Scout held his breath.

One more step forward.

Two more steps.

Lore shouted, "Now!"

McQueen opened fire. Tight three round bursts found the one-time god's reflection in the water, stitching it first on the left, then on the right, then in the back. Wherever the rounds sizzled into the water, impact wounds opened in the *daeva*'s golden-hued skin. It fell to its other knee, and still McQueen fired.

Lore climbed off her perch and slid into the water, which came up to her waist. She stepped to the side, firing her 9mm into the reflections before her.

Then it fell face first into the center stone.

Narco and Bully exchanged raised fists in victory from opposite sides of the room.

McQueen dropped his empty mag and inserted a full one with all the skill of a man who'd done it ten thousand times before.

Lore holstered her pistol in her chest rig and crossed her arms. Although she spoke softly, her voice rang loud in the rounded-roofed chamber as she repeated the Persian words that had been the clue to killing these creatures... the same words she'd tried to bang out of her head in her double-wide in Riverside. Only that had never really happened. She'd been in fugue, and someone, or something, had given her that clue. But to what end? To whose benefit? Had it been Faood? Had it been Sufi Sam? Had it been Rumi? Did it even matter?

McQueen raised his rifle to fire again, but Boy Scout put a hand on the barrel and gently pushed it down. Then he cupped his old friend's cheek and smiled at him. He held the gaze for a moment, then strode into the cistern. He slung his rifle on his back, then waded into the water. He swam to where the *daeva* had collapsed on the central rise on which Lore had previously stood. It still breathed, but barely. Well aware of the danger, he reached and pulled the bag free from its head. Its eyes were pallid gold and lacked power. The previous tell-tale glow in its throat was non-existent.

This close to the being, looking into its eyes, Boy Scout felt a somberness come over him. For a reason he couldn't ken, he reached out and cupped the *daeva*'s cheek, the same way he had with his friend's, and was immediately transferred to a street in Saigon where a monk had just set himself on fire. He could smell the burning skin mixed with car exhaust, a man's body odor and a curry dish being made on the street in an immense metal wok. The fire sparked, whipped and roared in a voice of its own. A car honked. A woman screamed. Flashes from cameras lit the scene. The monk burned before him, stoic and unmoving, staring at Boy Scout with all the volition of an angry god.

"Why is it you kill us?" it said.

"Why is it you kill *us*?" Boy Scout asked in turn.

"You are with the others. You use us—torture us with your dreams. Like this thing. How could you do this to yourselves?"

"It's my understanding that he did it in protest... something political."

The burning monk grinned. "He did this and you don't even know the reason why."

"This was not from my time. This was from before."

"And still you fail to learn from history."

"What are you really?" Boy Scout asked. "What made you?"

"The better question is who made *you*. We looked

away, then looked back, and there you were... shadows upon this world bathed in the light of creation. And like shadows, you bring darkness wherever you go."

"Some of us are warriors and some are poets," Boy Scout said, thinking of Rumi and Byron and Frost.

The monk said, "The words of a single poet can cause as much damage as the swords of a thousand warriors."

"And so we're back to my questions," Boy Scout said. "Why do you kill us and who are you?"

"We're not here to kill you. We came to get the one who was being tortured. We heard its screams and came to it now that it was no longer hidden."

Boy Scout noted the use of the word *it* rather than *him*. Perhaps they didn't have a gender. "So you have no desire to kill us?"

"We defend ourselves only. You weren't our creation, therefore we have no power over you."

"Yet you revel in our war against ourselves?"

"We try and seek understanding why a creation would try and destroy itself."

Suddenly a question formed that Boy Scout knew had to be asked. "Where are your creations?" The moment he asked it, he felt such an overwhelming sense of loss that he wept, a sob wrenching free.

"We don't know," the *daeva* said, the face of the monk burning away. "But we will continue to seek them until the last of us is but a memory to the first star."

Then Boy Scout snapped back to reality and watched the light die in the *daeva*'s eyes.

"God bless you, Thích Quảng Đức," he whispered,

invoking the name of the monk who'd died, suffering in the hopes that the torment of his fellow monks would stop, anguish they'd endured because of the politics of the South Vietnamese government. The similarities weren't lost upon him.

Then Lore and Boy Scout were by his side.

"You're crying, boss," Lore said.

He opened his mouth to speak, but another sob broke free instead as the *daeva* died and the last of its self-imposed perdition washed through him, multiplied into oblivion until the weight of it was enough to crush a planet.

"Bryan," McQueen said, uncharacteristically using Boy Scout's real name. "What's wrong? What's going on?" He grabbed Boy Scout by the shoulders. "What is it?"

Boy Scout let out a bone-rattling sigh. "It's all just so fucking sad."

"What?" McQueen asked.

"What's so sad?" Lore asked.

Boy Scout waved a hand, then noted he was still holding the being's fingers. He let its hand go with reverence and watched as it slid beneath the water. "This creature, for one thing. This whole set up. The burning monk. The falling man. The poor girl running from the napalm. All of it. Us, shadows on the world bringing darkness wherever we go."

He put a hand on McQueen's arm and turned away.

"Not this," Lore said. "Never this. This thing killed Criminal."

"No it didn't, Laurie May."

The use of her name startled her, but she continued. "What is this? What did it do to you?"

"It didn't do nothing. Just truth."

"I call bullshit," Lore said matter-of-factly. "Criminal was one of us, and it was one of these who killed it."

"No, that's not true, Lore. A creature who was being tortured woke up and lashed out. It was more of a prisoner than we ever were. Don't you see? It's not us. It's the dervishes. They are the darkest shadows of us all. They kept it here and brought people as lures to catch immortality. Do you have any idea how many graves are out there, how many bodies to share eternity with Criminal—Oscar James?"

"I remember," she murmured.

"Three thousand, nine hundred and forty-two." He grabbed her shoulder and spun her to look at the *daeva*. "This didn't kill them. *They* killed them."

She tried to tug free, but Boy Scout wouldn't let her.

So she pulled him in close. Now face-to-face, she said, "Then if they're so good, why is it I learned how to kill them so easily? Do you think Rumi or any of the other dervishes would have told us, wanted us to kill their precious fugue machines?"

"Who do you think told you, Lore? God?"

"I don't know. Maybe. It just came to me and I couldn't get rid of the damned words."

"And all while you were spiritually strapped to the *daeva*, who had the ability to shift and control what was happening," Boy Scout said. When she said nothing, he said, "Now you're getting it. Think about it, Lore. Why did you know how to kill them? Who told you that they have an Achilles' heel?" Her eyes widened and he pulled her close, hugging her. "Yes, the *daeva* told you. It no longer wanted to live."

"Suicide," she whispered.

He held her at arm's length so he could see her face. "It wanted to die and it chose you to give its greatest secret."

"Then how did Rumi know? Why had it become part of his legacy?"

"They've wanted to die for an eternity, I'm afraid." Then he added, "I think they put the words out there and instead of taking them literally, like we did, they turned the phrase into something about wellbeing and yoga pants. *The wound is the place where the light enters you,* like *it's always darker before the dawn.* It wasn't spiritualism. It was a prayer for the dying."

"Wellbeing and yoga pants." She laughed flatly. "Isn't that just like us."

Just then Faood came running in, out of breath, eyes flashing towards the dead thing in the water. "You killed it?"

"We got lucky," Boy Scout said, not wanting the dervish to know their secret.

"No time to celebrate. The QRF is almost upon us."

"You heard the man," Boy Scout said. "Partner up and spread out."

Everyone moved with purpose, but Boy Scout made them pause one last time. "And remember to count backwards in multiples of threes."

"Hear that, Narco?" Bully said, punching him soundly

in the shoulder. "Now's your chance to walk and chew gum at the same time."

He winced and gave Boy Scout a look that said, *This girl is scary.*

Chapter Thirty-Eight

BOY SCOUT WOULDN'T let them get any nearer the entrance than cistern number three. If he was leading the QRF, he'd have his team toss in flash-bangs or even grenades to clear the rooms. The attacking force would be on edge when they got to the first room, more so the second room. But by the time they got to the third cistern and still had no contact, he was hoping that their guard would begin to fall—they might even wonder if their enemies hadn't already been killed. Sadly, the idea that they'd already escaped couldn't be played with the TST vehicles still out front.

He wasn't sure where the others were, but he and Faood were on either side of the entrance to their cistern. Three was probably the smallest of the cisterns, with the exception of eight, which was no more than a foot pool. Three was no larger than a standard living room. There was space to walk around the edge, but the cistern fell to a depth of eleven or twelve feet, the water absolutely chilling. When they hadn't been in fugue, Boy Scout liked to dive in and hover near the bottom every morning. Not exactly a cup of coffee, but the cold shock definitely woke all of his senses.

He carried five magazines for his long rifle and three for his pistol. He also had two grenades, which he hoped to use when and if he could get the QRF to cluster.

They didn't have long to wait.

The attacking force did as he'd suspected they would, using a flash-bang in the entry chamber. When they entered, they'd see a dead *daeva* and rubble from the collapsed ceiling.

It didn't take them long to work their way to the sleeping chamber, where they used another flash-bang.

Then the place the TST used as a bathroom.

Flash-bang.

Then the first cistern. He could now hear one of them calling terse military commands in clipped Persian.

Flash-bang.

The second cistern.

No flash-bang.

At that moment, Boy Scout smiled. He pulled the pin on the grenade he held in his hand, let the spoon snap free, and after two seconds tossed it high in the air into cistern number two.

Two men cried out in Persian when they saw it, then came the explosion.

Boy Scout held out his hand and counted down from five so that Faood could see. When he got to one, they both leaned around the corner and picked out targets, using full automatic to increase the confusion. He saw two bodies in the water and two more rolling on the ground. Once his mag was empty, he and Faood turned and ran around the water and into cistern number four. He passed Lore and McQueen, who were waiting on either side of the opening, and continued running into cistern number five, where Bully and Narco had returned to their ledges. Instead of aiming mag lights, they were now aiming their HKs.

Boy Scout continued on until they were at the archway to cistern six. They slipped inside and then turned to look. He couldn't see all the way to where Lore and McQueen stood because of the elevation drop in cistern five, but he pictured them in his mind.

He dropped his empty mag, replaced it, and seated a round in the chamber.

Faood did the same.

Thirty seconds later, McQueen and Lore opened fire, taking turns at double tapping.

McQueen around the corner.

Blam! Blam!

Blam! Blam!

Lore around the corner.

Blam! Blam!

Blam! Blam!

Rinse and repeat.

Once their mags were empty, they beat feet into cistern five, then beyond, to stand beside Boy Scout and Faood.

"How many?" Boy Scout asked.

"I got two," McQueen said.

"Same here," Lore said. "One was dancing and I almost forgot to count."

"I saw it too. Started at ninety-nine," McQueen said.

"I saw four down from the initial, but could be more," Faood said.

"They have body armor," Boy Scout reminded them. "So some of the hits might not be lethal."

Thirty seconds passed. From where Boy Scout stood with McQueen beside him, he could see Narco up on a ledge, aiming into the archway.

"With their losses, will they still keep coming?" McQueen asked Faood.

"If I was leading the QRF, I'd call for reinforcements."

"Radios work inside here?" Boy Scout asked.

"Not even a little," Faood said.

"They'd have to go into full retreat to make the call."

"Narco?" Boy Scout called.

The man looked his way.

Boy Scout made the universal sign for *What's going on?* with his hand.

Narco shook his head. "They ain't coming, boss."

"Okay. Let's move by twos."

Boy Scout tapped Faood on the shoulder and they ran back into cistern five. They each climbed the ledges to get to the opening, then peered around the archway. Nothing moved in cistern four.

Boy Scout waved for the next two.

McQueen and Lore ran over, then edged around the water until they reached the archway to cistern three and took up position. They waved for someone to move forward.

Boy Scout motioned for Narco and Bully to join them. They climbed down. As they passed Boy Scout, each of them flashed him a grin. Boy Scout grinned back, noting again the Broney patch on Narco's body armor.

Then the room exploded, water and debris shooting everywhere.

Boy Scout fell back and down the ledges until he rolled to a stop at the water's edge.

He cursed himself for not being more careful. He should have waited longer before he committed his people forward.

His head was ringing as he climbed unsteadily to his feet. His body armor had protected him from flying debris. Still, he wobbled a little but found his rifle and climbed the ledges back to the entrance. He dreaded what he'd discover. Out of the corner of his eye, he saw Faood struggling to get to his feet.

Inside cistern number four was a slaughterhouse.

Bully lay face down next to the entrance, her head sheathed in blood.

Narco was in the left corner, sitting, as if he'd just gotten tired and plopped down. His head lolled back at an impossible angle, his eyes endlessly open, a piece of sharp stone protruding from his neck.

Both Lore and McQueen were face down on the other side of the cistern.

Everything was covered in water and stone dust. If Boy Scout had to bet, the QRF had used a block of plastic explosive with a remote detonator, which meant someone would have had to been watching.

As if on cue, a round whizzed by his ear like a supersonic hornet, then he got three in the chest. The hammer thumps knocked the wind from him. He thanked his body armor once more. Of its own accord, his right hand brought up his rifle and he fired from the hip as he fell backwards.

Rounds ate the wall behind where he'd been standing.

Feeling like he had a gorilla sitting on his chest, Boy Scout fought to get to his feet, then ran around the center of the cistern and pulled McQueen around the corner. Then he yanked out his pistol. Holding it in his left hand, he ran across the archway firing both weapons at the same time, seeking anything moving. He made it to the other side without being shot again and grabbed Lore. Just as he was pulling her, she kicked at him, catching him in the chest, then the jaw.

He fell back, grabbing at his face.

She twisted and brought her pistol around, aiming at his head.

Her eyes had the dull shine of someone still out of it.

"Lore—"

She fired at the sound, the round impacting the wall above his head, showering him in rocky dust.

"Lore!" he shouted. Her eyes cleared, then she blinked. Once. Twice. "Boy Scout," she whispered. Then realizing where she was and the circumstances, she whirled and saw the carnage. Her hand went over her mouth.

Faood climbed into the archway to cistern four and opened fire on a target. Then he lifted Bully's head, looked for a moment, then lowered it gently to the floor. When he saw that Boy Scout was watching, he shook his head. He glanced over to Narco and shook his head again. He made his way around to McQueen.

Boy Scout couldn't move.

Please God, no, Boy Scout thought. McQueen was his best friend. God, anything but that.

Suddenly several rifles began to fire into their cistern.

Boy Scout snapped out of it. He dropped both his weapons and pulled out his final grenade. He pulled the pin and let the spoon fly too late to note that he couldn't get it through the door in time.

Faood held out his hand and Boy Scout tossed him the grenade.

Faood caught it and threw it into the next room, then dove back behind the wall.

The explosion ended the gunfire.

Boy Scout scrambled for his weapons, shoving his pistol back into the chest rig. On hands and knees he made it to the archway. Then he took his rifle and went into a prone position, begging for a target to enter his sight. But there was nothing. No one.

He used the archway to pull himself to his feet and lurched around the water in cistern three. His ears still rang and he shook his head to shake the bells free. He moved with his rifle ready to fire. He didn't even pause as he entered the next cistern. Fucking dervishes were going to kill his TST. If there was any moment he wished he'd been in a fugue it was right now, so he could come back and everyone would be alive, but he knew better.

Then he heard a savage scream from the main cistern.

A bolt of golden energy shot across his line of vision.

Boy Scout lunged forward, ready to fire at anything.

When he reached the entrance to the main cistern, he

saw the *daeva*—the one they'd presumed crushed by the ceiling blocks—holding a dervish in its hands. The *daeva* roared as it ripped the man in half, human innards roping down to the water below.

Hearing movement, Boy Scout spun and saw a dervish squatting next to a wall, his arms around his knees, fear in his eyes as he sobbed. Beside him lay the remains of another man, this one burned and broken in half.

Boy Scout took three quick steps and placed the barrel to the man's head. He hesitated a moment, then put three rounds into him. He pushed him to the ground, lifted a boot, and brought it down on the detonator the man still held.

A presence suddenly loomed behind him and turned around slowly.

The *daeva* stared down at him.

Boy Scout lowered his rifle and looked up at the superbeing.

They stood there, frozen, for what seemed like an hour, then the *daeva* moved on, limping as it left the complex. After a moment of silence, there came a roar, brightness flared from the entrance, then it was gone.

Boy Scout seated the rifle into his shoulder and moved with purpose. By his count there was still one dervish missing and he wanted desperately to find the man, if nothing more than to explain the nature of American munitions and how a 5.56 round could etch an epitaph onto an evil man's soul.

Chapter Thirty-Nine

IT TURNED OUT that the last dervish was hiding in the same spot Boy Scout had used earlier to hide from the *daeva*. Weaponless and terrified, he was babbling in both Persian and English about the *daeva* tearing his friends in half. Boy Scout was prepared to fire when he heard a voice he recognized.

He turned to see his old friend McQueen, slightly worse for wear, standing at the edge of the water, helped by Lore.

Boy Scout slammed the butt of his rifle into the dervish's face, then ran to the last two members of his TST and embraced them. Together they cried for their fallen friends.

After a few moments, they cleared the cistern of potential danger. Once certain there were no survivors, they took their two fallen comrades into the desert and dug graves for them.

They buried Sarasota Chavez, aka Bully, convoy driver, MMA fighter, TST member, and friend to them all. She'd perhaps had the worst of it, taking care of them when they were in fugue as if she was the mother and they were her babies.

Then they buried Dakota Jimmison, aka Dak, aka Narco, arranger of things, TST member, and a regular pain in the ass.

Throughout the entire solemn process, Boy Scout remembered the scene in the Kenneth Branagh movie, *Henry V*. After the Battle of Agincourt, the king and his knights took up the bodies of Davy Gam and the others who'd died. During the burials, they sang the old Latin hymn first sung by the Knights Templar, *Non nobis, Domine,* which meant *Not unto us, Lord.* The idea was that the English army was happy they'd won the battle and the war, but were solemn in the notion that it hadn't been up to them and that God had favored the English that day. But to Boy Scout, the song meant much more. It was not only a nod to the bravery and sacrifice given to him by the members of his team, it was also his expression of humility as one who'd survived. He didn't sing it and he didn't hum it, but it played in the orchestra of his mind with all the grand fanfare of a major symphony.

As they stood and stared at the two filled graves, Boy Scout knew that the fugue had brought them all closer together. They hadn't merely done their day-to-day TST tasks. They'd traveled the world in their minds, run from the cops, chased bad buys, beaten up gang members, and even unleashed camels onto a downtown Phoenix highway. That those events never really happened had little bearing on the reality that at the time they'd all believed they *had*. The memories of those events were as real in their minds as anything they had ever done, and the doing of them bonded them closer than they would have believed. As a result, losing Narco, Criminal, and Bully wasn't like any other loss he'd experienced in his life... and Boy Scout had lost a lot of men in combat.

When they were done with their own, they went to Faood and helped with his dead. These they didn't bury; instead, they packed them into the SUVs they'd come in, posing them as if they'd died inside the vehicles. When they were finally done, Boy Scout took Lore and McQueen and they cleaned each other, wiping away the day's blood and sins. When at last they were dressed and geared up, Boy Scout spoke to them.

"We have a decision to make."

Both Lore and McQueen stared at him expectantly.

Lore had come through the battle with bruises and a ringing in her ears that wouldn't quite go away.

McQueen had a three-inch gash across the back of his left shoulder and enough bruising to make his skin blue.

"It's been more than seven months since we went missing. By now, they've found the remains of the general's vehicle. They won't have found ours since the dervishes removed the LoJack recovery system. For all we know, we're wanted men and women."

The others made no comment.

"What happened here, all of this, can never be discussed. They'd think we're crazy and probably lock us up, which means this location and unfortunately the location of the bodies of our fallen can never be revealed. As much as it saddens me, this is their final resting place."

"Cemeteries are for the living, boss," McQueen said, swallowing hard. "Especially military cemeteries."

No one spoke for a long minute as they digested that fact.

Then Lore said, "I thought you said we have a decision to make."

"We do, but I don't want to ask any more of you than—"

"We're in," Lore said excitedly. Then when Boy Scout seemed about to speak, she added, "McQueen and I have already talked about this. If you're about to say what I think you're about to say, then yes… hell, yes!"

"There's only three of us," Boy Scout said. He'd asked Faood if he'd help, but the man had replied that it was just too much. He was going on Hajj to find himself and to figure out who he needed to be.

Neither Lore nor McQueen said a word.

"We'll be outnumbered, probably ten to one."

Still, they remained silent.

"This is not a suicide mission. I'm not planning on any of you dying, but the reality is that at least one of us isn't going to make it."

Still not a word.

"When we get there, I'm going to free the *daeva* they're keeping."

Lore glanced at McQueen and fidgeted. She hadn't been expecting that, but she said nothing.

"Then, when it's all said and done, we're going to go home."

"We can tell them we were captured by the Taliban," Lore said. "You, and especially McQueen, look as if you've been starved to death. I probably do, too."

"Then we saw our chance and fought our way free," McQueen added.

"We'll have a lot of time to work on our story after the battle," Boy Scout said. "We'll have to be on foot when they find us to make it look realistic."

"How far do you think we're away from friendly forces?" McQueen asked.

"I figure fifty kilometers east and we could hit FOB Mitchum in Kunduz Province. Or we could go sixty kilometers west and hit Mez. It's a German base, but there are some US forces there."

"I'd rather go east," Lore said.

"Me as well," McQueen said. "Special Forces have a presence at FOB Mitchum. If it was them who found us, I could sell our story better."

"Then east it is," Boy Scout said, grinning slightly. Although FOB Mitchum was named after an Army private who'd died there, he couldn't help thinking of the classic movie *Night of the Hunter* starring Robert Mitchum. The actor had played the serial killing Reverend Harry Powell with the letters L-O-V-E tattooed on his right hand and H-A-T-E tattooed on his left. The movie was a classic, but that's not why Boy Scout thought about it. It came as a warning and he'd come to wish he'd heeded it.

"And to think that friendly forces were so close all this time," Lore said. "You know, it's a shame we couldn't just call this in." Then she hastily added, "I know. This is far bigger than anything. Can you imagine if the CIA got their hands on a *daeva*?"

Boy Scout nodded. "What's going on here is biblical. For all I know it was foretold in Revelations. Not that I'm a diehard believer or anything, but now that I know that these *daeva* are real and now that I've seen what I've seen, I'm far slower to discount the possibility of a belief being true."

"True word," McQueen said, nodding.

"Something is going on outside of our reality that can affect ours, and as much as I love the red, white, and blue, I'm not certain it's something that we need to be messing with."

"Are you comfortable with Rumi messing with it?" Lore asked.

"No, I'm not. But as much as I hate his method, I think his intentions are good. Plus, I can't do anything about him unless I go back in and that's nothing I intend on doing ever again."

Lore laughed hollowly.

"What? Am I missing something?"

"Know what Narco would say about that? *Don't hate the player, hate the game.*"

"That was so Narco," McQueen said.

They remained silent for a full minute as they each replayed Narco, Bully, and Criminal memories. The good times. The bad times. The fugue times. All of it.

"What about our prisoner?" McQueen asked.

"Faood's going to let him go."

Both Lore and McQueen seemed to consider dissenting, but thought better of it.

"What's left for us to do?" Lore asked.

"Gather our gear and *dee mao*," Boy Scout said. "The

dervishes are going to come investigate the area. We'll be gone and they'll have no reason to believe we're going to come for them. My guess is it's going to put them in an uproar. They probably believe we'll go to the first friendly forces we can find, spill our guts, then have a whole Marine division descending upon Kholm. If we're lucky, they'll be preparing to move operations and we can catch them in the middle of it."

"They might even have a Jump TOC set up," McQueen said, meaning a temporary tactical command center prepositioned in the place that they intend on going. "It would be better if we were already there and waiting. Then we could attack them on our terms."

"I'll have to discuss with Faood what their standing operating procedure is. If we have the opportunity to do that, then I think it's something we should do. Good thinking, McQueen."

"Spoken like the Special Forces badass he always was," Lore said with a grin.

McQueen's face reddened.

"You guys get the gear together and I'll find Faood."

Lore and McQueen both acknowledged his command and set to it.

Boy Scout went into the fifth cistern and found Faood, who was sitting with the captured dervish. They'd removed both of the *daeva* and left them out in the desert to be recovered by their own kind.

Faood said a quick word, then joined Boy Scout.

"*As-salāmu 'alaykum,*" Faood said, a hand over his heart. The words meant "Peace be with you," and Boy

Scout responded, "There's not much chance of that, but *wa'alaykumu s-salām* to you."

Faood nodded solemnly. "You ready to leave?"

"Fairly soon."

"You still going to attack?"

"That's our plan."

"Is there any way I can talk you out of it?"

Boy Scout raised an eyebrow and glanced over to where the other dervish sat. He thought it had all been settled. He'd thought Faood understood. "Why would you do that?"

"They are my people. I do not want to see them dead."

"You did a pretty good job killing in here," Boy Scout said.

"That is not the same. They were attacking us. I was defending myself."

"Sometimes the best defense is a good offense."

Faood wrinkled his brow for a moment, then said, "I think I understand that. Yes, what you say is true. But that's not the reason you want to fight. You are not defending anything. What you want, you will never be able to have."

Boy Scout sighed, already tired of the sermon he knew was going to come. "And what is that, Faood?"

"You want revenge. Let me tell you, my friend, you will go there and you will kill, and if you survive, your friends are still going to be dead. All of the killing in the world is not going to bring them back. You still will have lost seven months of your life. All of the killing in the world won't undo that. Revenge is hollow. Tell me, what will this give you that you don't already have?"

Boy Scout didn't even hesitate. "Satisfaction," he said.

Faood stared at him for a moment, then said, "Killing dervishes you don't even know will satisfy you? Killing men who have nothing to do with you will satisfy you? Why? Because they are dervish? Then you might as well kill me." He tore open the collar of his shirt and pointed to his chest. "Here. Shoot me here."

Boy Scout grabbed Faood's collar and tugged it back in place. "Stop the drama, Faood. You're embarrassing yourself."

"Me? Embarrassing myself? No sir, it is you who are embarrassing yourself."

"Because I want revenge?"

"Because you are acting like Taliban. You are acting like Al-Qaeda. You have a blood oath to kill dervish because dervish kill your people. You tell me, Mr. Boy Scout, how this is different."

Boy Scout stared at Faood, wanting to punch him square in the face. "It's different."

"How?"

Boy Scout shook his head. "I don't know. It just is."

Then he turned and trudged out of the cistern complex.

Lore and McQueen were geared up and waiting for him.

"Come on," Boy Scout said. "Let's go."

"What about Faood?" Lore asked. "Did he tell you what we needed to know?"

"He said some things," Boy Scout said.

"Were they helpful?" Lore asked.

Boy Scout got behind the wheel and slammed his door. "Hardly."

Chapter Forty

Kholm

THEY SHOULDN'T HAVE waited until night. When they got to the palace, it was empty. There were signs of an attack. Scorch marks, the kind that might come from a *daeva*, marred the side of the once pristine white palace. A Land Cruiser lay on its side, nothing more than a burned hulk, the metal cold. There were no bodies. There were no weapons. The place looked as if it had been deserted for some time.

Boy Scout realized that he'd never really been to the palace at all. The only time he'd come here he'd been in a fugue specially designed by Faood. Had the dervishes even been here at all? Was the burned out vehicle and damage to the building from a battle long ago? He kicked a paper cup that the wind was tickling and watched it fly a few feet away and land near a shoe.

Was he in a fugue now? He never should have gone to talk to Faood alone. When it had been evident Boy Scout wasn't going to be denied his revenge, did Faood fugue him? Then why were the others here? Were they in the fugue or a construct? God, but it was so confusing.

They returned to their Land Cruiser and drove back to the cistern complex. All evidence of occupation had been removed. The SUVs and the bodies were gone. The dead *daeva* were removed. There was no Faood, but there were bullet holes everywhere. The roof above the primary cistern was still caved in from the fight with the *daeva*, just as Boy Scout remembered. That, at least, led him to believe that he was in reality. But could he be sure? Would he *ever* be sure?

Lore and McQueen were as confused as he was. He could see fear in their eyes. To doubt whether you were really you or whether you were really present was a magnificent invention of the dervishes. To make reality itself recalcitrant was genius.

With nothing else to do, they headed east to FOB Mitchum. Without the dervishes to attack, they might as well take advantage of the road and drive right up to the FOB. They'd say that they were kept in the cistern. Without the dervishes and without the *daeva* it was just an old historical place where water bubbled up from the ground. Investigators would come and see evidence of the firefight. It would work.

They'd gone about thirty miles, Lore leaning forward between the two front seats, talking candidly, their excitement building, their ideas about what they were going to do, drink, and eat bubbling forth. They promised that they'd meet again when they got back in the world, which always meant America, if they got separated because of the investigation. They talked about all of this and more and were beginning to feel as if they'd finally escaped the horror of the last seven months when they hit the mine. The explosion wrapped a titanic hand around the SUV and slammed it onto the other side of the road. Lore's scream was the only sound Boy Scout heard in the silence after the boom.

Then his mind was filled with words made famous by Cormac McCarthy. The booming voice of James Earl Jones proclaimed, *It makes no difference what men think of war. War endures. War was always here. Before man was, war waited for him. The ultimate trade awaiting its ultimate practitioner. War is the ultimate game because war is at last a forcing of the unity of existence. War is god.*

Then all sound returned with the force of a private Armageddon.

Machine gun fire raked the undercarriage of the SUV.

Someone was screaming his name.

Lore had gone through the windshield and was laying on the ground several feet away, unmoving.

Something was pulling at him. Jerking him. Boy Scout turned to see McQueen, his face bloodied from a broken nose, yanking on him.

Boy Scout fumbled with his seatbelt but his hand was slick with his own blood. The airbags had deployed. His face felt like it had hit a wall and throbbed. He fumbled twice more, then found the release.

McQueen pulled him through the space where the windshield had once been, then reached in and grabbed Boy

Scout's rifle. He shoved it at Boy Scout, who looked at it as if it was about to bite him. Then his senses returned and he snatched it and checked to see if it was in working order.

"Where are they?" he shouted.

"Other side of the road. Five of them."

The SUV had landed on the passenger side. The damage had occurred at the driver side rear tire. The damage seemed minimal, which was how it was sometimes. Boy Scout had seen MRAPs turned inside out by an IED and Toyota Corollas only flipped. The damage depended on so much. The depth of the IED. The components involved. The skill of the bomb maker.

McQueen was standing and firing over the hood.

Boy Scout crawled around toward the back, his legs not responding to his commands. He managed to find a position that would allow him to peer around the edge without putting himself in further danger. He could see the enemy's position, but not a target. Then a head popped up and he put a round into it. Even blown up and shaken as he was, his marksmanship was still with him. He barely acknowledged the million rounds of ammunition he'd put down the end of a rifle, just knew that if it hadn't been for all of those mindless days slogging through training venues in swamps, mountainsides, snow-covered forests, and desert moonscapes, he'd never have made that shot.

"Get ready," McQueen yelled.

"For what?" Boy Scout yelled back. Feeling was beginning to return to his legs.

"Going to get Lore!"

Of course. "Ready!"

McQueen emptied his magazine in the area of greatest threat, then ran to where Lore lay.

Boy Scout took up the fire, sending three round bursts into the same area. Everything was working right up until the point his rifle jammed. A look of horror crossed his face and, in slow motion, he turned to see McQueen take three rounds in his side, then fall forward with Lore in his arms.

Boy Scout tore his gaze away from his friends and furiously cleared the weapon. Once he got the round out, he reseated the magazine, got a bullet in the chamber, and bent around the back of the SUV in time to see two men, faces wrapped with black and white checkered *keffiyehs*, stand and start across the road. Boy Scout fired, catching one and sending him spinning to the ground. But he missed the other.

Where was his marksmanship now?

He fell back just in time to see the enemy round the hood.

Boy Scout double-tapped him in the head.

With the blood returning to his legs, Boy Scout threw down his rifle and pulled his 9mm from the chest rig. He stood shakily, using his left hand to balance. Pain lanced down his left leg, but it somehow managed to support him. Something might be broken or twisted but he didn't have time for triage. Another Taliban came around the front and Boy Scout shot him, too. Then Boy Scout felt a sledgehammer to his back. He stumbled forward. His vest took most of the damage, all but the force of a 7.62mm bullet traveling at seven hundred and fifteen meters per second. Boy Scout spun and dropped to a knee.

The enemy fired, but his aim was too high.

Boy Scout shot him in the groin three times. The man folded in on himself, shrieking.

Then Boy Scout stood and, screaming with rage, tore around the hood and across the road. A man, barely older than a boy, sat there, working frantically to correct a jam in his AK 47. He looked up, fear skyrocketing in his eyes.

Boy Scout screamed, "War is God!" Then he fired his pistol until all he could hear were clicks and still he squeezed the trigger, screaming in the silence of surviving.

Epilogue

THE SECONDARY TITLE for *Blood Meridian* was *An Evening of Redness in the West*. Boy Scout had wondered at the need for two titles and it hadn't been until this moment that he'd figured out why the author had insisted on it. The first was the name of the book. The second was the warning. *An Evening of Redness in the West* had the same moral warning as the one that said *Abandon All Hope Ye Who Enter Here* from *Dante's Inferno*. If a book and a poem could have a warning, if a pillbox and a box of cereal could have warnings, then a goddamned godless place like Afghanistan should have warning signs at every corner.

The idea that Boy Scout had believed the Taliban had been the greatest threat they'd ever come up against was now laughable. The greatest threat wasn't even the *daeva* or the dervishes. No, the greatest threat of all was war, a goddess he'd once embraced and thought to master. He thought he could have her the way he wanted. A regular Good Time Charlie, doing with her what he would, then divorcing her or moving onto something else. No one had told him what a fickle, stone cold bitch she could be, letting him believe everything might be over. War. Fucking war. If there was any place on earth were war was *de rigueur*, it was Afghanistan, and now Boy Scout and his team were its most recent victims.

He'd also come to the conclusion that they were never going to be free of the fear that one day they might wake up and be back in the cistern, piss and shit coating the water as they sat dreaming of someone dreaming their life was real. This was a new form of PTSD altogether. They weren't affected by what they'd seen. They were worried that nothing was real. Were they even going to be able to make contacts, knowing that they might be gone in the wisp of a moment?

Then came the explosion.

Then the gunfight.

And then the truest pain of all.

So it was with his own pain firing down his left leg, carrying Lore's dying body over his right shoulder, leaning into McQueen—who by all rights should be dead with as many bullets as he'd taken—they stumbled down the middle of a lonely road on the eastern edge of Afghanistan.

One foot after the other.

One mile at a time.

No one passed them.

No one saw them.

In fact, not one of them said a word.

Still, Boy Scout listened because he believed he could hear whispering. It was just on the edge of his hearing, like over the horizon, or right behind him. The sizzling of a faraway radio station right on the edge of his ken. Worry crept into his consciousness as he realized what it might be. Then they turned a corner and saw the American flag flying over the FOB Mitchum and the gate with and MRAP parked in front of it and a soldier staring down at crew served weapons, wearing a United States Army combat uniform with an American flag on his right shoulder.

Help was only moments away.

Maybe they might live after all.

Maybe it wasn't a dream after all.

Maybe they could leave this forsaken place and never return.

Then the whispering began in earnest.

Acknowledgements

According to Erik Hage in his book *Cormac McCarthy: A Literary Companion*, Moby Dick is McCarthy's favorite book. Although I hadn't known this, it was of little surprise when I read it. Herman Melville's famous treatise on the inability of man to overcome nature left a raw wound in my psyche when I first discovered it, shattering the idea that man could do anything and that heroes always won. Then came McCarthy carving the same human inequities into his own anti-pastoralism. And it's all true. The inexhaustible qualities of nature far outstrip the abilities of any man or woman, even a team of men and women, to accomplish that which they must, which is the thematic element I attempted to capture in this book. So it is only right and honorable that I give thanks to Melville and McCarthy for their iconic contributions to literature and the idea that man will always be victim to nature, whether it be nature itself, the nature of man, or the nature of war. Thanks also to my first reader, editor and wife, fellow author Yvonne

Navarro. Thanks to my agent, Cherry Weiner, and the good folks at Solaris, Jonathan Oliver, Michael Rowley, David Thomas Moore, Kate Coe, Rob Power, and Ben Smith. Thank you to Jaycee Martin and Jen Germain for language support. A shout out to my mate Rob Knight for being the first reader while you were in Afghanistan— how's that for symmetry. Finally, I would like to thank all of the men and women who have spent all or part of the last sixteen years fighting in Afghanistan. It's a hell of a place, isn't it? I hope to God you never have to go back again.

About the Author

Weston Ochse is a former intelligence officer and special operations soldier who has engaged enemy combatants, terrorists, narco smugglers, and human traffickers. His personal war stories include performing humanitarian operations over Bangladesh, being deployed to Afghanistan, and a near miss being cannibalized in Papua New Guinea.

A writer of more than 26 books in multiple genres, his military supernatural series, SEAL Team 666, has been optioned to be a movie starring Dwayne Johnson. His military sci-fi series, which starts with *Grunt Life*, has been praised for its PTSD-positive depiction of soldiers at peace and at war.

Weston Ochse's fiction and non-fiction has been praised by *USA Today*, *The Atlantic*, *The New York Post*, *The Financial Times* of London, and *Publishers Weekly*.

T.S.T. WILL RETURN IN

DEAD SKY

COMING SOON FROM
WESTON OCHSE

'Weston Ochse is the new voice
of action science fiction'
New York Times bestselling author

WESTON OCHSE
GRUNT LIFE

A TASK FORCE OMBRA NOVEL

THE INVASION IS OVER. THEY ARE ALREADY AMONGST US.

Benjamin Carter Mason died last night. Maybe he threw himself off a
bridge into Los Angeles Harbor, or maybe he burned to death in a house
fire in San Pedro; it doesn't really matter. Today, Mason's starting a new
life. He's back in boot camp, training for the only war left that matters a
damn.

For years, their spies have been coming to Earth, learning our
weaknesses. Our governments knew, but they did nothing—the prospect
was too awful, the costs too high—and now, the horrifying and utterly
inhuman Cray are laying waste to our cities. The human race is a
heartbeat away from extinction. That is, unless Mason, and the other men
and women of Task Force OMBRA, can do anything about it.

This is a time for heroes. For killers. For Grunts.

'The new voice of action science fiction'
New York Times bestselling author Jonathan Maberry

WESTON OCHSE

GRUNT HERO

A TASK FORCE OMBRA NOVEL

THE EARTH HAS BEEN COLONISED.

Ben Mason fought the war and lost. The Earth has been taken by an implacable alien intelligence: our cities terraformed, our people broken.

Now Mason — back in the arms of task force OMBRA — needs answers to the most desperate questions. Can nothing be done? What do the invaders want with Earth?

When all hope of survival is gone, all that's left is to seek revenge...

WINNER OF THE 2016 LOCUS AWARD
NOMINATED FOR THE 2016 HUGO, NEBULA AND ARTHUR C. CLARKE AWARDS

When Captain Kel Cheris of the hexarchate is disgraced for her unconventional tactics, Kel Command gives her a chance to redeem herself, by retaking the Fortress of Scattered Needles from the heretics. Cheris's career isn't the only thing at stake: if the fortress falls, the hexarchate itself might be next.

Cheris's best hope is to ally with the undead tactician Shuos Jedao. The good news is that Jedao has never lost a battle, and he may be the only one who can figure out how to successfully besiege the fortress. The bad news is that Jedao went mad in his first life and massacred two armies, one of them his own.

As the siege wears on, Cheris must decide how far she can trust Jedao— because she might be his next victim.

 WWW.SOLARISBOOKS.COM

Follow us on Twitter! www.twitter.com/solarisbooks

CONFLICT IS ETERNAL

We have always fought. War is the furnace that forges new technologies and pushes humanity ever onward. We are the children of a battle that began with fists and sticks, and ended on the brink of atomic Armageddon. Beyond here lies another war, infinite in scope and scale.

But who will fight the wars of tomorrow? Join Elizabeth Bear, Indrapramit Das, Aliette de Bodard, Garth Nix and many, many more in an exploration of the furthest extremes of military science fiction...

 WWW.SOLARISBOOKS.COM

Follow us on Twitter! www.twitter.com/solarisbooks

FIND US ONLINE!

www.rebellionpublishing.com

/rebellionpub   /rebellionpublishing   /rebellionpub

SIGN UP TO OUR NEWSLETTER!

rebellionpublishing.com/sign-up

YOUR REVIEWS MATTER!

Enjoy this book? Got something to say?

Leave a review on Amazon, GoodReads or with your
favourite bookseller and let the world know!